THE CREDIT DRAPER

J. David Simons

Published by Two Ravens Press Ltd
Green Willow Croft
Rhiroy
Lochbroom
Ullapool
Ross-shire IV23 2SF

www.tworavenspress.com

ISBN: 978-1-906120-25-2

British Library Cataloguing in Publication Data: a CIP record for this book can be obtained from the British Library.

Designed and typeset in Sabon by Two Ravens Press.
Cover design by David Knowles and Sharon Blackie.

Printed on Forest [illegible] accredited paper by

About the Author

J. David Simons was born in Glasgow in 1953. He studied law at Glasgow University and became a partner at an Edinburgh law firm before giving up his practice in 1978 to live on a kibbutz in Israel. Since then he has lived in Australia, Japan and England, working at various stages along the way as a charity administrator, cotton farmer, language teacher and university lecturer. In his most recent guise as a journalist he has written extensively about the Internet and new media. He returned to Glasgow in 2006. *The Credit Draper* is his first published novel.

For more information about the author, see

www.tworavenspress.com

Acknowledgements

I would like to thank those who were there right from the start. My late step-father, George, whose childhood memories were the original inspiration for this novel. My friends Ish and Lorna whose patience, advice, criticism and guidance set me on the right path. My friend and editor, Steve, who over the years has not only constantly revised my work both fictional and non-fictional but provided me with an income that has allowed me to write. And for those that were there at the conclusion. Sharon and David at Two Ravens Press for putting their faith in the publication of this novel. And my partner, Sofia, for her love and support. In between, there have been those many family, friends as well as strangers whose advice, knowledge and encouragement have informed this work in so many different ways. To all those unaccredited contributors, I remain extremely grateful.

I would also like to acknowledge my enormous debt to the historical account of the Jewish community in Glasgow detailed in the book Second City Jewry by Dr. Kenneth E. Collins (Scottish Jewish Archives, 1990). Any deviation from the facts contained in his meticulous research are my own responsibility, either by error or design.

For George

Glasgow

1911

CHAPTER ONE

The crowd moved again and Avram let it take him, trundling him along among the damp shawls, the overcoats, the parcels, the pots, the battered cases, the rolled-up blankets. He strained to see something of the city, but from within the clutch of passengers all he could make out were the shadowy outlines of warehouses and cranes charcoaled into the early morning fog. Underfoot, the cargo ship swayed in its moorings with a gentle thud, thud, thud against the timbers of the pier. He felt so tiny. A thimbleful of soul lost in a vast adult universe.

A seagull swooped to perch on a line of rope stretching just above his head. Its feathers were streaked in grime, its beak snapped emptily ahead of tiny black eyes. The bird reminded Avram of the story of Noah, the message brought with the arrival of the dove. And then he warmed to the memory of his mother telling him the tale. Her two fingers marching across his body until he wriggled and giggled as she found refuge for her animals in his armpits, along his thighs or under his chin.

He wrapped his arms tighter around his chest. But for a few murmurs, the stamping of feet against the cold, the sob of a younger boy, the crowd was still and silent. Then came a surge and he felt Dmitry's hands guide him, stealing an inch here and there over the others.

The seaman's lips moved close to his ear. 'I have to help with the cargo.'

Avram struggled to twist his head back but Dmitry's firm grip at the base of his neck kept him facing forward.

'Don't leave me. Please don't leave me.'

Dmitry leaned in again. Avram felt the man's stubble graze his cheek.

'I've kept my part,' the seaman hissed.

'But ... but my mother paid you.'

'Bah! A few roubles to keep you company.'

Avram fingered the coins sewn into his jacket. The crowd shuffled forward, pushing him with it. He turned round but Dmitry had disappeared. A tightness forced its way through his chest and into his throat. He tried to gulp it down.

'Are you all right?'

He wiped his eyes. A fair-haired girl was staring at him, clutching a cloth doll to her chest.

'I'm fine,' he said, quickly pulling himself up straight.

'Where's your family?' she asked.

'I'm alone.'

'But I saw you with a man.'

'He works on the ship.'

The girl tilted her head to one side and then the other. 'You're very brave,' she said. 'Coming by yourself.'

'It wasn't hard,' he replied.

'I couldn't do it,' she said, more to her doll than to him. 'Where are you going?'

'I'm staying here.'

'We're off to America,' she said. 'On a bigger ship than this.' She held the doll even tighter. 'America, America, America,' she chanted, then squeezed herself between the two adults in front of her.

'*Shah*, girl,' one of them said.

Avram knew of this America. With its buildings so high they blocked out the sun, where people walked on golden cobblestones, where the land stretched free and forever. He was swept forward again in the crush, edging ever closer towards the head of the gangplank. He saw the girl's fair hair bob ahead of him. One time she turned, caught his stare and waved back at him, mouthing the words: 'America, America.'

Once off the boat, Avram perched himself on top of a capstan, his small case grasped tight to his lap. He was totally on his own now. He knew he had to do something, to make adult decisions about reaching his destination. But instead he distracted himself with his view of the dockside chaos as drivers forced their wagons through the melée of porters and passengers. A blinkered horse whinnied then reared up to the lash of a whip. Those closest pulled back from the clawing hooves until a porter grabbed the reins and calmed the snorting beast. Avram spotted some of the crew off his ship working on regardless of the incident, retrieving crates from inside the tangle of rope nets.

'Where's Dmitry?' he shouted, failing to disguise the desperate shrill in his voice. 'Where's Dmitry?'

The men ignored him except for one who swore, lifted his eyes to the upper decks, mimed the smoking of a cigarette. Then a hansom drew up and Avram watched the fair-haired girl scramble inside. She dropped her doll, and only her scream caused the cab to halt so she could step back out to pick it up. He thought about following her to America but instead he forced himself to move away from the ship. He approached a group of leering spectators who had appeared out of the fog. His hand trembled as he held out the letter his mother had given him. Curious fingers plucked the envelope from his grasp, smoothed out the paper, while heads drew closer to peer at the lettering. The address was passed around as he tried to grab back the envelope, anxious that the precious lifeline of ink-strokes should not be smudged or torn. These strangers, their faces like hideous puppets, smiled back at him over broken teeth, breathed alcohol onto his cheeks, patted his curls, pointed the way along dark tenement-lined streets. He picked up the case containing his few clothes and the one bottle of *schnapps* for his hosts, and started to walk into the thick mist.

'There's a tram to take ye where ye want to go,' a voice trailed after him. 'If ye've got a farthin'.'

He shrugged at the incomprehensible words and ploughed on.

Gas street-lamps struggled to light his way. Towering cranes hovered over him like skeletons signposting his route. An empty milk-bottle rolled and broke at his feet. Bare-footed children taunted him as their threadbare dog snapped at his ankles. A woman tried to give him food, but he shook his head, frightened that what was offered was not *kosher*. He heard a scream. Another time, piano music. Then the desolate echo from a foghorn on the river.

But it was the lack of colour that haunted him most. Everything was grey. The buildings, the people's faces, the mangy dogs. Even the air he breathed. It was a greyness that he felt as a terrifying pallor, clinging to his face and hands like the faint touch of cobwebs on his skin. He kept his attention on his feet, letting them walk him faster, pounding out the terror from his wildly beating heart onto the cobbled streets. The air drew thick and cold in his lungs, tightening his chest, causing his breath to shorten. He began to sweat despite the chill. With every few steps, he switched his case from hand to hand. His arms ached and his palms began to blister. He observed his feet moving him on, as if they had a consciousness of their own.

But the fog lifted and the streets grew wider, the buildings taller and the facades grander. A smear of sunlight crept into the morning. His head lifted too. He saw streetlights that were not lit by gas, but by some other miracle. He paused to wonder at the horseless trams and carriages. He passed shop windows crammed with merchandise. He lingered outside a bakery until the warm smell of freshly baked loaves was too much to bear. As he moved deeper into the city, the pavements began to fill up with pale, stern-faced people not unlike those from his homeland. He had no choice but to approach them, and with his cap in hand, he offered the envelope. Some guided him with elaborate hand signals, others walked him ahead to street corners before showing him the way.

It took him nearly six hours to reach the Gorbals. There, the first sight of a Hebrew shop-sign soothed his fears. An old woman who spoke Yiddish accompanied him to his destination. He entered the close at number 32, and grasping the heavy brass knocker on the door of the ground floor flat, tapped out his message of arrival. Still holding on to the envelope, he collapsed starving and exhausted into the arms of the woman who answered the door.

CHAPTER TWO

Avram felt the increased pressure of Madame Kahn's hand on his back and he stumbled forward almost dropping the bottle of *schnapps*.

'This is the boy,' she said. 'Rachel Escovitz's boy.'

Papa Kahn looked up from the picked-clean bones of a pickled herring, dabbed a napkin to his moist lips.

'What is your name, boy?'

'Avram, sir. Avram Escovitz.'

Papa Kahn popped an apple slice into his mouth and crunched slowly. The only sound in the room. 'You kept your mother's name?'

'I know no other, sir.'

'What about your father?'

'I have no father.'

'What do you mean? Of course, you have a father.'

'The Cossacks took him before I was born.'

Papa Kahn frowned as he chewed. 'Mmm. So that's how it is. How is she, your mother? Is she well?'

Avram didn't know if his mother was well. The last time he'd seen her, her eyes were red-rimmed with tears, her hands fluttering over his face like a blind woman, trying to imprint his face on her memory with her fingers.

'I don't know, sir.'

'Is she in good health?'

'I think so, sir.'

'And how old are you, Avram?'

'Eleven years and eleven months, sir.'

Papa Kahn smiled. '*Nu*. Come. Come closer. Let me have a look at you.'

He did as he was told, letting Papa Kahn cup a hand round his chin, drag his head from side to side in the light from the window. He wondered if Papa Kahn was in mourning for he only wore black. A black suit, black shoes, black tie and a black yarmulke.

'Teeth.'

Avram opened his mouth wide.

'The teeth are good. Bicarbonate of soda. Every day. Do you understand?'

He didn't but he nodded anyway.

'Now tell me, Avram. How were you allowed into this country?'

'I don't know, sir.'

'You must know. There are controls now. You can't just walk off a ship into this great country. This Great Britain. Where did your ship dock first? Before it arrived in Glasgow?'

'I don't know, sir.'

'Southampton?'

Southampton? He recalled the rush down the gangplanks into a large shed partitioned into sections by long tables. Braziers heating the chilly space. The other passengers brandishing papers, swearing in Yiddish, clamouring for the attention of the men in uniform. A medical examination, the doctor pressing the cold disc of a hearing device against his bare chest. 'Yes, sir. That was the name. Southampton.'

'And you spoke to an immigration officer?'

'Dmitry. Dmitry did everything.' Dmitry knew one of the officials. They were taken to one side.

'Who is this Dmitry?' Madame Kahn asked.

'My mother paid him to bring me.'

Papa Kahn shrugged and looked at his wife. 'Perhaps there were papers. Perhaps there was a bribe.'

'This Dmitry brought you here to the Gorbals?' Madame Kahn persisted.

'Only to the docks in Glasgow.'

'And the rest of the way?'

'I walked.'

She gave a short laugh. 'You walked from Clydebank? There is a tram.'

'Now, Martha. What does it matter? He is here now.'

She sniffed hard, then turned away from her husband to address Avram directly. 'Go on. Give Herr Kahn the gift.'

'My mother sends you this in memory of times past.' His mother's words. He held out the bottle.

'What is that supposed to mean?' Madame Kahn said to her husband.

'How am I supposed to know?'

'You're the one who knew her.'

Avram searched his jacket pocket for the letter. 'And this will explain the circumstances of my departure.' Again his mother's words. Among the last she had spoken to him on the Riga quayside. Give this letter to the Kahns. To the father. Not the mother.

'Let me see that.' Madame Kahn made a grab for the envelope but her husband held up the flat of his hand.

'No,' he said firmly. Then with his fingers, he beckoned quickly at Avram to hand over the letter.

Just as Avram passed over the envelope, the door opened and a pale, red-haired girl entered with a tray. She stepped awkwardly and Avram could smell her sweat as she passed him, her tray a nervous tinkle of tea things. She placed a glass of black tea and a bowl of sugar cubes conveniently on the table and retreated quickly from the room.

With his thumb and forefinger, Papa Kahn plucked a single cube from the sugar bowl, fixed it delicately in a wedge between his teeth, slurped a mouthful of tea through the dissolving sugar. He then replaced the glass, took a knife from his plate, slit open the envelope and spread two sheets of writing paper before him.

'Now, what do we have here?'

Avram saw the familiar cramped handwriting and bit his lip so hard slithers of flesh came away with his teeth. Papa Kahn kept reading and nodding with an occasional glance to his wife.

'What does this Rachel say?' she asked.

'She says she is sorry.'

'Sorry for what?'

'For sending the boy.'

'She has a *chutzpah*.'

'She had no choice. He was to be conscripted on his twelfth birthday.'

'What shall we do with him?'

'We must keep him.'

'What are you saying? We haven't enough room.'

'I must do what she asks.'

'But why? What do you owe her? This Rachel woman.'

'She is from *der heim*.'

'*Der heim*? Are we responsible for every stray waif drifting into Glasgow from your homeland?'

'He will stay with us. That is final. We can make up a cot for him in Nathan's room.'

'Did she say anything about money?'

'There is nothing written.'

Madame Kahn turned to Avram. 'Did you bring any money, boy?' she snapped.

He opened the front flap of his jacket to display the sewn-up pocket. Madame Kahn snatched the knife off the table and the tears just seemed to come as he watched her skilfully slit open the stitches of his only jacket. She pulled out a small pouch, spilled the coins and the small wad of notes into her palm.

'Almost worthless.'

Avram sensed the reproach, but Papa Kahn looked sternly at his wife. 'As I said. He will stay here. As family. As a brother to Celia and Nathan.' Papa Kahn turned to him, his voice kinder now. 'I agree to your mother's request. This shall be your home. Until we hear from your mother that you can return.'

Again, he felt a hand at his back as Madame Kahn guided him quickly out of the room.

'Mary,' Madame Kahn shouted.

Avram heard footsteps. The servant girl who had brought the tray scurried into the hallway.

'Make a bath for the boy. He is filthy.'

The girl glared at him. 'But Madame. It's ma evening off. I'm on ma way out.'

'Be a little late, then.'

Madame Kahn pulled him into a large curtained room lit only by the glow from a coal fire in the grate, pushed him down into a chair, and swished out of the door.

From somewhere behind him, the loud grind of a clock measured out the heartbeat of the room. He sat still, staring at the dancing flames until he heard the door open behind him. Mary came into view, dragging a tin bath half-filled with water across the carpet to the centre of the hearth. When the tub was in place, she clamped her hands firmly to her hips, turned towards him. Her young face was flushed, her rolled-up sleeves revealed thin freckled arms, their skin raw and reddened from housework. She swung one foot towards him, then the other, until she could grab the arms of his chair. He stiffened. She drew her face close up to his, her red hair and white face filled his vision. Green eyes peered into his own. He had never seen green eyes so close before. They seemed to reflect his image, not absorb like the brown eyes he was used to. He could feel the heat of her cheeks, hear the excited rasp of her breath in her chest as she scrutinised his face, muttering all the while in sing-song under her breath. He tried to push himself further back into the chair.

'Ye had to turn up just as I was leavin',' she half-whispered, her thin lips mean and narrow over yellow teeth. 'Like a bad penny.' She snatched his cheek between the knuckles of two of her fingers, twisted the flesh hard. 'That'll teach ye.'

His eyes teared, but he refused to let out a sound. She ruffled his hair and left the room.

He waited. His cheek burned but he didn't dare touch it. The clock beat louder. A coal shifted and crunched in the grate causing a minor avalanche of sparks and cinder. Voices chattered past the curtained window, followed by a woman's laugh, then silence. He shuddered to the sound of the door opening. Mary. This time with a large pitcher of boiling water which she poured into the tub. Again on her way out, she stopped, drew herself close to him. Again she grabbed the same stinging cheek with her knuckles, twisted the flesh. This time the pain was worse and he struggled not to cry out. She stepped back, humming to herself, rocking her head from side to side. She moved closer and he felt her hands on his abdomen, her fingers crawling under his jumper to lift the shirt from inside his waistband. He flinched from the coarse cold touch of her fingers on the flesh of his belly as they struggled with his buttons.

'Mary,' Madame Kahn shouted.

He kicked out, sending the girl tumbling to the floor. But quick, she was on her feet again, smoothing down the front of her apron, curtsying before her mistress. Madame Kahn snapped a few words at her servant before sending her out of the room. She then told him to get undressed and take a bath.

Avram was still shaking when Madame Kahn left, but he somehow managed the unwieldy buttons of his shirt. He stripped off the rest of his clothes, eased himself down into the scalding relief of the water in the tub. A gritty soap had been left for him and he rubbed hard at the grime of the last few days wishing his mother was there to wash his back, to soothe and comfort him from these new terrors.

As the water cooled he laid back to soak, surprised to recall that it was only early this same morning that his steamship had docked in this foreign land. He remembered clinging to the deck railings, peering into the fog as the ship had stumbled up-river with thin-bellied seagulls squawking at the stern. He realised he had no idea what kind of country this Scotland was. Only that he had emerged here, into this room, out of a river of mist and a tunnel of tenements. He nipped his nose closed and let himself sink down slowly into the tub, feeling the water test his lips for entrance, massage his eyelids, block his ears. In the black silence, he saw his weeping mother disentangle herself from his arms then push him away. His fingers had tried to claw at her jacket but Dmitry's strong arm had swept him on board. When he had been released on deck, he ran back to the gangplank but his mother had already disappeared into the darkness. This darkness.

He pushed himself up from under the water, kneaded his eyes open to witness a young girl about his age tapping a finger on the side of the tub. She wore a blue cotton smock, her hair tucked up in a headscarf except for a few dark curls escaped around her temples. With a tilt of her head to her shoulder, she stared unabashed at his nakedness.

'Celia,' she said, pointing at her chest. She then swivelled her finger menacingly at him.

He told her his name.

She placed the finger into the gap of her open mouth. 'Avram. English?'

When he shook his head, she folded her arms in annoyance. Then, as if contemplating all the wonderful possibilities his lack of understanding could present, she giggled.

He ducked under the water and when he re-emerged, he pointed at her.

'Celia. *Russki?*'

She shook her head and it was now his turn to mock her. She strutted around the tub, trailing a finger along its rim, causing him to twist his head in pursuit. She began to go faster, dragging her hand in the tub, then dipping in deeper to scoop water into his face. He splashed back. Shrieking, she ran faster, slipping and sliding around the bath. He ducked under the water again, but when he brought his head back to the surface she had gone.

CHAPTER THREE

Avram liked the way Celia held his hand. No girl had ever done that before. Just taken his hand in hers, easy as you like, suddenly a feeling of connection to another human being in this strange and alien world. So comforting, those tiny white fingers clasped warmly around his own as he followed her to the top landing of their close. There, he managed to grasp through her poor Yiddish and her gestures that when she was in position, she would call out his name from the landing below. He was to run down after her, try to catch her.

'You must shout the game's special words,' she instructed, so close he could smell her breath. He wondered if it was the bicarbonate of soda that gave her such a sweet fragrance.

'What are they?'

Her eyes darted at him in excitement. 'I. Did. It.'

'I. Did. It.'

'Good. Again. But faster.'

'I did it.'

'Perfect. Now, stay.'

He clambered on to the bannister, watched her skip down the stairway. She rang the doorbell of one flat, then the other.

'Avram,' she screamed up the stairwell. 'Who did it?'

'I did it, I did it,' he screamed. He flew down the stairs after her, ignoring the angry neighbours roused to their doorways until an old woman on the ground floor blocked his flight with the snap of a broom handle across his path. She grabbed him hard with a wizened hand, twisted his ear until he cried out. Then she led him to the Kahn's flat across the passage.

'Not only did he do it,' she complained. 'He even shouts out he did it. "I did it, I did it." This is what he says. What kind of *meshugga* child do you have here?'

'But Mrs. Carnovsky,' Papa Kahn protested. 'The boy can't speak a word of English.'

'You see,' Madame Kahn said, stepping out from behind her husband. '*Tzores*. That boy will only be trouble.' Her hands were stained purple from peeling beetroot, the earthy-sweet aroma of *borsht* drifting into the stairwell from the kitchen. Avram knew that smell. It was the smell of *der heim*.

Mrs. Carnovsky let go of his ear.

'*Feh, feh*,' she grumbled, as she shuffled back across the corridor into her flat. Avram waited for the punishment that surely must come. But instead Papa Kahn took him gently by the arm.

'Come,' he said. 'I want to show you something.'

The shop was only two streets away. Avram couldn't read the name on the sign but the size of the lettering for such a small store-front impressed him. Through the grainy window, he could see bolts of cloth set out against a curtain. To one side, a crude dummy of a male torso displayed a jacket, a dead rose in the lapel.

'Back in Russia I was to study mathematics,' Papa Kahn told him. 'You see, Avram, I was very good with numbers.'

'I am good with numbers too.'

'You are?'

'Yes, I like arithmetic.'

'Be careful of numbers. They have the power of truth. But in Russia they can betray you.'

'How can numbers betray you?'

'Quotas.'

'Quotas, sir?'

'Quotas restricted the number of Jews in Russia entering institutions of higher learning. Quotas demanded their numbers of Jews for the army. Then more and more numbers. Until they wanted me. Then more again. Year after year after year. Younger and younger numbers. Until now it seems they want even a young number like you.' Papa Kahn stopped talking, stared at the ground. 'Let us go inside,' he sighed.

The dim air of the workshop hung thick with the fluff and fuzz of fabric, prickling the skin on Avram's forehead, bringing him out in a sweat. Myriad shapes of discarded cloth, like tiny flags after a parade, began to attach themselves to his shoes as he walked in Papa Kahn's wake across the room. A young girl stood at a large work-bench building up the canvas of a jacket with padding. She greeted her employer with a slight curtsy. At another bench, an older woman pressed out a pair of trousers with a flat iron, her mouth bristling with pins. Papa Kahn introduced him first to the young girl, Sadie, and then to Mrs. Wallace.

'Take off your jacket,' Papa Kahn told him. 'Sadie will fix it for you.'

Avram attempted to show Sadie where the pocket had been sliced open, but she just snatched it from him, laid it out quick and efficient on her work-bench. He followed Papa Kahn into a back office. It was a narrow, tidy space with just enough room for a small desk. A Hebrew calendar hung on the wall with each day passed crossed out in thick black ink.

'So here I am,' Papa Kahn said, holding out his arms. 'Doing one of the few crafts open to a Jew who didn't want to roll cigarettes, upholster chairs or frame pictures. And who lacked the strength to build ships or go down the mines. I became a simple tailor.'

Avram felt instinctively that Papa Kahn was seeking a response, but he didn't know what to say. He wasn't used to an adult talking to him in this way. So directly. So intimately.

Papa Kahn sighed again, sat down slowly on the worn leather chair behind his desk. 'Don't judge me too harshly, Avram. Don't judge me too harshly.'

Avram looked at the calendar and counted the days to his birthday.

* * *

Avram squashed up beside Celia in the armchair, watched with fascination the glow from the match illuminate Uncle Mendel's face, further deepening the circles around the man's eyes as he sucked his pipe alight. Uncle Mendel boasted long side-locks and a thick beard, he wore a *yarmulke* on his head, but his skin was not the pale skin of the pious – this man's complexion was ruddy and weather-beaten, a man of the plough rather than the prayer book. Avram had no idea what Uncle Mendel did to make a living, except that his work took him off to the Scottish countryside for most of the week, until he returned for the synagogue service on Friday nights. When the Sabbath was over the following evening, Uncle Mendel would come downstairs from this tiny, barely-furnished flat to accompany his sister's singing on the piano. The man would hunch his large frame over the keyboard, squeeze his eyes shut and somehow manage to eke out a delicate tune with thick fingers that reminded Avram of the fleshy tubes of *vursht* hanging outside the butcher shop in his hometown. And as Madame Kahn sang operatic ballads from her German homeland, Avram saw her normally stern face so transformed with a spirit of joy that he too began clapping along to her song.

'So you are the son of Rachel Escovitz.' Uncle Mendel leaned back in his chair to consider this piece of information before returning his attention to keeping the tobacco burning in his pipe. 'And how old are you, this son of Rachel?'

'I am twelve years old,' Avram said proudly. 'Yesterday was my birthday.'

'*Mazeltov, mazeltov, mazeltov*. A birthday in your new homeland. We must celebrate.'

'And how will we do that, uncle?' asked Celia.

'With a little *schnapps,* perhaps, or a little dram of the whisky. And for you children, this wonderful baked fish. This herring. Fresh from the waters of Loch Fyne it comes.'

Uncle Mendel took a poker and with a skilful flick he turned over a parcel of damp newspapers baking in the white embers of the grate. Celia gleefully clapped her hands together. A curious combination of smells began to fill the room – that of wet paper drying and charring, the tantalising aroma of cooking fish, the essence of sweet, dark tobacco. 'And who also was the son of Rachel?' Uncle Mendel asked. 'Of Rachel and Jacob? Quick, quick, quick.'

Avram felt Celia poke him so hard he almost fell off the chair. He managed to steady himself. 'Joseph,' he replied. 'Joseph was the son of Rachel and Jacob.'

'So he was.' Uncle Mendel nodded his head around the room as if to some invisible audience. 'This is a good Jewish *boychik* who knows his Pentateuch.'

Avram waited for another question but none came. Instead Uncle Mendel continued to draw on his pipe, making gentle sucking noises as he did so, his watery, melancholy eyes lost to faraway places. After a while, the man turned his attention to minding the herring baking on the fire, tipping the bundle up here and there as if some special vision enabled him to see past the newspapers to the progress of the cooking flesh within. Avram tried to keep still but Celia wriggled in the chair. Avram had already heard Madame Kahn's complaints about Uncle Mendel's lapses into silence. She put it down to loneliness. *A man his age should have been married with grown-up children already,* she would say. *Too much time on his own. Travelling around the countryside, schlepping his parcels around. Or stuck up in that miserable flat of his. Or in that broken-down hut in the countryside. What does he do there all the time? Drinking that awful whisky. Or baking his herring. Baking his brain more like it. Too much time to think. Too much thinking is not good for you. He forgets how to talk to other human beings.*

'Only Joseph?' Uncle Mendel asked eventually, prodding the stem of his pipe at Celia.

'No, Uncle. There was Benjamin. The youngest of all Jacob's twelve sons. But only the second he had by Rachel.'

Uncle Mendel chewed on the white stem, drifting away on some memory.

'Uncle Mendel?' Celia prompted.

'Yes,' he sighed.

'Is Benjamin the right answer?'

'Of course it is, my dear.'

Celia folded her arms smugly while Uncle Mendel reverted to bobbing his head in rhythm to the consideration of some other thought. He pulled his pipe out of his mouth, drawing out a thread of spittle.

'Cossacks, Avram. The Cossacks still hurt our people?'

Avram nodded.

'It is a terrible thing. But here you are safe. Here are a good people.'

'They don't hate us here?'

'No, they don't hate us here. They don't have time to hate us here. They are too busy hating each other. Or hating the English.'

'But why do they hate each other?' Avram asked.

Uncle Mendel didn't answer, for known only to him some significant cooking threshold had been achieved in the grate. 'Aha! Dinner is ready,' he announced.

Uncle Mendel took up the poker, nudged the bundle of fish out of the fire onto a large plate. With dancing fingers, he unwrapped the package, the skin of the herring peeling away easily with the paper to leave the naked steaming flesh. Uncle Mendel then picked off a piece, passed it to Avram, and then another to Celia.

'Mind the bones,' he warned.

Avram popped the succulent flesh into his mouth. It was delicious.

CHAPTER FOUR

Avram discovered he had two lives now. Back in his homeland there had only been one integrated narrative, where the world of his senses was the same as the incessant chattering going on inside his head. But here in the Gorbals there existed not only this outer world involving these strangers with their strange language in this strange city: there was this inner world too, quite separate, the world of his dreams.

'What will happen to you, Mama?' he screamed across the chasm of water into the wild eyes of his mother. 'What will happen to you?'

'God will look after me, Avram. Don't worry. God will look after me.'

He clung on to the mast of a raft that was being lashed in its moorings by towering waves as high as a steeple. The sky was so grey it was impossible to see where the ocean ended and the air began. Water lapped over his feet, slapped at his face, drenched his clothes. Bodies of silvery fish, swept up in the swell, wriggled on the make-shift deck then disappeared over the side with the next sea-burst. There were other figures on the raft, men with vague bearded faces. Many men, far too many for such a small cramped craft, but miraculously the limited space coped with their presence. Papa Kahn and Uncle Mendel could have been among them or they could have been the prophets he had seen illustrated in biblical textbooks. Elijah, Isiah, Jeremiah, Obadiah, Zehariah. They were engrossed in tasks with winches and thick wet ropes that coiled and snapped among them like wild snakes as the raft slid up and down on the belly of this ocean beast. The men murmured as they worked, creating a deep bass tone that resonated like a synagogue prayer above the roar of the ocean. He reached out towards his mother, towards the harbour jetty which lurched in and out of his view with each heave and suck of swell.

'What will happen to you, Mama?' he shouted.

His mother spoke effortlessly, yet her words still reached him clearly over the buffeting wind. 'I told you. God will look after me. Why do I have to keep repeating myself? God will look after me.'

The raft rose high on a wave, dropping him back into the grip of a sailor, Dmitry's grip, the dark coarse cloth of the man's naval sleeve blocking his vision. A wave washed over them and he managed to drag the damp serge away from his eyes.

'What will happen to me?' he screamed into darkness. 'What will happen to me?'

Avram had written his mother and so had Papa Kahn, but they had received no reply. Yet he wanted to believe so much what she told him in his dreams: to believe God would look after her. That, after all, was what God did. Papa Kahn had told him this, too. How God had looked out for Joseph in Egypt, how He had guarded the Jews through the years in the Sinai, how He had even cared for the Gentile Hagar after Abraham had cast her out.

'The Almighty will look after your mother,' Papa Kahn pronounced. 'And when the time is right you will go back to her.'

Avram was not totally convinced. 'Why will God look after my Mama, when he didn't look after my Papa?' he asked. 'Why will God look after my Mama and not the other Jews being killed?'

'Because your mother is a good woman.'

Avram thought about this. 'Was my father not a good man? And the other Jews?'

'Yes, yes, they were probably good too.'

'Then I don't understand.'

'What you need to understand, Avram, is how hard it must have been for your mother to give you up so you wouldn't have to join the army. Some parents cut off their son's forefinger so he cannot fire a rifle. Others hide their sons in caves so they spend their youth living like animals. Your mother did none of these things. She gave you up in order to save you. That is what is important to remember. The unselfishness of her love for you.'

'I still don't understand.'

Papa Kahn sighed. 'Life is not for understanding.'

* * *

Avram's favourite task took place just towards the end of the Sabbath when he ran down to Arkush's bakery with Celia to pick up the pot of *cholent* left to cook overnight for their Saturday dinner.

The heat scoured his face as he watched old man Arkush open the giant oven door. The smell of baking meat, carrots, butter beans and potatoes flooded his nostrils. When the baker turned his back, Celia found her mother's pot among all the others, lifted the lid, dipped her finger into the steaming stew.

'Ours is the best,' she said.

'Not sure,' Avram replied, tasting the rich stew for himself.

'Then let's check again,' she giggled, licking her finger.

'Yes. You are right. It is the best.'

'And who stuck their dirty fingers in the pot?'

'I did it.'

He helped her carry the pot home, careful to follow her instructions not to step on the cracks on the pavement otherwise he would grow up to look like Uncle Mendel.

'And you will look like Mrs. Carnovsky.'

She laughed. 'I like you. You're much more fun than Nathan.'

Avram warmed to what he took as a compliment. Then he pondered a while on the image of Celia's young brother. How morose and introverted the boy was. And realised that Celia's words were not much of a compliment after all.

Once the Sabbath was over, the *cholent* eaten, the after-meal benedictions sung and said, Avram worked with Celia to help Madame Kahn quickly clear the table. Papa Kahn brought out the playing cards, Uncle Mendel pressed tobacco into his pipe with his thick fingers, Mrs. Carnovsky arrived from across the hallway, Nathan was sent to bed.

The adults sat around the table, Celia cosied up to her Uncle Mendel, Avram found a corner where he could rest his chin and watch the cards fly across the green cloth of the playing surface. He marvelled at the blur of Madame Kahn's skilful shuffles, the remarkable patience of the adults waiting for the deals to be completed before picking up their hands. Papa Kahn drummed the table with his fingers, Mrs. Carnovsky muttered '*Feh, feh,*' under her breath as she sorted out her hand, Madame Kahn held her cards tight in a fan just under her nose lest the Devil himself might sneak a look, Uncle Mendel alternated between holding his pipe, holding his cards, bringing a glass of *schnapps* to his lips. Then came the ordered placements of the cards in trebles and runs on the table, the surprise entrance of the magical and colourful jokers, a final flourish as the last card of someone's hand found its rightful place on the green cloth. Then shouts of 'Bah! What *Mazel*!', the throwing down of redundant cards into a messy confusion until the next dealer swept them all up again, worked them neatly into a pack, started the process all over again.

'Mere symbols of life itself the cards are,' Uncle Mendel told Avram through a cloud of pipe smoke during a break in the play. 'Hearts. They represent love. Diamonds are money. Clubs are work. And spades mean health.'

'Stop filling the boy's head with nonsense,' Madame Kahn scolded.

But Avram liked the idea. 'So if I have four aces,' he dared to ask. 'Does that mean everything in my life is good?'

'Four kings are better,' Celia insisted.

'No, my little piece of herring,' Uncle Mendel said. 'Avram is right. Aces are high not low. So, four aces give you the very best life has to offer.'

'*Nu*, Mendel,' Papa Kahn prodded. 'It's your deal.'

Uncle Mendel bent down to Avram's level. His breath flowed with the sweetness of the *schnapps*. 'Just make sure you're never low in hearts, *boychik*,' he whispered. 'Never be low in hearts.'

CHAPTER FIVE

In his Jewish universe that was the ghetto of the Gorbals, Avram found it was not difficult to survive day-to-day on a mixture of Russian and Yiddish. There were synagogues, Jewish shops, Jewish warehouses, *kosher* butchers and even a *kosher* restaurant. But Papa Kahn insisted he must learn English.

'And who will teach him?' Madame Kahn asked, with a sharp glance at Avram sitting across from her at the dining-room table. Avram knew just to remain quiet and listen to the almost incomprehensible discussion, until some other aspect of his future had been decided. For that was what adults did – they came to take him to their armies, they pushed him on to boats, they sent him here and there.

'I can help him with mathematics,' said Papa Kahn. 'But he will need a tutor for English.'

'What?' exclaimed Madame Kahn. 'We have no money to do this.'

'He will need English to go to school,' Papa Kahn insisted. 'We must educate the boy.'

'We are not a charity.'

'This is not charity. This is a responsibility.'

'For you, maybe. I know nothing of this Rachel Escovitz and her problems.'

'Oh, Martha, Martha,' Papa Kahn said in a more conciliatory tone. 'You were an immigrant once, too. You know how it feels.'

Madame Kahn appeared to soften. 'And how will you pay for this tutor?'

'I will barter for it. I know someone who was a schoolteacher from *der heim*. He speaks better English now than Asquith himself. I'm sure he would be happy with a nice, tailored suit.'

'You are clothing half the Gorbals for nothing already.'

'His education is essential. The boy seems to be quite bright.'

'And what about his *barmitzvah*? He is twelve years old already.'

'Let Rabbi Lieberman tutor him. That is his job after all.'

'And that will be another free suit.'

* * *

Papa Kahn drew him in close as they pondered the figures on the page. Avram could smell the man's hair oil, the balm used to soothe the skin after shaving. He could see the early evening stubble just beginning to appear on Papa Kahn's cheeks above the trim of his beard and he would rub his own smooth chin, wondering when the evidence of his manhood would begin to show. Standing like this, in the hollow of Papa Kahn's arm and shoulder, he felt protected, shielded from the harshness and complexities of the outside world.

'Appreciate the purity and simplicity of numbers,' Papa Kahn told him. 'Recognise the way these numbers fit together in your head, providing meaning where ordinarily chaos reigns.'

Avram could almost feel the figures settle perfectly into little slots inside his brain until they displayed the undeniably correct solutions he sought.

Papa Kahn went on: 'Consider the contribution numbers make to the value of currency, weight, height, distance, space and time. Consider the cosmic possibilities presented by their square roots, their prime and their common factors. But most of all, love their truth, the way they balance out, the way they never lie.'

'Numbers never lie,' Avram repeated softly to himself. He understood the concept, not only in his brain but in some deeper part of himself. As if a truth he had always known had been uncovered.

* * *

Avram took his *barmitzvah* lessons in a dank, dim room annexed to the main synagogue building where grim portraits of community elders watched over his progress. There he spoke in Yiddish, read in Hebrew and struggled to sing the *barmitzvah* portion according to the various ancient esoteric symbols of musical notation taught by Rabbi Lieberman. They worked until it was so dark Avram couldn't read the words before him and the rabbi was forced to put a flame to the gas mantles on the wall.

The rabbi sipped from a glass of black tea with lemon prepared by Mrs. Carnovsky. She would wander in and out of the room during the lesson, wiping and dusting, all the time chain-smoking cigarettes rolled with pastel coloured papers and gold tips. She offered Avram no tea, but eyed him with such a curious stare that he was sure she was trying to put a curse on him. It was a fear placed in his mind by Celia, who told him Mrs. Carnovsky was known around the Gorbals for her powers of prophecy and her expert reading of tea-leaves.

Along with his tea, the rabbi ate home-made strudel from a large tin adorned with a picture of Queen Victoria on the lid. Occasionally, the rabbi gave Avram some cake on merit but for the most part the sweet pastry and raisins found its way solely to the rabbi's mouth.

'Now your barmitzvah text pertains to the section of Deuteronomy known as "*Va-etchanan*",' the rabbi explained through a mouthful of strudel. 'Say it. Go on. Say it.'

'*Va-etchenan.*'

'And what does that mean? *Va-etchenan*?'

Avram shrugged.

The rabbi pointed a finger in the air, as if to the heavens. 'And I besought,' he translated in a spray of crumbs onto his beard and the table. 'It means "and I besought". So called, Avram, because the chapter begins with Moses begging God for a favour.' The rabbi used the sleeve of his robe to wipe away the flecks of pastry from the open pages of the Pentateuch and the relevant *Haftorah*. 'Besought. Beseeching. Moses beseeching, Moses begging, Moses down on his knees pleading for God in His mercy to allow him to cross over to the good land across the Jordan. To the Land of Canaan. The Holy Land. The Land of Israel. And how did God respond to this request? *Nu*? Come on. Tell me. Quick. Quick.'

Avram relaxed, for he knew he must possess the right answer. 'God agreed.'

'And why did God agree?'

'Because Moses was such a great man. He led the Children of Israel out of Egypt. He gave them the Ten Commandments.'

Rabbi Lieberman wagged his finger. 'Where did you learn such nonsense? Na, na, na, na. Moses was forbidden from entering the Promised Land.'

'But why?'

'As punishment for striking the rock in anger in The Wilderness of Zin.'

Avram was shocked. How could Moses not be allowed into the

Land of Canaan? How could that poor man be left sitting on top of Mount Pisgah watching the bedraggled Israelites crossing into the Promised Land, this land of rivers and palm trees after so many parched and dusty years in the desert? How did Moses feel then in his one hundred and twenty years? Was he bitter in the same way as Papa Kahn was bitter about quotas? Was he envious of his people? Did he still love his God?

The rabbi picked out another piece of strudel from the cake tin and continued. 'But the real importance here with your *barmitzvah* portion is in the reiteration of the Ten Commandments. And the confirmation of the oneness of God through the *Shema* prayer. Hear, O Israel. The Lord our God. The Lord is One.' Again the rabbi pointed, but this time the finger was directed at Avram. 'The Jews. We are a people of the law who both love and fear our God.'

The rabbi's final words troubled Avram deeply. As did the plight of Moses. The unfairness of God's refusal to allow the great man into the Promised Land disrupted his burgeoning understanding about the rationality of the world around him. The world of numbers, where everything was supposed to fit so neatly together. It also affected his relationship with his God, which up until now had been a watchful and protective one. A God that would look after his mother as He had Joseph and Hagar. Now this God was also a God to be feared. After all, what kind of God was this who could deny admission into the Holy Land to a stumbling, reluctant lawgiver who had taken on the might of the great Pharaoh, who had spent forty years leading his people in the Wilderness, who had commanded plagues to descend, seas to open and bushes to burn? If God treated His servant so harshly, what chance did Avram have in this world? He had no history of great deeds behind him and in his twelve years, he was sure he had done much more to provoke God than merely striking a rock in anger. Had he given his mother enough honour? Had he taken the Lord's name in vain? Had he observed the Sabbath day and kept it holy? Had he coveted Celia and Nathan's toys? Had he not wanted to steal some of the rabbi's strudel? Had all his food been *kosher* enough? Had he not wanted to lash out in anger? Not just at a stupid rock, but at another human being? He promised himself from this day on he would never be angry with anyone again. Not with his mother. Not with Celia. Not even with Mary.

For Mary still tormented him. She came to the household daily, slinking around in the shadows, scrubbing and dusting, helping Madame Kahn in the kitchen, taking the dirty laundry down to the 'steamie'. He often found himself alone with her in the same room, his exit blocked. She would approach then, drawing her face up near to his own, as she had done on the night of his arrival, never touching him now, but bringing her fingers so close to his cheek that he could almost feel his skin being snatched and twisted between her knuckles. He would back away from her until a wall, or the kitchen pulley or a piece of furniture gave him no escape and he was left to endure her muttering scrutiny of his features.

'Madame tells me ye'll be thrown out by end of week,' she often told him. 'Ye'll have nowhere to go but the backlands. The backlands. Back to where ye belong.'

He wanted to fight back. To grab her scrawny neck, shake her, drag her across the kitchen by her red hair until she screamed surrender. He was almost sure he had the strength to take her. But God might be watching him, monitoring his behaviour, waiting for that one moment of weakness, the flash of anger that would prevent him from entering the Promised Land, that would get him sent to the backlands instead.

For the backlands was Mary's version of hell. And he knew what she was talking about. He was aware the Kahn's flat was a luxury compared to other places he had seen – there were three bedrooms, a large lounge room with a triple-bay window looking out on to the street, the kitchen was big enough to host a table around which the children could eat. Papa Kahn even had a study. But Celia had shown him tenements at the end of the street where whole families were crowded into single rooms.

'Come, come,' she said, sneaking off in front of him into the dark close of one of these buildings.

'This place stinks,' he said, but followed her nevertheless.

They emerged into the rear yard of the tenement – the backlands. Celia crossed the drying green, entered the open door of a dilapidated outhouse. Again he followed her. There was no window, the place stunk of urine, empty bottles littered the straw floor. Poking out from under a blanket – it wasn't even that, just a piece of rough sack-cloth – he could make out the dirty faces of three children, much younger than himself. Celia began to cry.

'Avram. Give me something. Quick. Quick.'

'Give you what?'

'A farthing. A morsel of food.'

'Me? I've got nothing. You give them something.'

'What? I've nothing either. Wait.' She lifted her arms, undid the ribbon tying up her hair. 'Here,' she said, holding out the thin fabric. 'Take this.' A skinny arm snaked out from under the cloth, snatched at the ribbon. Celia turned back to look at him. 'They live like animals,' she said, continuing to sob. 'It's not right. It's just not right.'

'Come,' he said, gently taking her hand, feeling her warm fingers quickly lock into his own. 'We should go.'

Sometimes, Avram would awake in the middle of the night to the sound of a window rattling, the creak of a door or the clang of the ash cans being emptied, convinced that in the darkness he could see Mary's shadow approaching, ready to pounce and drag him off to the backlands. But even then, in these moments of his greatest fear of her, he remembered the fate of Moses the Lawgiver. He would clench his fists and whisper into his pillow 'I will not be angry with her,' until he fell back into restless sleep.

His only respite came at weekends when Mary had the Sabbath and Sunday off. Her last job on a Friday afternoon was washing the entrance-way to the close and when she had finished and departed for the weekend, Madame Kahn gave both him and Celia blocks of pipe clay to decorate the passageway. Together they tried to outdraw each other with elaborate patterns on the steps and the sides of the close to welcome Papa Kahn on his return from work.

'Which steps are nicer?' Celia would always demand of her father.

'This week I think your steps are nicer. But last week I remember Avram's designs were very good too.'

CHAPTER SIX

The silver-plated thimble winked at Avram from under an armchair in the lounge. He dropped down on to his knees, picked it up, tried the tiny cup on each of his fingers. As he settled it snugly on his thumb, he remembered how he had once done the same with a thimble of his mother's. The memory surprised him as it had been some time since he had thought of her. But that was how it was with her, suddenly these details popping up like little *dybbuks* at his shoulder, catching him off-guard, forcing the images of her to come flooding back, reminding him of the hole in his life where her love should have been. He pushed the thimble down on his thumb, began twisting it at an angle until it raised a welt on his skin. It wasn't enough. He wanted to pierce his flesh, see and smell his blood, but the edges were too rounded to produce the cut.

'You seem sad.'

It took him some time to realise Nathan had spoken. Such a small, pale, frail child who possessed the same dark circles under his eyes as his Uncle Mendel, a mark of birth that seemed to absorb the pain of the world around him into their blackness. Nathan was three years younger than Avram, yet his face bore all the anxieties of an old man, his head full of adult questioning.

'No, I'm not,' Avram countered a little too harshly, then felt guilty for startling the boy.

Nathan continued staring at him, head dropped to one side, eyes watery with concern. 'Yes, you are. I can feel it.'

'Feel what?'

'Your sadness.'

Avram shrugged.

'Why are you so unhappy?' Nathan persisted.

'I don't know.'

'Of course you do.'

'Maybe I think about my mother.'

'When was the last time you saw her?'

'In Riga. By the ship. She left me there.' He closed his eyes. He was back on the frozen streets of the Russian port listening to a sullen-faced fiddler play. The violin music pleaded at his ears while his mother held on tightly to his mittened hand, her face glowing red in the cold like a doll's painted cheeks as she spoke to him of his father and the music and when she was young. He stamped his feet against the chill as his mother talked on, her words soaring in the crisp blue air to the swirl of the bow or dropping to an agitated staccato as she muttered into her scarf. When the violinist stopped, his mother stopped too, somehow angry at the loss of accompaniment to her rant. She scattered a few coins into the battered violin case and moved off in the direction of the docks, dragging him with her. He turned to Nathan. The boy was sobbing.

'What's wrong now?' Avram asked.

'Mary.'

'Mary?'

'Listen.'

Avram held his breath. He could hear Madame Kahn's voice.

'Stay here,' he told Nathan. He opened the sitting room door, padded to the back of the hallway where Papa and Madame Kahn had their bedroom. The door was open slightly. From the reflection off the wardrobe mirror, he could see Madame Kahn. She was beating Mary with the back of a hairbrush. Thwack, thwack, thwack. Just like she might pound the dust out of a carpet. Mary was squirming on the floor trying to protect her head against the onslaught with her hands and her bare forearms. Madame Kahn, her face red, her hair hanging loose in a way Avram had never seen, knelt over the maid, swiping at her back and face.

'Why?' Madame Kahn screamed. 'Why? Why? Why? Why must you steal from me like this?'

'A bit of soap,' Mary sobbed back in a respite between the blows. ''Twas only a bit of soap, ma'am. Just a bit of soap.'

As her head tilted back, Madame Kahn caught a glimpse of Avram's reflection in the mirror. She spun towards him. He stared motionless at her angry maw as she shouted at him. 'Get out of here, boy. Get out.'

Such was the venom in her voice he wasn't sure if in that instant she meant get out of her bedroom, get out of her house, or even get out of Glasgow. He fled back into the hallway, found refuge among the various garments hanging from the coat-stand until his breathlessness subsided, consoling himself with the thought that God would never let such an angry woman into the Promised Land. He then returned to the lounge, eased down beside Nathan, watched in silence as the younger boy's back juddered every few seconds in spasms of tears.

'Is Mary all right?' Nathan asked.

'It's nothing.'

Later, when Avram had an opportunity, he slipped into Papa and Madame Kahn's bedroom with Celia. He picked up the hairbrush.

'How do you say this?'

Celia told him.

'Hairbrush,' he repeated, slapping the silver-plated head against the cup of his palm. 'Hairbrush.'

He asked Celia if there was anything wrong with Nathan.

'He's just sensitive,' she replied.

That evening, Madame Kahn was back to her usual self with her hair drawn up into a tight bun, hovering impatiently around the hallway in an evening gown and fox-stole wrap. Avram watched as she kissed her own children good-night before possessively taking the arm of her dinner-suited husband who escorted her out of the door.

'Where do they go?' Avram asked.

Celia pulled the gilt-edged invitation off the mantelpiece. She read haughtily: 'A charity concert by the Glasgow Jewish Choral Society in aid of the families of the victims of the *Titanic* disaster.'

Avram knew about the *Titanic*. He even felt a connection with the doomed vessel. For he had seen the newspaper pictures of the ship setting off on its tragic voyage from the docks at Southampton. Southampton. The very port where he had first landed.

'What is a Titanic?' Nathan asked.

'The biggest ship in the world, my love,' Celia said. 'Until it hit an iceberg.'

'What is an iceberg?'

Celia explained, then continued in an eerie voice. 'In the darkness of the night, in the middle of the cold lonely ocean, the giant ship, the *Titanic*, sailed on its maiden voyage. On and on. On and on. The glittering city of New York waited for its arrival. The orchestra played, the passengers laughed and danced and drank champagne, unaware of the tragedy about to happen.'

Avram watched Celia dance around the room to the sound of her own orchestra, her arms outstretched to some imaginary partner. He joined her, miming the playing of a violin and even Nathan stood up and began to clap out an awkward beat. Celia came to a halt.

'Hush.'

Avram dropped to the floor. Nathan stood frozen in silence.

'Listen. The wind stilled. The music played, the lights blazed, the ship steamed on into the night. All was well, when ... suddenly ... a strong shudder in the darkness.' Nathan shuddered too as Celia slapped her hands together. 'An iceberg. The ship had struck an iceberg. The side of the vessel tore open like a skin. Water flooded in. The passengers rushed for the lifeboats. But there weren't enough for everyone. It was women and children first. Women and children first,' Celia called, imitating the cry of a crew member.

Avram cupped his hands to his mouth, echoed her plea, a thin voice coming through the fog. 'Women and children first. Women and children first.'

Celia went on. 'But everyone panicked. People scrambled for the boats. Others jumped screaming into the freezing sea. The band played on. More water poured in. The band still played on. Play on, Avram.'

Avram jumped to his feet, scraped wildly at his extended forearm as he danced around the bewildered Nathan.

'The band played until the ship tipped up and up and up before sliding into the ocean depths. Down and down and down into the seabed, the *Titanic* plunged. It didn't matter if you were rich or poor, first class or steerage, everyone sank together. Hundreds of passengers were drowned.'

'What is drowned?' Nathan asked.

'It's when people can't breathe in the water, my love.' Celia placed a hand over her nose and mouth, sucked hard on the flesh of her palm. 'Then they die.'

Nathan's legs gave way underneath him, his small body crumpled to the floor. Avram started to laugh but he noticed the expression of horror on Celia's face as she looked down at the prostrate body of her brother. He watched in silence as Nathan remained sprawled motionless on the floor.

'He's not moving,' Celia howled. 'He's not moving. He's dead. We've killed him.'

Avram wasn't so sure, but Nathan's usually pallid expression had drained to an even sicklier grey.

Celia knelt down, twisted her head to Nathan's chest.

'I can't feel him breathing. Avram. Do something.'

'Uncle Mendel. I'll get Uncle Mendel.'

'No, no. He isn't at home. Go to Mrs. Carnovsky. Hurry. Mrs. Carnovsky.'

He flew out of the Kahn's flat and rang and rang the bell opposite until Mrs. Carnovsky cracked open the door and peered out. Her customary Balkan Sobranie cigarette hung in its bright pink paper from the shrivelled corner of her mouth.

'Oh, it's you. The *meshugga* orphan.'

'Come. Please, you must come.'

Mrs. Carnovsky poked out her head, surveyed the corridor of the close from side to side.

'What tricks are you playing?'

He grabbed her hand, tried to pull her across the passageway.

'What are you doing? Leave me. Leave me alone, child.'

'Not a trick,' he said, jumping up and down in frustration. 'Come. Please come. Nathan is ... is ... drowned.'

'Nathan drowned? Don't be silly. Calm down, child.'

'It's true,' he protested. 'It's true.'

'The Kahns? Where are Mr. and Mrs. Kahn?'

'They went to concert on the *Titanic*.'

'Enough of your nonsense. Off with you, child.'

Mrs. Carnovsky was about to close the door when Celia appeared.

'He's breathing,' she said. 'I think he's only fainted.'

'Feh!' Mrs. Carnovsky scowled at Avram. 'Fainted, stupid boy. Not drowned.'

She went back into her flat and returned to the Kahns with a bottle of smelling salts. Avram watched fascinated as the old woman wafted the blue opaque bottle under Nathan's nose, confirming his belief that she was a witch, with various magic potions at her disposal.

As Nathan twitched into consciousness his right hand began to jerk spontaneously, hitting out a beat on the floor in rhythm to his mumbled words: 'Hundreds drowned. Hundreds drowned. Hundreds drowned.'

Mrs. Carnovsky slapped her forehead. 'What's wrong with the children in this house?'

'He's just very sensitive,' Celia defended.

'Well, get him to his bed, the two of you. I'll wait here until your parents come home.'

Avram helped Celia pull Nathan to his feet, then together they half-dragged him into his bedroom to lie down. Nathan stayed there for a full week, speaking only occasionally to bemoan the tragedy that had befallen the victims of the *Titanic*.

CHAPTER SEVEN

Avram hung back in the shadow of the close watching the other boys play with a ball on the street. They called out to each other in names he'd never heard before. Not the names of the forefathers, the kings and the prophets he was used to. But Tam, Shuggie, Wullie and Billy, Wee Jimmy. Some played barefoot, their shoes left unscathed to one side. Others had no shoes at all. One boy's legs were bent from rickets. Not far from where Avram stood, three girls squatted on the pavement watching after a group of toddlers. Every so often, they'd look up at the game, shout out some sarcastic comment with a laugh and a sneer. The boy with rickets they called 'Bandy'.

One of the girls got up, walked away from her friends, pulled down her knickers, showed her white arse to the world, urinated in the gutter. When she'd finished, she turned round to Avram, flashed him a grin. Realising he'd been staring, Avram felt his cheeks go hot, turned his attention back to the game.

Suddenly, all the activity stopped and Bandy walked away. Another heavier, taller boy screwed up his mouth, shook his head, then spat forcefully to the ground. In his tattered yellow goalkeeping jersey, he stood out like a lighthouse above the ragged assortment who made up the rest of the street gang.

'You're always sneakin' awa' early for your tea, ya big Jessie,' he called after the departing Bandy.

'Fuck off, Solly.'

'Fuck off yersel, Mammy's boy.'

'Ahm no a Mammy's boy,' Bandy said, his voice turning whiny.

'That's 'cos ye've no got a Mammy. She's gone off with the sailors.'

'That's a fuckin' lie.'

'All right then. She's gone off with the soldiers.'

The three girls looking after the bairns laughed. Solly seemed satisfied with this outcome, let Bandy slink off, folded his arms high on his chest, looked around. 'Hey, you!'

Avram pointed a finger at his own chest. 'Me?'

'Aye you. D'ya wanna kick the leether aboot?'

Avram knew who Solly was. Solomon Green. Only son of Morris Green the bookmaker, or 'Lucky Mo the Bookie' as Papa Kahn called his neighbour and fellow-congregant from the synagogue. Papa Kahn always pronounced Mr. Green's profession softly with a quick glance to either side. Avram's mother had used the same gesture when she'd told him tales about the raids of the Cossack soldiers. He couldn't understand why a similar fear and reverence should be attached to a man who made books. And why someone who did so should be considered lucky.

Solly picked up the badly beat-up leather football, walked over. The rest of his gang shuffled after him.

'The leether. D'ya wanna kick the leether aboot?' Solly said pointing to the battered object resting in the crook of his arm.

Avram shrugged. Solly moved in closer, looked him up and down.

'Ah know you.' Solly sniffed, then wiped a sleeve across his mouth. 'You're the orphan the Kahns took in. Celia told me.'

Even in the darkness of the close, Avram could make out Solly's eyes. They weren't hard or cruel as he had expected. But they flickered impatiently.

'D'ya wanna play footba' then?'

'Please speak slowly.'

'He's wan o' those immgrants wha cannae speak English,' one of the boys shouted.

'Shut yer gob,' Solly snapped. 'Do-you-want-to-play-football?'

'I not play before.'

Solly grabbed Avram's arm, swept him out of the confines of the close.

'That disnae matter. We just need you to fill up the numbers. Just kick the leether in the direction I tell ye.' Solly mimed a kick as he brought him over to the rest of his gang. 'Just-kick-the-ball. Ye don't need to be Patsy fucking Gallacher.'

A couple of boys laughed but a look from Solly made them stop.

Avram stood off at the periphery of the game, watching the other dozen or so boys scramble after the ball. He didn't know what to do, yet he was happy to be with boys his own age, to be a part of something that wasn't just Celia and Nathan. He remembered the games back in his hometown. There was no ball then, just sticks for swords, poles for Cossack horses, the streets for their battlefield.

The play was rough, rougher than the game he was part of now. He still had a small scar above his left-eye to show where his friend Baruch had caught him once with a stick. The gash had spouted then, but he had played on until the blood had stopped running to congeal in a proud crust down his cheek. He wondered if Baruch was in the army now using real swords.

'Hey, orphan,' Solly shouted. 'Stop dreamin' and get stuck in.'

He looked back at Solly's frantic waving. Solly was in position guarding a goal scratched in chalk on a tenement wall. The rest of his team aimed for the space between two piles of satchels further along the road. When the ball was with his team-mates, Avram ran with them in a swoop on the opposite goal, but feared shouting for the final pass. Then he was back on the defensive, doing no more than getting in an attacking player's way, being pushed roughly aside. He was surprised therefore when a rebound placed the ball at his feet.

'Pass it over here, orphan.'

'Just fuckin' kick it.'

'Get it out to Billy, ye daft bampot.'

'Pass it to me,' screamed someone from the other team.

The blood pounded in Avram's head, blocking his ears until all had gone silent around him. The initial heft of the rough leather on his instep felt comfortable, his foot responding naturally to the weight and shape of the ball. His legs loosened, relaxed, adjusting their balance, preparing for their task. He felt he knew instinctively how to play this game – how to execute a dribble, weight a pass, curl a shot. Some of the other boys had started to move in on him, but they seemed to move slowly, mouthing words he could not hear, giving him time to act. He could see Solly behind them, arms signalling instructions from between his chalked goalposts.

With one swift movement, he dragged the ball back behind a clumsy tackle, rounded the prostrate body and continued forward.

'Pass it, pass it,' his team-mates screamed. He could hear their voices now, guessed their meaning but he drove on exhilarated. He weaved between two players, lost his balance on the road's uneven surface, stumbled, regained his footing, honed in on the piles of satchels. His shirt had come loose to a clawing hand and flapped behind him. An elbow aimed high tried to knock him off the ball but he managed to take one last desperate kick to squeeze the ball past the advancing keeper. He fell forward on the momentum, rolling over on the pavement, cutting a scrape along his thigh.

A cluster of boys gathered around him. A breathless Solly pushed his way through.

'I thought ye said ye hadnae played before.'

Avram rubbed his leg where the skin had come up red and raw. He looked up. Solly's yellow jersey gleamed in a burst of sunlight that had appeared suddenly from behind clouds. He noticed a bloody gash on Solly's shin, a faint scar that seemed to tug at his upper lip.

'Thank you,' Avram said. 'Thank you.'

'Thank you?' Solly laughed, held out a hand. 'Thanks for what?'

Avram shrugged, took the offered arm, let himself be hauled to his feet.

'Ye cut through these eejits like Patsy Gallacher,' Solly said, surveying his gang, grinning to the thought. 'That's what we'll call you. Patsy. Patsy Gallacher. The greatest dribbler Celtic's ever had. Aye, Patsy.'

Avram repeated the word to himself, savouring its softness in his mouth. He didn't know what it meant but it carried the sound of friendship.

From then on, it made no difference whether it was with a battered piece of leather, a bundle of tied-up rags and newspapers, a ha'penny rubber ball or with the much sought-after genuine article, Avram just loved to play football. It made no difference either whether the playing surface was cobbled street, sandy gravel or muddied grass. He discovered he had almost complete control of the object at his feet. With one movement, he could bring the ball under his direction, with another he could fly past an opponent, and with yet another he could direct the ball accurately on its way to its destination. He practised hard until he could catch and control the ball on his forehead, the back of his neck, his thigh or on the top of his foot. His record at keepie-uppie was close to one hundred, at least twice as many as anyone else in the neighbourhood.

'Once ye start school, Begg'll want ye,' Solly said, tossing a stone after a cat from their perch on a mound of wasteland near their street.

'Who's Begg?' Avram asked. He liked this, just the two of them, sitting together easy as dusk approached, sometimes silent, sometimes talking when an idle thought arose needing to be spoken.

'Ye'll find out soon enough.'

'I want to know now.'

'He's the gym teacher. A cruel one-eyed bastard. They say he was a prize fighter once, lost his eye in a bare-knuckle contest. Ye can see him sometimes at the back of the assembly hall, whalloping the shite out of a punch-bag. He does the same with the tawse.'

'What's that?'

'A thick leether strap. He'll wallop the shite out of ye with that too. Any excuse. I've seen him break fingers with it. I've even seen him burst open one boy's veins with it. All the blood spurting out.' Solly looked at him deadpan, miming with a sprinkle of his fingers a fountain of blood flowing out of his wrists. 'Like steaming piss.'

Avram got the message even though he didn't understand all of the words. 'You lie to me.'

'No, I don't. Ye'll see. He puts a towel over yer wrists now to stop it happening. Ye should see the line of sick notes for gym class. Begg takes it as a compliment.'

'Why will this Begg want me?' It was Avram's turn to pick up a stone. He looked for a suitable target, let fly at a broken wheel. The stone clattered off a spoke into a muddy puddle. 'He does not know me.'

'Coz yer a natural.'

Avram smiled. 'A Patsy Gallacher.'

'Aye, maybe. And d'ye know why yer so good?'

'At throwing stones?'

'At the football, ye daft bampot.'

But the connection between football and stones wasn't lost on Avram. For he recalled his initial inspired touch of the ball during that first street game in Biblical terms. He'd felt just how he imagined the young King David must have felt, kneeling down to pick up a pebble for his catapult. Feeling in his palm the smoothness, the roundness, the effectiveness of the selected stone. Knowing instinctively this was the object that would fit perfectly in his sling, that would fly most accurately, that would shape his destiny.

'God gave me a gift.'

'Don't get so big-heided.'

'What is it then?'

'Naw. It's not that, Patsy. It's something else. Something I've noticed.'

'Tell me.'

'It's that ye never take yer eyes off yer feet. Other boys'll look up to set up a pass, or a cross or a shot. Or they'll be put off by a defender rushing at them. Ye just keep yer eyes on yer feet.'

CHAPTER EIGHT

Celia skipped ahead, singing as she went:

'You'll never meet your mither till she's gone
Gone wi' yer claes tae the pawn
If you dinnae meet her there
You'll meet her on the stair
Blind drunk, wi' the ticket in her haun.'

Avram was caught between catching up with her or waiting for Nathan who was lagging.

'What's "the pawn"?' he called after her.

'Stupid boy. I'm not telling you.'

'Come on. What is it?'

'I told you. I'm not telling you'.

'You don't know, that's why.'

'Course I do.'

She stuck out her tongue at him then waltzed further ahead, singing 'Avram doesn't know what the pawn is,' her voice niggling him until he longed to chase after her, to prod and tickle her into confessing she did not know. But Nathan was groaning behind him, tangled up with the straps of his satchel.

'Are you happy or sad today?' he asked him as he helped the younger boy's arms through the straps.

The boy beamed at the question. 'Nathan is happy.'

'Why?'

'Because you are.'

He thought about this. Yes, he was happy. He had been looking forward to school for months now. His street friends were there. There would be proper football. Not just with a tanner ball on the streets, but on pitches with a real leather ball and goalposts. He looked forward to the lessons in a language and dialect he was beginning to understand. He looked forward to studying with numbers.

'Is Nathan happy because Nathan is happy? Or only because Avram is happy?'

'Nathan feels nothing about himself.'

He looked at the boy. He seemed so fragile. Nathan never played out in the streets. At the very most, he would sit on the close-step and watch. Never taking part, hardly speaking to anyone. He could become totally absorbed in scratching a stone on the pavement surface or watching the drip, drip, drip from a cleaning cloth left out to dry. And those deep circles around his eyes. So much pain hidden there, yet for the moment Nathan's lips were fixed in a serene smile.

Celia was back, running round in teasing circles. 'Avram doesn't know what the pawn is.'

'What's wrong with your brother?'

'You keep asking me that. And I keep telling you. There's nothing wrong with him. Are you all right, Nathan?'

Nathan nodded.

'See. He's even smiling.'

'But he's so quiet.'

She took Nathan's hand, pulled him along with her, chanting her taunt. Nathan twisted his head back awkwardly to look at him. He was still smiling.

* * *

'School's for bampots,' Solly said authoritatively, his mouth and tongue stained black from sucking on a liquorice stick. 'There's nothing worth learning. 'Cept reading and writing.'

'What about your times tables?' Avram asked.

'I already know ma 'rithmetic.' Solly boasted that since he was seven years old he could work out the return on a penny bet at thirteen-to-eight on the favourite at Ayr. 'That's about it,' he declared. 'The rest is a waste of time. I'm leaving soon as I reach fifteen. I'm going to earn a wage.'

Avram didn't agree with his friend. He liked school. He liked to learn. He liked his jotters and his blotting paper. He liked the double desks with their ink pots and ink stains, and to read and feel the deeply scored desecrations made on the hinged lids by previous occupants. He liked the display of maps on the walls from which he could constantly review the journey he had made to this country or wonder at the extent of the British Empire. He liked to monitor his progress in learning by his movement away from the front of the class.

As the new boy, he had been seated right next to the teacher's desk on the first day. But after each test he had slowly moved backwards until he was now well into the top half of the class. Sometimes there would be a space when someone died. Then the seat would be left vacant for a week with a black ribbon tied to the back before everyone again moved up a space. Nobody wanted to end up at a dead child's desk and Avram felt uneasy if he did, fearful to inherit the lingering of the deceased's disease. But very quickly, the spirit of the dead pupil vacated both the desk and the memory of the classmates, and he relaxed. On his academic ascent, he had passed Solly now but was yet to reach Celia who hid in the back row. She was the cleverest girl in the class.

'Escovitz!' screamed Roy Begg. 'Over here!'

Avram trotted off the pitch to face the school sports master for the first time. Roy Begg stood tall with thinning greased-back hair, long cheeks that gave his face an equine shape, and a mouth frozen into a constant scowl. Over one eye, Roy Begg wore a black patch on a thong etching a deep ridge across his forehead, while the other good eye seemed to weep in perpetual mourning over the loss of its partner.

'Sir.' Avram was surprised to hear his voice come out steady for his legs were shaking.

Roy Begg looked up from the list of players he had scribbled together for Sunday's game. 'You're in the team. Left wing.'

He watched Begg chew out other words, his jaw snapping like a seagull's empty beak. He noticed the cropped shadow of the man's shaving glistening with the sheen from some pungent lotion and he felt the glare of his classmates as they looked on. He wanted to turn round to them and shout 'I'm in the team' but he stood still with his fists clenched tight around his joy. For that was what Solly had told him. 'Don't show any emotion or he'll pick on you, like Wee Jimmie picks his spots.' They both had laughed at the joke but he knew the seriousness of the advice. Yet as he stood there petrified by Begg's one-eyed stare, his fingers stayed wrapped around his elation not just because of Solly's warning but because he never wanted to let it go.

Wallop. The slap across the top of his head stung him back to attention.

'Are you listening, boy?'

'Yes, sir.'

'I might even play you later in the senior team,' Roy Begg continued. 'But you're still a runt. You'll need to put on a bit of beef before I can do that.'

Avram remained tight-lipped. He would ask Solly later what a 'runt' was.

'And don't get any fancy ideas, Escovitz.' Begg stabbed a pencil in his direction. 'You've got talent, that's for sure. But it will need nurturing. And discipline. You're mine now. Do you understand? From now on, you're mine.'

'Yes, sir.'

'What are you?'

'I'm mine.'

He flinched to another slap across his head.

'What are you?'

'I'm yours.'

'That's better. And don't forget that.'

He turned to run on to the pitch but Roy Begg called him back.

'And one more thing you should know, Escovitz.'

Roy Begg stared at him with one watery blue eye until he was forced to ask:

'What is that, sir?'

'I don't like Jews, Escovitz. I don't like Jews.'

CHAPTER NINE

The sound of the brass knocker on the front door echoed in the cold, unlit hallway, intruding on the quiet of the Sabbath afternoon, rousing Avram's attention from the football cards spread out on the floor. Madame Kahn looked up from her book, clucked disapprovingly. Her husband had gone to lie down while she sat reading before the light of a fire of her own making, her bare legs blotched red from the licking closeness of the flames. Avram was surprised she allowed herself this transgression of fire-lighting on the Sabbath, but Madame Kahn always had the same answer to any comments about her sin. 'If our forefathers lived in the Gallowgate and not the Galilee, believe me they would light fires on *Shabbos*.'

Celia leapt to her feet, darted out of the room. She returned with a contrite-looking Solly.

'He wants to know if Avram can go out for a walk,' Celia announced.

Madame Kahn glowered at Avram, then at Solly, as if trying to detect some sinful conspiracy. She nodded. 'Go. But be back in time to collect my *cholent*.'

Solly bowed politely to Madame Kahn, then gestured with a flick of his head for Avram to come.

'Where do we go?' Avram whispered in the hallway.

'Ye'll see.' Solly grabbed a tammy from the hat-stand, threw it at his friend. 'Dress up warm. It's right nippy outside.'

He followed Solly out into the cold where the fresh air felt good on his cheeks, drawn deep into his stifled lungs. He let Solly race off, glad to run after him, to move his limbs, to use up the energy lodged stodgily in his stomach. His legs were stiff at first, almost reluctant to exercise on this Day of Rest, but soon he was racing along the Gorbals streets in pursuit.

'Where do we go?' he called out again, but Solly had turned a corner into another street. He followed but again Solly twisted away from him, raced ahead into an alley between the back of the tenements. Avram ran on steady, confident he could catch up with his heavier friend. But after a few more yards, he drew up sharp at the end of the pavement, as if it were the edge of a precipice he'd reached.

'Come on, Patsy,' Solly shouted. 'What's keepin' ye?'

Where Solly stood waiting on the other side of the road, shops were open for business, pedestrians crowded the streets, tramcars and buses plied their daily routes, horse-drawn wagons ferried goods through the city.

Solly crossed back for him, grabbed his arm. 'Get a move on. We have'nae much time.'

Avram stood his ground. 'I'm not coming.'

'What? Don't be a daft bampot. Come on.'

'No.'

'Why not?'

'It's not…' He struggled to find the words. 'I don't know. It's not *kosher*.'

Solly laughed. 'What are ye feart of?'

'Nothing.'

'Ye think God's looking down on ye or something?'

Avram wrapped his arms around his chest, said nothing.

'I promise ye He isnae.'

'What do you know?'

'I'll tell ye what I know. God's got better things to do with His time than worry about what Avram Escovitz does on a *Shabbos* afternoon.'

'Like what?'

'Jesus, Patsy. I dinnae know.' Solly shrugged, screwed up his face as he searched for an answer. 'Other people. People with big problems. People who are really suffering. Like … I dinnae know … like the Jews in Russia.'

Avram thought about this. 'Maybe you're right,' he said.

'Come on, then. We're late already.'

Avram took off uneasily at Solly's shoulder. But as they leapt in and out of the tramlines, the two of them racing across the south side of the city in the darkening afternoon, his burden of guilt was soon forgotten. They passed wagons being loaded in a railway goods yard, the belching towers of an electricity generating station, a giant hospital, picture houses splashed with matinee posters, a ballroom preparing for the night to come. They ran through the beery stench emanating from countless pubs, followed the tree-lined railings of a public park, then across a recreation ground of colourful crowded football pitches with their sidelines of staunch supporters.

'Almost there,' Solly panted.

'Where?'

'Round the next corner.'

Avram heard their destination before he saw it. A low rumble of voices conjoined into some audible life form, swishing and swirling in the air, rising sharply to a united gasp of disappointment, disintegrating into an outbreak of applause. He raced ahead past Solly, then stopped at the corner. There in front of him stood the stadium, pulsating from the presence of some vibrant beast locked within. A blanket of mist, cigarette smoke and steamy breath hovered above the stand and the terraces, the corrugated walls heaved from the bodies inside.

'Where are we?' he screamed, dizzy from the noise.

'Cathkin,' Solly said with a showman's flourish of his hands. 'Home of the Hi-Hi's.'

The Hi-Hi's. Avram knew the nickname of Third Lanark Football Club from the street games, along with others like "The Bully Wee", "The Jags", "The Spiders", and especially "The Bhoys" for Celtic and "The Gers" for Rangers. He knew the names of the players too, memorised off cigarette cards Solly collected from customers coming out of the tobacco shops, from punters mulling around in the lanes outside his father's betting premises. He knew these names better than he knew the names of everyday objects in the Kahn household. But the one card he had never seen was the one of his namesake, Celtic's Patsy Gallacher. That was a collector's item which never made it into Solly's begging hands.

'We'll soon get in,' Solly said. He'd joined a crowd of other boys huddled outside a paybox by a corrugated gate.

'I have no money,' Avram said.

Solly grinned back at him. 'Me neither. They open the gates twenty minutes from the end to let people out. That's when we nip in. Easy as you like.'

As Solly spoke, the gate was dragged aside, a few men in red scarves exited.

'What's the score?' Solly asked.

'Three-nil to the Bhoys,' one of them muttered sourly.

'The Bhoys?' Avram said. 'Celtic play in there?'

Solly grabbed him by the arm, pushed him through the gates along with the other boys who scattered like beetles into the rear of the crowd.

'Of course, Celtic are playing. I'm taking ye to see yer hero. Come on. Down to the front quick. Or we won't see a thing.'

Crouching down, Avram squeezed a path through a curtain of coat-tails, down terraces littered with the dregs of beef tea, cigarette butts squashed by feet stamping against the cold. The game carried on out of sight, but in his imagination he could see each move across the park from the noise above him and the straining of bodies in the direction of the ball. Just crawling through the forest of legs was a game in itself, finding a gap here and there to burrow through, avoiding the kicks and curses when he trod on a foot or grazed an ankle. Eventually he managed to twist out of the sea of spectators to arrive flat up beside Solly against the enclosure wall. It was as if he had emerged out of a caravan of stragglers into the Promised Land.

He gasped at the emerald expanse. 'It's so…'

Solly smiled. 'So … what?'

'So … green.'

'What did ye expect?'

'I don't know. Not like this.'

He couldn't believe how close he stood to the pitch. So close he could smell the earthy aroma of the churned up turf. The players loomed as shiny giants above him in clouds of snorting breath, baggy shorts flapping around their thick white hairy thighs as they came in close to take a throw-in or to drag a ball along the touchline throwing up divots with their studs. The thwack of boots on leather echoed in his ears and around this stadium bowl awash in the colours of Third Lanark red and Celtic green. The same colours moved around the pitch in a twist and a weave and a swoop as the players followed the ball. At either end the goalkeepers' bright yellow jerseys shone like warm beacons in the dying light.

Avram wrapped an arm around Solly's shoulder, the two of them jumped up and down screaming: 'Come on the Bhoys. Come on the Bhoys.'

'Where's Patsy?' Avram asked breathlessly.

'Him there. Standing right in front of yer bloody nose. And see the Hi-Hi's goalie.' Solly pointed to the far-end of the pitch where a long, lone, figure prowled between goalposts almost invisible in the half-light. 'That's Brownlie. Scotland's keeper.'

But Avram only had eyes for his namesake. Patsy Gallacher stood stomping eagerly by the touchline in his green and white hooped jersey, hands on hips. He seemed smaller, younger and skinnier than the other players with wide ears and hair that sat stiff on his head like a flat black cap. He didn't move for the ball but waited for the game to come to him. Boys closest to him were calling out to him but he just flicked a shy wave back at them as he kept his attention on what was happening on the pitch.

'Hey, Patsy,' Avram shouted, his excitement and the noise of the crowd giving him the courage to call out. 'I'm called Patsy too.'

'Shut yer gob,' said Solly.

But Avram persisted. 'Hey, I'm Patsy too.'

Some boys laughed, but Patsy Gallacher turned round. With hardly a pause, he seemed to pick out the source of the comment, looked directly at Avram, and smiled. Avram felt the heat rush to his cheeks. All he could do was raise his hand weakly in vague acknowledgement. Then there was a call to the player from the pitch, the leather ball thunked at Gallacher's feet and he was off jinking his way to the Hi-Hi's goal.

A huge roar lifted Avram out of his blessed daze.

'What happened?' he asked an hysterical Solly.

'Yer hero scored. That's what. A fuckin' beauty.'

Patsy Gallacher strode back to the centre spot, shyly accepting the hand-shakes of his team-mates. Avram joined in as the crowd around the ground chanted his name.

'I want to play for Celtic,' Avram said. The final whistle had gone, he was following Solly out of the exits, still wrapped up in the glorious excitement of seeing Patsy Gallacher play. Celtic had won four-nil.

'Aye. And so does half of Glasgow. The Catholic half.'

'I mean it.'

'Just coz Patsy gave you the wink.'

'It's not that. I really believe...'

A hand pawed at Avram's shoulder bringing him to a halt. A red pock-marked face leered over him.

'Whaur's yer colours, boy?' the man snarled at him with a blast of whisky breath.

He tried to shake away but the grip held firm.

'He disnae have any colours,' Solly answered.

'Ahm no taukin' tae you. Ahm askin' yer pal here.'

'He disnae understand.'

The man raised an arm at Solly as if to whip him. 'Ah said Ahm no taukin' to youse.' Then he took an end of his green and white scarf, shoved it so close to Avram's face he could smell the damp of the wool. 'Ah'll ask ye agin. Are ye a Fenian or are ye a Proddie bastard?'

Avram hung taut at the end of the man's arm, staring at his bulging eyes, not knowing what to say.

'Are ye green or blue, boy? Are ye for the Celtic or are ye a fuckin' Proddie bastard?'

'He's Jewish,' Solly shouted.

'Jewish? A Jew?' the man grunted. 'A bloody Jew.' He shook Avram hard as he considered this information. Then he snorted. 'Are ye a Fenian Jew or a Proddie Jew?'

Before Avram had time to answer, Solly snatched his arm, pulled him away. 'Run! Run for it!'

Avram ducked. The man stumbled, clawed out for support then fell to the ground. A bottle broke in his pocket. Avram watched as whisky poured on to the road in an amber trickle to mingle with blood from the prostrate body.

'Come on,' Solly shouted. 'Run! Run! Run!'

But Avram didn't want to run. He had witnessed far greater violence than this, delivered by men far more fearsome than this pathetic drunk. Instead, he stayed, hovering above the body. He wanted to kick this man. To feel his belly cave in softly against his foot, to hear the wheeze that would issue hoarse from the man's lungs. An act of revenge against the adult enemy, those vodka-fuelled riders who had come on skilful horseback to terrorise his village. But he had underestimated the tenacity of his opponent. A hand grabbed out from under the heap of overcoat on the ground, snared his ankle. He lost his balance, tripped over the man's outstretched arm. He threw out his hands to break his fall, but as his head swung close to the ground, he felt a cool slash to the side of his forehead. Then large adult hands came from above pulling him to his feet.

'Calm down, lad,' said one of those who held him. 'Just calm down.'

'He's cut,' said another. 'That drunken eejit glassed the boy.'

Avram thrashed vainly with his feet against his captors. Tears of frustration rose in his eyes.

'Fuckin' Proddie Jew boy,' the drunk shouted up at him.

But Avram finally managed to wriggle free, raced away, his heart beating a tom-tom rhythm up and down his chest. He dodged through the pockets of supporters, glancing back every few paces to see if he was being followed. But the path behind him was clear. He eased off his pace until the fingers of the crowd tapered out. Solly was waiting for him at the top of the road.

'For Christ's sake, Patsy. What's happened to you?'

'What do you mean?' Avram leaned forward, hands on his thighs, his breath pumping hard in his lungs.

'There's blood running all over yer face.'

Avram touched his cheek, his forehead, felt the warm stickiness on his flesh.

Solly had a hankie out. 'Dinnae worry. I havenae blowed any snot into it,' he said dabbing away with the cloth. 'Dammit. It's deep. And the blood's no stopping. Why d'ye no skedaddle when I telt ye?'

'I am fine. It not hurt.'

'Yer no fine, ye daft bampot. I'll have to take you to the Infirmary.'

'Infirmary?'

'Aye. The Vicky. The Victoria. A hospital, ye stupid bugger.'

'I don't want a hospital.'

'Yer going to need someone to stitch that. Ye've got a cut there as deep as the bloody Clyde. It'll no heal by itself.'

'I need to go for the *cholent*.'

'Forget the fuckin' *cholent*. Madame Kahn's going to kill us anyway. I'm taking ye to the Vicky. It's no far.'

Avram sat on a bench in the small waiting room, opposite a large set of brass balance scales and a cupboard full of medicine jars. The place stunk of carbolic. He had managed to staunch the bleeding with Solly's handkerchief which was now totally dyed red. Solly paced the floor like an expectant father as he plotted the story to be told to Madame Kahn.

'Ye just fell on some glass,' he said. 'Yes. That would be the easiest. We were walkin' down Albert Drive easy as ye like, chattin' away about yer *barmitzvah* next week and yer feet slipped on something, down ye went, a piece of glass on the cobbles, and there ye have it. Immediately I understand the seriousness of the injury, I cart ye off to the Vicky. Solly Green. Hero of the hour. So now it's yer turn, Patsy. Repeat the story. The way ye'll tell it to Madame Kahn. Which street were we walkin' along'?'

Before Avram had a chance to perform his piece, a nurse called him into a side room. She was a tall, thin woman all starched-up in her uniform, full of 'tut-tuts' and bustling efficiency. She pulled away the handkerchief, pecked away at his wound with her darting eyes, then dabbed the cut with some stinging liquid that made him flinch. But not as much as the six stitches she sewed straight into his skin with as much care and compassion as if she were fixing a button to an old shirt. His screams could probably be heard all the way back to the Gorbals. She then made him press a gauze pack smothered in iodine over her handiwork as she wound a bandage round his head.

Madame Kahn was waiting for them.

'So?'

'We were walkin' down Albert Drive ...' Solly began, but a stern look from Madame Kahn made him stop.

'Avram?' she asked.

'I fell, Madame. Solly took me to Vicky. The Victoria.'

'Is it serious?'

'She sewed me six stitches.'

'Hrrrmph. A small scar for your pains. Well, Celia and I had to go out to Arkush's bakery in the freezing cold. We brought back the *cholent* ourselves.' She wriggled herself up to her full height. 'You can go now, Master Green. I trust there will be no more of these adventures on a *Shabbos*. You, Avram, can go straight to bed.' She pointed to the doorway of the room he shared with Nathan. 'I always said you would be trouble. *Tzores. Tzores. Tzores.*'

But Avram didn't care. He was glad to have this time alone to consider the impact of the day's events on his young soul. For he no longer viewed this Glasgow as a blanket of grey mass shrouding his perception of where he lived. Beyond his previous boundaries extended a city that now had a purpose for his life and a palette of colour for his imagination. There was the red of blood and of the Hi-Hi's strips. There was the bright amber of whisky and of goalkeeping jerseys. And there was the deep contrast between the blue and the green.

CHAPTER TEN

The bookshelves in Papa Kahn's study swelled high to the ceiling, packed tight with volumes of Hebrew texts that seemed to reek of a musty holiness. Bolts of dark cloth lay on the floor among neat piles of manuscripts adorned with Aramaic or Cyrillic scripts or just simple rows of figures. Cluttered on to a small table were the religious artifacts Avram only saw on festivals and the Sabbath – a *menorah*, a filigree spice container, an *etrog* box and a pair of silver candlesticks that Madame Kahn boasted once belonged to her great-grandmother at a time when Emperor Napoleon ruled the world. And on the large mahogany desk stood an abacus with shiny ivory beads he yearned to slide along on their wires for the sweet *click, click* of their contact. Ensconced behind this desk sat Papa Kahn, absorbed in the book open in front of him.

'I am here,' Avram said.

Papa Kahn looked up from over half-moon spectacles.

'Ah, yes. Come. Come beside me.'

Avram went round to the other side of the desk where Papa Kahn put an arm around him, drawing him near. The fingers of Papa Kahn's hand played with a small box on the desk. The man's skin stretched parchment thin across the back of his hands, like the scrolls of the Torah Avram would read the following day in the synagogue.

'It is a pity about this ... ' Papa Kahn's hand drew circles in the air close to the bandages wrapping his wound. 'This ... this turban.'

'Celia said she make it look better tomorrow.'

'That would be helpful. You look like a soldier. A wounded soldier. A wounded soldier of the Torah.' Papa Kahn laughed at his own wit, then in a sterner voice. 'Are you prepared?'

Avram nodded.

'The rabbi says he is pleased with your performance. Are you nervous?'

'I only sleep little in the night.'

'That is normal. What you are reading tomorrow relates to an important part of the Torah.' Avram felt himself being pulled closer. 'I know it has been difficult for you,' Papa Kahn went on. 'Learning subjects in English while studying for your *barmitzvah* could not have been easy. But you have a young mind and young minds absorb these things more quickly. Now, for tomorrow, are you sure you truly understand the portion of the law? It is the part the *Shema* prayer comes from.'

There was one phrase among all the others that had pricked at Avram's consciousness. It was a phrase that pushed him to grapple with concepts beyond his youthful knowledge, yet intuitively he knew that these were important thoughts.

'I don't understand the part in the Shema where it says *et adoshem elokecha tira*.'

'*Et adoshem elokecha tira*,' Papa Kahn repeated. 'And thou shalt fear the Lord thy God. What don't you understand?'

'I don't understand why God wants to frighten me.'

Papa Kahn smiled. 'Such large thoughts for such a small boy. The Shema not only says you should fear God but you should also love Him. Fear and love together make respect.'

'But I don't want the fear. Is love not enough?'

Again Papa Kahn smiled. 'Imagine, Avram. Imagine God is the ocean. You can love the ocean, yes? Its beauty, its horizons, its taste, its smell, its refreshing quality. This love will make you want to be near the ocean, to protect it, to honour it. But the ocean can be fearful too. It has its typhoon swells, its thunderous waves. That fear makes you want to respect the ocean. It makes you take care of strong currents. It keeps you on the right path.'

Avram recalled his journey on the steamship to Scotland and realised he had no love for the ocean. He knew how a vessel could be tossed in its writhing belly, he knew the distance the waters could put between a boy and his mother, he knew the darkness in its depth that would be a hiding-place for his most terrible dreams. He wanted to ask how he could love such an ocean, when Papa Kahn sighed:

'There is something else.' Papa Kahn picked up the small box, spun it slowly around in his fingers. 'This is a gift,' he said, his voice drifting away. 'This is a gift. From your mother.'

Avram took the box, ran his trembling fingers over the smooth, dark amber of its casing as if it were his mother's face he was touching. 'Mother sends this?'

'For your *barmitzvah*.'

'My mother sends this?'

'Someone brought it a few hours ago. You were at school.'

'I don't understand. Who brings this box?'

'Dmitry. That was what he told me. Dmitry. He was in a hurry. A seaman. He was between ships. He pressed the box into my hands. "Give this to the boy," he said. "From his mother. For his thirteenth birthday." I begged him for more information, I even offered him money, but he said he knew nothing. He left quickly.'

'Dmitry.' Avram felt a panic rise behind his ribs, move up through his chest in a rush to beat at his ears, to threaten this new world he had carefully begun to construct. It was a world where he had no mother for she was locked away in some compartment in his heart he had chosen not to enter. Yet it seemed his mother was still there, knocking at the walls of this vault, registering her absence in this gift. She was not dead. And the ghost of her now began to stir in this compartment of memory. God had indeed looked after her, this God whom he both feared and also could learn to love.

'There is a letter?'

'I'm sorry, Avram. There is nothing else.' Papa Kahn kneaded his eyes behind his spectacles and then went on. 'I do not know what to say to you. I am of course joyous she is alive, as you must be, but for her not to tell us what is happening, not to ask for you to ... I just didn't know what to say. You are like family to us. A son. A brother for Celia and Nathan. I just don't know what to say.'

Avram was barely listening to Papa Kahn. With his nail he picked at the tiny clasp on the box, prising back the lid. Sitting on a bed of blue velvet gleamed a silver thimble.

He closed the door to Papa Kahn's study behind him, walked around the hallway, cradling the box in his hand like he might do a young bird. He didn't know where to go or what to do. His mother was alive. But it was a fact that existed somewhere else. Not here, where she might as well be dead if she did not come for him. He felt like throwing the box with its thimble away, then he changed his mind. He would show it to Celia when she came back. He wandered into the cold kitchen, sat by the table, took the thimble out of its box. It fitted neatly on his index finger.

'They say tomorrow's your bassmissva.' Mary stood at the doorway with a bucket in one hand, a mop in the other. 'They say tomorrow ye'll be a man. Bein' a man's no such a great thing.'

'Go away.'

'Go away, is it now. Now ye've got some English words on yer tongue. Now yer the Kahn's lovely boy, ye think ye can talk to me like that.' She put down the mop and the bucket which slopped grey water on to the floor, moved towards him, forcing him to scrape back in his chair.

'Leave me alone.'

'What's that ye've got there? A bit of jewellery is it? Been stealing some of Madame's jewellery, have ye?'

'I do not steal. It's mine. From my mother.'

'Now don't ye be telling fibs to Mary. Yer mother's dead. I've heard them say it. Come on, give us a look.'

He scrambled to his feet and backed away. 'She's not dead. She's alive. Alive.'

'If you havenae stolen it, ye'll want to show me then.'

He managed to stuff the box into his pocket before she grabbed both his arms, pinned them behind his back, drove him hard across the kitchen until he was forced back against a cupboard. He tried to twist his head away from hers as she leered in close, the bandages around his stitches beginning to loosen. With both his arms trapped against his own weight, he felt her withdraw one of her own from behind his back. She grabbed his chin.

'So, they says tomorrow yer going to be a man. Well, a man's got to learn to kiss the girls.'

Again he tried to wrench his head away but she held on to him firmly while her bony body kept him pinioned against the door behind him. The strength of her surprised him. He tried kicking out at her but she kept her legs well away. She pulled her mouth close to his, licked a tongue around her lips, then pressed them hard against his own. He felt her mouth moist and rough, he could taste the staleness of her breath mixed in with the taste of sweet Sabbath wine. In the darkness behind his clenched eyes, one word rose into his consciousness among all the other thoughts swirling in a panic inside his brain. He felt her pull away but she still had him pressed against the cupboard door. He sprang his eyes open, looked straight at her. Her breath heaved quickly in her chest, her green eyes glistened with excitement.

'Hairbrush.'

She stepped back. He repeated the word, confidently now, knowing he had discovered a combination of letters as potent as anything Papa Kahn might find in the Hebrew texts. He smacked a fist into his open hand, pounding out a rhythm as he taunted her with the power of his new vocabulary. 'Hairbrush, hairbrush, hairbrush.'

She retreated a step with each beat until she turned, ran out of the kitchen, slipping on the spilled water by the bucket. She stumbled, fell forward, regained her balance quickly, disappeared into the hallway. When his panic had died down, he let his body drop to the floor. He buried his head in the crook of his elbows and began to rock back and forth, back and forth on his knees. Between gulps for air, he began to sing. It was the first verse of his barmitzvah ceremony and he sang it over and over again:

Comfort, comfort my people, says your God.

He knew his words were in vain. He would never be comforted. By God, by his mother, by anyone. He had struck a rock in anger. He would forever be forbidden entry into the Promised Land.

CHAPTER ELEVEN

Avram heard the rabbi call his Hebrew name from the *bimah*. Uncle Mendel sitting beside him suddenly gripped his wrist.

'It is time, *boychik*.' The man's normally ruddy complexion was even more flushed than usual. 'When you return to your seat, no longer will you be a *boychik*. You will be a man.'

Avram stood up self-consciously in his newly tailored single-breasted jacket with matching waistcoat and short trousers, over which he wore an expensive silk *tallith*, the *barmitzvah* gift of Mr. and Mrs. Morris Green and their son, Solly. Celia had worked wonders with his bandage, reducing it to a small square which she had stuck over his stitches with fish glue. His hair covered most of the patch and he no longer felt like a wounded soldier of the Torah.

His time had indeed come. But somehow its passage was unfolding slowly in a tunnel of mental calm rather in a blurred panic, which was how he had always envisaged this day. He glanced up to the women's gallery where Celia sat on the narrow, steeply-angled seats, angelic in all her Sabbath finery. She waved to him surreptitiously. She wore gloves, which made her appear so much older than her years. Wedged upright beside her, Madame Kahn loomed motionless behind a black veil.

Deliberately, he gathered together the fringes of his *tallith* so that they would not snag on the edges of seats or jacket buttons. He squeezed past Uncle Mendel, Nathan and the rest of the row of male congregants who clacked back their hinged prayer-book ledges to let him pass. On the *bimah*, Rabbi Lieberman was waiting for him, resplendent in white robes, his silver pointer poised over the open scrolls of the Torah. And beside the rabbi, there was Papa Kahn who stepped forward, firmly shook his hand.

He felt himself ushered forward on to the step which provided the height for him to stand properly by the rabbi at the podium. When he was in position, Rabbi Lieberman cleared his throat and rattled off a series of mumbled Hebrew verses. As Avram waited for his moment, he looked out to the Holy Ark opposite which housed the other scrolls of the Torah. Across the top of the Ark, inscribed in gold lettering, beamed the words: *Know where you have come from and to where you are going.*

He shifted on the step, diverting his attention instead to the lettering inscribed in gilt on the blue velvet podium cloth in front of him. *Donated by Mr. and Mrs. Jacob Stein.*

The rabbi stopped his murmurings, indicated with a nod that it was now Avram's turn. A placard was placed before him. He already knew the blessings by heart. He half-spoke them, half-sung them in a low chant, pausing appropriately for the congregational responses. The synagogue then fell into silence as the space was created for him to proceed.

He gripped the podium with both hands, waited for the rabbi to settle the pointer on the Hebrew text on the rolled-out parchment in front of him. There were a few hissed 'Shushs' from the audience, a couple of empty coughs, then the whole congregation held its breath as he let out his own. He began slowly, his unbroken voice tentatively piercing the otherwise noiseless air.

Comfort, comfort my people, says your God.

Then another verse, the musical notation forcing him to quickly take up the gentle Hassidic lilt.

> *Speak to the heart of Jerusalem*
> *And cry to her*
> *That her time of service is ended*
> *That her iniquity is pardoned*
> *That she has received from the Lord's hand*
> *Double for all her sins*

His legs began to firm, his lungs shook off their anxious shallowness, he began to breathe more easily, more deeply, his voice growing stronger and stronger with each word. Rabbi Lieberman was pointing his progress across the scroll, but he had already abandoned the reading of the text. The words were inscribed in his head, branded painstakingly and indelibly into the parchment of his brain. His voice began to soar. The congregants who usually gave the *barmitzvah* boy two or three minutes of polite audience were stunned into listening.

His voice filled up the vaulted auditorium, the sound of his refrain spreading confidently outwards across the lower level of the synagogue, passing over Solly, Mr. Green, and the other wealthier male members of the community who sat at the front, closest to the Ark, closest to God. Then these notes of his moved backwards like a lapping wave, past the rows that included Nathan and Uncle Mendel, to touch the newer and poorer congregants modestly sitting in the shadows at the rear. He could hear his melodies reverently address the closed velvet curtains of the Ark, then wrap themselves around the synagogue's stout pillars to swirl upwards on vines of song to the women's gallery. There, for a sweet instant, his voice lowered to a whisper to caress Celia's ears before drifting on up through the roof. His song burrowed heavenwards through the muck, the soot and the grime of the city to be blown eastwards on the wind across clear blue skies.

His lungs may have been the driving force but it was the Aeolian harp of his heart that instilled his words with both joyous and wretched emotion as they sailed across purple-green hills, over Lowland mining towns and villages, followed railway tracks past distant rivers and lochs, and on towards the sea. As his melodies passed over shores of shingle, hardy fishermen looked upwards from tangled nets and shook their heads in recognition of the siren sounds that had haunted their sea-faring dreams.

From the coastline, his music was sucked up by flurries and squalls, protected by gulls and picked up by the mouths of doves. Ever eastwards, this flock of words and music flew on an airstream over the dark choppy surf, past shoals of shimmering fish, lone steamers and majestic fjords to the land of his birth. There, his mother, young and smiling and carefree, hugging herself in excited anticipation, waited to receive the gift of his song. Yellow flowers adorned her hair, silver thimbles patterned her pale blue dress that matched the colour of the sky. Her face filled with joy at the love conveyed in his music which whirled around her in an eddy of sound. Floating above her, the fiddler from the Riga streets played, his music matching Avram's own and together the words and notes broke off from their circular dance and soared in unison to the heavens. Higher and higher his song went, piercing the clouds, past the moon and beyond the stars, until his words reached the orbit of the Lord's countenance where they beseeched Him for the forgiveness he craved. By the time he had reached the fabulous crescendo to his *barmitzvah* portion even Mrs. Carnovsky who sat way back in the woman's gallery had forgiven him. Rabbi Lieberman stood motionless with the redundant silver pointer in his hand, Madame Kahn had lifted her veil, Papa Kahn's mouth was agape, Celia was smiling as tears ran down her face. Only young Nathan fully understood what he had heard.

Glasgow

1915

CHAPTER TWELVE

'You must forgive me for calling uninvited like this,' Jacob Stein said, as Madame Kahn took his bowler hat, gloves and umbrella. 'I have just been with Morris Green along the road. I thought I would come over. It is important business.'

Of course, it was important business. Important business was the least Avram could expect from such a man, who sat in the front row in the synagogue, who donated the books he studied at Hebrew School, who turned up unannounced in the middle of an evening ensconced in a fur-trimmed coat and the rich aroma of sweet brandy and cigars. Uncle Mendel called Jacob Stein a *ganze macher* – a big shot. After all, Jacob Stein was a bailie, a warehouse owner, a founder of the synagogue. And, of course, Jacob Stein was Uncle Mendel's employer. And although Avram did not know exactly what a bailie did, Uncle Mendel had told him it was the highest civic office any Jew had ever held in the City of Glasgow.

'*Komm*, Celia,' Madame Kahn said. '*Du auch*, Avram.'

He felt himself prodded by Madame Kahn into the presence of this large, rotund man with his thin moustache, sweet-smelling hair tonic and powerful voice that rumbled confidently from his belly.

'So, this is little Celia. Such a big girl she is becoming.'

Jacob Stein's tongue licked his fat lips as he bent down to tug lightly at Celia's black curls, then to squeeze her chin in his hand. 'So beautiful, too.' Jacob Stein pulled in close to Celia's face but she jerked her head away.

'Celia,' Madame Kahn hissed.

'Not to worry,' Jacob Stein said, unperturbed. 'Ah, yes. And this is the *barmitzvah* boy who once filled our synagogue so ... heroically ... yes, heroically, with his voice. This is ...?'

'Avram,' Papa Kahn interjected.

'Ah yes, Avram. You're quite a football player as well, I hear.'

'Nothing special.'

'Speak up, boy.'

'Nothing special, sir.'

'Hah. Nothing special. Such a modest boy. Only fourteen years old and playing for the senior team. That *is* something special.'

Papa Kahn cast a surprised look at Avram, then at Jacob Stein. 'You know more about the boy than I do.'

'I have my spies.'

'And what do they tell you?' Papa Kahn asked.

'They tell me what you and I already know. Football is not a career for a Jewish boy, eh?' Jacob Stein looked around the hallway. 'There is another boy, is there not?'

'Nathan. He's not so well at the moment,' Papa Kahn explained.

'I see. Nothing serious, I hope.'

'He feels things,' Madame Kahn said.

'Oversensitive,' Papa Kahn said, ushering his guest into the sitting room. 'Can we get you a little *schnapps*?'

Jacob Stein raised his index finger in salute to this suggestion. 'An excellent idea.'

Avram watched the adults move out of the hallway. The excitement was over. Homework waited for him back in the kitchen. But Celia grabbed him by the arm.

'Don't you want to know what this is all about?' she asked.

'I want to know why football isn't a career for a Jewish boy.'

'Stop with your football already. There's a war on. Come on.' She shepherded him to the half-open sitting-room door, pulled him down on to his haunches.

'Why isn't football a career for –' he whispered.

'Shush!' Celia scowled, placing a finger to his lips. 'Just listen.'

'Herschel and Martha, *l'chaim*,' Jacob Stein said, raising a glass of *schnapps* in turn to each of his hosts. Avram shifted in his crouch, feeling awkward yet curious to trespass on an occasion that merited the uttering of Papa and Madame Kahn's first names. He watched as Jacob Stein settled his bulky frame into Papa Kahn's armchair, the fingers of one hand drumming on the belly of his waistcoat, while the other gently swirled the amber liqueur in his glass.

'The war,' Jacob Stein sighed. 'It affects us all.'

'Yes, I know,' Papa Kahn said. 'But we are grateful for your contracts. We prefer to work in our shop making uniforms than in a munitions factory making shells. Don't we, Martha?'

'We thank you for your consideration, Herr Stein.'

'It is all part of the war effort,' Jacob Stein said. 'We must be seen to participate. And to volunteer to fight as well. This city raised a whole battalion in only sixteen hours down at the Tramways recruiting station last month. The patriotic urge to fight for King and country is overwhelming.'

Jacob Stein leaned forward in his chair, cradling his shot glass in his hands.

'But the Jews are beginning to suffer in all of this,' he said.

'In Poland and Lithuania,' Papa Kahn concurred. 'The situation is intolerable.'

'No, no, Herschel. The Jews here. Here in Glasgow.'

'In Glasgow?'

'Yes, in Glasgow. Our loyalty is in question.'

'But how? Why? We have shown our support. Jews have enlisted.'

'That is true. But there is something else.'

'What do you mean?' Madame Kahn asked.

'I mean...' And here Jacob Stein cleared his throat. 'I mean, it is the question of citizenship.'

'Citizenship? ' Papa Kahn said.

'Yes, citizenship,' Jacob Stein said firmly, easing back to languish fully in his chair.

'Citizenship,' Papa Kahn repeated.

'You know what I mean, Herschel. You are of Russian origin. You do not have British citizenship.' Jacob Stein paused. 'You are therefore ... in these times of conflict ... an alien.'

'What is an 'alien'?' Madame Kahn asked.

'*Zar*,' Papa Kahn snapped at his wife.

'Hmmmph,' uttered Madame Kahn. 'I have always been a foreigner here.'

'That may be so,' Jacob Stein continued patiently. 'But in war-time this is not so good. Especially in your situation, Martha.'

'My situation?'

'You are German,' Jacob Stein said.

'So?'

'I'm afraid that makes your situation more complicated. That makes you an enemy alien.'

Madame Kahn covered a gasp with her hand.

Jacob Stein went on. 'It is last week's sinking of the *Lusitania*. So many civilian lives lost. It has stirred up such anti-German feeling. There have been attacks against shops and individuals.'

'But how can this be?' Papa Kahn protested. 'I am working for the war effort. We both are. We are making the uniforms. How can we be aliens? We have lived here for years. How can Martha be an enemy?'

'It is the law,' Jacob Stein said. 'Listen, Herschel. Now is the time to decide.'

'To decide what?'

'To choose your nation. Are you a *Russki* or a Scot?'

Papa Kahn looked to his wife then back to Jacob Stein.

'Bah,' he snorted. 'You think this is a difficult decision? What do I owe Russia? Nothing. They gave me nothing and took away everything.' Papa Kahn rose dramatically from his chair. 'I am a Scot,' he declared. 'I am British. I am whatever you want! As long as I can be a Jew.'

Jacob Stein reached out, tugged on Papa Kahn's jacket, coaxing him back to his chair. 'Come, come. Don't worry. Of course, you can be a Jew. We can all be Jews here. They may try to convert us to Christianity but they do not try to kill us, eh?' Jacob Stein gave a slight laugh which changed to a cough. He continued in a more serious tone. 'I think we at the Jewish Representative Council can arrange to rush through your nationality papers but with you, Martha, it might be different.'

'How different?'

'I'm not sure exactly. It is out of my hands. Not a local matter. Not a matter for the Glasgow Corporation or the constabulary either. But for the Lord Advocate in Edinburgh, I believe. Or perhaps even the Secretary of State in London. We need to make representations. It will take time.'

'Time I have.'

'It's not that simple. You cannot stay here. You will have to go to some kind of camp.'

'Camp?'

'Yes, camp. All the enemy aliens living in Glasgow are being taken to a camp in England. Near Leeds.'

'I cannot go to a camp.'

Jacob Stein put out a consoling hand. 'I'm afraid you have to. The police or perhaps the army will come to take you there. You have no choice. It is best to prepare yourself for this.'

'Of course, I have a choice. I will not go.'

Jacob Stein ignored her and went on. 'Your brother Mendel is in the same position. He too is an enemy alien. But I shall do my best to make sure his work continues to keep him out of Glasgow. Away from the shipyards and out of trouble. He uses a small cottage in the countryside near Oban for his base while he's out travelling. He can stay there in the meantime. No-one will know to come looking for him.'

'Perhaps Martha can join him there too?' Papa Kahn suggested.

Jacob Stein looked at Madame Kahn. 'Well? What do you think of this idea?'

'I ... I ... I will not run away to the Highlands like some ... like some *kriminell.*'

'Hrrmph. Have it your way. But, there is also the question of the children.'

'The children were born here,' Papa Kahn said quickly.

'That is good. But what about the boy?'

'Which boy?' Papa Kahn asked.

'The footballer. Avram. Have you formally adopted him?'

'We wanted to,' Papa Kahn said. 'But we believe his mother might still be alive.'

'So he is not legally registered anywhere?'

'We are known as his guardians at the school. But officially registered? No.'

Jacob Stein thought about this information. 'Good. Then he will not be on their list. He is a nothing. A minor. A visitor. If the police come, don't say a word about him. He doesn't exist. He is a nothing.'

When the police came, Avram hid in the coal cellar. Through a grille just above pavement level he could still see and hear Madame Kahn as she was led away. 'I am not an alien,' she screamed, wrenching herself from the grasp of the accompanying constables. She walked proudly to join the rest of her compatriots in the horse-drawn police wagon. 'I am not an enemy,' she announced to neighbours who had come to watch. 'I do good works for this country. I make uniforms. I work hard for the war effort. I work until my fingers bleed.' She shook these very fingers at the onlookers. '*Jah!* I am not an alien. I am not a *kriminell.*'

Even after the police had gone, Avram stayed down in the dust and the darkness. He was as unafraid, unaffected and as unemotional as the lumps of cold black coal piled around him. When he returned to school the next day, he found he now belonged to a group of immigrant children taunted and branded 'aliens' by the others. But for him, the humiliation was far worse than that. For he knew that he wasn't even worthy of being an 'alien'. He was a nothing.

CHAPTER THIRTEEN

Avram crept into the bedroom. Nathan lay on his bed staring at the ceiling. Since the outbreak of the war, the boy had steadily become more morose, declining into a consistent melancholy until eventually he was confined to his bed.

'I know what's wrong with you,' Avram whispered.

Nathan turned to him, his eyes sunk deep into potholes of misery.

'Do you hear me, Nathan?' He wanted to shake him, to spark some life into the lethargy of the boy he now thought of as a young brother. 'Do you hear me?'

Nathan rubbed his head against the pillow in a nod causing a blob of spittle to escape from his mouth, roll down his chin.

'I learned this English language,' Avram said. 'And you lost your language. Don't you see? I have stolen your words. Do you hear me?'

Silence.

'And you are stealing my suffering, Nathan. Somehow you know how I feel. Deep inside. You know that I am a nothing. It is because of me you have all this pain.'

Nathan's dry lips began to mouth some syllables. Avram moved his head in closer, trying to decipher meaning from the hoarse rasp at his ear. He pulled away.

'I can't hear you. What are you saying?'

The sound from Nathan's throat breathed stronger and Avram leaned in again. He wasn't sure what he heard but he thought Nathan had said, 'I forgive you, Avram. I forgive you.'

'These are hard times,' Papa Kahn said, as he stood in the centre of the sitting room flapping a letter from Madame Kahn.

Papa Kahn had come to appear less grand to Avram now. The man's features had grown sallow, his beard untidy, lines that had once danced fleetingly on his forehead now formed permanent trenches of anxiety. He was surrounded by a perpetual gloom that buckled his shoulders, seeped into his spirit. On the rare times Papa Kahn was at home rather than in his shop, Avram would see him stooped in bowed vigilance at Nathan's bedside.

'Mary will work for us full-time,' Papa Kahn announced. 'With

Uncle Mendel kept away by these alien restrictions, she can take a room in his flat.'

Avram glanced at Celia. She looked exhausted. Since Madame Kahn's departure, he had helped out in the house where he could. He ran errands after school, beat the carpets, hauled in the coal, scrubbed the grate until it shone. But the real onus of maintaining the home fell more and more on the shoulders of Celia who looked after the rest of the flat as well as Uncle Mendel's, prepared the family dinners and tended to Nathan's needs. She cleaned out her brother's bedpans, changed his sheets, read him stories even though she was never sure if he was listening. Avram felt pained to see the weariness that grew around her eyes, the tightness contained in her brief smile of acknowledgement to him whenever he entered her presence.

Papa Kahn continued speaking, still with his wife's letter in his hand. 'But how can we even compare our own troubles to those of the Jews suffering in the Pale of Settlement and Galicia? We can live where we want, work where we want, worship where we want. We might be distrusted because of our nationality but we are not persecuted because of our faith. Think of your fellow Jews in Russia.'

Avram tried to think of his fellow Jews in Russia. He tried to think of his mother. He tried to think of Madame Kahn. But all he could think about was the fact that Mary's presence would now be permanent in the household.

Papa Kahn brought his wife's letter close to his eyes. 'And do you know what your mother writes, Celia? In the middle of all this war, all this *tzores*. She writes that she wants soap.' Papa Kahn read from the page. 'I do not care what my circumstances are, I will always retain my dignity. I will always bathe with expensive soap. Please, Herschel, send me bars of expensive soap. Lavender soap.' Papa Kahn held out his arms. 'Where will I get such soap in times like these? Avram? Are you listening to me?'

CHAPTER FOURTEEN

Avram shivered near the touchline as dark clouds skulked across the sky, dribbling their drizzle onto the red cinder recreation pitch. Some parents had come down to watch the semi-final against Victoria and Cathcart Boys' Club, and they now stood under umbrellas in scattered huddles along the perimeter. Papa Kahn wasn't among them. Papa Kahn wasn't even aware the match was being played. For he knew Papa Kahn had no time for such a frivolity as a game of football. So he stood alone and parentless in the cold, trying to salvage some joy from the importance of the fixture. If his team won today, they would play in the Glasgow Boys' Clubs final at Hampden Park, Scotland's national stadium. With real nets and white lines painted on rolled grass. With a capacity of close to 150,000 spectators for the big games, although the Boys' Clubs final would only attract a few hundred, maybe even a thousand. But Roy Begg said all the scouts would come to watch. Scouts from the big clubs. Though Avram knew there was only one club for him.

He was wearing Solly's boots, their too-largeness sorted by a couple of pairs of extra socks. His number eleven black and white-striped jersey clung damply to his skin. An older boy had worn it for a game the day before, and it remained unwashed. At least the rain would give it a good clean from the sweat and grass stains that endured. He preferred to play on grass rather than this cinder that gathered pools of water and scoured the skin on his legs if he fell in a tackle. Which was often.

'They'll try to snuff you out,' Roy Begg warned him. 'Bundle you out of the game early.'

It was a serious threat. Even though he was only playing a couple of years above his age, the rest of the players loomed like giants. Begg still called him a runt. He was too small to be of use through the centre where he lost out in the air or could be blocked easily by sheer physical strength. But out on the wing, he had space. Space to turn the size of his opponents against them, to weave their legs in a tangle, to outpace their lumbering forms. Until their frustration turned into desperate hacks and lunges he would have to try hard to avoid.

'Escovitz. What kindae fuckin' name's that?'

Avram looked up at his opposite number. A lanky, red-haired lad with a long, freckled face and teeth poking out at different angles that forced his thin lips into a permanent sneer. The boy was hugging himself in a twisted embrace to keep warm. It was as if his arms were all buckled up in a straitjacket.

Avram said nothing, knelt down, fiddled with the laces on his boots.

'Sounds like a Hun name.'

He tugged one of the loops into a tightness.

'It's a Gerry name. You're a bloody Gerry. A bloody Hun.'

'It's a Jewish name.'

'Jew. Hun. All the same.'

'It's not.'

'Ginger Dodds can smell a Hun a' the way from here to Parkheid.'

'I'm not a Gerry.'

'We'll see.'

The whistle went and a body blow from Ginger Dodds flattened Avram to the ground, expelling the air full out of him. From the touchline, he could hear Begg calling for him to get up and get on with it, but the strength had gone from his legs. He lay in the wet cinder, sucking in air in shallow swallows to avoid the pain that swamped his chest. The game went on above him. He managed to prop himself up on his arms but by the time he got to his feet, Victoria and Cathcart had scored. He patted his cheek, raw from a scrape in his fall. His jersey was soaked and streaked red from the cinder. Dodds was back facing him.

'Goal straight off, Hun boy. We're gonna fuckin' hammer you.'

This time Avram avoided the sweep of the elbow that came with the whistle blow. But Dodds stuck with him, tugging on his arm, pulling his jersey, running a boot down the back of his shin. Avram tried to twist away from his marker, find some space to take a pass, but the tall shadow stuck with him. He jogged backwards, sprinted forward, moved out of position but Dodds was always there, taunting, stinking of sweat, breathing his venom on to the back of his shirt.

When Avram eventually did get the ball, his legs were taken in a scythe from behind. He tried to push his hands out to break the fall, but not fast enough. He bounced onto his bruised chest, then spun over on to his back. He felt as if a giant anvil had settled in a crush against his ribs. It was difficult to breathe.

'You all right, boy?'

'My chest, sir.'

Begg was tugging at his shirt, rolling it up his body. His one eye took a worried swoop over the injury while his fingers prodded. Avram flinched from the searing soreness in his ribs.

'Hmm. Nothing broken.'

He felt liquid on his skin.

'This'll hurt before it gets better.' Begg massaged his ribs with some lineament. The pain made him cough until the firm strokes began to soothe. Then quickly his shirt was pulled down and he was hauled to his feet.

'It's no long to the end of the half,' Begg said. 'Try to keep out of his way. Then I'll sort you out.'

Avram jogged stiffly back on to the pitch. Dodds trotted up beside him.

'Next time, you won't get up, Hun boy.'

Avram tried to shrug him off, but Dodds stuck in close.

'Ye'll no get away from Ginger Dodds.'

And he didn't. Avram was marked out of the game. Wherever he went, Dodds would follow. And when the referee wasn't looking, there was always a tug at his jersey or a clip against his heels to remind him of the attention being paid. The only cheer to his miserable afternoon of frustration came when his team scored just before half-time to tie the game.

At the break, Begg grumbled as he rubbed in some kind of embrocation over his chest then wound a roll of bandages tight around his ribs.

'I can't shake him off, sir.'

'I see that.'

'But what can I do, sir?'

'Well, he's too big for you to take on.' Begg plucked at the thong that held his eye patch to reveal the deep ridge scarred across his forehead. Then his fingers moved to scratch the back of his bull neck in a thoughtfulness until he seemed to make up his mind. 'Stand right out at the touchline when you line up again,' he said.

Avram did as he was told. Ginger Dodds took up a stance opposite. Begg stood watching close on the side-lines. The whistle went for the start of the second half, but before Avram could move, Begg stepped forward fast between them and slammed an elbow into Dodds' face. It was a strike so swift in its execution that Avram could hardly believe it had actually happened. Dodd's cheek bone caved in from the ferocity of the blow and his legs collapsed from under him as he crumpled with a yell on to the cinder, clutching the side of his face. Begg was over him, dabbing a cloth to his cheek which was rapidly purpling into a swelling. Ginger Dodds spat blood, then a tooth.

'What's going on?' The referee had stopped the game and plodded over.

'He ran into that lad of mine,' Begg said. 'He'll be all right.'

'Lost something too.' The referee stooped to pick up the bloodied tooth. He pinched it between thumb and forefinger, brandished it at Avram.

'Dangerous play. I could have you off for that.'

'This one's been at him all game,' Begg intervened as he dragged his victim to his feet.

The referee seemed to ponder the difference in the size of the two boys.

'Well, get him off the pitch so as we can get on with it.' He flicked the tooth into a puddle, wiped his hands on his shorts then blew his whistle.

Begg shoved Dodds back on to the pitch. The boy's left eye was puffed up fleshy like a piece of raw liver and he wobbled on his feet. Avram wondered if Dodds knew who or what had hit him.

'Ah'll get you for this,' Dodds slurred at no-one in particular.

But from then on, Dodds kept his distance, finally giving Avram the space he craved to work the wing. He did his best to execute his tricks with the ball, but his injury had taken its toll. He couldn't move smartly or twist away. He took passes but he laid them off quickly. He shirked tackles. Almost in a mirror of his own frustration, the game dragged on with neither side able to pluck a victory out of the dreary afternoon. Then, against one of his team's few attacks, the Victoria and Cathcart full-back in a tackle scrambled the ball over his own bye-line for a corner.

All of Avram's team bar the goalkeeper came to jostle for position in their opponent's penalty area. Begg was behind the goal, pointing feverishly here and there at his black and white-shirted players.

Avram flinched from the pain that snapped across his bruised ribs as he bent to place the ball on the corner arc. He felt like David, the young shepherd boy, selecting the round, smooth pebbles that would fly the fastest and the most accurate towards their target. But instead of pebbles, he had a mud-caked soggy leather ball, split and torn in places along the seams so that he could see the taut pinkness of the blown-up pig's bladder within. He tried to pick out his centre-forward, Big Tam, who was racing back and forth across the goal signalling frantically at his cropped head. It was a head as tarnished and nobbled as any soldier's helmet. It was a head worthy of any Goliath.

But as soon as his foot swept through the ball, Avram knew he had hit the angle all wrong. Instead of his intended straight cross to Big Tam hovering around the penalty spot, he had put too much curl on his kick. Yet somehow he sensed that his own wrongness had diverted the leather sphere on to its true path. At first, the ball soared on a trajectory that looped high towards the goalmouth. It soared too high for Big Tam, too high for the goalkeeper who had come off his line to check Big Tam's run, too high for Ginger Dodds and a defender across the face of the goal who both leaped to head the cross but missed. Then, just as the ball should have faded away on a curl beyond the far-post, it seemed to stop and hang in mid-air as though waiting for its fate to be decided. The wind dropped and the rain ceased. A sheet of newspaper floated down into a puddle. The ugly vapours from the power station stacks lining the horizon sagged down into the grey sky. A skinny dog ran onto the pitch in pursuit of a mis-thrown stick. The players stood stonecast in their positions, set into their tableau with limbs akimbo, heads back and eyes wide-open. Waiting. Waiting for the ball to continue. Waiting for the curl. And when the ball did continue, when the curl did come, the ball didn't drift off behind the bye-line or over the bar as everyone had expected. Instead, it dipped and slipped into the goal just inside the far-post.

Roy Begg stood behind the goalmouth, staring blankly at the match ball which had bounced into his arms. The other players remained transfixed in their positions. The referee's whistle ripped through the stillness. A mass of black-and-white shirted players came to life and rushed towards Avram.

'Patsy,' Big Tam shouted. 'Yer a bloody genius.'

'I didn't mean it.' Avram looked at his feet, clad in their cinder-stained leather boots. The same feet that at eleven years old had once walked him from the docks at Clydebank to the Kahn's flat as if they had a mind of their own. 'I don't know what happened. But I didn't mean it.'

'Disnae matter,' Big Tam shouted, spluttering with excitement. 'Disnae matter you didnae mean it. Ten more minutes and we're in the bloody final. We just need to hang on.'

And hang on he did. Ten long minutes. With his chest aching from the bruising but blown up with pride.

CHAPTER FIFTEEN

On his journey home from the recreation park, Avram saw the lamplighter doing his rounds. He was a man as tall and thin as the pole he carried, clad in a dark Corporation uniform that merged with the encroachment of the night. The endless routine had honed the man's task to a minimum of skilled effort that made Avram stop and watch. First came the simple claw back of the lamp's glass door with the pole's hook. Then there was the neat flick on the switch with a twist of the same device. Finally, the smooth insertion of the flame through the glass entrance to ignite the gas jet. A whoosh and there was light, first blue, then softening into a yellow glow which melted the darkness like a warm bath on a cold night.

'Did ye win, lad?' the lamplighter said with a glance to the boots hanging around his shoulders.

'Yes, we won.'

'Looks like ye took a battering in the process.'

Avram nodded. 'The light on the pole? How does it stay on all the time?'

'A drop of water on the mineral. Some kind of chemical reaction I do not rightly know how to explain that gives off its own gas. Strike a light and ye've got a lasting flame. Same stuff for the lamp on a bicycle. Carbide, it's called.'

'I don't have a bicycle.'

'Maybe ye'll get one for Christmas.'

'I don't celebrate Christmas.'

The lamplighter cocked his head to the side in puzzlement. Then a look up and down the street seemed to bring him his answer. 'I see. This is the Jew neighbourhood, isn't it?'

Avram shrugged, always a bit fearful when his religion was separated out from the Protestant and Catholic faiths dominating the city. But the lamplighter seemed friendly enough and it was hard to avoid the facts staring him in the face. There was the synagogue on the corner, the *kosher* butcher with its Star of David painted on the window pane, the greengrocers further up with its sign in English and Hebrew lettering. Then came Papa Kahn's tailoring shop. Most of the neighbours he knew were Jewish.

'I suppose it is,' he said.

'The lads at the depot call this place "Jerusalem".' The lamplighter pushed his cap further back off his forehead and chuckled. 'Must be off, lad.' He patted Avram's shoulder as he passed. 'It's good to win. But savour it right, because ye could lose the next time.'

Avram walked on, thinking that if he couldn't be a footballer, he wanted to be a lampie. He would like to join them where they congregated around their depot near Tolcross, bantering and smoking, with their poles stacked against the storehouse wall, ready to fend off the darkness around Jerusalem.

'You look like the cat that got the herring,' Celia said as he entered the kitchen.

Her sleeves were rolled up and she had one hand deep in a blackened pot on the stove. He saw the skin of her forearms raw and reddened like Mary's.

'We're through to the final. At Hampden Park. Scouts from Celtic will come to see me play. To see me. Avram Escovitz. An immigrant boy from Russia.'

He wanted to pick her up, twirl her around in his excitement. But instead he told her all about the game and as he spoke, she stopped her scrubbing, took a seat by the kitchen table. With elbows on the surface, she clamped her chin between the palms of her hands and listened. He warmed to her interest. By the time he had personally triumphed over Ginger Dodds and scored the winning goal her eyes were lit up in a shine he hadn't seen for a long time.

'You are my hero, Avram Escovitz,' she said smiling. 'Now can this immigrant boy from Russia get cleaned up before Papa gets home?'

He wanted to tell her more. He wanted to tell her that this sitting here now, talking like this in the kitchen, was like a time before. Before the War, before Madame Kahn had been taken away, before Celia had become different, before he was a nothing. But suddenly Mary strode into the room.

'I'm in charge,' she announced breathlessly. 'Aye, I'm in charge. I'm yer mam now.'

'No, you're not,' Celia snapped back at her. 'My mother's not dead. She'll be back.'

'That may well be, young lady. But she isnae here to look after you now.'

'She'll be back. Then you'll be back too. In your proper place.'

'I dinnae want to hear none of yer nonsense,' Mary snarled. 'Nathan needs attending to. Leave the pots and go see to him. And when yer finished, wring out the washing and hang it up on the pulley. Go on. Go on.'

'You can't tell me what to do,' Celia shouted, as she got to her feet. 'You're only a servant.'

'That's where yer wrong, child,' Mary spat back. 'With Madame away, yer faither put me in charge. I'm no a servant. I am the housekeeper. So you does what I tell you. You can ask yer faither when he gets home. You can ask him if I'm lying.'

'I will.' Celia stamped her feet as she spoke. 'I will.'

'Yer brother needs seeing to. Like I said.'

'I'm going. But I'm going because I want to. Not because you told me. You bloody servant.'

Mary raised her arm quick, sent a slap sharp across Celia's face, the sound of flesh upon flesh snapping across the room. Celia stood frozen in the shock of what had occurred. Mary stared curiously at her own palm still inches away from Celia's reddening cheek. Eventually Celia lifted her hand to her face as if to check she had really been hit. She dabbed her fingers against the tender marks on her flesh in confirmation, then pushed Mary's hand aside and fled from the room.

Avram had been numbed by the shock of the slap as much as Celia. Now he felt his own anger rising but Mary turned on him quick with her green eyes blazing. 'Now see you. You listen to me. There are no bleeding hairbrushes any more. Just me. In charge.'

She pushed him backwards, throwing the boots from his shoulder. He tried to fend her off with flailing fists but she still managed to grab the flesh of one cheek between two of her knuckles and twisted tight. 'See! Mary's in charge.'

'Get your hands off me,' he shouted, wrenching her hand from his face.

'So, we're starting to fight back are we? Well, I'm going to make yer life a bloody misery.'

'See if I care.'

'You'll care.'

'No, I won't.'

'You think yer so damn clever. You'll care, all right.'

'There's nothing you can do to hurt me.'

'Yer mighty wrong about that.'
'What then?'
'Football.'
'What ... what about it?'
'There's to be none of it.'
'You can't forbid me to play.'
'Aye, I bloody well can. I'm in charge. No more football for you, d'you hear. From now on, you come straight home after school. There's work to be done. Same on Sundays. No more football. The Master agrees.'

That evening was the first evening of *Hanukkah*. The Festival of Lights. The Festival of the Rededication of the Second Temple.

'We are here to celebrate the miracle of the oil,' Papa Kahn said to Avram and Celia. He had taken the *menorah* into Nathan's bedroom so that his son could also witness the lighting of the first candle. 'The miracle of the oil when Judah and his Jewish warriors, the Macabees, defeated the armies of King Antiochus and reclaimed their Temple. There, in the profaned Sanctuary, the Macabees found only one small jar of purified oil. It was enough to sustain the *Ner Tamid*, the Everlasting Light, for just one day. But the oil miraculously lasted for eight days until a fresh supply could be found. That is why ... '

'... we celebrate *Hanukkah*,' interrupted Celia. 'By lighting a candle for each day of the miracle.'

Papa Kahn smiled. 'You know my speeches too well, daughter. *Hanukkah*. The festival of miracles and heroes.' Papa Kahn looked at the wasted figure of his son while Celia made the blessing and lit the first candle. 'The festival of miracles and heroes.'

Avram stared at the solitary burning taper adorning the *menorah* like a lone sentry. He remembered the same ceremony being conducted back in his home in Russia when it was he that was given the privilege of lighting the first candle. Then, together with his mother he would sing the same *Hanukkah* songs as he sang now with Celia and Papa Kahn, melodies that seemed to possess no geographical boundaries, melodies that somehow had wandered intact through the Diaspora locked in the hearts of his people. Was it like this in other homes in countries to which Jews had fled throughout the world? Singing the same melodies, like some universal code? He even recalled, in some vaguer memory, his mother giving him a few coins, the *Hanukkah gelt*, to celebrate the festival, and he remembered the joy he felt at being entrusted with such a wonderful gift of adult currency.

He half-shut his eyes so that the flame before him fractured into shards of light that beamed back at him. Perhaps the light would bestow on him another miracle. Or turn him into a hero.

'Now let us go into my study,' Papa Kahn said.

Avram had not been in Papa Kahn's study since the eve of his *barmitzvah*. The room not only appeared smaller but it had become neglected. The shelves of books around the walls seemed to sag both from their extra layers of dust and the weariness of their owner. Bolts of military cloth and boxes of military insignia now took precedence over everything else. It was here that Papa Kahn instigated the orders for the clothes that would turn ordinary men into soldiers. By the side of the desk, there lay a large opened box. He could see bars of soap stacked up neatly inside. The smell of lavender pervaded the room.

Papa Kahn slumped down into his leather chair behind the large desk. He flicked a hand back and forth across the top row of his abacus, following the rhythm of the beads until he was ready to speak.

'I put Mary in charge of the household,' he said eventually. 'You must do as she says.'

'But, Papa, she hit me,' Celia protested.

'She said you swore at her. Is that true?'

'She said she was my mother.'

'Did you swear at her?'

Celia said nothing.

'Avram?'

'I don't remember.'

'Very noble of you, Avram. Very noble. But your loyalty should be to me.' Papa Kahn turned his attention back to Celia. 'I don't know where you get this language from. Not from me or your mother. From the schoolyard, no doubt. From now on, you are to behave like a young lady, not some girl from the gutter.'

'But she provoked me.'

Papa Kahn sighed. 'Until Mother comes back, I need Mary's help. And I need you to cooperate. She has been with us many years.'

'Even if she strikes your daughter?'

'I will speak to her about that. It is an isolated incident and it will not happen again.' Papa Kahn looked at Avram. 'Is there something you want to say about the matter?'

Avram tried to keep his voice steady as he spoke. 'What ... what about my football, sir?'

'What about your football?'

'Mary says I have to come home straight after school.'

'If she needs you for errands or housework, she is within her authority to make such reasonable requests.'

'But they are not...'

'Enough!' Papa Kahn slammed his fist on the desk. 'Enough! Enough of your nonsense, both of you. Enough of this behaviour.'

'But Papa –' Celia interjected.

'I said it was enough. You must learn to get on with Mary. Much worse is going on in this world than your petty domestic squabbles.'

Celia turned away but Avram didn't move. The Glasgow schoolboy's final was only a fortnight away.

'Please, let me play football,' he pleaded. 'Just two more weeks. Please.

Papa Kahn looked up from his desk. 'You will not question my decision. You will do as I say. No more football.'

'But...'

'*Fertig*! Enough of this selfish behaviour.'

Avram felt Celia pulling at his arm and he let her lead him away. At the doorway, he turned back to see Papa Kahn stoop to reach into the cardboard box by the side of his desk and pull out a bar of soap.

That night, he had a dream he had not dreamt for a long time. His mother was watching him from the quayside as he clung on to the mast of a raft that was lurching in the suck and heave of a wild ocean swell. But this time the raft was no longer roped to the harbour. It had been ripped free of its moorings and was being rocked out to sea. He looked around where he expected to see the figures of men who looked like the Prophets, men wrestling with ropes and winches, their feet slipping around on the bodies of silvery fish that had been washed up on to the deck. But there was no-one. The craft was empty. He shouted back to the shore. 'What will happen to me, Mother? What will happen to me?' But his words were blasted back at him in the wind. He wiped the salt spray from his eyes and searched the horizon. His mother was nowhere to be seen.

He awoke to the sound of the ash-bins being emptied out of the back court. He got up and tiptoed over to the window from where he watched the glow from the distant foundry chimneys roast the night sky. He tried to imagine the colony of workers toiling in the heat. He saw the sweat on their skin and the strain in their muscles as they shovelled the ore, coal and limestone into the blast furnaces. Their lungs breathed shallow the air dense with coal dust and the sand from the moulds, their ears immune to the roar of the fans and the constant winching of the metal containers lurching under their load of molten ore. He saw their arms gloved in leather reaching up to ladle the scalding liquid into the moulds, each man bearing the marks of his carelessness where he had allowed the metal to spill and splash beneath his apron on to his skin. Out beyond the blast furnace rooms, tired workers crouched among the dull, lifeless shapes of their labour – the axles, the wheel hubs, the rail clamps, the engine blocks. They smoked their tobacco quietly, communicating the occasional vital word, grateful for the silence.

'The Devil's work in the furnaces of Hell,' was what Madame Kahn called it. 'That's where you'll go if you don't do what you're told,' she threatened. 'To the *fabriken*.'

Ribbons of clouds cleared from across the moon and as he followed the shadows of men emptying the bins into the wagon on the street, he wondered what would be worse. Working in the *fabriken* or not playing football.

CHAPTER SIXTEEN

Celia had once told Avram his footballing skills were a kiss on his feet from God. He chose to believe her. For where else could his talent have come from? He had not grown up with the game in Russia, he did not know that football even existed until that day on the streets outside the Kahns' tenement close. But what God had given, He could also take away. He knew that. He knew that this God was ready to punish the slightest sin, just as He had done to Moses. Just as He would do to him for his sin of dealing with Mary in anger, threatening her with the hairbrush. Or trying to talk back to Papa Kahn. But there was one man whose wrath he prayed might be equal to that of the Almighty.

'What do you mean you can't play football?' Roy Begg screamed. 'Don't stand there dumb, staring at your feet. Answer me, boy. Answer me.'

'I'm needed at home, sir.'

'Well, I need you at school. Our most important game is coming up. You have to play.'

He felt a droplet of sweat trickle from under his arm down the side of his rib-cage. 'I'm not allowed to play, sir.'

'No such thing, Escovitz. You're mine. Remember what I told you, Jew boy. You're mine. You play when I tell you.'

'There's too much to do at home, sir.'

'Why is your home so bloody special?'

'Because Madame Kahn is an enemy alien.'

'Who's this Madame Kahn?'

He explained.

'A German. A bloody German. Wouldn't you know it.' Roy Begg's face twisted into a scowl but he appeared to calm down. 'I don't think Mr. Kahn understands what a talent you have. It's a talent to be encouraged.'

'Mr. Kahn doesn't really know about my football, sir.'

'What do you mean?'

'I never talk about it, sir.'

'Why not? It's something to be proud of.'

'Maybe you could tell him that, sir.'

Begg scratched the back of his thick neck shedding flecks of skin on to his sweater.

'You'll play for Celtic one of these days. I'm sure of it. I've got my connections. I know the scouts. Don't you want to play for Celtic?'

'Yes, sir.'

'Good. You stick with Roy Begg and the colour of your jersey will be the green and white. Now you tell this Mr. Kahn of yours that Roy Begg is coming to visit. Tomorrow evening. At eight o' clock.' And then the gym teacher added. 'I'm coming privately, mind you. In a personal capacity. Not as a representative of the school. Make sure you say that. Personal capacity.'

It was not until the following morning that he found the courage to tell Papa Kahn about Roy Begg.

'Again with the football. What's this with the football? If Mary needs you to help in the house, then that is the priority. What business is it of a gym teacher?'

'He says he wants to see you in a personal capacity.'

Papa Kahn rubbed his forehead. 'All right, then. All right. But ask him to wait until *Hanukkah* has finished. I will see him next week. After *Hanukkah*.'

It was during *Hanukkah* that Rabbi Lieberman came to the flat. The visit was expected and the rooms were extra clean as if for Passover. Mary was asked to bake special cakes and Papa Kahn went to much effort to purchase a bottle of *kosher* wine for the occasion.

Avram was sitting by Nathan's bedside reading the boy a story when Papa Kahn entered with the rabbi. The two of them were flushed in their cheeks. Crumbs of pastry adorned the rabbi's beard.

'This is the boy,' Papa Kahn said, his voice louder than usual.

Rabbi Lieberman approached the bed. Nathan was propped up on his pillows, his head hanging loosely to the side on which Avram sat.

'He hears you when you read to him?' Rabbi Lieberman asked.

'I don't know, rabbi.'

'No acknowledgement? No sign? No movement?'

'Nothing, sir.'

Rabbi Lieberman moved in closer. 'Such a paleness and a thinness. Such dark circles around the eyes.' The rabbi placed the back of his hand on Nathan's forehead. 'And such a coldness. The doctor ... what does the doctor say?'

'Nothing physically wrong,' Papa Kahn said. 'A disease of the spirit. A melancholy.'

'He has always been like this?'

'In the last few years he has been worse. Before that, he was just a quiet child. Very sensitive to others around him. If they were happy, he was happy.'

'And if they were sad?'

Papa Kahn did not reply. Rabbi Lieberman put his hand on Papa Kahn's arm. 'I am just thinking, Herschel. Just thinking. But have you heard of the legend of the *lamed vav?*' The Rabbi turned on Avram '*Lamed vav*, boy. Quick, quick. What do the letters *lamed vav* stand for?'

'The number thirty-six.'

'Very good, Avram. I am glad you remember something of what I taught you. Now, Herschel, do you know of this mythology of the *lamed vav*? Of the thirty-six righteous men?'

Papa Kahn shook his head.

The rabbi continued. 'Some Talmudists believe that at any given time in this world there are thirty-six men who take on all the suffering of humankind. The *lamed vav*. They bear the burden of our misery. Without them, our collective grief over the condition of humanity would be so great we would not be able to endure living. These righteous *lamed vav* represent a great paradox. They must be sensitive enough to absorb all of our suffering yet strong enough to endure it on our behalf. They are truly righteous men.'

'You are saying Nathan is one of them?'

The Rabbi sighed. 'Na, na, na, na. It is unlikely. He would have to be part of a tragic dynasty of suffering passed down from one generation to another. Although the boy may not at first be aware he himself is a *lamed vav*, someone of the previous generation would have had to bear the legacy before him. Is there anyone in your family like that?'

'No-one.'

'Then Nathan will not be either. But perhaps he has some *lamed vav* blood in him. And therefore he is more sensitive to suffering. When this war is over as soon it must be and your family is reunited, let us hope God willing the boy will be returned to good health. Wait until then, Herschel. Wait until then and see what happens.'

The two men disappeared from the room leaving Avram to contemplate the righteousness of his companion. He picked up Nathan's skinny arm, feeling the lightness, almost a nothingness, before he let it drop back down on to the bedclothes.

'So, my little one of the *lamed vav*,' he whispered. 'I am giving you all my suffering. The suffering of a nothing. What do you say about that? Is it too much to bear?'

He shook Nathan's arm which only caused the boy's head to slump further sideways on the pillow.

'Well, tomorrow the suffering will stop.'

Nathan let out a groan. Avram realised he had been squeezing the boy's fingers too tightly.

* * *

The grandfather clock in the sitting room was still striking eight when the doorbell rang. Mary was working in the kitchen, Celia was out, and Avram was half-hoping Papa Kahn might go to the door himself. The doorbell rang again.

'Avram!' Mary called.

He ran into the hallway, wiped his palms along the sides of his short trousers, took a deep breath, then opened the front door. There stood Roy Begg in a brown three-piece suit, bow-tie and homburg. Roy Begg without his whistle, without his tawse, without his punch bag. Yet his jutting, strutting physical power seemed hardly constrained by the confines of his suit. The man loomed over him, now as a one-eyed civilian possessing a life outside of the school that allowed him to stride through the streets of the Gorbals in his brown and white co-respondent shoes, to ring doorbells and to hand over his hat and gloves.

'Sir.'

Begg grunted a greeting, twisted his neck in his collar, then sniffed the air. Avram sniffed too, taking in the thick aroma of boiling chicken drifting into the hall from the kitchen.

'Where is your ... Mr. Kahn?'

'I will tell him you are here, sir. Sometimes he doesn't hear the bell.'

But Papa Kahn was already at the door of his study.

'Ah, Mr. Begg. Welcome to my home.'

The two men shook hands. Side by side, they drew up to the same height yet Papa Kahn appeared dwarfed by the gym teacher. Avram turned to leave.

'No,' Papa Kahn said. 'Tell Mary to bring us tea in the study. Then you will sit with us. After all, this business concerns you most of all. Is that not correct, Mr. Begg?'

Avram sipped at his glass of lemonade, stared at Roy Begg over the rim. The curtains to the normally darkened study had been opened and a shaft of light shone through the dust to light up a sheen on the gym teacher's slicked back hair. He noticed that the usual black leather eye-patch had been swapped for a brown one which matched the colour of the man's suit and shoes. Begg sat stiff with a saucer palmed in one hand while his large fingers awkwardly hinged around the handle of a delicate cup. Papa Kahn drank his tea in his customary way, sucked through a cube of sugar wedged between his teeth. The gentle noise Papa Kahn made when he performed this action was the only sound in the room. Avram squirmed to each slurp.

'These are Jew things, aren't they?' Begg nodded towards a small table on which sat a filigree spice container, an *etrog* box and a pair of silver candlesticks.

'Yes, they are Jewish artifacts for specific festivals,' Papa Kahn replied. 'Would you like me to explain them to you?'

'No. It's all right.'

Silence again. Avram took another mouthful of lemonade, letting the liquid slip bitterly over his tongue into the dryness of his throat. Begg shifted in his seat and spoke again.

'Avram has a natural gift. Are you aware of that, Mr. Kahn?'

'A natural gift is something given by God.'

'I am a religious man myself. And I do believe Avram's talent is God-given.'

'This talent with a ball. You think this is something God cares about when there is so much suffering in the world?'

Begg put down his cup and saucer, braced his hands on his thighs. 'The war will soon be over and I am convinced Avram will have a fine career in football.'

'And what kind of career would that be, Mr. Begg?'

'When he leaves school, he can play for a Boys' Brigade club. I am associated with one myself. From there, he can get picked up by one of the big clubs. Glasgow Celtic perhaps. Third Lanark. I know some of their scouts.'

'You think this is a career? This Glasgow Celtic?'

'What are the alternatives? The mines or the shipyards? The factories? The mills?' Begg spread out his hands to indicate the bolts of cloth scattered around the room. 'No disrespect to yourself, sir, a tradesman?'

'I will ignore that comment, Mr. Begg, and tell you this. As a non-academic member of the school staff you may not be aware that Avram is an intelligent boy. He is particularly good with figures and mathematical concepts. In this respect, he is like me. But unlike me, he will not give up his studies. He will continue with his secondary education. Even a tradesman can hope for better things for his family. Isn't that so, Avram?'

Avram tensed to the question. And then finding a courage he didn't believe he possessed, he heard himself say quietly but firmly: 'No, sir.'

'No? What do you mean, "no"?'

'Tell him, Mr. Begg. Please tell him, sir.'

'Mr. Kahn. If Avram is to stay on to study, can we at least let him continue playing football as well? There is an important final coming up.'

'Mr. Begg. Football as a hobby. I have no objection to that. But it seems you have great hopes for Avram. That is your business and I appreciate your concern, although I don't want you filling the boy's head with ambitions he cannot fulfil. But my business is that I have great demands on my time and energy to supply military uniforms for our Forces, my wife has been unjustly interned and I have another son who is bed-ridden. I have doctor's bills and possibly school fees to pay. I need Avram to help in the home. Football is not a priority in the life of this family right now. Surely you must see that?'

Roy Begg poked a finger into his collar and wriggled his neck. 'Forgive me for saying, but if I came here and told you Avram was a genius at mathematics, I am sure you would allow him the extra time to study. Football has its qualities too. It is good for discipline and team spirit. It builds character. And Avram's ability should not be under-estimated. It can earn him a decent wage. There's young players pulling down three pounds a week. And it can earn him respect. It could make him well-known in this city. That surely can only be a blessing for an immigrant Jew. You should not mock it.'

Papa Kahn leaned forward on his desk. 'Tell me, Mr. Begg. Are you familiar with our ways?'

'You mean the ways of the Jew?'

'Yes, that is what I mean.'

'A little. Yes.'

'Then you should know that Avram can never be a footballer.'

'Why? Is it against your laws?'

Papa Kahn smiled. 'Not exactly. But this Glasgow Celtic and these other teams. They play on a Saturday, do they not?'

Begg nodded.

'Well, that is our Sabbath. Avram cannot play on the Sabbath. I forbid it. It is our day of rest. As long as he is a member of this household, he will never be a footballer. That is final.'

Begg rose to his feet. His face had purpled around the thong of his eye patch. 'Let me tell you something about you Jews. You should know your place. Coming from Germany with all your strange customs and special foods.' He grasped the top of Papa Kahn's desk. 'Look at your wife. Locked up as an enemy alien. You should be more contrite. You should be adopting our ways. You are our guests. You say you want to be part of this culture, but everything you do keeps you apart. Your food, your language, your holidays. In this country, you should learn it is the Sunday that is the Holy Day, not the Saturday.'

Papa Kahn had remained calm throughout the whole tirade. When he spoke now, his voice came out slow and even. 'Mr. Begg. I think you should leave. And you should know that even if I could spare Avram his football, I would never again allow him to practise under your tuition.'

'You should be more contrite,' Begg spluttered. 'You Jews should be more contrite.' He turned and strode out of the room. The front door slammed shut leaving Avram trembling in his chair. His lungs had tightened and he could only make his breathing come in short gasps. Papa Kahn came out from behind his desk and stood over him.

'I never want to hear you contradict me like that again. Do you hear me?'

Avram pulled his arms around himself.

'Do you hear me? Football isn't everything.'

'Yes, it is.

'I told you. Don't contradict me.'

'Please, Papa Kahn. Just let me play in the final. That's all I want. Please let me play. Without football, I am nothing.'

Papa Kahn placed a hand on his shoulder. 'This I will tell you, Avram. It is my final word on the subject. There will be no more football. Celia will come out of school. She is a very clever girl but I need her at home. It is a great pity, but this I must do. Nathan? I don't know what will happen to him. God willing, he will live through all of his troubles. But you, Avram. I want better things for you. I want you to stay on at school. To keep on with your studies. This is your chance to be a something, Avram. Not this ... *football*.'

CHAPTER SEVENTEEN

The weather had turned from a bleary drizzle to solid rain by the late afternoon, making a dark day even darker. Avram stamped his soles against the brick wall. Solly stood beside him, hands thrust deep in his pockets, glancing up and down the length of the back lane behind the tenement building a few hopscotch jumps from where they lived. Solly snorted out a foggy breath. Just like a horse in a dawn mist, Avram thought, recalling for a moment a fractured memory from a childhood visit to the Rumbula Forest outside Riga. His mother had lifted him up, settled him on the back of the horse. Or was it just a pony? He could feel the coarse hair, the powerful muscle and the warm life of the beast on the bare skin of his thighs. He remembered the texture of the mane in his hands – tough and matted, not fine as expected.

'Just like a little Napoleon,' his mother had said before swinging him back to the ground. His mother had laughed. She wore the same pale blue dress she always seemed to wear in his memories. Her teeth shone white in her laughter, not yellow and rotten like so many of the teeth he saw in this city's population.

Across the back green and up at a second floor tenement window, Avram could see Solly's father, Lucky Mo, his bald head round like a football, hunched over a desk in his shirt-sleeves, sorting out the betting slips in the cosy glow of a table-lamp. There was a cigarette fixed to the corner of the man's mouth. Sometimes when business was good, there would be a cigar. But not with the war on. 'Trains only for soldiers to front. Not for punters to tracks,' was how Lucky Mo summed up the wartime restrictions wiping out most of the season's racing card.

The room in the tenement was Lucky Mo's office. A single-room in a single-end that at night housed a whole family glad to receive the day-time rent. Solly was his father's runner. That was his job now he'd left school. Learning the business, picking up the bets, writing down the odds on the back of a garden shovel, keeping guard in case the polis came noseying around. Which, according to Solly, was often.

'I'd love to have seen Begg's face,' Solly said.

'It wasn't funny.'

'I know. But ye were Begg's big hope. He thought he'd discovered a new Patsy Gallacher. Imagine Patsy no being allowed to play 'cause it was *Shabbos*.'

'I got a note. I'm out of Begg's class for good.'

'Yer having me on?'

'Scout's honour.'

'Kids'd kill their mams for that. Yer one lucky bastard.'

Avram thought about this. He wouldn't kill his mother for anything. Not even to play football. He didn't think he would kill Madame Kahn either, even if she was an enemy alien. Papa Kahn had sent her another parcel of soap this morning. Avram had taken it to the post office for him. His hands still smelled of lavender.

'I'm not a lucky bastard. I missed out on the final.'

'Yer team lost six-nil. Ye wouldnae have made up that much of a difference.'

'Scouts from Celtic were there.'

'Just as well, then. Ye wouldnae have wanted them to see ye on the back-end of such a bloody hammering.'

'It was my only chance to…'

'Haud yer whisht,' Solly said suddenly. 'Somebody's coming.'

A figure had appeared at the far end of the lane in the half-light. Head bowed, cap fixed tight, hands in pockets. Solly let out a coded whistle and the lamp went out in the room on the second floor. Avram could still see the glow from Lucky Mo's cigarette.

'Get ready to run when I tell ye,' Solly said, checking out the other end of the lane.

The figure looked up, glanced from side to side, then proceeded up the alleyway. Head bowed again, feet avoiding the puddles that had quickly formed.

'Maybe it's the lampie,' Avram whispered. There was an open-flame gas lamp halfway between them and the approaching figure.

'Wheesht,' Solly hissed but then he relaxed. 'It's all right. It's just a punter.'

The man came closer. As he reached Solly, he handed something over quick, then he was past. Avram looked after the man's back retreating into the rainy darkness. He had never even got to see his face, just a whiff of beer breath. Solly whistled again. His father's light came on.

'The Mad Hatter,' Solly said as he unwrapped the piece of paper.

There were some silver and copper coins inside. He squinted up close at the writing of the bet.

'Who's The Mad Hatter?'

'Bernie Ross. Works at Mathieson's. Ye ken where I mean. Up at Gorbals Cross. Mathieson's Hatter, Hosier and Outfitters. The Mad Hatter. That's his *nom de plume*.'

'His what?'

Solly smugly repeated the word.

Avram managed a laugh. 'Sounds like you've got a bunch of marbles stuck in your gob.'

'I thought ye were the smart one learning yer fancy French and Latin.'

'Maybe if you pronounced it better.'

'Well, anyway. It means alias, like the criminals have. Nobody uses their real names with their bets.' Solly reeled off a list of names and their aliases. Avram was surprised how many of Lucky Mo's punters he knew. A lot of local shopkeepers and tradesmen. A lot of Jews. A lot of Irish.

'Then there's Baked Fish,' Solly said.

'Who's Baked Fish?'

'Come on. Ye ken who I mean.'

'Munro the Fishmonger?

'Try again.'

'I don't know.'

'Come on.'

'I give up.'

'Yer Uncle Mendel.'

'Uncle Mendel bets on horses?'

'Why not? It's no a sin last time I looked.'

'It's illegal.'

'Like I said, it's no a commandment. It disnae say anywhere – "Thou shalt not bet on the two-thirty at Ayr."'

'I can't believe it.'

'Well, there's a lot more ye wouldnae believe. We've got punters that cannae speak a word of English but can scan a racing card as fast as the Mourner's Kaddish. Where's yer Uncle Mendel anyway? He's no been around.'

'He's staying out of Glasgow until all this enemy alien stuff's sorted out.'

Solly checked out both ends of the lane again, then glanced up at his father's window. He snatched a cigarette from behind his ear, scraped a match against the dry underside of a lifted brick and lit up.

'It was my only chance to get spotted by Celtic,' Avram said, taking up his thoughts where he had left them before the arrival of The Mad Hatter. 'My only chance.'

'What are ye moaning about now?'

'Not playing the final.'

'There's nothing ye can dae about it.'

'I could run away. Play for a boys' club.'

'Dinnae be daft. Where would ye go? And anyway ye'd still need permission from Mr. Kahn to sign for a club. Ye'll have to wait till yer an adult. Adults do what they want. Want a drag?'

Avram took the cigarette, inhaled. The end was wet, almost soaked shut. He inhaled again, this time sharp, drawing strands of tobacco into his mouth. The smoke scratched hard in his throat and his lungs but he managed not to cough. He handed the cigarette back. 'I don't want to wait that long.'

'Lots of players dinnae play till they're in their twenties.'

'Not Patsy.' He knew Gallacher had signed for Celtic when he was eighteen. He would have been contracted earlier but the teenager had wanted to finish his apprenticeship down the shipyards. 'I want to play now.'

'Look at all the players breaking up their careers by enlisting,' Solly wheezed, managing to hold the smoke deep in his lungs and speak at the same time. 'God knows when they'll come back to the gemme. If they come back at all.'

'That's different. I told you – I want to play now.'

'Ye can play with the Jews. They've got a team. They play on Sunday.'

'The Jews? They always lose. Anyway, it's not the same. There's no future with the Jews. With a proper boys' club, I might get picked up by the scouts.'

'Yer a nutter, d'ye know that? A bleedin' spoiled nutter at that.' Solly stamped out the cigarette, laid his back flat against the wall, pulled his cap down over his face.

The rain was coming down heavy now. Avram didn't have a hat. He turned up the collar of his jacket, watched the sheets of water strafe the muddy pool at his feet. He wanted another drag on a cigarette.

'What do you mean, I'm a spoiled nutter?'

Solly ignored him, began a tuneless whistle.

Avram grunted, scuffed his shoes against the loose stones underfoot. A rain drop rolled off his cap and on to his nose. He wiped it off with the back of his hand. A light came on at a first floor window. A woman came into the room, hauled open the window.

'Ma bleedin' washin',' she moaned, snatching her laundry off the outside pulley.

Avram snorted a laugh as did Solly. He felt the tension between them ease.

'Aye, yer a spoiled nutter,' Solly sniffed. 'So what if ye dinnae get to play for Celtic? Ye can always play football for fun. The park's full of teams on a Sunday needing their numbers made up. Meanwhile, yer getting an education.'

'I don't want an education.'

'Dinnae knock it, Avram. Yer clever. Really clever. When ye came here ye couldnae speak the language, never mind kick the leether about. Now look at ye. Staying on for secondary. And yer always thinking about all that religious stuff. Ye could be a rabbi or something.'

'What? Like Lieberman?'

'Just dinnae be like me if ye can choose not to be. Standing out here in the rain waiting for the polis or the punters while my father's working illegal. Just dinnae be like me.'

Another figure appeared at the far end of the lane. Avram braced himself to run but Solly held him back

'It's the lampie, ye bampot.'

Avram peered down the lane at the tall, lanky, uniformed figure emerging from the drizzle with his lit-up pole laid over his shoulder like the rifle of a soldier coming through the fog on a French battlefield. Avram curled his fingers into the shape of a make-shift gun, sounded off a shot. Then, without saying goodbye to his friend, he ran off through the rain to his Hebrew class.

'Ah, it's you, Avram.' Rabbi Lieberman reluctantly sat back down. 'These lighting restrictions make everything such a darkness. *Nu?* I am in a hurry. Quickly, now. What do you want?'

'Today we studied from the Book of Samuel. The story of King David.'

'*Nu*?'

'There is something I don't understand.'

'*Nu*? Spit it out. Quick, boy. Quick.'

'Are there two Gods, *rebbe*?'

'What are you saying?'

'I just wanted to know if there could be two Gods?'

'How can you say such a thing? You of all boys, with the *Shema* prayer in your *barmitzvah* portion.' The rabbi pointed a gloved finger heavenwards. '*Shema yisrael adoshem elokenu, adshem echod*. Hear O Israel, the Lord our God, the Lord is One.' Then he turned his finger on Avram. 'Are you *meshugge*?'

The rabbi's histrionics no longer impressed Avram. Back before his *barmitzvah*, the pointed finger may have intimidated him into submission in the same way as Lord Kitchener's poster persuaded troops to enlist for The Front. But now, with the war into its third year and so many hundreds of thousands of lives lost, Avram's confidence in the authority of God and his earthly servants had eroded to the point of questioning everything he had been taught.

'It's just that it seems God loved David so much,' he said.

'This is true. David was an *eesh ahoov*. A beloved man.'

'But he broke two of God's Commandments, *rebbe*?'

'And what Commandments were those?'

'Adultery.' Avram said the word hesitantly unsure of the nature of a sin he assumed could only be committed by adults.

'Go on.'

'And then he had Bathsheba's husband killed by sending him to the front line.'

'That was Uriah. Uriah the Hittite. And, and…?

'Is that not murder?'

The rabbi began to fiddle with the straps of his briefcase. 'That is not for us to judge. *Nu*? What's the point? Get to the point.'

'Why did God treat him so kindly?'

'What do you mean, "kindly"?'

'Why did He allow David a life full of glory, when he was a sinner against the Commandments?'

'Na, na, na, na. God was not so kind to David. Their first child – the child of David and Bathsheba died in infancy. That was the punishment. The death of the child.'

'But after the first child they had another child, Solomon, who became a famous king. And look what God did to Moses when all he did was strike a rock...'

'Moses, David. David, Moses. What is it with you and Moses?'

'But Moses...'

'I will hear no more of this. It is not for you to question the ways of the Lord.'

That night, from under the warmth of his bedclothes, Avram heard Papa Kahn return from the shop. There was the double-locking of the door, then the slice of light into the bedroom as he paused to check on the breathing of his son. Then came the clanking of pots in the kitchen in the search for the food that Celia had left him, the scraping of a chair on the stone floor, the sound of grumblings, the smell of tobacco from the one cigarette before bedtime. There was a time when Avram would have risen from his bed to join Papa Kahn at the kitchen table, to stand in the crook of his arm and ask him if indeed there were two Gods. But he let the lights go out and the flat settle into silence.

CHAPTER EIGHTEEN

Avram liked the steamie. He liked the scald and hissing boil of the place, the bubbling vats, the scrubbed cleanliness, the stench of carbolic. But as the only male among the maids and housewives, he hated the teasing.

'Here's your boyfriend come to get you,' one of the women cackled.

Mary strutted out of the boiling mist. Her face was blotched red, her hair matted in strands to her cheeks. Sweat stained her dress in a yoke above her breasts. She placed a hand on a bony hip cocked in her teaser's direction.

'I need more of a man than that to satisfy me. And a rich one at that.'

'You know what they say about these young 'uns,' responded the teaser 'Plenty of powder in their guns.' Other women laughed.

'Master's son, Mary,' another voice chided. 'Don't go fouling yer own nest.'

Avram felt the shirt clinging to his back from the humidity and the heat of his own embarrassment.

'Come on,' he pleaded. 'Let's go.'

'He ain't the Master's real son,' Mary said. She looked straight at him. 'So I ain't be fouling my own nest.' With a tilt of her head, she indicated a large basket piled high with whites. 'That's ours.'

He took one handle, waited for Mary to pull her cardigan tight around herself then pick up the other side of the basket. After the steamie's concentrated heat and viscous smell, he breathed easier in the outside chill. It was only a couple of streets to home, a journey he tried to walk in silence, letting Mary babble out a mouthful of complaints about the housekeeping if she had to.

He sensed matters between them had changed since Madame Kahn's departure. Despite her threats, the tension was more between Mary and Celia now. He almost detected a softening in her attitude towards him. She never touched him and if she would have, he had promised himself he would hit her back. The last few months had seen him sprout taller too, putting his height on a par with Mary. There was down growing on his face and between in his legs, and a feeling growing inside him towards her that was not entirely unpleasant.

'I think you've got eyes for that cow,' Celia had accused.

'Away with you.'

'You want to go roamin' in the gloamin' with her. I can tell.' Celia burst into a teasing sing-song. 'Roamin' in the gloamin' on the bonnie banks o' Clyde. Roamin' in the gloamin' with Mary at Avram's side...'

'I hate her,' he said.

'You've got a funny way of showing it. You're always looking at her.'

And when he thought about it, so he was. Sometimes he would watch her working, the hem of her skirt retreating up the firm calf of her green woollen stockings as she reached for the pulley, or the heaving of her breasts as she sat in a squat on a stool to breathlessly scrub clothes up and down on the washboard. He watched Celia, too. But in a way that was different.

'You can help me mangle this stuff.' Mary sniffed the air just before they reached the close. 'But dinnae hang it out in the green after, though. I think it's going to rain.'

And she was right. Just after the work with the mangle, the rain came down in buckets. Mary went upstairs to her room in Uncle Mendel's flat to close the windows. He was left to take down all the dry clothes from the kitchen pulley, hang up the fresh wash. Celia came in, saw the newly-plucked dry stack in the basket, told him to put it in the bedroom for ironing. He did as he was told then remained to finish his homework by Nathan's bedside. He propped his schoolbook among the bedclothes and tried to work out the mathematical problems in his copybook. Nathan was asleep, his breathing coming in a light snore. Celia worked quietly in a rhythm with the steam iron.

'What's that you're doing?' she asked.

'Algebra.' He enjoyed the subject, the combination of numbers and letters offering up a different language, the discovery of unknown value through the knowledge of other values, the puzzle of it all. He could almost feel his mind visibly expand to accommodate the new concepts, like a muscle training and straining to lift a heavier weight.

Celia sniffed. 'That's all that stuff with 'x' and 'y' in it. I don't see the point, really.' As if to emphasise her statement, she slammed the iron hard down on one of Papa Kahn's shirts stretched out on the board. There was a warm spittle of hiss from the device which looked too large and heavy for her thin arms. Her hair was up under a head-scarf, her Paisley-patterned apron hugged in her waist, spread out tight over her hips. She muttered to herself as she worked, fussing with her fingers over buttons that had unthreaded loose or a stretch of material that wouldn't sit just right across the board. Her face was flushed from the heat and her brow was damp where it had crinkled into a frown over her task. She was only a few months older yet he thought how grown-up she had become since Madame Kahn had been arrested. So efficient. So bossy. So like her mother.

'I think you'd be good at it,' he said.

'Maybe I would. But I've got other plans.'

'What other plans?'

'Plans for when Mother gets back.'

'You'll still have to work here.'

'No I won't. Women are going out to work now. They're in the offices and the factories. That's one good thing about the war.'

'There's nothing good about the war.'

Almost as if in agreement, Nathan let out a groan and shifted in his bed, knocking Avram's school-book to the floor. Avram turned his attention to the figure twisted out from under the bedclothes. Nathan seemed to have wasted away to nothing. He ate little and sometimes Celia had to force-feed him. The skin across his collar bone where his nightgown had pulled down was dry and thin. His wrists hung out of his sleeves like chicken bones. Avram was certain Rabbi Lieberman was right. Nathan did have the blood of a *lamed vav*, pouring the suffering of the world into his veins.

And there was plenty of suffering around. Avram read the papers every day, sometimes adding up the published lists of the dead, mouthing quietly to himself the names of these men who had become no more than a two or three word item in a newspaper column. The totals were atrocious. Reports for the last three months showed three hundred and fifty thousand Allied soldiers killed at the Somme, along with some six hundred and fifty thousand Germans. There were one and half million Jews starving in Russia. Together that was three times the population of the city of Glasgow, half the population of Scotland. He tried to picture the streets of the

Gorbals littered with the bodies of the starving and the dead, and shivered at the image.

He thought that if he kept the newspapers away from the bedroom, Nathan would be unaware of what was going on. But then he realised that if Nathan was indeed related to a *lamed vav,* he would surely be able to feel the suffering without having to know about it. Somehow the pain would sink into him from the atmosphere, through radio waves, from silent screams or the reports of angels.

Even for Avram, it wasn't really necessary to read the newspapers to know about the tragedies occurring in mainland Europe. He could just go out into the streets to witness the men without limbs, with scarred faces, with the blank expressions of those who had seen too much and now only wanted to see too little. There was no rush to sign up for King and Country now. The war hadn't ended before Christmas. It hadn't ended before nearly three Christmases. Conscription had been introduced. Fifty thousand men were needed a month. He made the calculation in his head. Unless the war ended, in seven months all the new recruits would be dead at the Somme.

Celia picked up a shirt, tucked the neck under her chin, folded it just right.

'I want to be a clippie,' she announced.

'Course you do.' He rolled his eyes at her then tried to visualise Celia in a conductress' uniform. Black Watch tartan skirt, Corporation green jacket, her badge, the whirring ticket machine. 'Papa Kahn would never allow it.'

'Makes no difference. I'm still going to do it.'

'You're too young. You need to be at least eighteen to work with the public, handling money.'

Celia tucked a stray curl back under her headscarf. 'I'll lie about my age. Men lie to be in the war. Or I'll work in a factory. Girls of sixteen are working in factories. Making shells. Some are even fourteen.'

The door bell rang.

'Avram,' she said firmly, with a nod to the hallway.

At first, Avram didn't recognise the young woman standing in the doorway. She was hatless, her blonde hair wet and dripping. One hand was flat against the door jamb while with the other she clutched her chest beneath her coat, trying to calm her breathing.

'It's Mr. Kahn,' she managed between gulps for air.

Avram recognised her now. Sadie, from Papa Kahn's shop. He heard a gasp from behind him, then Celia's voice, suddenly shrill.

'What's happened to him?'

'He collapsed, Miss. Mrs. Wallace wants to call a doctor. Please come, Miss. She don't want to do it without yer permission. The cost and that. Please come.'

'Avram. Get Mary to come down and look after Nathan.' Celia snatched her coat off the hall-stand. 'Then come down to the shop.'

'Take an umbrella, Miss. It's coming down something rotten.' But Celia had already disappeared out of the close.

Avram raced upstairs to Uncle Mendel's flat. He didn't ring or knock but went straight in. The darkness of the hallway brought him to a stop as he tried to figure out which would be Mary's room. Even though Uncle Mendel had been away for months, the smell of pipe tobacco still lingered. He saw light where a door was slightly ajar. He meant to knock but the door swung open when he touched it. What he saw at first confused him. The sheets were in a sprawl upon the floor. On the bed, there was the bare back of a dark-haired man and the tangle of naked limbs. Mary was underneath, her red hair fanned out on the pillow, her eyes squeezed shut but her mouth slightly open, breathing out a moan. As soon as the door was full wide, Mary's eyes opened and she saw him. She pushed off the body from on top of her, made to yell at him but something changed her mind. He could see it in her expression as her lips moved into a strange smile. He had seen that smile before. He had seen it before in her wine-sodden kiss, he had seen it tell him there would be no more football.

'So look who it is.' Mary made no attempt to cover up her nakedness.

'Get him out of here,' the man shouted.

'No, I want him to see this.' She rose from the bed. Her whole body was covered in freckles except for the thatch of hair between her legs. She stepped towards him but he couldn't move. She came close enough for him to smell an odour he had never smelt before. Close enough to feel the warmth radiating off her so white skin.

'It's Papa Kahn,' he shouted. 'He's collapsed in the shop. You've got to come.'

'Yer lying.'

'It's true. Celia's gone to him already. We need you to look after Nathan.'

'Jesus Christ!' she hissed. She turned to the man who was busy putting on his underwear by the side of the bed. The mound of a crumpled uniform lay at his feet. 'For Christ sake, Brian. Get me a robe.'

Avram turned and ran out of the flat. As he sped down the steps and out into the rain all he could think about were Mary's breasts. Round nipples the colour of her hair.

CHAPTER NINETEEN

Avram arrived at the shop to find Papa Kahn slouched sickly on a rickety wooden chair, his blood-shot eyes open, staring vacantly at the floor. The man's collar hung loose, his shirt unbuttoned to reveal a hollow chest gulping air in a series of wheezes. Cuttings of different coloured cloth clung to his shirt like medal ribbons. Celia and Mrs. Wallace clustered on either side of him.

'Please, Avram,' Celia called. 'Come over here.' Her voice was steady but he could see the anxiety pinched tight in her eyes. He went round beside her. She put an arm around him, drew him in, dropped her head on to his shoulder. She had taken off her headscarf, her hair was lank and wet against his cheek. Her shoes looked sodden through. Underneath her coat, she was still wrapped up in her pinny. She was shivering. He knew he should be feeling anxious about her father. Instead, he felt glad to have her close like this, to be able to protect her.

'What happened?' he asked.

'I don't know,' she sighed. 'But the worst seems to have passed. He was still on the floor when I came. Sadie's gone for the doctor.' As she spoke a hansom drew up sharp outside the shop window.

Dr. Drummond was a plump, red-faced man with full mutton-chop whiskers who entered blustering and breathless under Sadie's hastily erected umbrella. He opened his bag, brought out a stethoscope, shooed everyone away from around his patient.

Avram felt Celia take his hand. It was cool and dry and he worried how his own palm must feel, still hot and sweaty after the running. He tried not to think about it as he watched Dr. Drummond make several placements of his hearing device on Papa Kahn's chest. The doctor tapped his patient's back a few times, requested a couple of deep wheezy breaths.

'There is pain?'

Papa Kahn shook his head.

'Tell me what happened.'

Avram could not hear the response. He could only see the terrible dullness in Papa Kahn's jaundiced eyes as the man strained to speak. Eventually, the doctor turned to address Mrs. Wallace.

'You are ...?'

Mrs. Wallace told him.

'And Mrs. Kahn? She is at home?'

Mrs. Wallace spoke quietly to the doctor.

'I see.' The doctor cleared his throat and addressed the room. 'I am pleased to say the pain has passed. Breathing has returned to normal.' He gripped his patient's shoulder as if he himself had bestowed the recovery.

'Is he going to die?' Avram asked.

Dr. Drummond scowled at the question. 'No, he is not going to die.'

Mrs. Wallace brought her palms together in a gesture of prayer. Celia let go his hand, moved to dab the spittle off her father's chin with a corner of her apron, wipe the sweat from his forehead.

'But he looks so pale,' she said.

Dr. Drummond ignored the comment and went on talking, barking orders to those assembled.

'I will write him a prescription for powdered digitalis. It may be obtained from the dispensary at the Victoria Infirmary. Meanwhile, most important is that he should have rest. Yes, bed-rest, bed-rest and more bed-rest.' The doctor returned to addressing Mrs. Wallace. 'I will take Mr. Kahn to his home in the hansom. Perhaps the children can go on ahead to the dispensary with the prescription. But first I will need help to fetch him into the cab. And then there is the matter of my expenses.'

The walk home from the dispensary took Avram and Celia through the park, past the deserted bandstand. The wet paths and the bushes sparkled in the lamplight, puddles sagged and cracked beneath their feet as the frost set in. It reminded Avram of the times he used to walk back with her from Arkush's bakery on the *Shabbos* eve, each of them carrying a handle of the pot of steaming *cholent*.

'There's no-one to look after us any more,' Celia said. She presented a strange sight, dressed up in a serge military tunic she'd borrowed from the shop to replace her sodden coat, her pinny hanging loose below the jacket hem. 'We'll have to do the looking-after now. It's as if we're orphans.'

'I've been an orphan for years,' he said.

'But your mother's still alive.'

'She might as well be dead.'

'Don't say that.'

'Why not? It's true isn't it?'

'You'll put the *ayin hora* on her.'

He didn't want to put the evil eye on his mother. But he knew the feeling of being an orphan even if he wasn't one. He knew what it was like to have his childhood snatched away for no-one being there to cherish his memories. He knew the desperation of lonely days on a ship to Glasgow when there was no-one to protect him from the terrors and vagaries of the adult world. He knew what it was like to be parentless and stateless. To be a nothing.

'We will manage,' he said, trying to put on his best grown-up voice. 'You and me together, Celia. Somehow we will manage.'

She smiled at him. And he wasn't sure if it was because she felt comforted or she was making fun of him.

'Adults will come around,' she said. 'I know they will. Anyway, it will only be for a short time. Papa will be well soon. You'll see.'

And then in that sudden change of mood he'd witnessed so often since her mother had been taken away, she began to sing. It was a song he remembered from his playground days before the war.

'Old Mother Hubbard, what a cold you've got
Drinking tea and soda hot.
Wrap me up in a great white shawl
And take me to the doctor's shop.
Doctor, doctor, shall I die?
Yes, my darling, so shall I.'

Celia fumbled in her apron pocket for Papa Kahn's prescription. *'Take this medicine, twice a day,'* she sang, shaking the paper bag of powders at him.

'And it will cure your cold away,' he chorused with her.

At the park gates, she bought a handful of chestnuts from the cart of an Italian vendor who complained to them, half in English, half in Italian, about the cold. They hung around with him by the warmth of the live coals in the brazier, clenching the shells in their fists to heat up their hands before cracking them open for the bitter-sweet softness inside. The air was bitter too but he felt warm inside. He could see stars in the clear sky and a moon come up over the tenements as round as a football, as shiny as Lucky Mo's bald head. Leaves glistened in the trees, moths flitted around the lamps of the cart. Two well-dressed women drew up on their bicycles, as did a butcher's delivery boy. The name of the butcher was painted bold onto a metal sign welded on to the mainframe. The chestnut vendor stopped his complaining and began to hum a tune as he scooped out the nuts into eagerly-cupped hands. Celia blew several times into her palms. Her cheeks were rosy red like a Russian doll. Avram thought she looked beautiful.

* * *

Celia immediately assumed control of the household. She took charge of the keys, she wrote out a schedule of chores, she made a shopping list for the next day. Mary was confused at first, but in the end she didn't seem to object.

'After all, it's only natural,' Mary said to Mrs. Wallace, who had come round to see if everything was all right. 'If I've taken Madame's part, then she's taken her faither's.'

It was to Celia that Mrs. Wallace gave whatever money there had been at the shop.

Avram, meanwhile, tried hard to avoid Mary's teasings. On the day after Papa Kahn's heart-attack, she had lifted up her skirts to him in the kitchen.

'Are you sure you don't want a better look?' she said, showing off her woollen-stockinged legs to above her knee. Later when she passed him in the hallway, she had other words for him, close to his ear so he could feel her breath flutter against his skin. 'What do you think of Mary's body, then?' And on another occasion, 'You know where to come if you want a taste.'

He was both embarrassed and enticed by her attention, until all he could do was wrap up warm and take a tanner-ball out into the street. He would keep to himself, kicking the ball back and forward off a tenement wall, ignoring the pleas of the other boys to join in a game.

Celia was right about the adults. They did come. But only for a few minutes at a time. Papa Kahn was still very weak and stayed in his bed, sleeping most of the time, only waking to eat little or to see the visitors. The weather had turned bitter cold, there was ice on the ground and on the windows. Avram sweated back and forward to the cellar for coal to feed the fires. Celia supplied metal hot water bottles to her two patients.

'It's like a bleedin' hospital and a tea-room rolled into one here,' Mary complained as she ferried another tray of tea things into Papa Kahn's bedroom. 'I'd be better off being a nurse at the Front.'

Solly came to visit with his father Lucky Mo, as did Mrs. Wallace and Sadie from the shop, and Mrs. Carnovsky from across the passage with a tin of strudel. Rabbi Lieberman called, along with Jacob Stein and a number of other men from the synagogue. The visitors also looked in at Nathan, who seemed to strengthen slightly from the attention paid and the general hubbub invading the household. Most of the time the guests didn't linger, but when Jacob Stein came, he huddled afterwards with some of his fellow congregants in the hallway where they ate cake and drank copiously from a decanter of Papa Kahn's *schnapps*. When it was time for the bailie to leave, Celia helped him on with his fur-trimmed coat. Avram brought his hat and umbrella. The handle was carved ivory in the shape of an open-mouthed fox. He let his fingers play between its teeth before handing it over.

'Such a pretty young lady you are becoming,' Jacob Stein said, bowing to plant a kiss. Celia twisted her head away. Herr Stein turned to Avram.

'Mr. Kahn wants we should talk.'

'About what, sir?' Avram asked nervously. Whenever he was the subject of adult conversation, it was usually to set him on a course he did not wish to take.

'Not now. I have to go. Come to my office. At the warehouse in Candleriggs. Tomorrow at four o'clock. We will speak then.' Jacob Stein wrote out a small card. 'Here is the address.' Then, in a less business-like tone. 'And the football? How is that now?'

'There is no time for football, sir. I am needed at home.'

'Ah, I see.' Jacob Stein thought about this for a moment. 'Anyway, not a career for a Jewish boy.' He fixed his bowler on his head and departed, leaving behind his familiar scent of sweet brandy and cigars.

With the visitors gone, Mary retired upstairs to her room in Uncle Mendel's flat. Avram remained by the window in the sitting room.

Ice coated the glass in thick sworls, and he leaned up close trying to melt the shapes with his breath. Celia sat in Papa Kahn's armchair knitting by a fire.

'Jack Frost,' she said.

'Who's he?'

'He makes the patterns on the window.'

He imagined a man not unlike the lamp-lighter visiting each house to paint the panes with his hoary breath.

'I'm going to start playing football again,' he said.

'You will not.'

'Who's to stop me?'

'I need you in the house now more than ever.'

'I promise I'll do everything you ask. You're the one in charge now. But I want to start going to practice again. And playing in the matches. If my chores suffer for it, I'll stop playing.'

He waited for her response but she continued with her knitting, her brow furrowed in a thoughtfulness over her task.

'I'll come with you tomorrow,' she said.

He went over to sit close to her. 'I'll be all right by myself.'

'It will be good to go into the city. To look at the shops.'

A coal shifted in the grate. Avram thought of Nathan and Papa Kahn asleep in other rooms, as if they were his and Celia's own children.

CHAPTER TWENTY

They took a tram. Even though it was cold enough for the snow still to be lying on the ground, they chose to sit upstairs huddled together in the uncovered area at the front just above the destination board.

'So we can see where we're going,' Celia said.

Avram loved the trundle and the rattle of the journey, especially the crackle and blue-white flash of the pantograph lighting up the otherwise grey day. Celia brought out a bag of sweets.

'Take a handful,' she said. And he did, happy in the conspiracy, knowing Papa Kahn's opposition to the irresponsible rotting of his children's teeth with soor plooms, lucky tatties and sugar-ally sticks bought from Glickman's on London Road. An opposition somewhat diluted by Papa Kahn's own habit of sipping tea through lumps of sugar.

Celia paid their fares to a young woman in a Black Watch tartan skirt who cursed them for making her come out in the cold to give them a ticket.

'I wouldn't complain,' Celia said when the conductress had gone back down the stairs. 'I'd always have a smile for my passengers.'

Over Glasgow Bridge the tram went, with the River Clyde flowing beneath, murky, swollen, barely visible in the mist. Tall electric lamps sentried the bridge's central aisle. On either side of the tram lines, streams of horse-drawn wagons laden with barrels, sacks, crates and loose coal trudged a weary track through the dirt-marbled snow. Pedestrians, swathed tight in scarves, mufflers and mittens, carefully picked their paths across the bridge's wide icy pavements. Avram tried to count the number of military men in their trench coats among the passers-by only to be interrupted by Celia pointing out the giant Paisleys store with the lettering – *Tailoring Establishment and Juvenile Outfitters* – displayed on the side.

'Papa supplies them sometimes,' she told him proudly, a fact he already knew from a hundred times in the telling.

He read off the other advertising billboards along the quayside – *Oxo, Bovril, Lux, Pears, Bryant and May, Whitbread's Stout, Colman's Starch*. He watched a steam train pull out from Glasgow Central on its own parallel bridge bound for somewhere south like Carlisle, Manchester, or even London. A couple of soldiers were leaning out of a carriage window. They waved and he waved back, feeling an overwhelming sadness as he did so.

The tram swung along its tracks into the city, the buildings came in tall on either side forcing him to arch his head back to wonder at the ornate balustrades and turrets of the banks, the stores, the merchant chambers and the hotels. He held himself tight and marvelled at the sheer grandness of it all.

Avram was shown into a large office lit only by dull winter rays filtering through tall windows. To the rear of the room, he saw Jacob Stein slumped fat into a leather armchair behind his desk, his fingers tapping the buttons of his waistcoat. Avram's own fingers were just beginning to flow warm again. As were his feet in the dampness seeping through the soles of his battered shoes. He swept off his cap and approached, wondering whether to sit down on the chair in front of the desk.

It was so quiet he feared the frantic thumping of his heart was audible to his host. His apprehension lasted only a few seconds until the silence was broken by the screech and clatter of a tramcar tackling the snowy slope of the street below. A crackle of a spark from the overhead wires electrified the room for an instant, making Jacob Stein's face flash blue-white and ghost-like in the dimness. The warehouse owner stirred, motioned with a flick of his hand for him to sit. He did as he was told, holding himself stiffly in his chair as Jacob Stein leaned forward, slowly placed his hands on the desk. A burnt-down cigar lay wedged between two of the man's fingers. Avram looked down at his feet. Just as he felt the whole interview was to be conducted as a silent scrutiny, he heard Jacob Stein clear his throat.

'First there is some good news,' the warehouse owner said.

Avram looked up.

'I have just heard this morning,' Jacob Stein continued, 'that Madame Kahn is to be released. I expect she will be back in Glasgow within the next few days.'

Avram tightened his fingers around his cap.

'Are you not pleased, boy?'

He did not know how he felt. People who disappeared from his life were a common occurrence for him. For them to come back again was unique.

'You, of course, must give this news straight away to Mr. Kahn.' Jacob Stein retreated into the luxury of his chair and sighed. 'It was not easy to obtain her release. Glasgow, with all its shipyards and munitions factories, is a prohibited area for aliens. But the appeals of the Jewish Representative Council fell on sympathetic ears. The so-called enemy alien members of our community can be registered under our protection.' Jacob Stein raised his arms to his sides as if to weigh the worth of what he was to say next. 'Justice and fair-play. Never forget that, Avram. We Jews have been treated well here. Madame Kahn, after all, was persecuted for her nationality. In other countries, we are persecuted for our religion. In other countries, to be a Jew is to carry a death sentence over your head.'

'I know that, sir.'

Jacob Stein's normally steady gaze wavered for a moment, then returned to fix on him hard. 'Of course, you do. And do you know why Scotland is such a fine place for us?'

'No, sir.'

Jacob Stein leaned forward again. 'There is so much hatred between the Protestants and the Catholics.' His voice lowered to such a conspiratorial level that Avram had to strain to hear. 'And when they are not hating each other, they combine to hate the English. Hah! What a wonderful city Glasgow is. No-one has any hatred left over for us Jews.' Jacob Stein clapped his hands together as if it were he himself who had manipulated such a ploy. He then struck a match, puffed and sucked the remainder of his cigar alight. 'There is something else,' he said. 'You are now going to secondary school?'

'Yes, sir. Papa Kahn wanted me to stay on to study. He thinks I could sit for the university.'

Jacob Stein waved a hand in dismissal, causing some ash to drop onto the desk. 'Well, you can forget about that.'

'I'm sorry, sir?'

'I said you can forget about that. Education costs money. Mr. Kahn is in no position to fund your secondary schooling. He is in no position to even run his own business for the present. I have arranged for temporary management of his affairs until his condition improves.'

As Avram struggled to absorb the impact of this new information on his life, his gaze wandered to the three tall windows beyond

Jacob Stein's head, each stained on the upper third with the identical emblem. He recognised the badge as being the same as the one engraved on the fountain at Glasgow Cross. He remembered the school-yard riddle Solly had once taught him.

> *Where's the tree that never grew?*
> *Where's the bird that never flew?*
> *Where's the fish that never swam?*
> *Where's the bell that never rang?*

'On Glasgow's coat-of-arms, ye daft bampot.' And there they were now, emblazoned on each of the three windows – the tree, the bird, the fish and the bell. Underneath scrolled the motto: *Let Glasgow Flourish.* Avram had first thought it meant Glasgow should be like flour. Clean and white and soft. Not the dirty, dark and hard city that it was. But Solly told him the real meaning of the word. Let Glasgow flourish. When would anyone let Avram Escovitz flourish?

'Are you listening, boy?'

'Yes, sir.'

'Do you know what a credit draper is?'

He shook his head.

'Do you know what Moses Cohen does?'

'I don't know Moses Cohen, sir.'

'Don't be stupid. Of course you know who Moses Cohen is. He is Madame Kahn's brother.'

'Uncle Mendel, sir.'

'He's not really your uncle. Yes, Uncle Mendel, then.'

'He works up north somewhere. That's all I know, sir.'

'It's more the north-west. Around Oban. Well, anyway, he is a credit draper.'

'Sir?'

Jacob Stein explained how he gave Uncle Mendel goods from his own warehouse at a wholesale price and on credit. Uncle Mendel then sold the same goods on to his West of Scotland customers at a profit, also usually on credit, on terms worked out between Uncle Mendel and the customer.

'The trick,' Jacob Stein said, 'is for Mendel to recover the price and a profit from the customer before he has to pay me. Usually within two months. Then he makes a living. That's how we Jews help each other. Do you understand?'

Avram nodded.

'Herschel says you are a smart boy. Good with figures?'

'Yes, sir.'

'Excellent. With the strikes at the docks, there's not much money around Clydeside to support a credit draper. So Mr. Kahn and I have agreed you should join your Uncle Mendel. You need to learn the business. When you can do that, when the strikes are over and the workers have some coins in their pockets, you can return to Glasgow and work here.'

'I have to go to Oban, sir?'

'Not exactly Oban. Oban is the nearest fishing village. Moses has a small cottage or a hut tucked away in the countryside somewhere. A *but and ben*, I believe, is the Glasgow expression for such a place. It will only be for a few weeks at a time. Every so often, one of you will come back for new samples, to fill the orders and so on. Moses needs to return anyway, to sort out his status. Do you understand?'

Avram didn't understand. He could make no sense of the whims of the adult world that pushed him on to ships, that took him away from the game he loved to play, that substituted his education for tramping around the Scottish countryside with his Uncle Mendel as a peddler of Jacob Stein's wares.

'Any questions?'

'Do they play football there?'

Jacob Stein smiled for the first time. 'I don't think so. Perhaps there is a small Highland league team. Shinty is the sport up there, I believe.'

'Shinty?'

'It's like hockey. With bigger goal-posts. That's all I know about it. Football is the game for me.'

'Hockey,' Avram sighed.

'Well, cheer up. It's not like you're being sent to the Front. Boys your age are enlisting.' Jacob Stein held out a hand to the room. 'I started like you, too. A credit draper. It is a beginning. A small beginning, but a beginning nevertheless.'

Avram followed the direction of the outstretched arm. An enormous safe as large as a linen press dominated a corner, the paint around the brass lever-handle worn to the metal. A far wall boasted a framed portrait of the warehouse owner decked out in some civic finery. Jacob Stein stood up and walked his bulky frame over to stand beneath his likeness.

'Last year, they made me a bailie.'

Avram flicked his eyes between the portrait and the real man. The figure in the portrait was slimmer but the painter had captured the certain smugness of his subject.

'Bailie,' Jacob Stein said, sucking on his cigar. 'I am only the second Jew to rise so far in this great city. A young man like you can be something too. With a lot of hard work and a bit of this.' Jacob Stein tapped a finger at the side of his own head.

'Yes, sir.'

Jacob Stein snorted. 'I have telegraphed your Uncle Mendel to tell him you are coming. Take some new samples with you when you leave. My secretary will show you what to do.' He stubbed out the cigar in an ashtray, waved a hand at him. 'Now, go. *Gie gezundheit.*'

After Avram had closed the door to Jacob Stein's office, he saw another young boy seated next in line to go in. A red-headed lad with lanky limbs who hardly looked up to register his entrance into the passageway. It was only when he reached the cubicle housing Jacob Stein's secretary did he remember who that boy was. The vicious winger from Victoria and Cathcart Boys' Club. Ginger Dodds.

Celia was waiting for him in the warehouse yard.

'What's in the parcel?'

'Samples.'

'Samples of what?'

'I don't know. Aprons, shirts, pullovers.'

'What on earth for?'

'They're for Uncle Mendel. I've to become a credit draper.'

'Stop a minute, Avram. What is going on here?'

'I told you. I've to become a credit draper.'

'Like Uncle Mendel?'

'I've to go and work with Uncle Mendel. In some place near Oban.'

'What about school?'

'I have to leave. There is no money to continue with my education. Papa Kahn and Jacob Stein decided it. I'm like a goods train. Shunted here, there and everywhere. Now I have to go to some damned place they don't even play football. Just bloody shinty.'

Celia stamped her feet in the snow.

'You can't leave me.'

He looked at her face, at the two familiar lines frowning her forehead between her eyes. He didn't know whether to be glad or sad that these lines were caused in his honour. 'Why not?' he asked.

'You're all I have.'

'No, I'm not. You're mother is coming back in a few days.'

'What?'

'I forgot. Jacob Stein told me. He just found out this morning.'

'Mother is coming back?'

'Yes. Under the protection of The Jewish Representative Council. You don't seem happy.'

'Of course, I'm happy.'

They walked on in silence.

'I hate Jacob Stein,' she hissed eventually.

'So do I.'

'Why do you hate him?'

'Because he pushes people around. Why do you hate him?'

'He's always trying to kiss me. And he thinks he's such a big shot. Ever since he was made a bailie. He'll want a knighthood next.'

'Jews get knighthoods?'

'I think so. In London.'

She tugged at his arm and directed him towards the bridge spanning the River Clyde that led them southwards out of the city.

'Let's walk home,' she said.

He buttoned up his jacket to the full, then looked down to follow the path of his shoes as they negotiated the wet cobbles alongside Celia's own petite laced-up boots.

CHAPTER TWENTY-ONE

Madame Kahn arrived home with a matter-of-factness that suggested she'd just come back from Arkush's bakery on Abbotsford Place rather than from over a year at an internment camp near Leeds. But the differences between the person who had left and who had returned were substantial. First, there was her hair. Or what was left of it. No longer did Madame Kahn boast those long thick locks that Avram had witnessed hanging loose as she struck Mary with a hairbrush. In fact, Madame Kahn had no need for a hairbrush at all, for her hair had been shorn to within a farthing's-width of her scalp. She looked much smaller, too, and her skin sagged on her face in the same way that her clothes hung loose on her body. To Avram, it wasn't as if she had just reduced in size compared to his own growth over the last year. It was as if her whole presence had diminished. She had lost her stature. There was a nervousness about her. He had seen the same look of insecurity in the eyes of the soldiers who had returned from the Front, their perception of the world shattered, their place in the new regime no longer assured.

She shook hands with him, lightly embraced her daughter, sniffed around the hallway, ran a finger over a table top then disappeared into her bedroom, leaving a trail of lavender behind her.

After a few minutes, she re-entered the kitchen, looking even paler than when she had arrived.

'How has Papa been?' she asked Celia.

'He is getting stronger.'

'Good. Soup. He must have soup.' She bustled over to the range and started to lift the lids of pots. 'Is there any soup?'

'There is chicken soup, Mother. But he has just eaten.'

'I see.' A lid clanged to the floor. She ignored it. 'And Nathan? Has he eaten too?'

'Nathan hardly eats.'

'I see.'

Madame Kahn flopped down into a chair, took a handkerchief from her sleeve, dabbed her eyes.

'You can always wear a headscarf, Mother,' Celia suggested. 'Or even a *sheitl*?'

Madame Kahn laughed, a short almost hysterical cackle. 'See.

See the wonderful ways of the Lord. I go to a camp as an enemy alien and return as an Orthodox Jew wearing a wig. No, I will not wear a *sheitl*. A headscarf, maybe. But a *sheitl* made of horse-hair? Never.' Then, she seemed to calm herself. 'Camps,' she said quietly. 'No-one should have to endure such a thing. And, Avram, you are to work with Mendel?'

'Yes, Madame.'

'And when will that be?'

'I have to go at the end of the week.'

'I see.' Then in an unexpected display of affection, she held out her arms to Celia. 'Come, daughter.'

Celia approached hesitantly and was bundled into the bosom of her mother. 'How are you, my little one? You have grown so much. You have become a beautiful young woman. And Mary? Where is Mary?'

'She's wringing out the laundry in the back,' Celia said from within the smother of her mother's grasp.

'Well, when she comes in, tell her the hall furniture needs dusting. Now, I must go and attend to Nathan.'

* * *

Avram laid out the new stock samples on his bed. A jumper, a couple of work-shirts, a girdle and a full-length apron. He hadn't known what the girdle was until the woman who checked out the samples served up an explanation in a thick tobacco-scratched voice that made him blush. But it was the full-length aprons that were the big sellers.

'Why are you packing now?' Celia asked as she came into the room.

'I don't have anything else to do.'

Celia picked up the girdle, held it against her body. 'What do you think?'

He glanced at her, then turned away from her coquettish pose.

'This will be your most popular item,' she said. 'They are replacing the corset all over Europe.' She smoothed the fabric against her belly and her thighs. 'I'm not sure if the Oban fishwives will go for them. What do you think?'

'Aprons are the most popular,' he muttered.

'I think you'd rather see the young lassies in their girdles than in these long pinnies,' she teased.

'Leave me alone.'

She looked at him fiercely, then stomped out of the room. Within a few seconds she was back again.

'Why can't you be nice to me?' she complained.

He shrugged. 'I do want to be nice to you.'

'Well, let's go and see Mrs. Carnovsky then. You promised.'

'Now?'

'Yes, now.' She took his hand and pulled at him. 'I told her we were coming.'

He let her drag him through the flat out into the close, where she rang the bell of the door opposite.

'Well?' Mrs. Carnovsky asked through a cloud of smoke in the half-opened doorway.

'It's me. Celia. I said we'd come at three.'

'*Komm. Komm, bubeleh*. I have made some tea. Ah, it's you. The *meshugga* orphan. You can come too.'

He followed Celia and the old woman down a narrow hallway lined with framed pictures, their subject matter indiscernible in the darkness. The living room was not much lighter, with the closed curtains holding out rare mid-afternoon winter sunshine while the gas lights remained unlit. Only an electric lamp, shrouded in a red cloth, bled any light onto a table where an unattended cigarette burned in an ashtray, and a set of tea-things sat prepared for the three of them. He pottered around the room picking up photographs and ornaments here and there while Mrs. Carnovsky staggered in from the kitchen with an enormous teapot for the table.

'So what must we do?' Celia enquired.

Mrs. Carnovsky stubbed out her cigarette in an ashtray littered with gold tips, immediately lit another one.

'First, drink your tea. But don't finish it all. Leave a *bissele* in the bottom of your cup for me to work with.'

Avram sat quietly, sipping at the strong brew. Celia had told him all the stories. The tea-leaf images of a snake and a dagger close to the rim of poor Harold Levy's teacup that made Mrs. Carnovsky beg him not to enlist for a war from which he never returned. The picture of a man near the handle of Beatrice Arkush's cup predicting the imminent arrival of Meyer Shapiro as a suitable husband for the baker's daughter. The juxtaposition of the sun and a purse that encouraged Abe Abramson to give up his slipper-making business to become the very successful *kosher* butcher he was today. Solly told him his father had once sat with a list of horses from the next day's racing at Ayr hidden under her table until he could match her interpretation of the random pattern of leaves to the name of one of the runners. The horse won, but when Mrs. Carnovsky discovered the illicit use of her powers, she never spoke to Lucky Mo again. It was rumoured she had even put a curse on the bookie, but until now the supposed hex had no effect on the success of his business. Although Solly reported that, since the incident, his father had suffered severe attacks of gout.

'Celia tells me you go to work with your Uncle Mendel,' the old woman said.

Avram nodded.

'Selling goods for that Jacob Stein,' she hissed, then turned her head to the side to emit a couple of dry spits to the floor. 'Feh! Feh! to that man,' she said, then turned her attention to Celia as if nothing had happened. '*Komm*. Let me see.'

She took Celia's cup, swirled the tea-leaves around three times anti-clockwise, then in one swift movement, flipped the cup upside down in its own saucer. She waited a few seconds then ground the cup around three more times anti-clockwise until it rested with the handle pointing directly at Celia.

'So what does the future hold for my little Celia? For my little *bubeleh*?' Mrs. Carnovsky discarded the cloth covering the lamp, picked up the cup and began to examine the patterns close to the glow.

'You are sure you want to know?' she asked.

Celia giggled. 'Yes, of course, I want to know.'

Mrs. Carnovsky sucked hard on her cigarette then exhaled the one word: 'Sacrifice.'

'Sacrifice,' Celia repeated. 'What do you mean? Where?'

'Here,' Mrs. Carnovsky said, pointing a yellow-stained finger to the inside wall of the cup.

Avram peered at the pattern also. 'What is it?' he asked.

'A cross.'

He looked again. The display of leaves could have been a cross but also … 'A dagger,' he said. 'It could be … a dagger.'

'A dagger is worse. It means danger,' Mrs. Carnovsky said, scowling at him. 'But it is a cross. Sacrifice.'

'What kind of sacrifice?' Celia asked.

'What kind I don't know.'

'Why are the leaves always miserable for me?' Celia pleaded. 'Why are they always bad for me? Why can't they be about love or success or happiness?' Her dark eyes danced nervously as she searched for an answer in Mrs. Carnovsky's stony face. 'What do I do to deserve this? Why can't I have marriage or success or good news?'

Mrs. Carnovsky shrugged. 'I can't make it good for you, *bubeleh*. The leaves just tell me how it is.'

'It's just hocus-pocus,' Avram said. 'Don't get so upset about all of this ...'

Mrs. Carnovsky continued unperturbed. '... And the pattern is closer to the rim rather than to the bottom of the cup. That means the sacrifice is not far away.'

'How soon?' Celia asked.

'That I don't know.'

'Everyone has sacrifices to make in the future,' Avram said. 'Look at me. I have to make sacrifices all the time.'

'Sacrifices are not always a bad thing.' Mrs. Carnovsky snatched at his cup, quickly repeated the same movements as she had done with Celia's. With the handle facing menacingly at him, she snapped: 'You want to know your future or not?'

Such was the intensity of her stare that he thought she was putting a curse on him there and then. Even with the cigarette smoke passing over her face, her watery eyes refused to blink.

'Please, Avram,' begged Celia. 'Please. You said you would do it.'

Mrs. Carnovsky continued to look at him.

'Fine. Tell me my future then.'

The old woman picked up the cup, inspected it carefully, dipping the white bone interior in and out of the glare of the light.

'What does it say?' he asked.

'There is a pattern,' she said. 'Very clear.'

'What is it?'

'It is good news. You want to know? You want to know this hocus-pocus?'

He nodded.

Her old eyes looked at him triumphantly. 'I see a bird. You have the shape of a bird very near the rim. A bird. That is good fortune and it will come soon. Very soon. A bird.' She closed her eyes but continued to speak. 'A large bird, a strange bird, the likes I never saw in my life before.'

* * *

Madame Kahn was not interested in crosses, daggers or strange birds. Or any of Mrs. Carnovsky's antics with the tea-leaves.

'Life in the present is hard enough,' she complained. 'Who needs to worry about the future as well? *Alles beshert*. Everything is fate. What will be, will be. This is what I learn from the camps. What will be, will be.' She was sitting up close to the open fire, so close it was hard for Avram to believe the skin on her legs did not curl up like wood-shavings and burn from the heat. She was also knitting in a frenzy, the needles clicking and whirring before him in a blur as she fashioned woollen balaclavas for the troops in the trenches. Celia sat beside her, engaged in her own knitting task, one eye on the pattern-book provided by the Red Cross, but no match for the speedy production of her mother.

'They treated you well in the camps, Madame?' Avram asked.

'My treatment was fair. But it is the humiliation. It is the not knowing what will happen. It is to be punished for what? For being a spy? That's what it is. They think we are all spies. They think we will steal their secrets. Poison their water. Suffocate their children in their sleep. Gas their homes. Do I look like the kind of person who would do such a thing? Me? A spy? Martha Kahn. Who worked my fingers to the bone to make uniforms for our soldiers. But to put people in camps. God forbid it should ever happen again.'

'Of course, it won't happen again…' Celia said.

'…And what was my punishment?' Madame Kahn continued, accompanied by a more spirited attack on her task. 'What was my punishment for being an enemy alien? This is my punishment. This knitting and darning. Knitting and darning. Knitting and darning. What else was there to do? Some daily chores to keep the camp clean. Play cards if we were lucky. But we were civilians. Not prisoners-of-war. Not enemy soldiers. Just civilians unlucky to be born in a foreign country. *Alles beshert.*'

Avram had remained silent throughout Madame Kahn's tirade, staring into the fire, letting his thoughts wander in and out of the tunnels, passageways and crevices created by the burning coal. But he could feel his anger simmering away like the embers in the grate.

'Everything isn't fate,' he said quietly.

Madame Kahn stopped her knitting. 'What did you say, boy?'

'It's because you are a Jew,' he muttered. 'Not a civilian born in a foreign country. But a Jew.'

'What are you talking about?'

He was shaking now, shaking with a rage he never knew he possessed. 'That was why they took you,' he said, rising to his feet, then wishing he hadn't for he could feel his legs trembling under him. 'They say it was because you were an enemy alien. But I know the real reason. I know the truth. They took my father because he was a Jew. And now they took you. It is because we are Jews. Being Jewish is the source of all our troubles.'

Celia sat staring at him with her mouth open, although somehow she still managed to continue with her knitting. Madame Kahn pointed one of her needles directly at him.

'How dare you talk back to me,' she said. 'And shame on you for your words. Shame on you, shame on you, shame on you. How can you say such a thing? Of course, it is not because I am a Jew. Who cares about such a thing in this country? Now, get out of my sight. How dare you speak like this? After all I have suffered. How dare you? *Gie, gie, gie*. Get out of my sight.'

But Avram was already on his way out of the door.

CHAPTER TWENTY-TWO

Avram kicked the small rubber ball ahead of him, then it was Solly's turn. That was the game. No double hits allowed. Even if the ball rolled out on to the road or into the tram grooves or under the hooves of horses – only one touch. Not one touch to stop it, another to pass it on. Just one pass. Even if it rolled into the slow trodding path of mourners, which it did now. Avram stopped and Solly did too as they watched the ball get shuffled around among the newly shined-up shoes. Not one of the procession glanced at the ground. Only straight ahead at the tiny coffin being borne aloft. A single wreath of white flowers jiggled on top with the lightness of it all.

'Billy McKechnie's little sister,' Solly said flatly, as if it were a sack of coal he was watching being carried along the street.

Avram saw Billy among the mourners. His former class-mate was wearing his school cap, a too-tight jacket, a black band around his upper arm.

'Do Jews wear black arm-bands?' Avram asked.

'Naw,' Solly said, yawning his reply. 'Dinnae think so. But they get to rip their clothes. Or at least the rabbi does it for them. Cuts their jumpers and jackets with the nick of a knife. That's the Jewish sign of mourning.'

The ball came to rest at Billy's feet. He stooped to pick it up, then looked around, his mouth screwed up in puzzlement like a small question mark. He saw Avram and Solly, smiled, tossed the ball back. A woman in a black coat and a black veil walloped Billy across the back of his head. Billy paid no attention to the slap, and waved.

Avram wanted to wave back but when Mrs. McKechnie lifted her veil and scowled over, he bowed his head instead. And so did Solly.

'Daft bampot,' Solly said under his breath. 'That's about the fourth one to die since I've kent Billy. He was always getting off school to go to a funeral. If he was a bloody Jew, all his clothes would be ripped to shreds by now.'

'There must be about seven of them left. Which one died?'

'The youngest. She wasn't even two.'

'Shame for Billy.'

'Aye. Billy's all right, tho',' Solly said thoughtfully. 'He was brilliant at wood-work.'

'You better make sure you don't die. You've got no-one to take your place.'

Avram wished he hadn't said the words the moment they'd left his lips. Solly wasn't sensitive about much, but he cared about being an only child when everyone around him had a football team of siblings. Or even just Celia and Nathan.

'Ye'd better start running, orphan, or I'll beat yer bloody heid in.'

Avram took off, dodging around the tail end of the funeral, with Solly chasing after. But Solly's threat was an idle one because Avram knew he was always too fast for the heavier boy. Nevertheless, the hurt in the words needed to be run out, and when they were, Avram found himself in the public playground beneath the high stone embankment that led up to the railway track. The place was deserted apart from two girls playing peever and the parkie who blew his whistle and shouted when Avram started kicking the ball off the wall of his shed. Through the dirty window, he could see a hung-up rake and spade. In the summer, the man would sit in the doorway in his shirt-sleeves reading the paper, puffing on his pipe, with a vase of cut flowers by his chair. Avram thought the shed must be a cosy place to live, bedded down on a mattress in the light of a paraffin lamp among the loose bulbs and the smell of dried mud and fresh grass on well-oiled cutting blades.

'Can ye no read signs?' the parkie shouted.

Before Avram could shout back, Solly turned up out of breath, grabbed the ball and sat down on one of the leather cradles that swung around the maypole in the centre of the playground. Avram followed and did the same. He liked the feel of the worn smoothness of the leather and the brass studs against his bare thighs. The parkie relaxed and retreated to his shed. Solly pulled out a scrunched up cigarette from his pocket and lit up.

'So,' Solly said. 'Yer finally joining the working classes.'

Avram kicked off lightly on his cradle, let it swing. He felt proud in front of Solly that he had a working wage to come. 'Give me a couple of years and I'll be a millionaire,' he said. 'Like Jacob Stein.'

'Naw. Like Rockefeller. He's the richest man in the world.' Solly laughed then spat some loose tobacco at his feet. 'Well, I'm thinking of enlisting.'

'That'd be a daft thing to do.'

'Serious. Cross my heart.'

'Come on, Solly. You're too young.'

'I'll lie. They're desperate now. They're none too careful.'

'You don't look like eighteen.'

'I do so.' Solly stood up off the swing, pulled himself up full. He was a big lad with a look of knowing life in his eyes far older than the rest of his almost seventeen-year-old features.

'You can stretch as much as you want, you still don't look eighteen.'

'That's only yer opinion.'

'What do you want to enlist for?'

'I was born here. I've a feeling to defend my country.'

'Don't be a mug. You'll get yourself killed.'

Solly scratched his head, and with thumb and forefinger drew something out from among the roots of his hair. He scrutinised the louse, then flicked it away. 'Aye, maybe.'

'Maybe? Maybe you'll lose a leg or an arm. Or an eye.'

'Or everything. I'll just be a stump with a heid.'

'A big potato.'

'A neep.'

'Not much difference from now, then.'

Solly feigned a punch. 'Ha bloody ha.'

'Got another?' Avram jerked his head at Solly's cigarette.

'Finish this.'

He took what was left and sucked, swinging back and forward on the leather cradle, scuffing his boots aimlessly along the ground in line with his thoughts. It was all happening too fast. Leaving Glasgow to work with Uncle Mendel. Solly now wanting to leave too. Papa Kahn's illness. No chance to play football. Celia. Celia? His world was shifting and sinking under his feet. He was back on the boat again, floating on the dark belly of a beast to an unknown destination. He felt small, hollow and scared.

'Lassies go for men in uniform,' Solly said.

'Like you said. Men. Not boys.'

'Maybe Molly'll let me go all the way. Give me a fuck for going off to the Front.'

'That's just like you. Getting yourself killed just for a ... fuck.' Avram still wasn't used to the word. It didn't come out comfortable like it did when Solly said it, like he had earned his right to employ it. But it felt good to say it anyway. It was a word for a working boy.

'Maybe it's ye that needs a fuck before ye go away? Maybe Celia will let ye have it?'

'Celia's family.' He tried to feign indifference, though he knew the sudden flush to his cheeks showed otherwise.

'No, she isn't. She's just yer ... I don't know what she is. What is she to ye? Nothing really.'

'She feels like family.'

Solly laughed. 'How do ye know what she feels like? Ye been touching her up?'

'She's family.' He took a last drag on the cigarette, snatched a look at the parkie, and tossed it.

'Give me a chance and I'd fuck Celia,' Solly said. 'Family or not.' He thrust his hips back and forward. 'Oh Solly, please fuck me. Please.'

'Stop it.'

But Solly didn't let up.

'I said "stop it".'

'Make me.'

Avram pushed Solly hard. Harder than he thought he really meant to. Solly fell to the ground, but he was up on his feet quick, fists clenched, drawn back, ready to punch. Avram stiffened, drew up his own fists. A train steamed along the embankment and they both stood locked in a silent, motionless glower until it had passed. Then the parkie's whistle shrilled, but Solly had relaxed anyway, the violence gone from his eyes as fast as it had come.

'Never thought ye had the guts to hit me, orphan.'

Neither did Avram. He was surprised at the feelings that had led him to strike his friend.

Solly brushed off the caked dirt, some twigs caught in the wool of his jumper, then sat back down on the leather cradle. The two of them swung around for a while until Solly spoke:

'Why don't ye come out with me and Molly tomorrow?'

'No thanks.'

'Why not?'

'Don't want to play raspberry.'

'Gooseberry, ye daft bampot. Come on. I'll get her to bring Fiona. Time ye started winching.'

'Fiona Cameron?'

'Aye. Fiona Cameron.'

Avram knew Fiona from school. Small, pretty girl, with a pale, milky skin – the kind of complexion Madame Kahn described as a '*milcheke*' face. She had eyes that were kind, but a mouth that was thin and cruel – a curious combination that meant he could never tell what she was thinking. Despite her petiteness, she had a lofty confidence with the boys, always teasing them and flicking their hair. She had done that with him once. 'Lots of girls would die for curls like these,' she told him with that expression on her face he didn't know was cruel or kind. "Go on, let me touch some more." But he wouldn't let her, even though he wanted her to.

'She won't go out with me.'

'Aye, she will. She's Molly's best friend. They go everywhere together. We can go to the pictures.'

'I don't know. What's on?'

'Chaplin. At The Eglinton.'

'I've got no money.'

'Have ye no jelly jars?'

'I don't know. Maybe we have. But Mary usually takes them.'

'Well, find out. If ye don't, I'll lend ye. Ye can pay me back when yer working. I'm flush.'

'I thought you said there was hardly any betting.'

'The war's thinned out the racing but the punters still want a bet.'

'A bet on what?'

'Anything with a result at the end of it. Especially the football. Seniors, juniors. The boys' clubs. Even the school games.'

'What? On teams like ours?'

'Aye. Even that. Come on. What d'ye say about Fiona?'

'I don't know.'

'Come on.'

'I wouldn't know what to do.'

'Ye don't have to do anything. Just talk to her nice. Tell her how pretty she looks. Hold her hand in the pictures. She might even let ye have a feel if ye tell her yer enlisting. She doesn't need to know yer off to the Western Highlands and no the Western Front.'

CHAPTER TWENTY-THREE

Avram watched Solly swagger along the pavement towards him. Molly on one arm, Fiona Cameron on the other. Fiona Cameron with her *milcheke* face, her tartan skirt, her fair hair tied back in a red ribbon, her breasts jutting out beneath her faded pink cardigan. Molly, the taller of the two girls, with her auburn hair and full-bodied features that even Avram realised gave her a sexual allure now that would probably collapse into plumpness later on.

What Avram knew of sex, he had learnt in the school yard. And that was not much. He had seen Mary naked and for a while that had given him a lot of credibility among his peers, for actual knowledge was rare. He knew he had to "stick it up her" but he wasn't sure exactly how or where. None of the girls he knew went all the way anyway. Even Molly – and Solly would have been the first to have told him if she did. But he didn't want that anyway. He would be happy just to hold hands. To fix a kiss on Fiona Cameron's pale cheeks would be an absolute triumph.

'Couples should be made up of people with rhyming names,' Solly announced. The girls were giggling.

'What do you mean?' Avram asked.

'Like us. Solly and Molly. Molly and Solly. We're already in harmony.' Solly squeezed Molly's arm. 'We were thinking of someone for you but we couldn't think of a girl's name that rhymed. With Fiona neither.'

'What about Jonah?' he suggested, pleased at his contribution to the conversation.

Molly clapped her hands together. 'Fiona and Jonah. Jonah and Fiona. I like it.'

'Well, I don't,' Fiona said, screwing up her mouth in distaste. Avram noticed she was wearing lipstick. 'Makes me think of a whale.'

'Let's go in,' Solly said, guiding Molly to the tail-end of the queue. Avram shuffled along beside Fiona, desperately trying to think of something to say.

'Do you like Charlie Chaplin?' he ventured.

'Course, I do. Or I wouldn't have come, would I? Are you paying for me?'

'Yes.'

'Good. But that doesn't mean you can try anything.'

'I wasn't going to.'

'That's all right then,' she said, but then her tone softened. 'Solly says you've joined up.'

'What?'

'Solly says you enlisted.'

He looked to his friend but Solly was busy buying the tickets. 'I suppose so,' he said.

'Well, either you have or you haven't?' She tilted her head to one side. 'You're not trying to be modest, are you?'

He shrugged. 'I have, then.'

'I was wondering why you'd left school. You used to be really clever.'

'I still am.'

'Course you are.' Fiona laughed. 'But you're not even seventeen.'

'They need everyone they can get.'

'But what about your folks? What do they say?'

'I don't have family.'

'I thought Celia was your sister.'

'He's an orphan,' Solly turned round to say.

'Stop interrupting,' Fiona said. 'Is that true?'

'I don't know the truth. I never knew my father and I haven't heard from my mother in over three years.'

'Oh.' She stared off into the distance and when she spoke again it was more to herself than to him. 'I lost two brothers in this war.'

'I'm sorry,' he said. He felt as if he had betrayed their deaths with his lie.

'It's all right. It was a while ago now. Right at the beginning.' She looked at him. 'Don't worry. I'm not going to start greetin' on you. When do you go?'

'The day after tomorrow.'

'That doesn't leave much time.'

'Time for what?'

'To get to know each other.'

He was glad of the darkness inside the picture house until Solly insisted they took seats along the back row. Solly immediately wrapped himself around Molly, despite her protests that she wanted to watch the film. Avram sat next to the cavorting couple with

Fiona on his other side, leaning slightly towards him so that their shoulders almost touched. Her fingers tapped a rhythm on her knee to the music of the piano. He watched the cigarette smoke billow out elaborate sworls on the projector's beam as the film crackled and flickered to a start.

Avram sat still, feeling awkward for not being able to share in the rest of the audience's hilarity over the antics of the little tramp. He just could not understand why the butt of this slapstick should cause such amusement. Even Solly was forced away from his amorous manoeuvrings so that Molly could see what all the fun was about. Fiona's shoulder rubbed against his own as she wriggled with laughter.

'Are you thinking of the army?' she asked him.

'No … I'm just…'

He shuddered as he felt her quickly squeeze his hand. Her palm lingered, soft on his skin.

'Try to enjoy the picture,' she said, before returning her hand to rest on her knee. He brought his own hand to lie close by on his thigh. He imagined he could feel the heat across the short distance between their fingers, yet the gap between them still seemed so achingly far. He decided he would count to three, then place his hand on hers. He tried to discreetly rub his palm dry along his thigh. One. Two. Three. He lifted his hand on to hers. Her wrist immediately twisted on contact so she could entwine his fingers in her own. He let out the breath he realised he had been holding for a long time.

He clutched on to Fiona's hand for the rest of the film then clung to it proud as they all bundled out of the picture house. It had rained while they had been inside. The streets were wet, the air unseasonably clammy.

'What now?' he asked Solly.

'Let's go for ice-cream,' Solly declared to the company then whispered in Avram's ear: 'Don't worry, soldier boy. I'll pay.'

Solly took them to Valentino's where they were greeted by Carlo, the proprietor, a small worried-looking man in his mid-sixties who was also one of Solly's punters. Carlo waved them to the rear where Avram finally let go of Fiona's hand so she could slide into one of the red-leather booths. As Avram moved into position beside her, Solly leaned over the table.

'Listen to what I say, soldier boy. And don't look behind ye.'

'Stop your messing,' he said with a quick smile to Fiona.

'It's Begg,' Solly whispered. 'He's just come in. He's at the counter.'

'You're having me on.'

'I kid ye not. It's the one-eyed monster himself. Keep low and he won't see ye.'

Just the mere mention of Begg's presence made the tension crawl up Avram's spine. He hunched over Valentino's elaborate tasselled menu, trying to concentrate on the list of ice-creams as if it were some dense tract from the Torah. He could imagine his former gym teacher waiting tense for his order, kitted out as he had been on the evening he had visited Papa Kahn – three piece suit and homburg, with his thick neck straining for release from the confines of its unaccustomed collar.

'You've gone awfully quiet,' Fiona said.

Avram shivered as he sensed a figure approach the table.

'You like to order?' An elderly square-faced woman in an ill-fitting waitress uniform stood poised with a notepad. 'We have mostly nothing.'

Molly laughed loudly. 'What do you mean? Mostly nothing.'

The waitress remained impassive. 'Just plain we have. Plain scoops.'

'That's all?' Molly said, her mouth in a pout.

'Don't ye know there's a war on?' Solly chided his girlfriend. 'A soldier in the trenches can only dream of a scoop of ice-cream.'

'It's just that I really wanted…'

'Escovitz!' boomed a voice the length of the cafe. Avram didn't turn round but he heard the footsteps click across the tiled floor. Then Roy Begg's face appeared at his shoulder so close he could smell the man's hair lotion, see the web of broken blood vessels across one cheek. 'The ice-cream here *kosher* enough for you, Escovitz? That is the word, isn't it? *Kosher*?'

Avram stared straight ahead.

'We could've won the cup last season. But for you and your Jew customs.'

Avram turned to look at his tormentor. Roy Begg's eyes were blood-shot, there were clusters of stubble around his cheeks and jaw. He wasn't dressed up in a three-piece suit either – just an old sweater and trousers wet around the turn-ups from the rain. He held an ice-cream cone in his hand.

'That's not true,' Avram protested. 'It wasn't my fault we lost six-nil.'

'Oh aye it was. Aye it was, most definitely.' Begg pulled back, swayed slightly on his feet. The waitress looked on anxiously as he grabbed the ledge of the table for support. 'You were my best player. You had it all. You could have played for Celtic.' Begg held out his arms to the otherwise empty cafe. The ice-cream cone had started to drip on to his hand. 'And you threw it all away. All for your bloody Jew Sabbath.'

'Excuse me, Mr. Begg,' Solly interjected. 'But please don't swear in front of these young ladies.'

'Fuck you, Green.' Begg wiped a hand across his mouth. 'Excuse my French, ladies.' He turned the attention of his one eye back to Avram. 'You were a coward, Escovitz. You could have faced up to … to that Jew Kahn. But you backed down.'

'Don't you think I wanted to play? Don't you think I miss the football?'

'That's your own fault. You were a bloody coward.'

'No, he isn't,' Fiona said, the colour flooding into her milky cheeks. 'He's enlisted.'

'Enlisted?' Begg's neck bulged at the collar. 'Enlisted? A cowardly little runt like you?'

Avram clenched his fists, wished for the courage to rise to his feet to hit this man he'd once seen pulverise a punch bag in the school gym, rip the flesh off a classmate's palms with six swipes of his tawse.

'Let him be,' Solly said. 'He's drunk.'

'He's a better man than you,' Fiona shouted at Begg. 'Others are dying while you're drinking.'

Roy Begg drew back as he tried to focus on the source of the insult. 'Why you little …' But Carlo had approached purposefully from the counter, his sleeves rolled up, a dish towel slung over his shoulder. He took Begg's arm and with a few persuasive tugs managed to lead him back from the table towards the door.

'It was my eye that did it for me.' Begg twisted his head to call back. 'But for my eye I'd be out there with the boys. Out there in the trenches. Fighting with the boys. But for my eye.'

It was dark by the time they left Valentino's. Solly proposed they should walk the girls home like proper gentlemen. Avram was walking ahead hand-in-hand with Fiona when he realised Solly and Molly were no longer behind them.

'They've gone winchin' up that close,' Fiona said. 'The lamp not working makes it a favourite.' She turned to face him square and close, rocking back and forward in front of him so that her breasts just brushed lightly in a rhythm against his chest. 'Do you want to join them?'

He stood awkwardly, trying to hide the growing hardness between his legs. 'If you like.'

'Of course, I'd like. Or I wouldn't have asked. Come on.' She pulled him by the hand to the entrance of the close. He stumbled after her in the darkness through the front passage, past the doors of the ground floor flats, under the stairwell and into the corridor that led to the back green. The moonlight came in from the rear and he could see Solly pressing Molly hard against the close wall.

'Joining us, then?' Solly said, pulling away from his embrace. Even in the moonlight, Avram could see Molly's face flushed, her clothes dishevelled. Her cardigan was open, the buttons hung loose on her blouse. Solly's shirt flapped free under his sweater.

'Aye,' Fiona said matter-of-factly. And she moved up to a couple of yards from her friend, turned her back to the tiles, beckoned for Avram to come into her arms. He moved in close and she put a hand around the back of his head, pulling him in towards her. He buried his mouth in her neck, feeling the softness beneath the collar of her blouse. He recalled for an instant the soap-smell of his mother's neck as he held on to her at the quayside and he felt as if he could stay like this forever, his lips nuzzled against Fiona's skin, any girls's skin, it hardly seemed to matter.

Fiona wriggled slightly in his grasp, then pulled his head up. She looked at him straight, her eyes questioning, her lips thin and tense.

'Kiss me,' she said.

He heard a giggle from Molly.

'Give her a Frenchie,' Solly said.

Avram pressed his lips flat and hard against Fiona's. His face was hot and he had one arm awkwardly around her back against the cold slime of the tile. He kept his mouth pressed against hers until he felt her lips open slightly. He responded, letting his mouth fall into the contours of hers. Then he pulled away gasping for breath.

'You got to breathe through your nose, silly,' she said.

He pressed in again, this time with his mouth open. He brought his free hand between them, flat against the soft contour of her breast. Fiona moaned slightly, pushed hard against him. He felt her fingers tug at the waistband of his trousers, pulling out his shirt. Then, her fingers cold against the flesh of his stomach. The sensation was too much.

'Oh God,' he moaned. He snatched his hand away from her breast, leaned against the wall as his penis pumped and pumped its discharge into his underpants.

'What's going on?' Fiona gasped.

'I'm sorry,' he muttered. Then he turned away and fled out of the close, feeling the warm wetness spread over his groin as he ran.

CHAPTER TWENTY-FOUR

All was silent in the room except for Papa Kahn's hoarse breathing. It was an awful sound. A wheezing inhalation, then a pause during which Avram was not sure if the outbreath might ever come. He wondered how Papa Kahn must feel at that instant when his lungs were poised between life and death. Before the sudden relief followed quickly by the fear of death again. Inhale, pause, exhale. Life, pause, life. Papa Kahn appeared to be listening to the sound too. His head was tucked to one side as if the muscles in his neck had completely given up their function, exposing an ear cocked to the sound of his breath. His beard had grown ragged compared to the precise cut of healthier days when he was a man of such sharp contrasts, of glossy black cloths and shining white shirts. Now everything was grey. His hair, his eyes, his skin, his nightshirt. Even the air in the room.

Avram stooped to help Papa Kahn struggle to raise himself straight. He could smell the soiled warmth of the man's nightclothes, the sick desiccation of skin reminding him of the palm-sweated mustiness of old prayer books. The man's bones hung brittle and lifeless as he settled his hands on the bedclothes.

'You are angry with me,' Papa Kahn said. The sound of his eerie battle for breath filled the room. 'Ever since that business with the football. Go on. Say it.'

Avram shook his head.

'Say it.'

Still Avram said nothing.

Papa Kahn lips parted into a lop-sided smile. His teeth were stained a yellowish-brown. 'Anger can sometimes be a good thing. It can push you on.' He eased back into his pillows, coughed hard, his lungs heaving under his nightshirt like a pair of battered bellows. 'Pass me some water.'

Avram took the cloth off a jug on the bedside table, poured out a glass, placed it in the man's hands. Papa Kahn sipped slowly until his breathing relaxed.

'Remember what I told you about numbers?'

'Numbers never lie.'

'Good. And they don't lie now. Numbers show I cannot afford to send you to school. They are stopping your education. Just as quotas did mine.' His voice trailed off and his head fell back into the pillow. 'But numbers will also help you in your job with Herr Stein. And when I am well again, we can see what we can do to return you to your studies.'

'I don't want to go back to my studies.'

'Of course, you will return to your studies. You are a smart boy, Avram. Don't throw away your chance to learn.'

'I have other plans.'

'What other plans?'

'I have to go,' Avram said, turning away from the sick figure. 'My train leaves at…'

'Wait.' Papa Kahn's voice was hardly a whisper now. 'Do you ever think of your mother?' The man's jaundiced eyes were wiped with a sudden brightness. 'Yes, your mother. Dear Rachel. Do you ever think of her?'

The question surprised Avram. He stopped at the door. 'Yes, sometimes. Sometimes she comes to me in my dreams.'

'I can see her in you. I couldn't before, but now I can. I can see her in your eyes. And in your forehead.' Papa Kahn cupped a hand around his own mouth and nose so that Avram was left only with the sight of the upper half of the sick man's face. A pale, feverish forehead, dull eyes in dark sockets. He waited until Papa Kahn's head had sloped sideways and his eyes had shut. Then he went in to see Nathan.

The boy lay semi-conscious on his bed. On a nearby table there was a tray of breakfast dishes from which Celia had tried to spoon-feed her brother. Avram picked up Nathan's hand. Such a weightless thing that rested in his palm like a few dried twigs.

'Your father doesn't understand. But you do, don't you?'

Unlike his father, Nathan breathed easy, pleasant puffs of spittle through his lips, as effortless as a young baby. His neck was arched back slightly to reveal the white slithers of his half-opened eyes. A red rim to his nostrils was the only sign of colour on the bloodless face. Avram felt a slight pressure on his palm from the boy's bony fingers.

'You can hear me, can't you, my little *lamed vav*? You can hear me.' He watched as Nathan's hand twisted around in his own. 'So let me tell you something. A little secret between you and me. I am leaving you. I am leaving Glasgow. And I am leaving being a Jew. Being a Jew only brings me trouble in this world. You can see that, can't you, my little *lamed vav*? So I am leaving. And you will suffer less when I am gone.'

* * *

The tram clattered to a halt at the bottom of Buchanan Street. Avram jumped off, Celia skipped down after him. Together they walked the few yards to the hitching-post where carthorses were gathered for the haul of their wagonloads a quarter-mile up the easy slope to the station. A young boy wandered in and out of their steamy flanks with a brush and shovel sweeping up the hot manure.

'Give us a ride, please,' Avram shouted to one of the drivers who was getting ready to pull off with a half-load of grain sacks.

The lad turned to look at him, then at Celia, pushed his already rolled-up sleeves even further up on his brawny arms, let out a shrill whistle. 'I shouldnae really ... och, aye ... hop on.'

Avram swung on his bag and parcels first, then heaved himself on to the rearside of the wagon. He held out his hand. Celia grabbed it, pulled herself on board.

'Mind yer dress from the wheels,' the driver shouted. 'Don't want to be getting yer skirts dirty. Yer young fancy man wouldn't be wanting that.'

'He's not my fancy man.'

'Right then.' The driver gave his brace of Clydesdales a flick and the horses began their plodding ascent.

'Oh, Avram,' Celia said. 'This is such fun.' A Salvation Army band had struck up as they passed St.Vincent Place, and she began pumping her elbows in time to the brass. 'I'm sorry, Avram. I should be feeling sad about you leaving but the weather ... the music ... and the people. It all makes me so happy.'

'It's all right,' he said. 'It's good to see you like this.' And he meant it. She had become so serious these days, always rushing around intent on her chores, staying up late to read in the kitchen, hardly a smile to lift the frown from her brow. Political tracts, she read. Manifestos and socialist commandments. There were piles of them, printed up on cheap ink that came away on her fingers, smeared her eyes when she rubbed the tiredness out of them. She devoured them all. As greedily as Solly could swallow down a jelly piece.

The wagon pulled up sharp as a large group of women and children waving flags and banners swarmed around them on a march across the road. At their head, two stern-faced matrons held up poles stretching a white sheet declaring the procession's purpose in bold, red lettering – *Defending Our Homes Against Landlord Tyranny.* The cloth brushed over the pricked-up ears of the horses but the beasts just snorted, wriggled their thick necks, jingling the buckles and straps of their halters. A boy in a sailor suit ran alongside dwarfed by his own giant placard demanding: *Rent Strike Against Increase.* Despite the sunshine and the buoyant blare of the band, an angry mood pulsed through the marchers. Avram could sense it in the bark of their slogans, in their pinched faces, in the thrusting shake of their banners. This was no Sunday stroll up Buchanan Street. The lined-up constables twitching their batons were testament to that.

The wagon-driver sprang half-way up from his bench. 'I'm with you,' he said, pumping a clenched fist. 'Bloody landlords.' Then, as if he felt the need to give some explanation, he twisted his head back. 'On their way to George Square. For the big demonstration.'

'Brave women,' Celia said.

'They are that, bless 'em.' The young man gave her a broad smile then cracked his whip. The team started moving again. Avram saw that Celia's cheeks had reddened. She began to swing her legs back and forward over the side of the wagon.

'Are ye gettin' any increases where ye are?' the driver asked over his shoulder.

'We're from the Gorbals,' Celia said. 'We're too far away from the shipyards. Where are you from?'

'I'm from Partick.'

'That's one of the worst areas.'

'Aye. There's a big housing shortage with all those workers from outside floodin' into the steel and engineering works. Landlords are rubbin' their hands together like they're kindlin' fire with sticks. Meanwhile ma faither's in France and I could be off there any day now. Fightin' for King and country. And the factors want our families out on the streets to make room for all these new folks if we cannae pay the hikes.'

'It won't happen,' said Celia with some assurance. 'You've got a lot of support. Especially from these women. The Government will pay attention. These wifies will make them.'

'That's a fine way of thinking ye've got for being a lassie.'

Avram was leaning against the sacks, head back to the weak sun, listening to the conversation. He had never heard Celia talk like this before. She was all riled up, her face and neck in a flush. He eased a knee against her back.

'These pamphlets you read? Is that how you know all of this?'

She turned to him. Droplets of perspiration had formed just above her upper lip. 'I read the papers.'

'So do I.'

'You just count the numbers of the war dead. And every spare minute you're out in the streets kicking that daft ball about. Or winching that wee Fiona Cameron.'

'Who told you about Fiona Cameron?'

'The whole of the Gorbals knows. You should be ashamed.'

He swallowed hard, frightened to ask what exactly he should be ashamed of.

'Telling her you were enlisting,' Celia continued. 'You know, Avram Escovitz: you may be smart, but you're not thinking. There's so much going on right now. Not just the war. And not just the football. And not just the winching.'

'Like what?'

'Well, these strikes for one. And a revolution happening in Russia.'

'What revolution?'

She raised her eyes in a mock gesture of despair. 'You can ask Uncle Mendel when you see him. He's a socialist.' She called to the driver. 'Can you stop, please.'

'Whit faur, lass? We're almost at the station.'

'Please stop. I want to go to the demonstration.'

The driver pulled up the horses and Celia eased herself down off the backboard. Avram quickly gathered his baggage together in a scramble, jumped off after her.

'Celia,' he shouted. 'Wait!'

She stopped, spun back at him. Her bonnet had slipped back off her forehead, her whole face luminous with the excitement of what she was doing.

'I have to go,' she said.

'I'll be back,' he said.

She looked at him quizzically. 'Of course you will.'

'I'll be back to get you.' He fumbled in his pocket, pulled out the small box he'd been saving for her. 'Here. I want you to have this. Take it.' He clawed back the lid to reveal the silver thimble.

She stared at his outstretched hand. 'I can't. Your mother gave it to you.'

His mouth should have been full of all the fine phrases he had been rehearsing in his head all morning. But instead all he could manage was: 'Please.'

'I just can't.'

'Please. Please take it.'

'No, no. I can't.'

'Why not?'

'It's all you have left of her. It's too precious.'

'That's why I want you to have it.'

'Oh, Avram. You'd better go.' She leaned forward, brushed his cheek with her lips. Then all he saw was her back as she disappeared quickly and purposefully into the crowds, leaving him with the amber box clasped painfully tight in his fingers.

CHAPTER TWENTY-FIVE

Unlike Uncle Mendel, the train had arrived at Oban right on time, the driver deliberately holding back until the station-clock struck the hour before allowing the engine to kiss the buffers. A hundred-mile journey churning away at a steady sixty, then these last few inches so sweet and so slow. Avram saw the station-master snap his pocket-watch shut, smile in satisfaction as the train hissed down in its berth. That was over two hours ago. As he waited, he could feel his anger sloshing around inside his stomach like a mug of hot tea quickly swallowed. And he was not sure how much was due to Uncle Mendel's lateness or to his memory of Celia's figure, retreating towards the demonstration in George Square.

From where he stood under the clock tower at least he had a fine view of the town, he had to be thankful for that: Oban was far bigger than he had ever imagined. In his mind's eye he had conjured up a wee village with a post office, a few cottages scattered around, perhaps some sheep grazing the weeds by the railroad platform, a couple of fishing boats tied to a run-down jetty. Instead, he looked out on a sprawling harbour-town boasting a whisky distillery, a high street, two stout piers, one with a giant excursion steamer drawn up alongside. There was an esplanade bordered by a grand hotel and a string of mansions, proud in their squat of their gardens as they admired the view across the bay like retired sea captains with plundered wealth and time to ponder. And presiding over all of this from its hillside perch sat a strange, out-of-place stone structure, looking like a smaller version of Rome's Colosseum, which he recalled from a photograph in his Latin textbook.

'And that's the Isle o' Mull o'er the water,' a sour-faced man selling toy windmills had told him, with Ben Mor facing back defiant at the town. But it might as well have been a heap of slag for all Avram could see of the mountain under the grey clouds. Still, the air was pure and he could almost taste the salt on his tongue. Better than the soot and ashes he was used to.

There was a stink of herring about the place too. The stench would waft in at him now and then from the fishing boats unloading their cargo from the dock just behind the station, the screech of the gulls alerting him to when the catch was in. The smell reminded him of the very same fish baking inside a bundle of newspapers on Uncle Mendel's grate while he and Celia had looked on excited, curled up together in an armchair by the fire. The thought made him feel more kindly about the man he was waiting for. But not about the young woman who had rejected him.

There she was again, with her back to him as she was swallowed up by the marchers and their banners. The same way he had watched his mother disappear from him into the port-side chaos at Riga. He remembered how he had tried to cling to her as Dmitry's naval sleeve wrapped damp around his chin to force him away. And within the tension of that struggle – her pushing, his pulling, the screaming, the sobbing, the drag of his shoes on the timbers of the pier – one moment had etched itself on to his being. A precise moment of a death and a life wrapped up into one. A moment when his young soul had closed up over the loss and his spirit had desperately adjusted to survival without her. And he knew he would have to draw on that very same moment again as he embarked on this new life without Celia. Without the support of the Kahns. And without being a Jew.

He glanced up at the clock, estimated a decent time had passed, took out Uncle Mendel's letter, re-read the instructions. Written in that familiar English with Germanic phrasing. He could almost hear Uncle Mendel's voice as he read: 'Allow a decent time to pass, and if come I have not, then this you must do.'

He went in search of the station-master, spotting him at the far end of the platform in conversation with another man. The two of them seemed to be arguing about an object lying at their feet. As Avram drew near he realised the topic of discussion was the severed head of a dead stag, the lifeless eyes of the beast unswervingly observing his approach.

'Mind it don't bite you,' the station-master said, guiding him with large hands around the splayed-out antlers.

'More like mind it don't butt you,' wheezed a prosperous-looking gentleman with an impressive walrus moustache who returned to observe the kill as if it were a sack of potatoes lying on the platform.

'What will you do with it?' Avram asked. The cut across the stag's neck was ragged, matted with patches of dried blood, the eyes glazed with a sadness.

'It's no up to us,' the station-master replied. 'It was the Laird's kill. He's having it sent down to London.'

'What for?'

'Stuffed and mounted, lad. That's whit for. As much a waste of money as that bloody sight for sore eyes.' The station-master's chin jutted a nod beyond the station's glass canopy towards the Colosseum-like structure on the hill-top.

'Ye know what that is, lad?'

Avram shook his head.

'That's old John McCaig's Tower. A half-finished testament to the vanity of man. A folly is what they call it now. A cursed folly.'

'Ach, dinnae mind the station-master here,' the walrus-moustached man said. 'He'd have the Laird's castle and all the castles in the land struck down and raised again as cottar's lodgings if he'd half the chance.'

'And Donald the chemist here would dae everything to stop me.'

'Ye ken my feelings on these matters.'

'Aye, Donald, I do. But God gave the land to his children. Not to the Laird or his ilk in some divine covenant.'

Avram saw Donald's face tighten. But then the man relaxed, chuckled at the station-master. 'I do believe you're turning into one of those Bolsheviks.'

The station-master shrugged his broad shoulders. 'What is it ye want, lad?'

'I need to get to Glenkura.'

'Well, ye'll need to get yerself to Connel first.' The station-master pulled out his pocket watch, squinted at it from arm's length. 'There's a train in one hour and fourteen minutes. Or ye can leg it in that direction. The tips of the Connel bridge will guide ye. Six and half-a-dozen depending on yer fancy. Donald here is taking the train. He's got a mug of tea to sup with his Bolshie comrade before he's off.'

The road north took Avram under the shadow of the station-master's accursed McCaig's folly, then wound past the distillery, through its cloying fumes. Away from the merchant buildings on the seafront, the town began to close in on itself, hemming up tight into spindly lanes and alleys where inns crouched side-by-side with shops selling goods he'd never seen before. Goods of the sea, goods of the countryside, not the stuff of the Gorbals. Ship chandlery, yachting requisites, pebble jewellery, hunting rifles, rods and reels. In their turn, these store-fronts gave way to rows of railway cottages with their clipped gardens and drenched flower-buckets until quicker than expected he spilled out of the town and into the open countryside.

No more the narrow, sun-starved vistas of tenement streets. His eyes widened to the sweep of the horizon, the rough, stubborn beauty of the landscape. Hillsides awash with the yellow of whin, the branches of the shrubs bowed like old men burdened by the shape of the prevailing wind. Clumps of heather sprouted stubborn here and there in cracks between rocks, violets clung to their petals in the stiffness of the breeze. Off in the distance, he could just make out his marker – the two triangular peaks of the cantilever bridge. By the time he reached Connel, hardly a village at all, just a huddle of houses, a woollen mill and a general store, the sun was close to dipping beyond Ben Mor and the range beyond. There was already a pinkish glow spreading across the firth, glinting off the girders of the bridge.

'If ye wannae get across, ye'll have to go now,' the guard at Connel Station warned him. 'It's the last wan o' the day.' Like a proud showman, he presented with an outstretched arm the unusual vehicle parked on the tracks alongside the platform. It resembled some kind of charabanc, except with wheels modified to run on rails. A glossy red and green covered the side panels. Avram couldn't resist running his hand along the gold lettering, freshly-painted. *The Caledonian Railway Rail-Motor Service*. Donald from Oban Station was already seated on board.

'Where are ye bound, laddie?' the guard asked.

'Glenkura.'

'Well, ye won't make it before dark. This'll only take ye as far as Benderloch ... unless ... Mr. Munro here ...' The guard called out to his only other passenger. 'Are ye off hame, Donald?'

'Aye.'

'Can ye take the laddie?'

'If it'll do him.'

'Mr. Donald Munro can take ye as far as Lorn. Will that help?'

'Do you know a Mr. Kennedy of Lorn, sir?'

Donald Munro pulled his pipe from his mouth. 'Kenny Kennedy.

Ach, of course, I do. And what business do ye have, laddie, with the gamekeeper to the Laird himself? Ye don't look like kin.'

'He's one of my uncle's customers, sir. I was told I can stay with him for the night.'

'And who might yer uncle be?'

'Mendel Cohen, sir.'

'A strange name for these parts. Cannae say it rings a bell.'

'Jew Moses,' the guard chimed in. 'It'll be Jew Moses the tinker, I'll wager.'

'Ach, the Jew,' Donald said in a long sigh. 'Is that right, laddie?'

Avram looked from one man to the other. Donald Munro chewing hard on his pipe, his large moustache circling with the movement. The guard, stern-faced, glowering at him over his spectacles.

'Dinnae be feart,' Donald said. 'Yer uncle may be a Jew. He may also have socialist tendencies. But he was responsible for this fine suit I'm wearing.' Donald stood up and held out his arms. 'Fit for the Laird hisself.' He hovered uneasily on his feet as he opened out the jacket in an exaggerated display of the tailoring. Avram recognised the *Kahn & Co* label on the inside flap. Then Donald grasped one of the canopy poles, dropped back down into his seat. He pulled a thin silver flask from his pocket, undid the cap, took a swig. He wiggled the flask at the guard. 'A wee dram?'

'Not on duty.'

'Come on. Who d'ye think would report ye? This young laddie?' Donald tipped his flask in Avram's direction. 'Whit's yer name?'

Avram told him.

'Ach. One of the forefathers.'

'More than my job's worth,' the guard muttered as he shuffled Avram on board the vehicle. 'Take them away, Davey,' he said to another uniformed man who had emerged onto the platform.

The sun was setting across the firth as Davey steered the passenger vehicle over the Connel cantilever bridge and the swirling waters of the falls beneath. A liquid coolness rose from the churning currents below, adding to the chilliness of the evening air. Across the estuary, Avram saw a lone deer on the hillside scramble along the scree in a retreat from the engine noise. Dislodged pebbles hurtled down the slope to strafe the water below. The gloaming began to creep into the sky bringing with it a calmness that stilled his thoughts as gently as it erased the day. Shades of purple deepened across the horizon. Beside him, Donald had dozed off, clutching his whisky flask to his chest with both hands. It was only when they reached the village of Benderloch, a couple of miles over on the other side, did he gently shake Donald awake in time to greet the woman waiting at the station on a horse-drawn wagon.

'This is young Avram. Jew Moses' nephew,' Donald said, steadying himself with an arm against Avram's shoulder. 'My wife. Mrs. Jean Munro.'

Avram thought she looked more like his daughter, her young face wrapped up in a coarse beige shawl against a cold wind risen quickly on this side of the water. Even in the dusk, he could see the wildness of her eyes, the reddish brown hair flowing out from the back of her shawl to whip around in the wind. She reined in her horse, shook her shoulders in a quizzical gesture at her husband.

'He's bound for the Kennedys',' Donald explained, then bowed his head so close to Avram he had to lean away. It wasn't just the whisky. There was another smell, too – from his skin, not his breath. Like an ether.

'The wife. She disnae speak. Not a word. But she isnae daft either. Mind that. Just that her thoughts collect in her head rather than being wasted on the folk round here.'

Mrs. Jean Munro drove her wagon hard with her husband sat up beside her. Donald Munro tried to rest his head against her shoulder, but the lurch of the ride forced him to keep upright, grab on fast to his perch. Avram sat in the back, careful to avoid the metal arms of the seed plough shifting and sliding with each bump of the road. A couple of neeps and some linseed slabs bounced around at his feet.

The gloaming had faded fast into a starless sky, night closed around them quickly. There was neither a lantern on the wagon nor the light of any houses around and he couldn't remember ever having seen such a thick darkness. Even the moon was blotted out by the clouds scudding across the sky. Branches scored and scratched him on either side but neither the horse nor Mrs. Munro flinched as they ploughed on into the night. The horse must have known the road blind just as Mrs. Munro knew the world dumb.

He shivered in the blackness, sensing beasts and insects all around him. Eyes stared at him out of the depths of the forest. The swift brush of air close to his cheek could have been the swipe of a branch or the swoop of a bat-wing. Then came the hollow pleading cries of owls, the screech of some other fearful creature, the threat of ghosts and spirits, cackling as they circled the vehicle, spooking the horse on to its wild gallop. He clung on to the sides of the wagon with one foot securing the seed plough. A turnip jumped over the back flap, was swallowed up into the darkness.

Mrs. Munro finally slowed down her charge. The trees thinned out on either side of the road, a few scattered islands of lighted windows began to appear. Behind a cluster of crooked gravestones, he could make out the outline of a kirk set off the road. The horse snorted and panted.

Donald Munro twisted his head round. 'Lorn,' he said, his breath showing in the night air.

The wagon clattered to a halt outside a long cottage. A dog barked from somewhere behind the building. Mrs. Munro kept her gaze ahead. Donald turned round again. 'We'll wait.'

Avram gathered up his parcels and knapsack, leapt out of the wagon. There was light in one of the windows, the sound of voices inside. He tapped lightly on the cottage's wooden door.

'Ye'll have to dae better than that,' Donald shouted.

He struck again more firmly, skinning his knuckles in the process. The door creaked open and he had to squint against the light.

'Aye?' said the tall figure of a man stooping over him in the doorway, a paraffin lamp swinging in his large bony hand. He held out the lantern to the wagon. 'Donald. Jean.'

'Are you Mr. Kennedy?'

'Aye.'

'Mendel Cohen told me to come, sir. He said you would look after me.'

Kenny Kennedy bit his lower lip, sucked in some air. He looked back at the wagon.

'Jew Moses' nephew,' Donald said.

Kennedy nodded his head in broad sweeps. 'Och aye,' he said. 'Och aye.'

'Are ye taking the boy or are ye no?' Donald shouted.

'Away with ye, Munro.' Kennedy flapped a hand at the wagon. 'Night, Jean.' Mrs. Munro flicked her whip, drove off back into the darkness.

CHAPTER TWENTY-SIX

'Ye'd better come in, then.'

Avram followed the long back of Kenny Kennedy into a kitchen lit by a paraffin lamp at the window, a blaze in the hearth. Socks in a line across the fireplace filled the kitchen with the oily smell of drying wool. There were two box beds, one with the curtains closed. A shotgun lay against a wall, and at the rear of the room, cured ham hung from hooks in the ceiling. Through the opened top-half of a split door Avram could see into a byre where a couple of cows shifted to the sense of an intrusion in the household. The stench of warm animal bodies, dung and straw strayed into the kitchen. For a moment, he thought he was going to be sick.

Kenny Kennedy wiped his hands on his breeches, surveyed his own kitchen with a sigh, as if he were registering its cosiness for the first time. He pulled a chair out from under the kitchen table, set it firmly in front of the fire, opposite a rocker.

'Place your things and sit down.'

Avram did as he was told. Kenny Kennedy fixed his hands on his hips, stared at him with sad eyes, his face struggling with a thought that seemed to be forming in his long skull. He scratched the top of his head, thinly covered by a few streaks of oiled-back hair.

'Wait here,' he said suddenly. 'I'll get Mrs. Kennedy.' And he lumbered out of the room.

Before Avram had time to settle, a woman as small and plump as her husband was tall and bony skittered into the kitchen with a bundle of knitting in her hands. Her husband followed, then behind him came a girl of about sixteen. Avram stood up quickly.

'This is the boy,' Kenny Kennedy said.

'I can see that. What's his name?'

Kenny Kennedy shrugged and his wife dug an elbow into his ribs.

'What are ye called?' Mrs. Kennedy asked.

'Avram. Avram Escovitz.'

Behind her mother, the young girl giggled.

'Haud yer wheesht,' Kenny Kennedy said, raising a hand half-way to his daughter.

'Heat some broth, Megan,' her mother said quickly. 'And show some politeness.' She put a hand around her daughter's neck, shoved her forward into the kitchen. 'Ye'll have some barley soup, Avram? And some bannocks? Yer uncle keeps his own dishes here. Special ones.'

It took Avram a few seconds to realise what she meant. 'I don't need special dishes, madam.'

Mrs. Kennedy looked puzzled. 'I thought it was the Jew custom. *Kosher*, yer uncle calls it. Isnae that right? Everything has to be *kosher*. Even the crockery. The knives and forks and spoons. Not that we have any forks, mind. Just the spoons.'

'It's my uncle's custom. Not mine.'

Mrs. Kennedy scrunched up her lips, made a strange kissing noise as she considered this piece of information. 'That's fine with me,' she said. 'Ye can eat out off our good Christian plates then.'

Kenny Kennedy settled into his rocker, his wife fussed with the crockery, Megan dragged herself around in her tasks. Avram was left standing like a maypole in the centre of the room until he was called to sit before his meal at the table. Mrs. Kennedy scraped up a chair beside him while Megan sat opposite, elbows on the table, her head resting in the cup of her hands, staring at him as if he were a creature that had walked into the cottage from the African continent. For his part, he had never seen hair quite as beautiful as Megan Kennedy's. Long chain-links of tight blonde curls, reflecting the glow from the fire behind her. From whom Megan inherited such glorious locks he could not begin to guess. Her father hung on to a few loose strands of interminable colour somewhere between grey and ginger, while her mother had an untended mousy fuzz underneath her cap.

'Yer uncle expecting ye, then?' Mrs. Kennedy asked.

'I was to meet him at Oban Station,' he explained, conscious all the time of Megan's scrutiny. 'I waited for ages but he didn't turn up.'

'When was Jew Moses last here?' Mrs. Kennedy asked her husband.

'Must be ten days gone by. He was on his way up to Glencoe. I think he mentioned the boy might be by.'

Mrs. Kennedy chewed her lip. 'Yer uncle's probably hit some bad weather. That's what's kept him.'

'I'll take the lad up to the cottage tomorrow,' Kenny Kennedy said. 'I'm passing Glenkura on my way to the castle.'

'Hmmph. That's settled then,' said Mrs. Kennedy. 'Stop staring, Megan. Ye'd think you hadnae seen anyone from Glesca before. Ye'll need to show better manners if yer to work for the Laird.' Mrs. Kennedy folded her arms, turned to Avram. 'Off to work for the Laird tomorrow, she is. Fourth housemaid.'

'Fifth,' Megan snorted. 'A slave.'

'That's no true,' her mother said.

'It is so. I'll be the servants' servant,' Megan said. 'Ye cannae get much worse than that.'

'It's a good start, daughter,' Kenny Kennedy intervened. 'Ye should be grateful to her ladyship she took ye. Ye've a much better prospect working as a housemaid.'

'I'm a gamekeeper's daughter is what I am. My only prospect is to find an ugly husband with plenty of gold sovereigns in his pockets.'

'Dinnae mind her,' Kenny Kennedy said, unperturbed by the outburst. He continued to rock silently. Mrs. Kennedy picked up her knitting. Megan continued staring.

'Where's yer wee cap?' she asked the instant Avram had laid down his spoon.

'Dinnae be rude,' her mother said.

'I was only askin'. Jew Moses is never without one on his head or under his hat.'

'He's just more religious than the rest of us, that's all,' Avram said. 'Most Jews in Glasgow don't wear those things. I'm not religious at all.'

'So yer not a Jew?'

Avram hesitated. 'No ... not really.'

'Well, ye either are or yer no. Which is it to be?'

'... I'm not.'

'Whit are ye then?'

'I don't know.'

'Ye must be something. A Wee Free? A Catholic?'

'I'm a ... nothing.'

Megan smiled. 'A nothing. So ye eat bacon?'

'... yes, of course.'

'Well, yer uncle disnae. Like it's a sin or something.'

'It's not a sin. It's just against the law.'

'So it's a crime then?'

'It's a religious law. Like a commandment.'

'But breaking a commandment can be a crime. Thou shalt not kill. That's a crime if ye…'

'Yer uncle's a good man,' Mrs. Kennedy interrupted with a fierce attack on her knitting. 'Good manners and clean. If truth be told, faither here fair enjoys his company. They talk and play cards. And he always has a wee dram on him.'

'Mither here bought a few bits and pieces from him at the start,' her husband added. 'Work shirts and the like. Saves her going over to Oban. And then he asked if we'd give him bed and board for the night when he's down in these parts. So we have an arrangement.'

'Do I have an arrangement too?'

'Aye, lad,' Kenny Kennedy said, grinning. 'We'll just put ye up in the byre with the coos and ye'll be nae trouble at all.'

Kenny Kennedy led him into the cowshed with a lantern, laid out a blanket, dragged over a sack of grain for a pillow.

'Night,' the gamekeeper grunted and the lantern was gone.

A wind whinnied through the cracks here and there, forcing Avram to burrow deeper into the straw to keep himself warm in his thin blanket. Every now and then, he could hear the heavy shiftings of the two beasts tethered in the stalls to one side of him, then a snorting of breath, a settling down to silence. He also heard the Kennedys talking softly, the damping down of the fire, the creaking of the box bed on the other side of the stone wall. Then their lamp went out and the light leaking into the barn disappeared.

Again, there was such a darkness. He closed his eyes, opened them again, hardly noticed the difference. There were scurryings among the straw, swift movements in the grass outside, the creaking of branches, the whispering of the leaves in the wind. He could hardly believe that only one night ago he had lain in his bed in a Gorbals flat with Nathan's light snorings beside him. There was no hum of the city, no clanking of the ash-cans, no late night carriages or pedestrians, no sirens from the foundries. Just an earthy silence in which he could hear the barley filling out the stalks, the mushrooms exploding out of the humus, the moss growing between the drystanes, the flicks of the cow tails keeping the spirits and thoughts of Celia at bay.

CHAPTER TWENTY-SEVEN

It was hardly daylight when he woke to the sound of Megan's low singing. Wearily, he raised himself on one elbow. Through the slates of the byre, he could see her hands pumping the udders of one of the cows, squirting the milk into her bucket. She was sat in a squat on her stool on the far side of the swaying beast, the skirt of her smock hiked up to her knees to reveal her woollen socks, some bare shin just below the knee. The same way Mary would sit over her washboard.

Her head suddenly appeared in a twist under the belly of the cow so that her hair hung to the ground in a shiny golden wave.

'Her name's Fladda, if ye're asking.'

He wasn't asking. He laid back down on the grain sack, listened to her heavy breathing, the tinny squirt of the milk against the bucket coming more fiercely now.

'Well, ye should be asking,' she called out. 'After all, ye've just lain beside her a full night.' The cow stirred up restless, its flank knocking against the stall. 'D'ye no think Fladda's a strange name for a cow?' The squirting ceased. Her head was back under the slats. 'Have ye no a tongue in yer heid?'

He said nothing.

'Yer just wan of those stuck-up Glesca folks.'

'No, I'm not.'

'So ye can speak.'

'All right then. I think Fladda's a bloody strange name for a cow.'

'That's because it's the name of an island, daftie. We name all of our cows after the isles. It's my faither's idea. There was Iona and Lunga and Ulva and Gometra and Coll and Tiree. This other beast here is Colonsay. Now, get out of yer kip. Ye could take one of these buckets into the dairy for me.'

'You're very cheekie for a young girl.'

'I'm past sixteen.'

'Did no-one teach you to respect your elders?'

'Hah! Ye cannae be much older than me. Or ye'd be off to the war with the rest of them. There's hardly a hair on yer chin. And what there is ye'd hardly call lint in a cowherd's pocket.'

'Megan.' Her father's voice from the kitchen.

'Slave here, slave for the Laird. Whit's the difference.' She picked up her bucket and left.

Avram took the pail into the small milk-house on the other side of the kitchen from the byre.

'Och, ye gave me a right fright,' Mrs. Kennedy said when he went back into the kitchen. 'I thought ye were Jamie standing there.' She told him there was another child, an older boy, but he'd enlisted a couple of weeks before.

'I pray for him every night,' she said. She was frying up some bacon in spitting lard on top of the range.

'He'll be back for the harvest,' her husband promised, wandering in with a plunder of eggs cupped into his large hands. 'Sit down, lad. Have some breakfast. Then we'll be off.'

Mrs. Kennedy put a plate down in front of him. Avram eyed up the rashers framing the two fried eggs. The bacon was curled up crispy along its edges, glistened greasy in the middle, the colour of a raw burn. He had never eaten bacon before, although Solly swore it tasted better than the pickled brisket from Abrahamson's the *kosher* butcher. Suddenly, the laws of clean and unclean animals he'd studied in Hebrew class started to prod at his conscience. He remembered Rabbi Lieberman's pastry-crumbed lips form the words of warning, his finger pointing to the heavens as he spoke. 'Leviticus. Chapter Eleven. Every animal which is not cloven-hooved or which does not chew the cud shall not be clean to you.' That was the rule, complicated as it was to understand given the three negatives in Rabbi Lieberman's sentence. But the consequences were clear. Cows, sheep and goats were *kosher,* for their hooves were entirely split and they chewed the cud. And pigs? Yes, their hooves were cloven, but they did not chew the cud. Definitely not *kosher*. He imagined God hovering in the rafters of this small cottage waiting to punish him for eating this forbidden flesh. The smell was already tickling his nostrils, stirring up the saliva in his mouth. It was a smell he knew from neighbouring houses in the Gorbals to which Madame Kahn responded by slamming the window down and uttering the word '*Treife*' as if it were the disease tuberculosis itself wafting into her *koshe*r kitchen.

Avram cut himself a piece, placed it slowly in his mouth. The texture was slippery yet pleasing. There was a thick, concentrated, salty yet still meaty taste that awoke a new vocabulary of sensations in his mouth. A non-kosher vocabulary. A Christian vocabulary. A New Testament vocabulary. Tastes that made him know what *kosher* was because now he was experiencing what it wasn't. A profound flavour compressed within layers and layers of succulent bloody pig flesh, so unlike the anaemic meat from Abrahamson's. He chewed slowly, glancing up to the rafters for the punishment that might be inflicted. But none came. He wolfed down his portion and asked for more.

After breakfast, fortified by the pig meat and lard flowing in his veins, he helped Kenny Kennedy load slabs of peat on to his wagon.

'They're only freshly cut,' the gamekeeper told him. 'Ye'll need to lay them out proper and turn them regularly. If ye dinnae, they'll be as worthless as the udders on a dried-up cow.'

'What's "lay them out proper"?'

'Yer uncle has a kind of a shed out there. Lay them out flat under that. Not one on top o' the other. But mind to turn them. And another thing, while I mind...'

Kenny Kennedy disappeared behind his cottage and returned pushing a bicycle ahead of him.

'Yer uncle told me to look one out for ye. I got it off the factor's boy. He's off to the war with Jamie. It's a wee bit rusty. But oil it up, give it a shine and it'll look braw. Tell yer uncle he can settle with me next time he's by.'

Avram rubbed his hand over the well-worn saddle. 'It's ... it's ... it's just great.' No-one except his mother had ever given him a present before. Even if it was the rusting hulk of a second-hand bike. 'Thank you. Thank you.'

'Dinnae thank me. Thank yer uncle. He's paying for it. Can ye ride it?'

'I've never had one before.'

'Well, the country's a good place to start. They'll be no broken bones for falling on your backside. Yer uncle says ye'll need it for work.'

Kenny Kennedy loaded the bicycle onto the wagon beside the peat, then called into the house. 'Are ye ready, Megan Kennedy?'

Gone was the gamine Avram had seen at milking. Instead, emerging from the cottage came a young woman in a dark tartan skirt, a tight little jacket and a white blouse underneath it, secured at the collar with a brooch.

Kenny Kennedy heaved his daughter's trunk on to the back of the wagon.

'Sit up front, lassie.'

'I want to sit in the back with the Glesca boy.'

'Ye'll dae as yer telt. I dinnae want yer claes all soiled before ye get to see her ladyship.'

Uncle Mendel's cottage was a ways off the main track. Kennedy's wagon leaped and lurched so much in the rutted path across the fields that Avram stepped down and walked among the sheep scattered across the hillsides.

'Mind that dress,' Kenny Kennedy called after Megan who also jumped down from her perch. She hitched up her tartan skirt and ran after him the rest of the way.

He reached the cottage before her. Tucked into a hillside, it was an isolated building made up of drystane walls, a thatched bracken roof supported by free-standing cruck frames. A burn flowed close by, rushing down the slope to a small loch about a quarter of a mile away. Avram called out his uncle's name as he pushed open the door.

Uncle Mendel had done what he could to make the one room habitable. A tartan rug covered the box bed, a vase of dried flowers sat on top of a small dresser. There was a blackened pot, a kettle and a poker by the hearth, a bundle of newspapers for kindling and no doubt wrapping up herring for the baking. A large girnel took up one corner while a couple of fish-liver oil cruisies served to provide the light. A pair of faded curtains hung loosely at the window, their hems soiled where the rain had leaked in. Under the window ledge, there was a table set with a wooden bowl, a milk jug and two simple candlesticks. He noticed a *mezuzah* had been fixed to the door frame. He picked up the note that lay under the milk jug and read the familiar untidy scrawl.

> *Boychik. If this note you are reading, I am delayed up north. By Shabbos I will be back.*

'This'll dae,' Megan said as she entered the room. 'But it could dae with a sweep.' She picked up a broom fashioned from twigs, thrust it in to his hands. Avram pushed it away, let it fall to the floor.

'I thought *you* were the fifth housemaid,' he said.

'Suit yerself. So what does yer uncle say?'

'Back Friday.'

'That'll give ye a couple of days to learn to ride yer bike,' Kenny Kennedy said, stooping under the lintel. He walked over to check the girnel.

'Well, I see ye've got oats for yer porridge,' he said. 'I've brought some bannocks, eggs and milk from Mrs. Kennedy. There's plenty of fish in the loch. Can ye sling a rod?'

'I've only fished for tiddlers in the canals.'

'Jew Moses will have a line and hook somewhere. Ye won't starve.' The gamekeeper poked around here and there with his boney fingers, opening a drawer, lifting up a curtain, pressing the slabs of peat lying by the fireplace.

'Aye,' Kenny Kennedy said as he opened another drawer. 'Matches. Some tools. Good.' On his way out the doorway, he ran his fingertips over the simple oblong shape of the *mezuzzah*. 'What's this?'

'It contains parchments of holy prayers.'

Kenny Kennedy looked as if he was set to ask another question but instead he just shrugged and said: 'Help me get the peat off the wagon.'

It was close to noon by the time Megan left with her father. Avram walked them out part of the way until the wagon could pick up some speed, then he waved them off. Walking back, as the wagon drifted out of ear-shot, he realised how still and quiet everything was. There was hardly a ripple across the face of the loch, the few clouds hung motionless, there was not a bird in the sky. Even the gurgling of the burn was too far away to be heard. The few black-faced sheep on the hillside stood stationary watching his every move. He quickened his pace until he was running back to the cottage.

The bicycle lay on the ground where Kenny Kennedy had unloaded it. He lifted it up, propped it against a wall, thought about what he could do to make it right. He found some sandpaper to scrape off the rust. A rag dipped in fish-oil from the cruisie greased up the chain. He was ready to go.

There was a rough furrow in the hillside for about a hundred yards above the cottage, a dried-up bed from when the stream would overflow. He used that slope and groove to give him both the momentum and the opportunity to kick out at the small banks on either side for balance. The gamekeeper was right. The countryside was a good place to break his fall, for that was all he did – hurtle down the slope until he pitched to one side or the other, sending the bicycle clattering to the ground. Then he would get back on his feet, push the bike up the slope, start again. After two hours, he could ride down the hillside without losing his balance a score of yards more than when he had started. He had a bloody knee and scratched forearms, but he felt more cheerful for his pains.

He cleaned himself up in the burn, ate the bannocks, some milk and left-over cheese for his lunch. He discovered a pit dug out as a latrine, evacuated his bowels over the hole, wiped himself with some ripped-up newspapers. Before covering over his deposit with loose soil, he noticed no difference in either colour or consistency from his usual stools and wondered if Mrs. Kennedy's bacon had yet made its contaminated journey through his system.

Late afternoon, he prepared a small fire on the grate then went down to the loch with the hook, rod and line the gamekeeper said he was sure to find. Following a path of flattened reeds, he reached a flat rock which his uncle must have used as his fishing perch. For bait, he cut off a slice from the tube of *vursht* Madame Kahn had sent with him for her brother. He cast off as best as he could and waited, letting his thoughts drift with his line.

'So what do you think of this, Celia Kahn?' he said to his reflection in the loch. 'Here I am fishing for our supper. What are you doing up in the cottage? Sweeping the stone floor and making scones? Boiling a kettle for my tea, are you, Celia Kahn? Are you milking the cow and scratching after the chickens for eggs? Are you sewing up my socks, cutting up your skin for lack of a silver thimble on your finger?'

He foraged in his pocket for the amber box, letting the smoothness rub up and along his palm as he concentrated on his fishing. Then, quickly, as if his hand was acting independently of his thoughts, he grasped the box, tore it out of his pocket, pitched it hard over the loch. He watched it fly until it hit the water. The box bobbed on the surface for a few seconds then sank. He imagined it floating down in the darkness, nudging past the snouts of hungry fish until it rested among a tangle of reeds at the cold bottom of this silent place. He gulped down the tightness that had risen like a pebble in his throat, shook himself straight and recast his line.

He settled back down, decided instead to concentrate on practical thoughts. He thought of stoking up the fire and turning the peat. He thought of putting the jug of milk out overnight, bringing in a pitcher of water from the burn, soaking some oats for the morning. He thought to bring out the bedding and letting it air in the sunshine.

There was a plop in the water. He felt a swift nibble at his line. He pulled the rod up sharp, it caught and he whipped the line out of the water. A fish wriggled frantically on the hook. He was so excited he almost let go of the rod as he swung the creature round to the flat of the rock. The fish must have been at least two feet long and he could see the hook gnawing right through the flesh of its mouth. He wasn't used to the slippery skin. The scales felt rough and slimy in his hands. The unblinking eyes registered terror. He squeezed a couple of fingers into the silky gulping purse of a mouth, wrenched out the hook in a scrape of flesh and blood. Holding the writhing body down with one hand, he searched around his perch until his fingers settled on a small rock. The trout or salmon or whatever it was almost wrenched free, but quickly he slammed the rock down on to its head. The struggle immediately went out of the creature although the tail still wriggled with a life of its own. Tiny bones had ruptured the flesh, blood smeared the rock. But the eyes were still intact. They looked back at him with both fear and compassion. Fear of the death. Compassion for the killer. He realised he knew that look. He had seen it encompassed by the dark circles around Nathan's eyes. He thumped the rock back down on to the fish-head. And again. And again. The fishing perch was now a mess of bone and silver scale and blood and flesh. A yellow eye clung to the rock in his hand. He stopped pounding now, grinding the rock against the squashed remnants as he waited for his breathing to settle. He scraped what was left of the fish back into the loch, scooped some water up to clean off the stone surface. Next time, he would bring a knife to cut his catch's throat swiftly and without fuss.

Everything had died down into stillness again. A dying sun cast shadows across the glens, darkened the reflections on the water. Clouds of midgies hovered and swooped above the loch. A hawk beat a silent path across the sky. He turned and looked around him. There could not have been another soul for miles. On the journey in the Kennedy's wagon up from Lorn to Glenkura, there had not been sight nor sound of another cottage or steading. He knew that when the light began to fade, the night would bring its own terrors for him. But he had built his fire to fend off his fears as best he could. For now, it was so quiet he thought he could hear the silence. Like a hum vibrating through his soul.

That night, the black emptiness of the countryside provided an unwelcome vacuum for his dreams. From his raft adrift on the horizon, he still could recognise the figure of his mother at the quayside. But she was faceless now. There was no storm either, just a vast expanse of water, eerie in its stillness. Papa Kahn stood by his side, as did Jacob Stein. On a bed in the centre of the craft lay Nathan. The boy was conscious, his face bruised, bloodied and terribly disfigured.

'I gave you my pain,' Avram admitted.

'No, Avram, it is the war,' Nathan said evenly, despite his immense suffering. 'So many have died.'

'So many have died,' Papa Kahn repeated solemnly.

'But not you, Avram,' said Jacob Stein. 'For you are to be a credit draper.'

CHAPTER TWENTY-EIGHT

It was deep into the night when he awoke to a light thudding sound at the door. At first, he thought the noise came from the snout or claw of a wild deer, a fox or even a sheep, but then he realised it was the scratching of a hand searching the cottage door for its handle.

'Uncle Mendel,' he whispered.

There was no reply. Just the click of the handle as it turned downwards.

'Uncle Mendel?'

The door opened. Backlit by the moon, a shrouded figure stood at the entrance.

'Uncle Mendel?' His voice shook from the realisation that the shape standing in the doorway was far too small to be that of his adopted uncle. He slipped his hand from underneath the bedclothes, his fingers searching desperately for the iron poker lying in the hearth. The figure took a couple of steps into the cottage.

'I've got a poker,' he shouted.

The intruder stopped. 'No, ye havenae.'

'Bloody hell! It's you.'

'Is that a way to greet a lady?'

'What are you doing here?'

'Have ye no a match to light a cruisie?'

He wrapped himself in his blanket, got out of bed, scrambled for the matches on the table by the window, lit the oil-soaked wick. The flame flickered to life, showing up Megan standing in the middle of the room, dressed in a maid's uniform, a shawl drawn around her face. Some burrs clung to her black stockings. Her shoes and the lower part of her apron were splattered with mud.

'What happened?'

'I've run away.'

He saw she was trembling.

'I'll get us warm,' he said. He quickly set about stoking up the fire, set a kettle above it when the flames took to the peat. Megan sat on the edge of the bed, leaning her head against the wall, watching him. She let her shawl drop around her shoulders, her hair shining in the flickering light as if it were her own personal beacon.

'Are you hungry?'

She nodded.

He brewed a pot of tea, cut her some slices of *vursht*. She looked at the meat suspiciously.

'It's German sausage,' he explained.

'I thought we were at war with them.'

'More for you, less for the Germans, then.'

He was glad to hear her laugh for she looked so close to tears. She folded the slice of meat in half, popped it into her mouth. Her hands were still shaking.

He passed her a cup of tea. 'Put your palms around that. It'll warm you up. I've got some milk if you want it.'

'Black's fine.' She took a sip to wash down the meat. 'Yer no bad with the fire for a city boy.'

'I'm better with coal. I'm not used to this peat. So what happened?'

'I dinnae ken what I've done. But I just cannae take it there.'

'What? You were only there half a day.'

'Aye, it's all right for you to say. I saw from the first moment how it was going to be. Her ladyship was fine. She kent faither from him being the gamie. And I was all full of curtsies and 'yes and no, your ladyship'. But I'm no workin' for her. Like I said, I'm to be a servant's servant.'

'It can't be that bad.'

'Oh, aye it can. The worst mistresses are servants themselves. Ordering me to do this and that for no more reason than to look down their long noses at me. A few hours into my uniform and the butler and the clerk of works with no hands for their tasks, but plenty for pushing me against the pantry wall and pushing up my skirts.' She plunged her face into her hands. He had a feeling to reach out and touch her but held back. Instead, he watched the firelight display their lanky shadows against the wall opposite until the shudders in her back subsided.

'What will you do now?' he asked.

She lifted her head. Her cheeks glistened red from the fire's heat and the salt of her tears. 'I didnae leave with any grand plan. It was either here or Jean Munro's place. But that was too far in the night. I can go hame but ma faither'll just beat me raw and send me back. I might go back to the Laird myself. Or I might find my way to the city. I'll ken better in the morn's light.'

'Well, you can have the cot.'

'That's kind of ye. But I wouldnae want ye to kip on the cold stane floor.'

'It's not so bad. Last night I slept on a bed of straw. With two cows for company.'

She laughed. 'We could try a wee bit of bundling.'

'Bundling?'

'Aye, bundling. Ye wrap yerself in yer blanket and I'll wrap up meself in my shawl and we'll share this mattress together like two good Kirk-going folk.'

She stood up, stretched to unhook the back of her uniform. 'If ye don't mind damping down the fire, I'll need to take this off. I may need it in the morn if I decide to return.'

He turned away to sprinkle some water on the flames, tidy up the hearth, but his attention was more on the sound of Megan's clothes falling to the floor than on any fireside order. He heard the cot creak and he put out the cruisie. Wrapping himself in his own blanket, he lay down beside her.

The cot was narrow, but lying on his back he managed to keep a good inch between himself and Megan's rolled-up frame. He watched the moonlit shadows play across the bracken roof, thought of Solly and how he would probably have an arm around Megan by now, giving her a 'Frenchie'. He twisted his head slightly in her direction. Her breathing had eased to regular, her eyes were closed, her shift had fallen slightly off her shoulder exposing just the hint of the furrow between her breasts. He looked away, too excited to contemplate sleep. He listened to the night roll on to its deepest point before it sighed and moved on towards the dawn. There were no eerie noises from ghosts and beasts to be heard, just Megan's soft breath soothing him until he eventually drifted into slumber.

When he awoke, she was gone from the bed.

At first, he thought she had left him completely. But there was a fire burning in the grate and the cottage door was left open to let in a shaft of the morning sunshine and the sound of her singing. He dressed quickly, rushed outside. She sat hunched over the burn, her shawl draped over her shift, scrubbing her apron clean on some rocks. He stayed back and listened.

'... I am my mamie's ae bairn
Wi' unco folk I weary, Sir
And lying in a man's bed
I'm fleyed it make me eerie, Sir.

I'm o'er young, I'm o'er young
I'm o'er young to marry yet!
I'm o'er young, 't wad be a sin
To tak me frae my mammie yet.

I am my mamie's ae bairn
Wi' unco folk ...'

She looked up from her task, smiled at him sweetly as if he were her very own husband standing before her. 'Good morn,' she said.

He picked up a pebble from the side of the stream, threw it in the direction of the loch. He watched it fall way short of its destination. He had no idea why he had done that. 'Have you made up your mind?' he asked.

'Are ye weary from me already?'

'I just wanted to know.'

She stopped her scrubbing. 'Dinnae worry. I'm going back to the Laird's castle.'

'Are you sure?'

'Why? Would ye like me to stay here?'

Avram blushed. And she smirked at him as if she had achieved some little victory.

'Look, I've nae choice,' she said, not waiting for his answer. 'I cannae go hame. I cannae stay here with yer uncle coming back. Not that I've asked yer permission, mind ye. And the stories of young girls alone in the city are not pleasing. I'll return to the castle to suffer my fate.'

'All things considered,' he said, 'that seems the best thing to do.'

'That's very sensible of ye. Ye sound like ma faither.'

'You told me your father would beat you raw for what you've done.'

'Aye, yer right. I'm sorry.' She stood up, held out the hem of her shift and performed a mock curtsy. 'I thank ye for yer hospitality, kind sir.'

He ignored the gesture. 'How far is it? To the castle?'

'Six miles or more. Depends if ye fly like the crow or ye canter along the bridleways.'

'I'll see you part of the way then.'

'That's kind of ye.'

'But I'll need to be back here before the Sabbath starts.'

'By tomorrow morn?'

'No, no. The Jewish Sabbath. This evening when the first star appears.'

'That's a fine custom,' she said. 'It has a common sense about it.'

Even dressed in a maid's uniform, she strutted beside him with a sense of ownership of the land worthy of any laird. She could name the birds from their song, place each sheep with its owner from the brand on its flanks, point out the shielings for the summer shearing. She stopped to pick bluebells for her hair, a feather off the ground to wave as she walked. She was full of stories of the shire, the gossip of the villages, the scandals at the castle. He envied her this rootedness in place for he drifted over this world like the mist on the hillside. Like a wandering Jew. Like a credit draper.

With a nose for the direction of her destination, she led him on paths no more than sheep tracks across the hillsides, ways she knew from playing as a child with her older brother. She described Jamie as a big lump of a lad but handy with a rifle. Just a glimpse of a tail or a snout was all he needed to find his target. She imagined him picking off easy any German soldier who dared put his head above the trench line. That was how she preferred to visualise Jamie's war. As a sniper. Hidden away from the action. Invulnerable. Always the hunter, never the hunted.

By midday, the coach-road came into sight where it split west for the Laird's castle, north for Glencoe, south for Lorn and Glenkura. They scrambled down the scree, turned into the Laird's estates where the terrain changed immediately. Fir trees were set out orderly to mark the road, there was an orchard of apple trees standing among its shed blossom, the stone walls were properly maintained, the land was flatter, given up to acres of barley and cattle, not just sheep and crofts. She dropped away from him a few paces, became silent.

He heard the dull humming noise first, dismissed it as a party of bees hovering around a hive or a cluster of pollen. And as the drone grew louder so did the size of the swarm in his imagination. Megan cocked an ear to the sound too and soon she was scanning the sky.

'Bees?' he asked.

Before she had time to answer, the flying machine burst into view, skimming through the tops of the trees lining the road. Instinctively, he dived for cover under the gorse bushes on the side of the road. Megan fell in right behind him. The bi-plane passed overhead, its engine coughing as it circled the open field beyond the whin.

'It's an aeroplane,' he shouted. 'It's a bloody aeroplane.'

'Is it a Gerry?'

'Don't be silly.' But he checked the red, white and blue roundels on the wing to be sure. 'It's one of ours,' he yelled. He clambered out through the gorse, ran out into the field, his eyes fixed to the sky. The plane circled again and he could see the pilot lean out of his cockpit to inspect the ground. The engine stuttered then picked up again. The pilot took his machine on one more long loop away from the field, lined up straight then dropped down to land. The plane bounced and skidded as it hit the uneven surface, hit a bump and veered over dangerously so that its lower wing scraped the ground, throwing up a spray of earth. Avram saw the pilot wrestle with his controls, grinding the rudder against the swerve. Then the aeroplane twisted to one side and came to a halt just before a row of bushes. By the time Avram had reached the craft, the engine had coughed and died but the propeller was still cranking down. The pilot eased himself up on to the back of his cockpit, swept off his leather helmet and goggles.

'It's an aeroplane,' Avram yelled.

'Well, it's not a bloody Zeppelin,' the pilot said in an English accent. 'But it's a thirsty one.'

The pilot slid himself onto the wing, dropped to the ground. Avram was surprised how young he was; there couldn't have been more than four of five years between them, his blond hair thick but cut short, still matted down from the tightness of his helmet like a field of wheat flattened from the lying in it. The skin on his forehead and around his blue eyes shone pinkish-white in contrast to the rest of his face ruddy from the wind, streaked with oil.

'And is this your very own servant?' the pilot asked, raising his eyes in the direction of Megan running awkwardly in her uniform across the field.

'No, that's Megan Kennedy. The gamekeeper's daughter.'

'What happened?' Megan asked breathlessly.

'Ran out of petrol,' the pilot replied. 'On a reconnaissance test up from Carmunnock. Thought I had enough to get out and back. Must have been way off in my reckonings.'

'Reconnaissance,' Avram repeated, savouring the length and importance of the word. 'What does that mean?'

'Just having a look-round. A reckie. For the RFC – Royal Flying Corps – that is. Scouting the terrain. Doing the same against Gerry in France. Once the tests are finished.'

Avram ran his hands over the silver-painted wing. 'What's it made of?'

'Metal body. Wings covered with fabric.'

'What happens when it rains?'

'The fabric's coated against letting in water. Otherwise the wings would get too heavy from absorbing the moisture. It's just the poor pilot gets soaked.'

'Can I get up?'

'On you go.'

Avram hauled himself up on to the wing close to the fuselage. Clinging on to one of the struts, he swung his body round so he could sit down and let his legs dangle underneath.

'Just sit steady,' the pilot said. 'No clambering around.' He handed Avram the leather helmet. 'Try this. And you too, young lady? Take the goggles. I can put you on the other side.'

Megan let herself be lifted up on to the opposite wing. Then the pilot stepped a few paces back from the nose of the plane so he could view his two passengers.

'Like bookends,' he pronounced.

Avram found himself observing the scene from the pilot's perspective. He could see himself perched on the wing, legs swinging back and forth underneath, with the helmet hanging loosely over his head. Megan, on the other side, goggles strapped over her mane of hair, laughing as the pilot pretended to film them with some imaginary crank-handled two-reeled camera. The pilot was speaking to Megan but he couldn't hear what was being said, his sense of sound muffled as if he were hearing everything from underwater at the Corporation Baths. Movement seemed to have slowed too until the whole scene crystallised. This was it. Of course, this was it. This was the strange bird Mrs. Carnovsky had read in his tea-leaves. The bird the likes of which she'd never seen before. He must hold these moments tight to his memory – the spring sunshine glinting off the aeroplane fuselage, the amusing antics of the pilot, Megan's disembodied laughter, the feel of the rough nap of the wing fabric under his palms, the sense of lightness that pervaded his whole body. Then the voice of the pilot, clearer now, asking him a question.

'Can you tell me where I might find some petrol?'

'Megan could tell you. She's from around here.'

Megan had dropped down from her side of the plane, scrambled up from underneath the body.

'The castle must have some,' she said breathlessly. She had pushed the goggles back off her face to form a strange band across her hair. 'The Laird keeps automobiles and motorbikes there.'

'The Laird, eh?' the pilot said. 'How far is this castle?'

Megan pointed in the general direction. 'Not two miles straight down the avenue there. I'll take ye there, if ye want.' She turned to Avram. 'Ye can leave me here,' she said. 'Best ye get back for yer Sabbath.'

Avram watched her disappear across the field. The pilot ambling beside her, one hand shouldering his leather jacket, the other supporting Megan's elbow as he guided her over a stile. He ran after them.

'Wait. Wait a moment."

'What is it?' the pilot asked.

'My name is Avram,' he said, stretching out his hand. 'Avram Escovitz.'

The pilot snapped into mock salute. 'Sinclair it is. Flight Lieutenant Charles Sinclair.'

CHAPTER TWENTY-NINE

Uncle Mendel was naked. Bathing in the burn, the folds of his flesh wobbling to the splashing, his shrivelled-up penis wriggling like a mouse in a hole. Avram just stood there, not sure how to approach.

'*Willkommen, willkommen, boychik*,' Uncle Mendel said, noticing him for the first time. 'Welcome to my country estate.' Uncle Mendel bowed, then grabbed the metal bucket from off the bank, dragged it against the current, poured some water over himself. He let out a shivering yelp as he did so. Avram laughed.

'What is so funny, *boychik*? Next in line you are.'

'I'm not getting in there.'

'Like a bath in the front room it is.'

'It's freezing.'

'If supper you want, get in.'

A few minutes later, Avram was soaping himself down in the icy water. Uncle Mendel, now dressed in a singlet and trousers held up with a length of string, watched on from the cottage door. His flesh shone pink in patches. Take away his *yarmulke*, Avram thought, and he could have been a blacksmith with nothing more to do than watch a horse led in for shodding.

'Scrub harder,' Uncle Mendel shouted. 'As clean as a *Shabbos* angel I want you.'

It was only much later, dressed in all the clothes he had brought with him, that Avram managed to stop shivering in his huddle in front of the hearth.

'Why didn't you come to meet me?'

'Bad weather up north,' Uncle Mendel said vaguely before handing him a steaming bowl of barley soup. 'But with only an address from Russia to the Gorbals you came. To this cottage from Glasgow must be easy for you. *Nu?* Now everything you must tell me. All the gossip. I like to hear all this – how do you say? – tittle-tattle.'

Avram shakily scooped up the warming broth with his wooden spoon then spoke of Papa and Madame Kahn, Celia and Nathan. To each piece of information, Uncle Mendel rocked a rhythm in his chair, fingering and twisting one of his loose sidelocks as if to bind the details in his memory. His gaze became lost to distant visions. When his attention did finally return, Avram told him of his stay with the Kennedys.

'Young Megan Kennedy ran away from the castle,' Uncle Mendel said.

'How did you know that?'

'The villagers tell me all their tittle-tattle this morning.'

'She has gone back now.'

'And you know this how?'

'Because ... because she came here.'

'And she did that why, I wonder?'

'I don't know. She had nowhere else to go, I suppose.'

Uncle Mendel nodded his head in a slow surveillance of the room as if he might discover some tell-tale sign of Megan's visit. 'I see,' he said, poking his pipe into life. The smell of the sweet tobacco took Avram back to the flat in Glasgow where the aroma used to mingle with the fleshy fragrance of baked herring. 'Now these parcels you bring. They are from Herr Stein? I must see what samples and brochures he sends me. And this *vursht*? A little circumcised it has become, don't you think? But of such things later. Now let us prepare for the *Shabbos*. Then we can talk some more.'

Avram helped tidy away the parcels, set out the table. There were fresh supplies of eggs, cheese and bread, a jar of honey as a special treat. He took two chairs outside so they could sit and scan the early evening sky in search of the first star, the sign to mark the arrival of the *Shabbos*. Uncle Mendel came out too, sat down, prepared his final pipe before the Day of Rest began.

'I hear some kind of football player you want to be,' Uncle Mendel said quietly.

'That was in the past.'

'Herr Stein mentioned this to me.'

'What does Herr Stein know about my football?'

'In these things, Herr Stein takes an interest.' Uncle Mendel lit a match. The tobacco hissed in the bowl as he puffed his pipe alight. 'A very good player, he says you are.'

Avram shrugged. 'It makes no difference. I have no opportunity to play now.'

'I see.' Uncle Mendel drifted off for a while on some reverie. 'You know what *beshert* is?' he said eventually.

'Yes. It means fate.'

'Well, if for you to be a footballer is *beshert*, then a footballer you will be. Even if all kinds of obstacles life puts before you. Somehow and in some way, what is meant to be will be.'

'And if it is *beshert* to be a credit draper?'

'Then a credit draper you will become,' Uncle Mendel chuckled. 'Just like me.' He paused then cupped a hand to his ear. 'Now, listen, *boychik*.'

'I don't hear anything.'

'Ssshhh.'

'What is it?'

'The sound of the Lord.'

'I still don't hear anything.'

'Sshhh. Here it is easier to discover Him than in the city.'

A sense of a hush and a holiness drifted down from the hillside. A stillness settled on the loch. Even the sound of Uncle Mendel sucking on his pipe had ceased. All became silent. The Sabbath closed in. Stealthily. Like a mist.

'There it is,' Avram shouted, pointing at the merest pinpoint of light in the sky.

'Ah. So it is.' Uncle Mendel reluctantly put aside his pipe. 'Come. It is time to welcome the *Shabbos*.'

Avram followed Uncle Mendel back into the cottage. As the older man passed through the doorway, he pressed his fingers to his lips, then to the *mezzuzah* fixed to the lintel.

'Please say the *bracha*,' he told Avram.

'Do I have to?'

'Do I have to? Do I have to light the *Shabbos* candles? What kind of question is that from a Jewish boy?'

'I don't feel like doing it.'

'Why? Because it is women's work?'

'No. I just don't want to.'

'Now, don't make me angry. You are a guest in my home. It will please me greatly if this you do for me.'

Avram relented, went over to the table, lit the two Sabbath candles in their holders, an honour usually reserved for Madame Kahn or Celia. Once the wick had caught, he covered his eyes, made the blessing.

When he had finished, Uncle Mendel grasped his hand, shook it vigorously. 'Good *Shabbos*, *boychik*. This is such a delight. Usually I am all alone for the *Shabbos*. We must make a *kiddush*. Wine I don't have. But a *biesele* whisky I can give you.' He rattled open a drawer, brought out a bottle and a glass, poured out a large measure, quickly said the blessing for wine.

'Only one glass I have,' he said, offering it to Avram.

Avram took the whisky, tried a sip, felt the liquid harsh in his throat before it warmed him all the way to his stomach. He took another sip. His eyes began to water. Uncle Mendel snatched back the glass, downed its contents in one gulp. '*L'haiim*,' he said, pouring himself another glass. 'I am going to sit outside.'

Avram stayed behind, pulled up a stool to the table, watched the candles flicker and drip. He could still taste the whisky in his mouth, feel his head slightly giddy from the alcohol, the overall sensation being one of pleasant contentment. He squinted at the candles, creating shards of light beaming back at him. He was sorry he had argued with Uncle Mendel about the blessing. Perhaps the man was right. God was easier to find in the countryside than in the city. For this was the God he loved. The God who created the beauty of this place. The God who brought peace and comfort to his soul. The God who looked after his mother. Yet he knew also that out there in the approaching darkness was the other God. The Jewish God that punished Moses. The Jewish God that demanded rituals of Sabbath blessings and *kosher* food. The Jewish God he feared.

He went outside. The sky was now a black mass pricked with thousands of stars. An awesome spangled firmament in a night humming with the stirrings of small insects.

'It is the *Shabbos*, Avram.'

'Yes. It is the *Shabbos*.'

'About our work together I have much to tell. But until the *Shabbos* has passed that must wait. For now is a time for rest, not for work. Even the talk of it.' Uncle Mendel paused, distracted by a scurrying in the darkness, and then returned to his topic. 'Like a young bride the *Shabbos* comes. And bachelor though I am, I must stay with her until she has passed. This is my time for reflection. So if this time I do not spend with you, do not feel neglected.'

And with that last remark, Uncle Mendel stood up, walked off towards the loch, whisky bottle in hand. Hours later, Avram felt the man's return when he heaved his large frame on to the bed, forcing him to scrunch up to the wall, to listen to the man's heavy breathing quickly turn to snores. When Avram finally fell asleep, gone were the dreams of his mother and rafts drifting off to the horizon. Instead, he dreamed of soaring, circling airplanes with Megan Kennedy, in helmet and goggles, as the pilot.

After a cold breakfast, Uncle Mendel recited the morning prayers for the Sabbath, then left on a long walk. Avram went out for his own stroll around the loch, seeking out the flat rock he had used as a fishing perch where he lay down to catch up on his lost sleep.

Uncle Mendel returned just before dusk, sat with him outside the cottage until the first star arrived. Then, he retreated inside, lit the fire, re-heated the broth.

They ate in silence but when the meal was over, Uncle Mendel prepared a pipe, brought out two packs of cards and a box of matches.

'A game of *kalooki*?'

Avram nodded.

'Tinkers. That's what they call us here, *boychik*. Tinkers.' Uncle Mendel dealt out two hands of thirteen cards each, divided up the matches between them. 'So about us tinkers what do you know? About us travellers? About us credit drapers?'

Avram searched through his cards arranging a set here and there. It was quite a good hand. 'A little.' He related what he remembered from his meeting with Jacob Stein. He then picked up a card. A joker. He tried to conceal his joy. He threw away a useless card in its place.

'Also, the code you will need to learn.'

'The code?'

'Yes, the code. The code is at the heart of everything.'

'Jacob Stein didn't tell me about any code.'

'The mark-up is what the code tells you.'

Avram played and listened as Uncle Mendel explained how his profit margin depended on his discretion, his relationship with the customer, how much he thought the customer could afford.

'From me, this is what you need to learn. And how to sell the stock. Although in these parts, things sell themselves for lack of choice.' Uncle Mendel laid down three sets in a flurry.

Avram tried to remain calm. He needed just one card until he could lay out his whole hand. Double payment. That was the dilemma. To put down now and expose his cards. Or to hold back, risk being caught with everything, but receive double payment if he won.

'You're very quiet, *boychik*.'

'You didn't tell me what the code was.'

'A Polish Jew.' Uncle Mendel found a pencil stub in his pocket, wrote the words down on the reverse side of a scrap of paper, all the while keeping his four remaining cards in a fan close to his chest. *A POLISH JEW.* 'Each warehouse has its own. Herr Stein's uses *A POLISH JEW.* Goldberg's uses *CUMBERLAND*. Always ten letters, no two letters the same. A mark-up of ten percent each letter shows. If beside a customer's name a letter *A* I write like this...' And here Uncle Mendel circled the letter *A* on the paper. 'Then the mark-up is ten percent. The letter *P* twenty percent, and so on and so on.' He continued circling each letter along the word until he came to the letter *W*. 'One hundred per cent. So if with an *L* beside it I write a customer's name, that is a mark-up of...?'

Avram picked up the scrap paper. As he twisted it around in his hands examining the code he noticed the front side was a cancelled betting slip. The word *PAID* had been written across the face of the bet underscored with a scrawl he immediately recognised. *Solomon Green.* It was Solly's signature.

'*Nu*? With numbers I thought you were good.'

'*L* is forty percent.'

'Excellent.' Uncle Mendel picked up another card, fussed over his hand. He squinted at Avram for a good few seconds before putting down another set of three cards. He shielded his remaining card in the hollow of his large palms. 'One card left.'

Avram sucked in his breath, concentrated on the fan of thirteen cards in his hand. Should he wait for his one card, or lay down what he had? He needed an ace of hearts or a nine of spades. Or a joker. He decided to take a chance.

'Why do you need a code?' Avram asked as he picked up a card from the top of the deck. King of hearts. High in hearts. That was what Uncle Mendel always told him to be. Lucky in love. But it was only a king. Not high enough.

Uncle Mendel relaxed, continued talking. 'Around here the code is not so important. Just a personal record of my transactions. Working in Glasgow it is more necessary. If the customer wants to go direct to Herr Stein's warehouse to pick a size, a colour, a style, I give them a line – a line of credit – for a dress or a shirt and so on and so on. My customer can't buy from the warehouse direct unless he has a line from me. And the warehouse knows what to charge my customer for the goods how?'

'You write the code on the line?'

'Very good.' Uncle Mendel picked a card now. He did so very slowly, slipping it off the top of the pack and along the table. He bent back a corner – a sin of card abuse that in the eyes of Madame Kahn would have meant expulsion from the table.

'Bah!' Uncle Mendel threw away the nine of spades which Avram promptly picked up. He gleefully laid out all his cards.

'Oy, *boychik*. What happened?'

'I won.'

'All out in one.'

'Double payment.'

'So they tell me.'

Avram picked up the cards, shuffled while Uncle Mendel wrote down his score and passed over two matchsticks.

'The bicycle you can ride?'

'Nearly.'

'Nearly is not good enough. Tomorrow we start. Follow me on my rounds for a few weeks. Listen and learn.'

'I will try.'

'If you can't ride, you can run. After one month, you are on your own.'

'On my own?'

'Here you will stay and visit my customers. Collect payments. Get more orders. I must go back to Glasgow.' Uncle Mendel explained how he needed to sort out his alien status, fulfil orders, look at new samples. 'When I come back, it will be your turn to go down there to complete the orders. The goods you can carry, you bring back from Glasgow with you. The rest you send on to the Post Office in Lorn.'

'Can you make money just by selling shirts and aprons and girdles?'

'See. Already a business head you have. No, we also measure up suits for my brother-in-law's shop. And larger items we also sell. Furniture. Dressers. Linen presses. Chests of drawers.'

'How can we do that?'

'From brochures. The transport the warehouse arranges. Some new brochures I'll bring back with me to show the customers. Now, deal, *boychik*. How do you say? The night is young.'

CHAPTER THIRTY

The weather was kind to Avram those first few weeks. He didn't get to experience what is was like to be holed up soggy and shivering waiting for the rain to pass, or to be lashed by sheets of it as he moved across the countryside pushing a bike laden with parcels. He didn't get lost in mists, pounded by sleet or have to squelch through mud that sucked the boots off his feet. Still, the work was hard and Uncle Mendel kept a tough schedule. They often walked or cycled up to twenty miles a day on terrain not known for its flatness. But it was healthy work, and day by day he felt his muscles build and his lungs expand.

They were always fed at the end of their treks and, as with the arrangement with the Kennedys, Uncle Mendel had organised accommodation en route where he stored some *kosher* dishes, where there was always a bed of straw for the night. No matter how early he woke, Avram would always find Uncle Mendel standing in some corner of the byre or barn, under the cover of his *tallith*, his *tefillin* perched upon his forehead and wrapped around one arm, rocking backwards and forwards to the rhythm of his mist-breathed prayer. At times like these, Avram would lie still among the straw listening to the man's muttered intonations as they lulled him back into a comfortable half-sleep. There, he would dream of a small synagogue where *tallith*-cloaked men droned their prayers in a ghostly undertone. The most elaborate glass lanterns hung at various heights from the vaulted ceiling, the white silk-covered scrolls of the Torah with their silver ornaments shone from the nest of the Ark like the display of some fabulous treasure. In such a scene, Avram could feel his body rock too – not to the lilt of prayer but to the swing of his mother's arms as she observed the scene below from her place in the gallery. And when later in the day of such a dreaming, after their hosts had sent them on their journey with a pocketful of eggs, a loaf and a hunk of cheese, fragments of his dream would rise to his consciousness. The synagogue he knew belonged to his Russian past. And he dared to imagine that somewhere within the shrouded congregation, stood the man who was his father.

As they traipsed around the countryside from customer to customer,

Uncle Mendel taught him how to properly measure a jacket or a suit, how to discuss the stitching and the cloth, how to calculate the price based on individual swatches. Avram learned about the different styles of collars and cuffs, the endurance of the fabric, what was in fashion and what was out. He became informed about aprons and bed-linen, wardrobes and dressers and even lost his shyness when talking about girdles. He became adept at writing out orders, noting the mark-up according to the code, handing out invoices and the proper receipts. Uncle Mendel recognised his ability with figures and left him alone to work out percentages, total amounts outstanding, profits made. Avram memorised the details of each customer, where they were located on his route, how much of a mark-up they were entitled to, the number and names of the children in the family, how old they were, who was married to who. And Uncle Mendel would test him on each customer until he knew their life stories as well as he knew his own.

Avram also discovered there was another side to the credit drapery business when Uncle Mendel brought out a small black notebook different from the one he usually used to mark down a repayment from a customer.

'What is that for?' Avram asked, trying to peer over his shoulder.

'This is not your business.'

'If you want me to look after things when you are away, I need to know everything.'

'Perhaps,' Uncle Mendel said, putting away the notebook. 'You see, *boychik*,' he sighed. 'Sometimes I lend the customers money on credit so they can buy on credit. Even when from me they buy nothing, I will lend them.'

'So, you are a money-lender?'

'When in Glasgow I do business, it is more common. There, because my customers are near, I can keep my eye on them more closely, I can visit every week to collect. Here in the countryside, only rarely will I lend them. But if they are good customers and they are in need.' Uncle Mendel shrugged. 'How else can a person survive out here?'

'Do you want me to lend money too?'

'Never,' Uncle Mendel said sternly. 'To do that is only for me. But the instalments you may collect.'

And it was unusual for a customer not to make due payment. Even if a farmer or his family were not at home, the money was often left in prearranged locations around the croft or farm-house.

'Cash is all we take,' Uncle Mendel warned. 'No bartering. And be careful of...' He cleared his throat. 'Sometimes the man is away and if there is no money ... the wife might offer...'

'Offer what, uncle?'

'You know what I mean.'

'What?'

'It doesn't matter. Just take cash. That's all to remember. Cash only. We only deal in cash.'

But Uncle Mendel didn't just lend money, trade in clothes, haberdashery and furniture or measure up suits for Kahn & Co. Avram saw that he dealt in another important commodity too. As they passed from village to village, farmhouse to farmhouse, croft to croft, Uncle Mendel became a carrier of news and gossip. With relish, he would pass on details of labour to be found, the dates for the spring and autumn feeings, prices fetched at market, bairns born, couples wed, old biddies passed away. Perhaps he would hand on a letter, a newspaper, a small package. But always he had a bottle of Scotch in his basket so he could furnish his hosts with a dram or two mixed in with a wee drop of scandal. Or a heated discussion on politics. After all, he was a man who not only knew the Torah in Hebrew but had read Marx in the original German.

'What is socialism, uncle? Celia is always talking about it.'

'Ah. A big question, *boychik*.'

'Can you explain it to me?'

'In simple terms, it is the political philosophy of putting people before profit.'

'That doesn't happen now?'

'No. Now it is profit first and people second.'

'Is that bad?'

'In theory? No. Men like Herr Stein and the Laird become wealthy and then perhaps to charities and their employees they give generously.'

'That seems very fair to me. What's wrong with that?'

'You forget human nature, *boychik*. People are too greedy to make such a system work. They get rich and their wealth most of them keep for themselves. But socialism allows everyone to progress together by sharing the profits of their labour equally. Can you see the value in that?'

Avram thought he did. But then again, he knew he had nothing and it was easy to share nothing. He wasn't so sure how generous he would be if he had wealth to give away.

'Does that make you a Marxist, uncle?'

Uncle Mendel laughed. 'Karl Marx was not even a Marxist. He was a bad-tempered German Jew who lived off his friends and worked not a day in his life.'

'Are you a Bolshevik then?' he asked, remembering what the chemist Donald Munro had called the Oban station-master.

Uncle Mendel laughed. 'Look at me, Avram. I carry bags of aprons and girdles around the Scottish countryside. You think I look like a professional revolutionary?'

Before Avram had a chance to ask more, Uncle Mendel diverted to one of his favourite themes.

'Do you know what I like about Scotland, *boychik*?'

'Tell me, uncle.'

'Look at how strange I must look to these people. Yet, still they accept me. Here I have the freedom to be a Jew.'

'Is that all?'

'*Nu*? Is that not enough?'

'Not for you.'

'Well, there's the herring…'

'Is that all, uncle?'

'There's the whisky…'

'Is that all?'

'It's enough for me, *boychik*.'

'What about the horse-racing?'

'What about it?'

'Solly told me you make bets. Under the name of "Baked Fish".'

'That Solly should keep *shtum* about my business…'

* * *

They had been cycling south along the coach road when a horse-drawn wagon sped past forcing them to cover their eyes from the dust. A hundred yards or so further up the road, the wagon-driver pulled up and waited.

'Why, it's Jean Munro,' Avram said.

'Ah, so it is.'

When they caught up, Uncle Mendel raised his hat, revealing his *yarmulke* underneath.

'Good afternoon, Madame Munro. Fine weather it is. A drop of rain I do not see for two weeks now.'

Jean Munro nodded to both of them. Across her shoulders, she wore the same beige shawl Avram recalled from the first time he had seen her on his wind-swept arrival off the Rail-Motor service. She looked so young, even younger in the daylight, not much older than Megan. Yet there she was married to Donald Munro, a man Avram reckoned to be older than Papa Kahn. With deft movements of her hands, she inquired of their destination.

'The Kennedys at Lorn,' Uncle Mendel told her.

She motioned for both of them to get on board. Avram piled the bicycles into the wagon, heaved himself up on to the back while Uncle Mendel pulled himself up beside Jean Munro. She half-stood on her perch, slashed with the whip and they were off at a gallop. He hung on to the sides of the wagon. What looked like the same collection of neeps and linseed cakes from his first trip on this wagon bounced around to keep him company. He leaned back and let the sky flash by above him, glad to let the horse take him the next few miles.

At the Kennedy's farmhouse, he waited as Uncle Mendel tarried by the wagon, exchanging words and gestures with Jean Munro. Eventually, he was asked to join them.

'Next week Madame Munro wants you to call round when I am in Glasgow. Delighted with his suit her husband was. Now another one he wants. I have his measurements. Just take him over the swatches.'

With another set of gestures, Jean Munro arranged the day and time of the visit. Then, another swipe of her whip and she was off. Uncle Mendel looked after her.

'A fine young woman,' he said, rubbing his *yarmulke* across the top of his head. 'But such a sadness.'

The Kennedys were pleased to see them. The gamekeeper led Uncle

Mendel into the parlour while his wife ushered Avram into the kitchen.

'I'll cook ye up some rashers,' she said. 'Ye fair swallowed them down the last time.'

'I can't. My uncle would kill me.'

'Well, they didnae do ye no harm, did they?'

'They were delicious.'

'Well, dinnae worry about Jew Moses. He has his ways and ye have yer ain ways. If I fry up some bacon, the smell always keeps him well out of the kitchen. And if I leave some slices on a plate there on the table ... well, if they happen to disappear, so be it. I'll no tell a soul. And if not, well I'll be havin' them meself.'

She let out out a little wheeze of pleasure, then busied herself in her preparations. He settled himself on a stool.

'Do you hear from your son, Mrs. Kennedy?'

'Aye, we had a letter. Someone wrote for him. Didnae say much.'

'What about your daughter? Megan.'

'She's no ran away again?'

'I just wanted to know how she was.'

'She'll visit in her ain time.'

Kenny Kennedy appeared in the doorway, quietly rubbing the bristle on his chin, watching his wife fuss at the stove.

'Smell's good,' he said eventually.

'What d'ye want, faither? Standing there like a big lump of tatties.'

'Twa glasses.'

'It's a wee bit early to start yer drinkin'. There's milking to be done.'

'I'll manage.' He took a couple of shot glasses from the dresser and returned to the parlour.

'They'll be at it all night,' she said. 'Rambling on about politics. Jew Moses gets faither well excited with the talk of it. In my mind, there's enough to be worrying about with the war on.'

Mrs. Kennedy went quiet then her body heaved with a massive sob.

'Are you all right?' Avram asked.

Tears were streaming down her cheeks. One even splashed with a hiss into the frying pan. She gave a loud sniff as if to snap shut all her upset. 'I'll be fine. I just get to thinkin' about Jamie, that's all.'

Despite the drinking, Uncle Mendel was up fresh and cheerful in the morning, helping with the milking after his daily prayers. It was the gamekeeper who seemed the worse for wear, bleary-eyed and moaning as he pulled at Fadda's udders.

'I could dae with ye at harvest, Moses,' Kennedy said.

Uncle Mendel shook his head. 'Not me. But maybe the *boychik*? What about picking potatoes, Avram?'

'Back-breaking work,' Kennedy interrupted, coughing up some phlegm and spitting it into the hay. 'If ye want it, ye can have it. Better wait until the war's over. We'll be back shooting pheasants instead of Huns. Then ye can be a beater.'

'A beater? What's that, Mr. Kennedy?'

'Scaring the pheasants into flight. For the gentry to shoot them down again. All the lads round the estate dae it.'

'I'd like that. Does it pay well?'

'A few baw-bees. Enough to keep a young lad like yerself out of mischief.' Kennedy gave up on the udder. 'Fadda's done. We need to go, Moses, if yer to catch the Rail-Motor.'

Before setting off for Benderloch station, Uncle Mendel gave Avram his cloth money-belt, showed him how to fasten it hidden below his waistband. Then there were the instructions. A list of customers to be visited, parcels to be picked up from the Lorn Post Office, the swatches to be taken over to Donald Munro

'In a fortnight I'll be back,' Uncle Mendel said as he pulled his bulky frame up on to the gamekeeper's wagon. 'A message for the Kahns have you? A letter perhaps?'

Avram shrugged. 'Just tell them I'm fine.'

CHAPTER THIRTY-ONE

'Whit dae ye want?' toothless Mad Aggie screamed, brandishing a skillet from the doorway of her cottage. Bits of feathers adorned her frazzle of grey-white hair standing up on her head like teased-out steel wool. She wore a tattered woollen coat buttoned top to bottom, her feet stood skinny in a pair of enormous boots.

'I'm Jew Moses' nephew.'

'Och aye. And I'm the Pope's auntie.'

'I'm telling you. I'm Jew Moses' nephew.'

'Och aye. And soon ye'll be wanting money out of me.'

'I've brought some nice samples in my parcels.'

She scratched her chin where a few grey hairs sprouted. 'Ye'll still have to prove ye are who ye say ye are. Afore I let ye take one step further.'

'I've got some fine blouses. Different colours.'

'Prove yersel' first.'

'How am I supposed to do that?'

'Tell me something about Jew Moses. Something secret only ye and me ken.'

'I don't know. He likes baked herring.'

'And so do I.'

'He likes a bet.'

Mad Aggie shrieked. 'Along with half o' Scotland. The non-church-going half, that is. Ye'll have to dae better than that. Or ye can turn yer bike round and get yer arse back down the hill. Well?'

He searched for something to say. 'Sheila McKechnie just had twins.'

'Och really?' She lowered the skillet. 'Lads or lassies?'

'One of each.'

'Ye'd better come in, then.'

He entered her cottage and was immediately set upon by four hens and one boisterous rooster. The air in the one-room was choked with the smell of warm fowl and chicken-shit, but he could detect something else as well. Urine. Whether human or otherwise he dared not guess. Wings flapped around him, feathers fluttered in the air. Mad Aggie began toasting oatcakes on the open fire, and as each one was done, she flung it wildly on to the bed where it lay singeing the wool of her coverlet. It worried her none, for she paid him the money she owed and ordered a new blanket for his next visit. As he reached for the door handle, she clawed at his shoulder.

'Will ye no stay for a mug of tea?'

'I need to get to see Tam MacIsaac.'

'Go on. I'm awfully lonely.'

'I'm sorry. I have to go.'

'Jew Moses sits with me for a while.'

'I can't,' he said, closing the door hard on her pleading.

'Aye, she's been going quite mad up there. Since Alistair passed on.' Tam MacIsaac stroked his long beard which when unravelled from the tip could be teased out beyond his waistline. It was a beard as woolly as any of the man's unshorn sheep and just as thick and oily. Avram had heard Kenny Kennedy suggest it would do Tam no harm to have his whiskers dipped at shearing time, for Lord knows what was hidden there among his hairy foliage. Spare change, pencils and bicycle clips, Avram imagined. 'Can't take the loneliness,' the bachelor shepherd said. 'Not like me.'

Old Tam stayed silent after that, nursing his glass of Oban malt in front of the fire. Avram was happy for the quiet with only the wind against the shutters, the spitting of the peat to accompany his thoughts about poor Mad Aggie. He loved Old Tam's place, crammed full of artifacts sculpted out of the odd pieces of wood found on the hillsides. Hat pegs, a footstool, spoons, strange ornaments, a pipe rack and the pipes themselves had all been crafted by Tam's patient knife. There was not much else to do up there in the hills with only his collie, his flock and Mad Aggie as his nearest neighbour. So when Tam spoke, his words were as deliberately whittled and fashioned as any of his wooden creations.

'Claes 'gin the rain,' the shepherd said.

'What was that?'

Tam sipped at his malt, then went on: 'Dinnae think I'm no grateful. All these workshirts and jumpers and socks ye and Jew Moses bring are all grand. But it's claes 'gin the rain I need.'

'You mean clothes that keep out the water?'

'Aye, that's whit I'm meaning.'

'Waterproof clothing?'

'If that's the word.' Tam smiled at this new learning. 'Waterproof.'

'You'd need a special fabric for that. Made up right.'

'I didnae need a Sunday suit, son. A smock or a jerkin is what I need. Not just me. All of us hill folk round here with the rain to batter us wet and cold like Noah in the Great Flood.'

'What about leggings?'

'Leggings would be grand.'

'And maybe a hat?'

'Aye, a hat gin the rain. That'd be guid too. Think about it, son.'

He did think about it. And it was with such a day-dreaming of waterproof clothing that later that same afternoon he got lost in the pine forests around Loch Etive on his way to the Kennedys. He pushed his bike in and out of the trees, looking for a proper logging path or a deer trail to guide him out, when he stumbled across a granite quarry. There at the entrance gate he was accosted by a dark, bearded man with a heavy length of pipe in one hand, the strained chain on a snarling dog in the other.

'What's yer business here?' the man shouted, holding a broad stance to keep his hound at bay. The man's cap was fixed so low and his beard grown so high on his cheeks, that there were only two dark eyes to show there was a face at all.

'I haven't got any business here,' Avram replied, keeping his distance. 'I'm lost.'

'What's that ye've got in the basket? In the parcels.'

'Stock samples.'

'Are ye a tinker then?'

'You could say that.'

'I will say that. Off with you then. This quarry's got its own stores. We dinnae want yer kind here.'

'What kind do you mean?'

'Jews. With all yer fancy transactions. Ma sister's still paying off that Jew Moses for stuff she disnae need. Fuck off. Or I'll set this dug on ye.' And the man loosened the chain so the dog had a few extra inches to leap and be pulled back. Avram steered round his bike as quick as he could and rode off along a wagon-road out of the forest.

CHAPTER THIRTY-TWO

With only the swatches to take over to the Munros, Avram decided to go by foot from the Kennedys on a crow-flies shortcut over the hills, which according to the gamekeeper would be twice as lenient on his shoe leather as sticking to the roads. He passed the village kirk, and where the church wall had crumbled he clambered through the rubble and out into the open countryside westwards towards the sea. Half-way through his journey, he saw the storm clouds roll in from the islands and cursed Kenny Kennedy for persuading him not to take his bike and to keep off the road.

The sky darkened but the rain refused to come. The wind blew in strong, blustering stiffly off the sea on to the exposed hillside. There was a heaviness in the air and he dropped to lower ground for shelter among the trees. The leaves shook and hissed on a rush of air through the woodland sending the branches creaking all around him. A crack of lightning split over Ben Mor and the subsequent thunder blasted through the thick, warm atmosphere like a cannon shot.

The sky's mood was dirty black and the day felt like night but still the rain didn't come. He skirted a distance away from the woodlands, fearful of any lightning that might strike. He was running now, clutching his book of swatches under his jacket, looking for the abandoned castle Kenny Kennedy had cited as a landmark for his journey. And then he saw it through the trees – a four-turretted granite fortress – a smaller and humbler edifice than he expected from a castle. There were few windows, and those that had been built into the walls were narrow and mean to both light and view. But as the rain began to spit, the gloomy construction presented shelter nevertheless.

He found the front entrance, a large boarded-up double door with a nailed-up sign too faded to show its message to the public. The windows, though some were broken, were set too high in the unscaleable walls to afford any chance of intrusion. Instead, he found shelter in the half-collapsed stable, just before the rain dropped heavily in a hot rush flooding the ground immediately with its gasp. He waited for the sheer pelt of water to ease off, listening as it soaked into the bracken above him. Then, as the exhausted rain faded to a drizzle, gently strafing the puddles already formed, he heard a sound from the castle. The noise was faint and at first he thought it was just the low moan of a door-hinge being swung open and shut on the wind. But, as the sound grew louder, he realised he was listening to an instrument being played. Whether it was a sustained breath through brass or a drawn-out chord on strings he could not make out, but it was most definitely music he was hearing. Not some classical piece or even a lilting Scottish melody. But a plaintive eerie lament that shivered and slithered hauntingly along his spine. He raced out of the stables and crashed back into the woodlands.

The music seemed to follow him as he ran, teasing its way through the trunks and branches to leap and dance at his ears. He raised his arms up around his head, for protection both against the melody and the boughs that scraped him. The leaves shook their watery drops over his clothes and skin as he slipped and slid and scampered through the trees. The more he put distance between himself and the abandoned castle, the more the music drove towards a crescendo. He dipped through an arch of branches and suddenly the forest cleared. The music miraculously ceased. He found himself on a narrow, gravel road that cut through the trees on either side. And there was Jean Munro, cloaked and on horseback, with another horse tethered to her own, cantering in a search along the forest wall.

He didn't have the strength to call her or to lift a hand in recognition. He just stood at the roadside bent over, gasping to find a rhythm for his breath. He heard the clop and crunch of hooves as she trotted over. Leaning off the neck of her horse, she brushed a hand against his hair so he was forced to look up at her.

'Music,' he panted. 'I heard music from the castle.'

She seemed unconcerned by his words. In a slow sweep, her green eyes scrutinised his face as if his nose and mouth, forehead, chin and cheekbones could give her better clues to his condition than his eyes could. Then she motioned with her head for him to mount the other horse.

'I can't ride,' he confessed.

Jean Munro dismounted in a swift, neat movement. She was smaller than he expected, her hooded head only just rising above his shoulder. Her face was pretty, but set in dourness, with lines of frowning already scratched across her forehead. Life had settled hard on this young woman, leaving her with a bitterness and impatience reflected in her gaze.

He felt her hands, small but firm, on his waist as she helped him clamber up into the stirrup, then swing over onto the saddle. She showed him how to place his grip on the pommel, then re-mounted her own horse. She swooped to grab the reins of his mare and set off in a canter. As he bounced along behind her, the salty drizzle stung his eyes and dried his lips but he did not once raise his arm from the pommel to wipe the rain from his face.

The Munro residence was not far. A lone, squat, two-story mansion house stuck out on a peninsula lashed by a murky sea's relentless battering of stubborn grey rocks. When the sky was clear and the sun shone on quiet waters, it would be hard to imagine a more beautiful spot on earth. But in this dirty weather it was a cold, wind-swept, foreboding place.

On reaching the gateway to the house, Jean Munro dismounted, her face pale but calm now. She led the two snorting horses to the stables at the rear of the building, and then helped him climb down. She showed him into her home.

He was guided into a well-furnished parlour, rendered even more grand by the presence of a gramophone with its large silver trumpet pointing directly at him. There were fine carpets on the floor, a low table set with a china tea-set, two china spaniels guarding the fireside, and an elaborate wall-clock hung opposite a sampler of Queen Victoria. Embroidery must have been one of the ways Jean Munro amused herself, for there were at least four unfinished works of indeterminate personages spread about the room on armchairs and foot-stools. Two cane chairs were set side-by-side by a large bay window which looked out on to the Firth, and he could easily imagine the young bride seated there with her stitching, Donald Munro by her side with a glass of whisky in his hand.

It was only when Jean Munro approached him and tugged at his jacket did he realise that his clothes were soaked. She tugged again, harder this time, dragging the cloth off his shoulder. When he resisted, she stepped back, mimed for him to take off his clothes, then leaned forward to rub at the damp material and to point out the mud on his trousers. He fixed his jacket more tightly around him. She stamped her foot and disappeared out of the room. He heard her clumping around upstairs before she returned with a blanket. She left the room again, but not before giving him such a stern look he knew he would have to strip and let her take care of his outer garments. He slipped the book of swatches, still dry, out from underneath his waistband and undressed to his underwear. He pulled the blanket over himself, sat down in an armchair in front of the fire.

Jean Munro returned with a tray set with a pot of tea, a jar of honey and a decanter of whisky. She placed these items by the chinaware on the low table and proceeded to pour out one cup of tea. With deft movements, she added the whisky, stirred in the honey, gave him the cup.

'When will your husband be home?' Avram asked.

Fishing into the pocket at the front of her skirt, she pulled out a silver fob chain with a large gentleman's watch attached. She showed him the masculine face with the thick Roman numerals. Almost three o'clock. Her finger moved from the three to the six.

'Half-past three?' he asked.

She shook her head.

'Six o'clock?'

She nodded.

'But you told me to come at three. I thought Mr. Munro would be here by then. What with it being half-day closing in Oban.'

Before he had time for further protest, she scooped up his clothes and flounced out of the room

He snatched up his cup, strode across to the bay window where the wind rattled the panes, flopped down on one of the cane chairs. The storm had come up wild now, chopping up the sea, thrashing the rain against the glass like thrown buckets of water. There was nothing out there but a greyness. He wrapped the blanket tight around him, sipped at the hot toddy. The wall clock chimed three. He thought of the music from the castle. An intruder perhaps. A tramp or a tinker taking shelter, finding an instrument among the stored furniture. A violin, a child's trumpet. Nothing more. He felt soothed by the thought, comforted by the drink. He put the cup down, bundled his bare feet up under the blanket. Three hours to wait with a mute for company.

Suddenly, there was darkness. A pair of hands over his eyes. Soft palms, rough fingertips, but female hands nevertheless. He brought up his own to drag them away but the grip was strong. Nails dug into his skin. He moved his hands up to thin wrists. Then there was a breath close to his ear.

'Who do ye think it is?'

She let him pull her hands away as she walked round to the front of the chair.

'Megan.'

'Aye, Megan.'

She stood before him, hands fixed on hips, a sly smile on her face. She was dressed, not in her maid's uniform, but in the white blouse and dark tartan skirt she had worn for her first interview at the castle. Her head lowered, she looked up at him from beneath bowed eyes, waiting for him to say something.

'What are you doing here?' was all he could manage.

'I came to see ye.'

'How did you know…?'

'I arranged with Jean. It's my day off.'

'You mean Mr. Munro doesn't want…'

'Oh aye, Donald Munro wants his new suit. But we've got three hours before that old drunk of a chemist gets here.'

She stepped forward, dropped herself on to his lap. Just like that. Without asking his permission. As though she had licence for such intimacy. But it felt good and he was glad she behaved so comfortable with him. For he was nervous and excited and a whole bundle of other emotions he couldn't begin to describe. She wrapped an arm around his neck and he felt her fingers play lightly with his hair.

'Yer all dark from the sun,' she said, moving her hand to his forehead, sweeping back his curls. She scrutinised his hair-line close, her chin almost touching his nose, her fair hair sweeping soft against his cheek as she examined the paleness behind each of his follicles, almost angry to see such a change in his skin in her absence. Her hair was freshly washed, smelled of lavender. He snaked an arm out of the blanket, held her around her waist, fingering the hint of plumpness that rested there. She eased herself into his embrace.

'I like that,' she said.

He moved his hand further up her back, feeling each nodule of her spine through the thin material of her blouse, ready for any resistance. But none came. He eased his head back, pressed her closer. She let out a soft moan, brushed her lips against his. He was just about to pull her more firmly into his body when she backed off, stood up abruptly.

'What…?'

'Come on,' she said, holding out her hand to him.

'Come on where?'

'Upstairs.'

'Upstairs?'

'Aye, upstairs. And wipe that glaikit expression off yer face, Avram whatever-yer-name-is. Ye don't think we can sit here winching in the Munro's front parlour, do ye? It's no the back seat of the pictures.'

'I suppose not.'

'Well, come on then.'

Megan led him out to the hallway, up an impressive stairway bordered by portraits to a narrow landing. There were four identical doors off and without any hesitation she took him through one of them into a small bedroom. The counterpane on the double bed had been turned down, there were fresh flowers in a vase by the window, a peat fire struggled to defeat the chill. He imagined Jean and Megan preparing the room for his arrival, laying out sheets and blankets.

Megan went over to warm herself with her back to the grate. They both stared at the bed as if it were a sacrificial altar confronting them. Suddenly, Avram felt a tension between them that hadn't existed downstairs in the parlour. He knew he had to act like a man – but in a way his *barmitzvah* had never taught him. He tried to imagine what Solly would do. Moving across to her, he nervously placed his hands on her shoulders.

'Let's get into bed,' he said. 'It's freezing.'

'That's because Jean's already got ye half-naked afore I arrived.'

'My clothes were soaked,' he protested.

'Aye, I believe ye. Tho' thousands wouldnae. Get in yerself. And turn yer heid.'

He slipped under the counterpane, turned on to his back, eyes closed, stiff as a corpse, listening to the rustle of Megan's clothes. Then the creak and sag of the mattress as she moved in beside him, but still keeping a distance of icy sheet between them that seemed as wide as the Clyde in winter.

'Just one thing,' she said. 'Ye can kiss me. And ye can get in close. But I don't want ye … I don't want ye putting … anything inside me.'

He heard her words with a sense of relief, the boundaries being set no further than he had it in his imagination to go. 'I'll come in close, then,' he said. He slid over the few inches of linen, lay face to face, mouth to mouth, breath to breath with her across the pillow. He felt her skin hot and clammy where their arms touched, where their thighs touched. But her feet were cold.

'Let me warm them on yours,' she said.

He flinched slightly to her touch, then caressed her feet with his own. They felt so smooth and tiny.

'You're very pretty,' he said.

Her eyes smiled at his. Pale blue eyes. Eyes that were a map of the Christian world. Church-going eyes. Eyes that sat under Sunday bonnets and read from hymn books. Eyes the colour of an Easter sky. And he kissed her. On her broad mouth that could name all the hundreds of islands of the Inner and Outer Hebrides. Lips closed then slightly apart. Her arms came round him as she cleaved to him. He felt her breasts, pressed against his vest. He ran his hands over her slip and down her back. She smelt of lavender. And silver polish. And furniture wax. She tasted of spearmint. And of a Scotland that wasn't the soot and stink of Glasgow, but mountain streams and thick gorse, dark loam and deep forests, wild stags and black-faced sheep, cottages and castles, bannocks and bacon.

Her embrace was tight. Tighter than was comfortable for him. As if she never wanted to let him go. He felt the sweat between them. And he broke away from her lips. She was panting and so was he. He thought of Jean Munro's pair of horses doing the same. Sweating, snorting, steaming. He kissed her again. This time, as they embraced, he kept his upper body away from hers so he could bring his hand round to touch her breast. He did so slowly, feeling the dampness of her underarm, then again the fabric of her slip.

'Yer tickling me,' she murmured into a half-kiss.

His fingers froze, but when she started kissing him again, he edged them round to feel the underside of her breast beneath the thin cotton. His whole body relaxed in the heft of this deliciously soft orb in his palm. His objective had been achieved. This small victory among life's challenges.

He moved his thumb upwards with confidence now, circling, until he located the button of her nipple. Megan moaned and he thrilled at his ability to create such pleasure for her and for himself. He continued to caress her there, feeling the small tight bud of her erectness. Her breath was held tightly in her rib-cage as was his. He felt the heat between them and he pulled away, still holding on to her breast. The tension subsided in the mingled exhalation of their breaths.

She looked into his eyes. Searching for something he hoped was there for her to see. For at this moment, his heart was full of great affection and gratitude towards Megan Kennedy. She moved closer and he twisted his groin away from her so she wouldn't feel his hardness. Her heart beat against his own. He wanted to stay like this forever. On this grey afternoon. With the rain lashing the small window as it tried to intrude on their cosiness. With her breast still cupped in his hand like a ripe plum. With Megan's fingers resting lightly against his thigh.

The sound of horses woke him. Megan was by the window, brushing her hair in long sweeps. Over her shift which rose to above her knees she wore the blanket Jean Munro had brought for him.

'Jean's gone to fetch him,' she said.

'How long will she be?'

'Half an hour. If the Rail-Motor's on time.'

'She doesn't mind us ... using this room?'

Megan came over to sit on the bed.

'She wants us to. She wants to see at least one happy person in this miserable household.'

'When will I see you again?'

'I dinnae ken. I'll try to get a message to ye. Through Jean. Maybe we can meet here again.'

'My uncle comes back to tomorrow to replace me. I'm supposed to go down to Glasgow.'

'How long for?'

'I'm not sure. A fortnight perhaps. But I don't want to go back. I don't want to go back to Glasgow ever again.'

She leaned over and kissed him on the nose. 'Now get up. I need to make this room tidy. Yer clothes should be dry by now.

CHAPTER THIRTY-THREE

'How's yer uncle, then?' Donald Munro asked, as his wife lifted the cloak off his shoulders. He roughly brushed some rain drops from his tweeds, then re-inserted his pipe into his mouth. 'Well?'

'He's fine, sir,' Avram said, smelling the faint whiff of ether off the man. 'He's been in Glasgow. Back tomorrow.'

Donald Munro walked over to the fire. 'Glasgow, eh? He'll be all riled up about the demonstrations, then.'

'Is that about the rent hikes, sir?'

'Ye ken about the rent strikes?'

'A bit, sir.'

Donald Munro grunted as he poured himself a glass of whisky from a crystal decanter. He swept one of his wife's samplers off an armchair and sat down. Pipe in one hand, glass in the other. 'Go on.'

'It's about the women protesting the landlords putting up the rents when their husbands are away fighting. It's about socialism.'

'Socialism, is it,' Donald Munro snapped. 'What do ye ken about socialism?'

Avram wrung his fingers behind his back. He recognised Donald Munro's anger. He had seen it flash across his face at the station-master in Oban Station.

'It puts people before profit.'

'It's nothing of the kind, boy.' Donald Munro drank greedily then refilled his glass. 'It's about a few teetotallers hungry for power. And using the ignorance of the workers to achieve it. If it's true ethical guidance yer after, boy, better look to the kirk than to the Independent Labour Party. Or wherever it is you Jews go to for yer morality. Now show me these samples.'

Avram hastily brought over the book of swatches.

'Jean,' Donald Munro screamed. 'Come in here.'

Jean Munro hurried into the room, wiping her hands nervously on her apron. Megan arrived behind her, and Donald Munro's features visibly softened.

'Megan. I didnae ken ye were here.'

'Mr. Munro,' she said with just the slightest curtsy.

He turned his attention back to his wife. 'When is dinner

ready?'

Jean stepped forward with her watch in the flat of her hand and showed him.

'Good. They will stay to eat.'

Jean nodded.

'Now what do you think of these cloths?'

Avram stood on one side, Jean on the other, as Donald Munro turned over the pages of swatches. Every so often, he would pause at a particular material and she would nod or shake her head until a choice had been made. Avram tried to offer his own opinion, but his advice was met with a grunt of dismissal. Instead, as Donald Munro fussed and his wife stood anxiously behind him, he listened to the sound of Megan setting the table in the other room. He imagined her fingers placing the cutlery just right or straightening a napkin, the same fingers which only a short time ago had tugged urgently at his vest, touched his lips, caressed his skin.

'Good,' said Donald Munro. He beckoned Avram over and indicated his choice. Then he snapped the book shut. 'Now, let's eat.' He stood up, took his wife's arm, and Avram followed as together they walked into the dining room.

By the time dinner had finished, Donald Munro was slumped florid in his chair, a decanter standing empty by his limp hand and unlit pipe. It had been a joyless affair, centred around the man's deteriorating speech, until there was almost no conversation at all. Jean Munro had hardly touched her plate and sat staring at it with a look of sadness that Avram felt a thousand words on her lips could not describe. He tried to imagine what it must be like when guests were not present. Jean Munro's dumbness matched by her husband's stupors. A monstrous weight of silence – with no sound but the waves attacking the rocks, edging ever closer to this isolated mansion before swallowing it whole into their grasp.

Megan leaned forward across the table. 'Jean telt me what happened in the forest.'

Avram smiled. 'How can she tell you anything, Megan Kennedy? She doesn't speak a word.'

'I can read her signs. I've kent her for so long … it's like she's talking to me. Isn't that right, Jean?'

Jean nodded.

'She telt me you heard music.'

'An intruder in the castle maybe. It didn't half scare me.'

'It's happened before. Jean's heard it many times. Since she was a bairn. Me too. But just the once. It's only when there's a storm and the wind's coming from a certain direction. Off the sea. Like today.'

'So what is it?'

'When we were little, we went in. There was a way in then. Not all boarded up like now. It was Jean's idea. She made me follow. I didnae want to go. It was real dark at first. We could hardly see anything. Just the grand staircase. And this sound. A musical sound. Not a tune. Like a jew's harp. Long notes.'

Jean sat fiddling with a fork but her eyes showed an interest.

'Like a moaning,' he said, recalling that awful sound.

'Aye, like a moaning.'

'So go on. What was it?'

'Haud yer wheesht and let me finish. We climbed the staircase. Jean first, then me hauding her hand. And it was getting lighter, for there were spaces in the roof. Where the tiles had loosed or dropped away completely. And everything was covered up with sheets. It was like a snow palace. And all the time, there's this sound. Getting louder all the time. And my heart is pumping like a piston on wan of these steam engines. And I dare say I can hear Jean's doing the same. But she carries on, dragging me with her. Along these corridors full of portraits watching our every step with their dead eyes. Until we come to this doorway. Double doors. And whatever is making the sound is behind it. I'm greeting now. Pulling her hand. Take me home, I'm moaning. Take me home.'

Megan glanced at her friend. 'But Jean Munro is no feart. Not Jean Munro. She's a strong lassie, that one. Full of courage. She'll take on even castle ghosts. She lets go of my hand and pushes down on the two handles. I think to running away, but my feet are stuck to the floorboards like I'm standing in a bowl of cold porridge. Jean pushes open the doors and goes in. There's a wind rushing through that room. Off the sea, like I said. And I see her pointing at something I cannae see. I move forward with wee steps along the side of the door. And the noise is coming loud. And Jean is still pointing. I get to the edge of the door and peek round. And what do ye think it was?'

'A ghost. A ghost playing a musical instrument.'

'It was a musical instrument all right. It was a harp. A big beautiful harp. With its sheet fallen down by the broken window. But no ghost was playing it. Just the wind. And ye should see yer face, Avram whatever-yer-name-is.'

Megan was laughing. And so was Jean, with her eyes. The two of them hugged each other. And he began laughing too. Donald Munro stirred in his seat, but no-one paid any attention.

When the rain eased off, Jean Munro drove Avram and Megan on her wagon back into Lorn, dropping them off by the kirk near to the Kennedy's cottage. Standing in his doorway, Kenny Kennedy scratched his head when he saw them, dishevelling the few strands of hair that lay there.

'How come the two of ye arrive together?'

'Jean Munro picked me up on my way back from the Laird's castle,' Megan said. 'Avram was in the wagon ...'

'... I'd been taking the swatches over to Mr. Munro.'

'Aye,' Kenny Kennedy said, with a stare at Avram. 'Aye.'

'It's nice to see them both together, isn't it, faither?' said Mrs. Kennedy.

'Aye.'

Avram slept in his usual spot in the barn with Fadda and Colonsay for company. The noises of the nights didn't worry him now. Instead, they linked him to Megan awake in the cot-bed in the parlour, listening to the same sounds. Even though he woke early the next morning to catch her, she was already gone back to the castle and it was the curious face of her mother who greeted him as she came to milk the cows.

Later that same morning, Avram took the Rail-Motor service back across the Connel bridge, then tramped across the hillsides to Oban. He found a different route into the town and it was just as well he did, for if there was one thing to take his mind off Megan, it was the sight that greeted him now. A field laid out with goalposts. And a clubhouse with a sign above the door. *ARGYLL THISTLE F.C.* Kicking a ball around in one of the muddy goalmouths were youngsters about his age and he guessed the real members of the club were signed up to some Pal's Brigade at the Front dreaming of the times they would be back thumping a ball up and down this very ground. He stopped to watch, eager to join in, to feel again the curve of the leather on his instep.

'I thought shinty was the game here?' he called out to one of the boys running in close for a throw-in.

'Who's askin'?'

'I'm not from these parts.'

The boy sniffed hard then spat out the clear mucus on the ground. He was a long-necked, tousle-haired lad with a smell of fish about him. 'Where are ye from then?'

'Glasgow.'

'Glesca boy, eh?' He looked Avram up and down, measuring him carefully. 'Rangers or Celtic?'

'Celtic.'

'Ye'll have to keep yer gob shut about that.'

'Why's that?'

'We're all Proddies here. 'Cept for a few Baptists. But I'll forgive ye. Aye, shinty is the gemme. But there are a few wee fitba' teams about. This one's one of the best. Argyll Thistle. Like it says on the shed.'

'Is there a league?'

'Aye. Can ye play?'

'A bit.'

'Let's see then.' The boy held out a muddied hand. 'My name's Archie. Archie Campbell.'

Avram had never played on a full grass pitch before. He had a dream of it once, when he thought he might make the schoolboys final at Hampden Park – but that was another life-time ago. This pitch had been left uncut for some time, the long and greasy blades giving an edge to some of the other boys with proper studded boots. But once he had adapted himself to the surface, he felt the old moves come back to him.

Argyll Thistle were professional enough to have nets for their goalposts, and though they were torn here and there or patched up with blue fishing mesh, they were full enough to gather the sting of his well-hit shot. It still thrilled him to see the bulge of the net, to hear the cord stretch taut in a stringy cradle before spilling the ball harmlessly onto the ground. And it was not just the thrill of scoring a goal. There was also an essential beauty in seeing all the power he had diverted to the ball absorbed and rendered harmless by the net's embrace.

'Where did ye learn to kick the leether like that?' Archie asked.

Avram shrugged. 'On the streets. School team, sometimes.'

'Well, ye can play with us any time. We're awfully short these days.'

'I'm not in Oban much.'

'Disnae matter. Just when ye can.'

'When do you play?'

'Saturday mornings. If I'm no here, I'll be at the fish markets by the pier. I'm an apprentice cooper for my faither.'

He thanked Archie for the offer and rushed to the station. The Glasgow train had already pulled in.

'*Boychik*. I'm glad to see you.' Uncle Mendel was checking several parcels at his feet, reconciling them with some list in his head. 'Take these, these and these. I'll take the rest.'

CHAPTER THIRTY-FOUR

The Oban Arms was a small, white-washed pub with a low lintel of thick oak beam that Avram had to crouch under to enter. The interior was dim and smoky, with most of the rickety tables occupied by fishermen who paid little attention to the entrance of an Orthodox Jew and his armful of parcels, save for an arched eyebrow or a disinterested glance. Some of the men played dominoes, some warmed their drinks in the palms of their hands, others just sat staring at the walls with the far-away look of men used to vast empty horizons. There was not much chat.

The barman eased towards them with a generous wipe of a cloth across the counter. 'Moses?'

Uncle Mendel pulled out a small bundled handkerchief from his pocket, unwrapped it to reveal a shot glass which he placed carefully on the bar top.

'Whisky. And for you, *boychik*?'

Avram looked around at what the others were drinking. 'Beer?'

The barman glanced at Uncle Mendel.

'For my young business partner, a half-pint.'

Avram followed his uncle in laying down his parcels, resting a foot on the brass rail, placing an elbow across the bar, still damp from the barman's rag. The drinks were poured. Uncle Mendel tossed back his, ordered another.

Avram sipped at his beer. It came warm and sloppish with hardly a head on it. But it was the first he had tasted and he felt more of a man for it, even though the hoppy taste was not particularly to his liking.

'The belt, *boychik*. The belt. Pass it over. Slowly. So no-one can see.'

Avram turned to face the bar, hitched up his sweater, unbuckled the money-belt under the cover of his jacket. Uncle Mendel snatched it from him, quickly wrapped it around his own waist under his jacket and cardigan. He then fiddled one of the pouches open, wriggled out some coins with his thick fingers.

'Wait here.'

Uncle Mendel went over to a corner of the bar. A lone drinker sitting with his pint and newspaper looked up, registered the approach with a nod and a blink. The man's eyes sat tiny on either side of a large tuberous nose, and across his red-raw ravaged cheeks bruised veins flowed ready to burst. Avram saw him put a hand into the top pocket of his jacket, pull out a wad of papers, sifting through them with a licked finger until he presented one to Uncle Mendel. Uncle Mendel took the slip, scrutinised it for a moment, then shook the other man's hand with both of his. Watching on, Avram was sure Uncle Mendel had passed over the coins with his grasp.

'Good,' Uncle Mendel said, slightly breathless on his return. 'Now, tell me about business.'

'Who is that man?'

'Just a *goy*.'

'You gave him money.'

'I said just a *goy*. Now, business.'

Avram handed over the order book and Uncle Mendel proceeded to flick through the pages, running a finger up and down the columns, suggesting a bigger mark-up here, a longer time to pay there. He dwelt longer on the totals, made some quick calculations which he wrote into another page with a pencil stub, then snapped the book shut.

'Not bad, *boychik*. Not bad for a first time.'

Avram relaxed, downed the rest of his beer. His cheeks burned hot as the warm liquid sloshed uneasily in his stomach. But he felt cheery in his heart, and a kindly disposition towards the dim cosiness of his surroundings. He accepted another drink, listened as Uncle Mendel spoke of Papa Kahn's slow recovery and Madame Kahn's return to running the household. Mary came in daily, but no longer lived upstairs. Only Nathan's situation remained unchanged.

'A conversation you cannot have with him,' Uncle Mendel said as he stuffed his pipe with tobacco from a leather pouch. 'Yet I am sure what you say he understands.'

Avram waited for more but Uncle Mendel had retreated into his own world as he savoured the first draws on his pipe.

'How is Celia?' Avram asked. It was strange to utter the name. He flushed to the sound of it.

'Ah, Celia.' Uncle Mendel sighed. 'One of these suffragettes she is becoming. A rally here, a rally there. Handing out leaflets. Martha is frightened she will be arrested. But these days, everywhere Martha sees enemies. I don't tell this to my sister. But of Celia I am secretly proud.'

Avram imagined Celia standing on street corners, distributing her propaganda, her earnest face shining with the same excitement he had seen as she turned towards the demonstrations in George Square.

'Wouldn't you like to take part in all these demonstrations, uncle?'

'I'm helping. In my way.'

'Helping to promote your socialism?'

'The ordinary working people, they are angry. Not just because of the rent increases and the evictions. But the poverty and the lack of housing. For Jew and non-Jew alike.' Uncle Mendel shrugged then went back to noisily sucking his pipe. 'I am not in Glasgow often. What can I do?'

Avram glanced out of the inn's open door to the harbour where the usual swarm of seagulls hovered and cawed above the fishyards. A few craft bobbed around quietly in the bay as the weak afternoon sun cast a gentle glow over the whole town. He looked to his feet, his boots scuffed and dirty from the football. He could feel his toes scrunched up into the too tight fit. He would buy himself a new pair. That would be his first purchase. Then another pair just for the football.

'You could go back to Glasgow,' he said hesitantly.

Uncle Mendel looked at him with eyes red and bleary from the drink and the smoke. 'What's that you say, *boychik*?'

'I'll stay on here. You go back.'

'What nonsense are you saying? I just arrived.'

'I'll remain here to do the rounds of the customers. Come back like you did today and check on me. Collect the money. Take the orders. Bring me samples. I can stay here.'

'I can't let you do that.'

'Why not? You said you could do more if you were in Glasgow.'

'What will Herschel and Martha say?'

'They can't say anything. I am not their son. I am a nothing to them.'

'That is not true.'

'Well, then?'

'You are too young to run a business.'

'What have I just done for the last fortnight? I could enlist at my age.'

'Even so.' Uncle Mendel scrutinised the shot glass cradled in his large hands as if the answer lay somewhere floating in the amber liquid. He stayed like this for sometime and Avram was not sure whether he was pondering the offer or he had just disappeared into some daydream.

'Let's have another drink,' Uncle Mendel said eventually. 'And I will think about it.'

Still woozy from the beer, Avram supported his uncle back to the station for the three o'clock train to Glasgow. The man rested heavy and awkwardly on his shoulder, singing some Hassidic melodies close to his ear. Once, Uncle Mendel's legs slipped, nearly toppling both of them and it was only with the help of a passer-by he managed to get his uncle back on his feet again. At the station platform, Uncle Mendel attempted a clumsy embrace before stepping on to the carriage steps of the train. Avram was ready to wave him off, but Uncle Mendel stepped back down on to the platform. His black hat was swept back far off his sweaty forehead, his *tsitsis* hung out in a tangle from beneath a loose shirt flap. The money-belt stretched tight around his waist like an unwieldy girdle. It should have been a comical sight but instead Avram found it tragic. It was as if he suddenly could see right through to the drunken heart of the man. 'Tuck yourself in. Or someone will rob you.'

Uncle Mendel made an exaggerated effort at stuffing his shirt back into his waistband. Then, a moment of clarity seemed to sweep over his eyes and he poked a finger at Avram's chest. 'Don't forget.'

'Don't forget what?'

'Don't forget you're a Jew.'

'Yes, yes, yes. Of course, uncle.'

'It's easy to forget who you are out here.'

'Yes, yes. Now please get back on the train.'

'Promise me,' he said, grabbing Avram's jacket by the lapels. 'Promise me.'

'No. I don't want to.'

'Promise me.'

'You're drunk. And you need to get on this train.' The station-master's whistle blew and Avram pushed Uncle Mendel back on board.

He sat down on a station bench, closed his eyes, listened to the last churn of the engine pull out of earshot. He dozed like this for a while, letting the alcohol sweep through his bloodstream until he found himself with a clearer head. Then he rose and squeezed his way along a fenced-in corridor between the station and the edge of the pier until he found a gap in the wooden slats. From there, he could see into a yard where a group of young leather-aproned women were gathered round an enormous trough overflowing with the silvery-grey bodies of captured herring. The women chatted and laughed as they greedily dipped their rag-bound hands into the salty mass of bodies and scooped out fish for gutting. As quickly as the fish were gutted and tossed into baskets, fishermen off the boats re-filled the trough with more creels of herring. Behind the trough, he saw men in suits, their trousers tucked into Wellington boots, lay out the fish for sale on the washed-down concrete while others packed the remaining fish into barrels. Archie Campbell was among another group hooping up and sealing the barrels.

'Didnae expect to see ye so soon, Glesca boy,' Archie said.

'Me neither. When's the next game?'

Argyll Thistle were playing at home the following Saturday; Avram promised he'd be there. He then left to collect his parcels from the Oban Arms, hitched a ride on a horse-drawn cart back to the Connel Bridge.

As he lay stretched out on the back of the wagon, he saw the clouds scurry overhead, sensed the approach of rain. He sorted out his parcels so as to defend them best against the wetness to come with a cover of empty potato sacks. The temperature dropped quickly, the greyness closed in like a heavenly wraith. He wrapped his jacket tight, pondered the events of the last two days. Windows of real hope had opened up for him and he knew he had to take his chances quick for fear they might close up again. He thought of Megan and wondered how soon it would be until they could be together again. He thought of the prospect of playing proper football on a Saturday with Argyll Thistle. He thought of the coins he'd have in his pocket from treading the countryside as a credit draper. He pulled his arms around himself as if to keep this sudden good fortune from escaping. Or from keeping the evil spirits at bay. The rain started to spit and he warmed to the vision of the shelter lying ahead of him at the Kennedys' cosy hearth. He closed his eyes, felt his taste buds moisten to the imagined smell of Mrs. Kennedy's rashers sizzling in the pan.

CHAPTER THIRTY-FIVE

It took one week for news of the end of the Great War to reach Avram. And when it did, he wondered how peacetime would affect his life. The conflict had rumbled on at the edge of his consciousness like a thundercloud on the horizon without it ever really touching him directly. In the last few months, he had merely borne witness to the countryside mourning the loss of its menfolk who had not returned and pitying the plight of those who had. But the women had rolled up their sleeves, tethered the ploughs and got on with the farm work. They had raised the bairns, grown the crops, milked the cows, sheared the sheep, tied up the stooks and rocked in their chairs waiting for the return of their husbands and sons both with a sense of longing and with an air of defiance. Now these same women lined the streets of Oban, standing stoically under their umbrellas and the sodden bunting, waiting for the peace parade to turn into the main street. He stood with them, football boots slung over his shoulders, his knees and shins muddied from the game just played. In his pocket he carried Celia's letter collected earlier from the Post Office. The noon-time twenty-one gun salute from HMS Cumberland anchored out in the bay boomed over the town sending the seagulls into a whirling frenzy above the fishyards. He could hear the sound of the pipe bands, the appreciation of the crowd for the parade's approach along the esplanade. Yet part of his attention was not on the direction of the music, but on the vacant doorway to Donald Munro's pharmacy.

The front phalanx of the procession swept into view to the moan of the bagpipes, with the Laird at the forefront in his tartans leading the other gentry of the county. It was the first time Avram had set eyes on the man. Even without knowing beforehand that the region's wealthiest landowner would be leading the procession, he would have recognised him from his bearing. He stood straight-backed – a good inch or two taller than his land-owning counterparts – and his stride was brisk and purposeful as he tapped his walking stick to the drumbeat. Under thick tufts of eyebrows standing out from his face like hanks of cotton wool, the Laird's gaze was fixed forward in a blinker against the crowd. And the expression on the thin, mean lips of his long face was so grim that a naïve observer might have thought the man to be leading this procession into war rather than in a celebration of peace.

Behind the Laird came another line of civilians, including Donald

Munro, then the marching band, then the soldiers. Alongside ran the children, waving flags or dancing around fathers they'd almost forgotten. The men walked proudly, yet there was a fear in their eyes as they took in the support of the crowd. It was not just the fear of war – for that was forever bombarded into their hearts and minds. It was the fear of knowing that the life they had once left behind had been altered irredeemably. And that the source of that change rested in the bosoms of their womenfolk.

Avram finally spotted Megan. She had pulled away from the crowd following the procession, taken refuge from the rain in the pharmacy doorway. Jean Munro was with her, and he watched them both huddled together like sisters under their single umbrella, waving to the columns of soldiers as they marched by. Megan was on tip-toe, on a look-out for him, stretching her neck in a twist here and there, not caring for the drops of rain matting strands of her hair to her cheeks. Even under her long coat, he could see she was a full woman now. As did many of the soldiers in the march who momentarily lost their rhythm to let out a whistle or to glance admiringly at the two young women in the doorway. And he felt proud, too. Proud that she was his. Proud in the knowing of that figure under the coat. The whiteness of her body as it wriggled and writhed beside his own. The dampness of her passion under her armpits and between her thighs. Knowing each birthmark, each freckle, each follicle, each fold of flesh. Yet their coupling remained unconsummated. She had relented to the insertion of his fingers into her moistness. But she wouldn't allow him to do the same with his erect penis, even though she was happy to pump away at it until he spilled his seed in a moan all over her stomach and across the tops of her thighs.

'Just like milking Fladda,' she would say as she wiped the stickiness over his chest. If she had the experience to know the difference between his circumcised penis and any others she might have handled, she did not say. And he chose not to ask for fear of the answer. Instead, he persisted with his usual question.

'When will you let me inside you?'

To which he received the usual reply. 'I'll be a virgin lass till I'm married.'

He had Jean Munro to thank for continuing to host these sessions with Megan, watching over them like some patron saint, a proud hen with her brood, until she had to drive off into the night to fetch her drunk husband. Sometimes she would return alone with an empty wagon and an easier whip to the horse. Then the lights would go on throughout the mansion and they would sit by the French window where he taught the two young women to play cards while the stars lit up across the black water.

'And the important thing is,' he would tell them, 'never be low in hearts.'

Megan looked up from her delicately fanned-out hand. 'Aye, I like that,' she said. 'I like that.'

In return, Megan would coach him in the ballads of the Highlands while Jean Munro, for all she couldn't speak, expressed herself fiercely on the Jew's harp. They would drink whisky from Donald Munro's crystal decanter until the fire was in their cheeks then dance flings, reels, jigs and ridiculous hornpipes to Jean's frenzied plucking of the harp's tongue. If the weather was dry and the night warm, they would open the doors and race whooping across the lawn to the peninsula's edge. He would watch the two friends cavorting in their shifts on the grass like two banshee and knew it, as much as the girls knew it, that these moments were precious. And as he followed his round of customers in the days after, he would be forever poised in a tension between anticipation and disappointment, never knowing when or where Megan's message would be waiting for him again.

He continued to watch her in the doorway as she strained to catch sight of him, her brow scrunched in a frown at his lateness. He remembered Celia's letter in his pocket.

You have been away too long, she had written in her hurried script. *The war is over and life is changing for all of us. For the better, thank God. Papa's health has improved and he goes into work a couple of times in the week. Mama even sings again to Uncle Mendel's banging on the piano. Solly visits often and asks for you … But the biggest change is with Nathan. He is so much better now. He wants to see you. We all want to see you. Please come back to visit us, Avram. We don't understand why you won't come. We miss you.*

When he thought of Glasgow now, he didn't think of the people he knew in the way that Celia listed. Instead, he felt Glasgow as a mixture of winter darkness and warmth. Not the warmth of the Kahn's flat, for that was always draughty. But the warmth of the Sabbath candles, the bowls of *borsht*, the chestnuts from the brazier, the fingers frantically fiddling with playing cards, the huddled bodies of the football crowds at Cathkin, Nathan's brow, Celia's fiery cheeks, Fiona Cameron's hand in his inside the picture house. Never summer and light. But winter darkness and warmth. That was Glasgow. That was the Gorbals.

He felt for the letter in his pocket, crumpled it up in his hand. He still had a hankering to see Celia again, face up to her as the young man he had become – stronger and taller, his cheeks and chin smooth from the razor, his body more confident in a woman's touch and presence. But he had his own plans now. And he couldn't wait to tell Megan.

Twenty-one shillings a week. That was his weekly pay. The rest of the contents of the money-belt went back to Glasgow for stock, and no doubt some of it drifted into the hands of Solly under the *nom de plume* Baked Fish. But twenty-one shillings. One pound one shilling. One guinea. With not a lot to spend it on. Except the box of linen handkerchiefs that he now held in his hand. Each embroidered with a tiny delicate thistle in one corner and the letter 'M' in another.

He waited for a gap between regiments, then ran across to Megan. But someone else reached her first. A young soldier swept off his cap, lifted her high in his arms. She let out a yelp, beat the hoist down with her fists on the man's back until her pounding softened into an embrace.

'Oh, Jamie,' she said, collapsing her head on to his shoulder. 'Ye've come hame.' Then she pushed him away, urgently patted his body under the loose cape of his coat. 'Are ye all in one piece?'

Jamie fully opened his greatcoat. 'Aye, every bit of me. I only lost one thing in my travels. And that's not for me to be telling my wee sister.'

Jamie's hair may have been cropped so it showed no resemblance to Megan's lavish locks, but Avram could see his smile was identical to his sister's. And it was with that smile Jamie turned to tease Jean Munro.

'And who is this bonnie lass ye have alongside?'

For all her frozen emotion from an icy marriage, Jean Munro's cheeks warmed to the attention. And even a kind of squeal escaped her mute lips when Jamie Kennedy lifted her in the same way he had his sister.

'Jamie,' Megan said, pulling him towards Avram. 'Here's someone to meet.'

Jamie towered over him. Broad-shouldered, well over six-feet, with a face that could have been hewn out of a Glen Etive quarry. What could have been there in years between them? Three at most. Yet Jamie seemed a generation older. There was a war between them. A war that had shown Jamie what death was. And courage. And horror. And fear. When Jamie shook his hand, Avram realised he knew nothing of these things. He felt small and naïve before the returned soldier. He felt like a nothing and knew nothing. Except that three years and a war made a big difference.

'Who d'ye play?' Jamie asked, eyes narrowing in his scrutiny of the muddied boots hanging over Avram's shoulder.

'The Army. A friendly to mark the celebrations.'

'Well?'

'Well what?'

Jamie glanced at his sister and laughed. 'Well, did ye win?'

'It was a draw.'

'That'll please everyone and no-one.'

'It'll please us. We didn't think we had a chance.'

'Who's that?'

'Argyll Thistle.'

Jamie let out a whistle. 'The Thistle were really useful before all this began.'

'We still are. We're in the Cup this year.'

'With a bit of luck, ye might bring wan o' the big teams to the town. That would be grand.' Jamie gathered the two young women into the wings of his greatcoat. 'Well, we're off to celebrate.'

'Avram's with us,' Megan said.

Jamie's look made Avram feel something he hadn't felt for a long time. He felt Jewish.

* * *

The celebrations strayed long into the clear night. A night lit by the HMS Cumberland in the bay, its hull, deck and masts festooned with fairy lights so that its outline shone against the hills of Mull like some wonderful fairground attraction. Suspended from wires slung between the ship's two masts hung a giant illuminated crown – His Majesty's crown shining over his Majesty's ship. The crown of victory for King and country.

'It looks like the moon,' Megan said from her perch on the

esplanade railings.

Avram could see the real moon beyond; a full moon it was, too, but shaded by thin clouds it shone in pale comparison to its bright sovereign counterpart. He greedily sucked in the clear air, glad to be out of the smoky swelter of the Oban Arms. The place was packed, all the pubs in the town were packed, their trade swelled by military pay packets and coins scavenged out of jam jars, biscuit tins and old teapots just for the occasion. Jamie was still inside, shouting himself hoarse over the froth of beer and the piano music at old friends. Kenny Kennedy was there too, his lanky face lit up from the whisky and the proud pleasure of having his son back unscathed. The war was over and the gentry would be flocking back to the Western Highlands, where a gamekeeper's life would be a busy one.

Despite the hour, the esplanade was busy with couples taking in the night air, the occasional groups of soldiers and sailors strolling and staggering, clinging desperately to their male camaraderie, taunting each other with their rivalry. But the main party was in the centre of the town. That was where the ceilidhs were. And the cluster of pubs belching out frenzied reels, jangling tunes and drunken clientele. That was where the fights broke out between the different regiments as they turned their aggression on each other, now that the enemy was defeated. That was where the young women let themselves be pulled into dark alleys for anxious, penetrating gropes by long-missed male hands. Here on the esplanade, the pedestrians had come for a respite from it all. They had come to reflect on what had been and to consider how things would be in the morning once the streets had been cleared from the drunks and the debris with life in peace-time grinding on anew.

Avram was ready to move on with his life too. His head had been full to bursting with plans ever since the parade. But there had been Jamie and the celebrations and no time to tell Megan. Until now. Now it was quiet, and Megan was rocking back and forward gently on the railings, humming lightly, her face as pale and beautiful as any full moon or illuminated coronet.

'Remember the day we saw the airplane?' he said.

'Aye. It was like a dream that day. Seems a lifetime away.'

'I saw the pilot in the parade this morning.'

'Aye, I remember him. What was he called again? Charlie? Charlie Simpson.'

'Sinclair.'

Avram had noticed Sinclair in the town, preparing to fall into the parade. Charles Sinclair of the Royal Flying Corps. He hadn't recognised the pilot at first. Even when Sinclair had waved at him, he thought the gesture was nothing more than a distracted acknowledgement of the crowd. But then Charles Sinclair had shouted something at Avram and started to mime the action of a crank-handled two reeled camera. 'Just like bookends,' is what Charles Sinclair had said on that spring day, and close to what he shouted again from the parade. 'Where is the other bookend?' And the other bookend was sitting beside him now, swinging her legs from the railings just as she had done from her seat on the wing.

'What did he say?' she asked.

'I didn't really speak to him. But he reminded me of something. I knew at the time that day was important. I remember trying to commit every single detail of it to memory. And now I know why.'

'Because I was part of it.'

Avram smiled. 'Of course, you were. But there was also the matter of the airplane wings.'

'The airplane wings?'

'Yes. They were made out of a waterproof canvas. That's what I need. Waterproof canvas. There must be rolls of the fabric somewhere. And with the war over, the aircraft manufacturers can't be needing them any more. Where did Sinclair say he'd flown out of? Carmunnock, I think it was. I just need to contact the factory there. Buy the fabric from them or their suppliers. Yards of it. Miles of it.'

'And what would ye dae with fields of waterproof fabric?'

'Remember I told you about that idea of Tam MacIsaac? Waterproof clothing. That's what he said he needed. I can have Papa Kahn's shop make up the garments from the material. Claes gin the rain for Tam and all the hill-farmers and shepherds in the West of Scotland.'

'All because of the pilot ran out of petrol,' Megan said dreamily, her lack of enthusiasm disappointing him. She had turned her attention to the ship in the bay. He looked too. The HMS Cumberland was an impressive sight. With its garland of lights glinting on the still water, it seemed to reflect all his hopes for the future. Mrs. Carnovsky had read the tea leaves right after all. A strange bird would bring him good fortune. And his young soul hummed vibrant from the excitement of it all.

CHAPTER THIRTY-SIX

'Six tanks, *boychik*,' Uncle Mendel exclaimed from his sprawling stance at the bar of the Oban Arms. 'Six tanks.'

Avram sipped at his beer, his attention absorbed by the purple-red bruise that now marked one side of his uncle's face, running past one eye and upper cheek before seeping underneath the man's beard. The injury reminded him of the liver-like swelling Roy Begg had once administered to Ginger Dodds. Uncle Mendel had received his bruising when a policeman's truncheon had thwacked him to the ground in George Square.

'Go on,' Avram urged, enjoying the bitter-sweetness of the dark ale. A stout taste to match this first-hand account of Uncle Mendel's attendance at the now infamous 'forty-hour strike' demonstration. An event he had read about in the Oban Gazette. This was men's talk. Socialists' talk.

Fuelled by the malt, Uncle Mendel continued more loudly than before, gathering in attention from the normally taciturn clientele. 'Six tanks in the Saltmarket. At the citizens of Glasgow they point their guns. A machine-gun at the Post Office.' Avram followed the direction of a hand, shot out to where the gun-nest might have been. Uncle Mendel swivelled, pointed with his other hand to a spot above the inn door. 'See, Avram. A howitzer on top of City Chambers. Why? Only because a job and a roof over their heads the workers want. To Donald Munro tell that, the next time you see him. Tell him soon is the revolution. With my own eyes I saw it.' Uncle Mendel raised the front of his hat, wiped a handkerchief across the sweat of his excitement. 'Six tanks. *Glaubst du das*?'

Avram tried to believe it. Tried to believe that these metal monsters he had seen in newspaper sketches driving the Germans from their trenches were now being turned against their own citizens for fear of their protest.

Uncle Mendel drew up closer and whispered. 'Worried is what we have them. Two months ago, about Marxist John MacLean's release they worried. Three days ago, about the Bloody Friday demonstration at the Square they worried.'

'Who is worried?' Avram whispered back.

'Lloyd-George. And his Government. Wait until the next General Election. The leftists will run Glasgow. The Red Flag we will sing all the way to Westminster.' Uncle Mendel started to hum the first few bars.

The barman sauntered over. 'There'll be no hymns of revolution sung here. I'm surprised, a religious man like yerself behaving in such a manner.'

Uncle Mendel turned to face the publican. 'Justice,' he said as if that explained everything. 'Justice.'

The barman moved off to serve some customers in the snug. 'Aye, Moses, if ye say so. Justice.'

Uncle Mendel called after him. 'A people of the law we Jews are. A people of justice. Look at Manny Shinwell.' He turned to face the bar-room again. He was in full swing now, chest pushed out with his moral sense of it all. 'Manny Shinwell. Leader of the seamen. He's a Jew. A month in jail he got for standing up for men of the sea like you.'

'Sounds like a bloody German,' shouted one of the drinkers. 'Just like you.'

'I'm not a German,' Uncle Mendel shouted back. 'I'm a Jew.'

'Whit's the difference?'

Uncle Mendel ignored the comment but the heckler slammed his empty shot glass hard on to the table-top and stood up. The man's cloth cap was pulled down low over his forehead, his dark beard covered his face high on his cheeks so only his fierce eyes showed. He wore a rough tweed coat belted in a twist dragging almost to the floor. Through black mitts, naked fingers clenched in tight fists. The man's drinking companion pawed at his sleeve.

'Leave the Jew alane,' he pleaded but the heckler shook him off.

'Whit's all this shite ye're talkin' about revolution? Where were ye, Hun, when the war was on? Makin' profit off of our poor folk that's what. Ma sister's in hock to ye up to her eyeballs. For fancy pinnies and Paisley patterns ye push in front of her greedy eyes.' A finger pointed sharp at Avram. 'And the young 'un's at it too.'

Avram recognised the antagonist. The guard at the quarry with the chained dog. 'I don't like this,' he whispered, but Uncle Mendel had already raised himself from his slouch at the bar.

'Who is this sister you talk about?'

'Flora. Flora MacPhee.'

'Madame Flora MacPhee I know. A good customer she is. Never

a problem.'

'Aye. That's because I'm aye stumping up for her debts, ye German traitor.'

'I'm British.' Uncle Mendel fumbled in his inside jacket pocket. 'There are papers I have to show it.'

'Fuck yer papers,' the man snarled as he pushed aside a chair, moving in closer, close enough for Avram to see the white quarry dust clogging the man's nails, the dog hairs lying thick on his coat. 'Yer papers don't count for shite.' The guard sniffed in a swagger around Uncle Mendel, flicking with disdain one of the tassles hanging out of his shirt.

'Yer blood's German. And yer nose is the big nose of a Jew.' He laughed hard at his comment, looking round the bar for support

'Come on, uncle. Let's go.'

But Uncle Mendel was not to be insulted so easily. 'My nose is big,' he said, 'so pigs like you I can smell.'

'Fuck ye.' The guard snatched an empty bottle of ale off a table, lunged forward. Uncle Mendel was ready but not ready enough. He twisted his head away from the blow but the bottle cracked down, smashed off his shoulder. The guard stumbled forward with the momentum of his own strike. Uncle Mendel turned, grasped the back of his attacker's neck, slammed his head down on to the splintered glass covering the wooden bar top. The man's head bounced off the surface and Uncle Mendel plunged it back down again into the remnants of the bottle. The guard screamed as a shard of glass sliced open the side of his cheek.

'Leave him, Moses,' the barman shouted, as he wielded a mace-like club in one hand. 'Or ye'll be having this.' With the other, he threw a bar-cloth at the guard's drinking companion. 'Here, Rob. Stop yer man's bleeding.'

Uncle Mendel's face had drained of his usual flush and he stared at his offending hand. 'Please. Please forgive me,' he said, as he tried to approach his victim. 'Forgive me.'

Rob pushed him away. 'Ye've done enough damage.'

The guard moaned as he held the blood-stained bar rag to his slashed cheek. Pieces of glass were stuck to his forehead in surface cuts.

'Ye'll need to get yer pal stitched,' the barman said to Rob. 'Aye, ye'll need to get him stitched.'

Rob began to shepherd his friend out of the pub, but not before the bloodied guard could turn.

'This is no the end, Jew. It's no the end.'

The bar door swung shut to a few whistles and cheers from the rest of the drinkers.

'Ye'll no be putting yon Wallie MacPhee on yer Christmas list then,' the barman said to Avram.

'Is that what he's called?' He repeated the name as if he was remembering a curse word. 'Wallie MacPhee.'

'Ye ken him then?'

'Bumped into him once on my rounds.'

'Once is enough if ye ask me. There's a violence in him even without the drink.'

'Give me a dram,' Uncle Mendel said hoarsely.

The barman poured out a whisky. 'Is that what ye call justice then?'

Uncle Mendel brushed the beer and glass from his jacket. The barman nodded to Avram. 'Ye'd better get yer man Marxist Moses MacLean to sit down. Before he gets intae any more bother.'

Avram led Uncle Mendel to a far corner. No-one paid them any notice. The behaviour of the guard Wallie MacPhee didn't speak for these no-nonsense people. If the mood had been against them here, it would have been Uncle Mendel who would have had to leave. He and his uncle, for all his strange garb and customs, were welcome here. Or if not welcome, at least tolerated.

'I'm ashamed,' Uncle Mendel muttered. 'Ashamed, ashamed, ashamed.'

'Well, I'm proud of you.'

The speed of Uncle Mendel's movement took Avram by surprise. At first, he thought it was going to be a slap. Then a hand to his chin, fingers grabbing him around the jaw, bunching his cheeks, forcing his gaze straight ahead. 'Look at me, Avram. Look, look, look at me. What do you see?'

Sad eyes. Nathan's eyes. It was difficult to talk. The grip was loosened. 'I don't know.'

'A religious man do you see? A socialist? A man full of compassion for other human beings?' Uncle Mendel let go his grasp, picked up his whisky glass, poured the contents on to the sawdust floor.

The yellowish puddle soaked up fast. Like urine. 'No, a man full of vices is what you see. Only anger I showed. For that God will punish me.'

'But the other man started it.'

'Once to hit him perhaps is justice. An eye for an eye. But to continue to rub his face in the glass...'

A drift back into a silence. Avram watched the light outside begin to fade, the imprint of Uncle Mendel's grip still lingering on his skin. The pub took on a mantle of cosiness as the lamps came on and the fire was stoked up in a welcome of the evening. A violinist picked up the mood with a jaunty melody. Someone with a mouthie joined in. A couple of men tapped their dominoes to the beat.

'Come, *boychik*,' Uncle Mendel said wearily. 'A walk before I return to Glasgow.'

Avram shivered to the feeling of snow in the air. Like a thick cotton blanket, high above him, ready to fall out of a trap-door. Fairy lights were strung along the esplanade in celebration of the Christmas festivities to come, scattering diamonds in a sparkle across the dark water. Cold crept in to the tips of his new boots. He thrust his hands deep into his coat, searching for any warmth there. Christmas. *Hanukkah*. Festivals of light for the winter darkness. Uncle Mendel beside him, saying nothing.

They ambled along the seafront, stopping only to marvel at the decorated fir tree dominating the square outside the station, the carol singers gathered around its base. A few of their customers, in town for the shopping, paused to wish them season's greetings. Uncle Mendel raised his hat to them, cheering to the mood and to the attention. They reached a bench on the station platform, sat down. Uncle Mendel leaned forward, head in hands, staring down the track. Avram let him settle.

'I have an idea for the business, uncle.'

'*Nu*? Tell me.'

'Waterproof clothing,' Avram said and began to eagerly outline his plan. 'Jerkins and leggings. Maybe hats too. All made from waterproof fabric. The material they used for airplane skins during the war.'

'And this fabric will come from where?'

'I think the planes were made in Carmunnock. We should be able to get the fabric cheaply now the war's over. We can start a new business.'

Uncle Mendel sat up, shook his head. 'I can't do that.'

'Why not?'

'Jacob Stein wouldn't like it.'

'What has Jacob Stein got to do with this?'

'Do you think to Jacob Stein's customers you can sell your own goods?'

'It's none of his business.'

'Everything is Jacob Stein's business.'

'Why?'

'Because he owns the customers. And he owns me.'

'How does he own you?'

'He just does. That's all.'

'Then I'll do it myself.'

'No-one can stop you. But your own customers you must find. And capital too.'

'What kind of capital?'

'For the fabric. And the making up of the clothing. Samples for the customers. It all takes *gelt*.' Uncle Mendel rubbed his thumb and forefinger together to indicate the invisible banknotes. 'Where will you get it?'

'You could lend me money.'

'I don't have any.'

'What about the profits from the credit drapery business?'

'There is nothing.'

'What? There must be something. After all these months of traipsing round the countryside. The money can't all have gone in stock.'

'I said there is nothing. If capital you need, you must save for it yourself.'

'Why are you making this so difficult for me? This is a good idea. The farmers and shepherds around here are desperate for this kind of product.'

'Perhaps.'

Uncle Mendel looked away to watch the Glasgow train hiss and steam into the station like some fiery dragon. Passenger-doors opened spilling out the country-folk, full of excitement and chat, arms filled with wrapped-up Christmas presents from their big trip to the big city. Avram kept his eye on the prosperous-looking gents with their fine tailored tweeds and shiny shoes, their deeds of profit sitting snug in their leather brief-cases, and knew he wanted to be like them.

'You could do me one favour, at least,' he said, shouting at his uncle over the noise of the train winding down from its journey.

'What is that, *boychik*?'

'The airplane fabric. Can you find some for me?'

Uncle Mendel picked up his suitcase of samples. 'All right. All right. I'll ask some questions. But you should be the one to do it. To return to Glasgow, it is time. It's not right you should stay away like this.'

'Why should I go back? There is nothing for me there.'

'What about the family? So much they want to see you.'

'You tell me everything I need to know.'

'You remember the servant Mary?'

'Of course, I do. She used to torment me so much when I first arrived.'

'About Mary I forgot to tell you.'

'What happened?'

'She died. From influenza. About two weeks ago.'

CHAPTER THIRTY-SEVEN

It was Archie who spread the news. The announcement had come over the wires when he was at the Post Office and he raced to tell his father and his cronies down in the fishyards. All the men in the yard cheered, as did the women gutters. Even Archie's father who never opined on any subject apart from the state of a barrel said:

'Just what we need to put the heart back into this town.' And then he returned to welding the metal hoop in front of him without another word on the subject.

Archie then rushed to inform the driver of the post bus, who whistled all the way to Connel thinking about the prospect. He passed on the news to Davey of the Caledonian Railway Rail-Motor Service, who in his turn carried the information across the swirling Firth to the doorstep of Kenny Kennedy in Lorn. Mrs. Kennedy reported later that her husband immediately pulled his only bottle of Oban malt from behind the dresser and toasted Davey, the Lord and Lenin in that order for bestowing such good fortune on the town.

'It'll be like wan big holiday,' he said after sharing a few more drams with the train driver.

Later that day, Jean Munro heard the news when she dropped by the Kennedys on her way to pick up her husband from Benderloch station. Jean chalked the magical words down on a slate for Megan the next afternoon when she was down on her day off from the castle. Megan couldn't wait to tell Avram.

'I've got something to tell ye. And it's the biggest news ye've ever heard in yer life.'

Avram lay on the bed waiting for Megan to get in beside him. He knew her tendency to get overexcited about the least morsel of gossip, but she did really look fit to burst from whatever it was she had to reveal.

'Go on then, tell me.'

'Give me a kiss first.'

He hadn't seen her for two weeks. He had thought about her every moment his mind wasn't full of conversation with customers or totting up figures and percentages in his head. His body craved her now as she stood in front of him, her breasts heaving in excitement underneath the coarse cloth of her shift.

'Tell me first.'

'No. Kiss me first.'

He shook his head.

'It's really important,' she said, clutching her chest to quell the information that was forcing itself to rise out of her lungs. 'Really, really important.'

'I don't want to know. It'll just be some tittle-tattle from the town.'

'Much, much mair than that.'

'I'll tickle it out of you.'

Megan folded her arms even more tightly across her chest. 'Wild beasts couldnae drag it out of me now.'

He leapt for her, pulled her to the bed, started pinching her waist.

'I'm no tellin',' she screamed as she wriggled her legs, riding her shift to above her knees. A hand over her mouth to muffle her shouts from Jean downstairs. The other hand into the warm flesh of her thighs.

'Tell me.' He felt himself go hard from the furious heat between her legs. He let his other hand go free and continued to pinch her. 'Go on. Tell me what it is.'

'I'm gonna be sick.'

He eased off slightly. 'I'm not interested in your gossip.' His erection poked out between the buttons of his long johns. He thought he might ejaculate over her there and then. All over her shift and the Munro's starch linen bedclothes. He tried to catch his breath. 'I just want you, Megan,' he said, leaning gently over her so that he could slip his erect penis up between the tight cloth of her shift where her legs were now stretched wide apart. He pushed back her hair, breathed into her ear, licking and nipping the fleshy lobe as he spoke. 'Let me inside you. Please.'

Megan's breath came as quick as his own. There was a red flush across the yoke of her shoulders and up her neck. A taut mound of one nipple pushed against the cotton of her shift. He placed a hand against that one breast, rolled the teat between his fingers, feeling it harden even more. Megan twisted under him, let out a small moan as she turned her head one way on the pillow and then the other, spreading out her hair in a golden arc. He felt himself stiffen even more. He couldn't remember being this hard. There was a heady combination of her pleasure, mixed with this sheer physical power he had over her. His stiffness pushed against the moist slit between her thighs.

'No,' she breathed, even as her legs seemed to part more for his entry.

'Please, Megan.'

'I dinnae want to.' Her hands were at his shoulders pushing him away. But he continued trying to enter her. What she wanted didn't seem to matter any more. This was all about him and his pleasure. Her hands, clenched now, beat at his upper back yet he continued to press against the reluctant membrane between her legs. Her slip had risen to above her waist, he felt the sweat of her thighs dampen the cotton of his underwear. He was ready to explode.

'Oh God, Megan. Please let me inside.'

'No.'

'Please.'

'Celtic,' Megan panted, almost biting the word into his ear.

The word came at him from a distance, not registering at first. But he pulled back slightly, not knowing why she was saying this now.

'What?'

'It's Celtic.'

His pause had allowed her to come back in control, letting her slow down his heaving torso, wriggle her legs closer together so that his penis was trapped between her thighs. He peeled himself off from her body, unplugging himself from the clench of her.

'What are you talking about? It's Celtic?'

'Like I said. It's Celtic. Argyll Thistle against Celtic in the Cup.'

'Honest?'

'Cross my heart.'

'Glasgow Celtic?'

'There's no' another.'

'Home or away?'

'Here. Here in Oban.'

He jumped off the bed.

'Yes,' he shouted, his now flaccid penis wagging in time to his dance around the room. 'We've got Celtic in the Cup.' And then he stopped, sat back down on the bed. 'I don't believe it, Megan.'

'Well, it's true.'

He took her hand, stroked her palm. The flesh was rough and hard. 'Do you know what this means?'

'Aye. I can imagine.'

'It means everything to me. I'm going to be playing against my hero. Against Patsy Gallacher. Me and Patsy on the same pitch.'

'Well, I'll tell ye something. Something that means everything to me too.'

'What's that?'

'Just dinnae do that again.'

'Do what?'

'Try to get into me.'

'I'm sorry. I just got too excited.'

'Well, it's no excuse. Excited or no, dinnae try that again. Or ye'll never set eyes on me again, never mind yer clammy fingers. I dinnae want any fatherless bairns running around the place. D'ye hear me? Dinnae try that again.'

CHAPTER THIRTY-EIGHT

For Christmas Eve, Avram stayed alone at Uncle Mendel's cottage where flecks of snow had threatened a heavier fall throughout the day, the frosted turf crunched pleasantly underfoot, and a light film of ice coated both the rain barrel and the loch. He spent the late afternoon down by the waterside, pressing his boot sole at various points against the frozen surface until it split and the crack ran out across the icy expanse to disappear in the empty dusk. No birds grazed the freezing sky and a hushed bleakness hovered over everything. Nothing stirred. Except for his breath in a cloud in front of his face. Here was a loneliness he had never experienced before. An isolated Jew in a Christian land at a Christian time of year.

Under the lean-to, the slabs of peat had frozen together and he had to hack them apart with an axe. A splinter from the handle embedded itself deep into his finger, but such was the cold he felt no pain in digging out the skelf with the blade of a penknife. He watched with detachment as the blood flowed until it clogged in a pool in the cup of his palm. With a rough bandage over the wound, he stoked up a fire in the cottage. He dressed in every item of clothing he possessed, wrapped himself in all the bedclothes, but still the cold chilled his bones. Pondering the sputtering flames, he ran through in his head the speech he would make to the gamekeeper the following day. And when the thought of that troubled him too much, he tried to warm himself to a day-dreaming of the cup-tie against Glasgow Celtic.

He remembered how he and Solly had snuck into Cathkin stadium to watch Celtic play for the first time. There on the touchline, Patsy Gallacher had smiled at him from out of the mist, picking him out from the crowd as if to say 'I know you. You are like me.' There had been a war since, players went and never returned, but Patsy had survived to turn out for Celtic. Opposite numbers they were now – inside forwards – left and right. He and Patsy. Soon they would be standing by each other on the centre line of the Argyll Thistle pitch, jersey sleeves pulled down tight against the cold. Letting go to shake hands before the whistle. Patsy with his flat cap of slick hair and an old pro's wink. And he wanting to tell the Celtic player how above a fireplace in a cold cottage a few miles north there stood a well-preserved cigarette card of his hero.

The Oban press had been full of the magic of the Cup, how it could pit a football giant like Celtic against a wee West Highland league club. Avram had read how the hotels in the town were booking up quickly as supporters from Glasgow sought to turn their away game jaunt into a full week-end with their pals. Canny town-folk were turning their dwellings into temporary bed-and-breakfast establishments, and the pubs were ordering in extra barrels from the distillery. In the letter pages of the Oban Gazette, some readers complained about this Fenian invasion of Covenanter soil. Others suggested the banning of the Irish tricolour or the Celtic green from a twenty mile radius of the town.

But out on his rounds, Avram's customers were full of pride, slaps on the back and advice. Even Tam MacIsaac had heard the news from his watch on the hillside. As the old shepherd ran his fingers in a comb through his long oily beard, he said nothing would stop him coming down for 'the big gemme'. That was how everyone called it now. 'The Big Gemme.' As if life didn't exist before and after, and that everything would stop for it. A reporter had even sniffed Avram out at the cottage, and with a licked stub eagerly poised over pad he asked how if felt for a Glasgow boy to play against one of his city's two greatest clubs.

'I'm not a Glasgow boy,' he told the reporter.

'Where are ye from then?'

'Russia.'

'Like the Revolution?'

'You could say that.'

'I don't think I will.'

Avram rose at dawn on Christmas day and part-walked, part-cycled his way in the bitter cold along the ice-rutted paths. The stars had faded away and the firmament was now shot with a blue as light and pure as any he had ever seen. The hillsides lay sprinkled with a soft layer of snow. Like the frosting of flour on Madame Kahn's rye bread. What he would do now for a slice of it dipped in the sauce of a sweet herring. He felt his fingers welded to the handlebars and the puss-filled cut from the previous day's skelf throbbing in the cold. Inside his boots, his toes were chunks of ice. By the time he reached Lorn, the kirk bell was tolling the festival day and some village-folk, bundled up so thick as to be unrecognisable, were already slipping and sliding along the road on their way back from church.

Megan seemed nervous when she answered the door.

'What's wrong?' Avram asked.

'Ye'll see.'

He followed her into the warm kitchen. Kenny Kennedy sat in his rocking-chair, a poultice pressed against his cheek.

'He's had the ache since yesterday's morn,' Mrs. Kennedy said in a fuss about her husband. She was still dressed in her Sunday best but with a full apron to cover her finery, her everyday kitchen-cap perched on her head. Megan in a crouch by her father's chair, adjusting the blanket over his lap.

'The sudden cold snap is what did it,' she told Avram. 'Is that not so, faither?'

Kenny Kennedy's face, the colour of sour milk, was still covered in a morning stubble. The gamekeeper dipped a bony finger into a shot glass of malt, squirming as he coated the painful tooth with the liquor.

'The Captain said he'll drop by,' Jamie said, with a stoop into the kitchen from the byre, two pails of milk carried light and easy in his large hands. 'I spoke to him at church.'

A knock on the door. Avram stepped out of the way as Jamie crossed the kitchen, his bulky frame throwing a shadow across the room and the rest of the family. Even Kenny Kennedy stopped his moaning.

Avram knew the Captain well enough. One of his best customers. A retired ship's doctor, usually well-oiled with drink, who swayed and stumbled through the village as if he still roamed the lurching decks of his vessel. For once, Avram was grateful for Papa Kahn's supervision of his family's teeth. Bicarbonate of soda every day. Keeps the Captain away.

The Captain positioned Kenny Kennedy in a chair by the cold sunlight of the window, twisted the gamekeeper's head this way and that, peering into the open jaws.

'I can tell what ye had for dinner last night.'

Kenny Kennedy rubbed his aching cheek. 'What are ye saying, mon?'

The Captain ignored him. 'Tweezers. Are there tweezers in the house?'

Megan ran to fetch a pair.

'Scald them with water,' the Captain shouted after her. 'And ye, Kennedy. Swill yer mouth out with some whisky.'

'I'm no having ye pulling anything.'

The Captain laughed. 'What? With tweezers?' He hauled open Kenny Kennedy's mouth, started to poke around. Megan stifled a giggle as her father roared and writhed in his chair.

'Give us a hand, young man.' The Captain beckoned for Avram to come close. 'Hold down his arms.'

Avram took a stance in front of the gamekeeper, leaned forward and grasped the man's wrists to the arms of the chair. The Captain came at his patient from the side, armed with the pair of tweezers.

'Hold still,' the Captain shouted. 'And I'll have ye fixed in a moment.'

Avram felt Kenny Kennedy's body lurch in the chair, then relax. The Captain withdrew the tweezers snapped tight in a pluck. 'There!'

'What is it?' Avram asked, struggling to see anything in the tweezer's grip.

'A herring bone. Wedged between tooth and gum.' The Captain turned triumphantly to his patient, wiggled the offending bone in front of his eyes. 'Swill out with whisky. If ye've any cloves in the house, press them on to soothe the pain. Ye'll still ache for a while.' He flicked the bone to the floor. 'Now, Avram. Yer quite a star for the Argyll Thistle, I hear. The whole shire's full of talk about the cup-tie. Well, make sure ye do the United Free Church proud against these Papists.'

'United Free?'

'I forgot. Yer no' one of us.'

CHAPTER THIRTY-NINE

Christmas lunch took place in the 'front room', as Mrs. Kennedy always called it, although Avram never quite understood why, given that the whole cottage was built in a single row of rooms all facing the front. He helped Jamie move through the kitchen table, which Mrs. Kennedy covered with a fine cloth and laid out with the best dishes to receive the roast chicken and potatoes. Avram tried not to think of the task ahead as he tucked into the hot meal, washing it down with several glasses of dark ale. At the top end of the table, Kenny Kennedy was slumped down in his chair in a half-glazed stupor. The man had hardly touched his food and was half-singing, half-mumbling to himself one of the Psalms from the church service.

Avram was about to stand when there was a hard rap at the door.

'Who could that be?' Mrs. Kennedy asked.

Jamie rose. 'I'll get it.'

'Aye. Get the door,' Kenny Kennedy slurred.

'It's one of the Laird's men,' Jamie announced on his return. 'Adam Baird.'

'Well, show him in,' said Mrs. Kennedy.

Baird was already stood in a crouch behind Jamie, with his cap clutched in front of him. His bald crown shone red from the cold like a burnished hillock. He poked his head round Jamie's frame.

'I've some gifts for my Master's gamekeeper,' Baird said. 'Christmas appreciation from the Laird of the shire to his loyal servant.' He nosed his gaze from Kennedy at one end of the table to Mrs. Kennedy at the other, then back to the middle. 'Miss Megan,' he said to his fellow employee. 'Ye'll get something back at the castle.'

'Well, Baird from the Laird,' Kenny Kennedy shouted. 'Show us what ye've got.'

'I'll need a hand.'

'I'll help ye,' Jamie said and went back outside with Baird. Mrs. Kennedy stood to straighten her cap and dress. Jamie returned with a large wicker basket of apples with several bottles of ale spread across the top. Baird held a bottle of whisky in his hand.

'That's very kind of the Laird,' said Mrs. Kennedy. 'Isn't that right, faither?'

'Aye, so it is. Ye must stay for a drink, mon.'

'I cannae,' said Baird. 'I've mair rounds to do.'

'Just a wee dram,' Kenny Kennedy insisted.

'Come on,' Jamie said. 'It's awfy cold out there.'

'Aye then,' Baird said, placing the whisky bottle on the table.

By the time Baird left, Avram was drunk. The whisky and beer had taken hold so that the room and all those in it glowed pleasantly in a light sway in front of him. Even the throbbing from his infected finger had ceased. Megan's hair shone back at him in a golden shimmer from across the table. He tried to focus on her features but her face just remained as a beautiful blur. With a fascination, he observed the movement of her wrist as she cut up slices of chicken for her father, then the profile of her head as she turned to laugh at something her mother had said. He struggled to his feet, bending his knees slightly so he could grip the arms of his chair. From his position, he managed to turn his head slowly towards the head of the table. All activity in the room appeared to cease. There was a silence except for the beat of the wall clock. The sound held his attention for a few seconds until he realised he had to speak.

'Something I want to say.' Avram wasn't sure if the words had actually come out or had remained trapped inside his fuzziness. 'Something to say,' he repeated just to make sure. 'Something to say.'

Kenny Kennedy looked up from his slump. One eye open. The other squeezed tight over the ache in his gum. 'Go on, lad. Get on with it. Speak yer piece.'

'Thank you. Thank you all for this Christmas dinner. It was delicious.'

'Well said,' the gamekeeper shouted, thumping the table with his fist. 'Short and sweet. Now sit down and haud yer whisht.'

Avram felt the sweat form on his forehead. Then the thought to take a hand off the chair arm to wipe his brow, followed by the fear he might fall over if he did. 'No, no. There's more.' He moved his head back to look at Megan, struggling with the formation of what he hoped was a smile on his lips. 'I'd like to ask permission to marry your daughter. Yes. That's it. Permission to marry your daughter, sir.' His head flopped towards his shoulder as he tried to look at Megan. From this sideways angle, he thought he saw her hands flash to cover her mouth. These same hands moved away to reveal her lips – an oval shape whichever way he looked at her. 'No,' he heard her utter, a pleading edging her voice he cared not to register. 'Oh no.'

'He's fou.' A voice behind him now. Jamie. 'And he's talkin' shite. Megan's no going to marry him. Not over my dead body.'

Avram stretched out his arms towards Megan. 'What is it? What's happening here? What is happening…?'

'It's Jamie,' she said. 'It's all because of Jamie.'

And it was Jamie who wrapped his arms round Avram from behind, pulled him backwards over his chair which fell away to the side. Avram tried to claw out of the grip but the hold was too strong. As he was dragged out of the room, he heard Megan scream. Kenny Kennedy was shouting too, vocalising the same thoughts Avram was having: 'Whit's going on with ye women? Whit's going on? Will someone tell me whit's goin on?'

Everything seemed to move slowly for Avram as he was bounced along the hallway. He noticed the empty milk buckets in the dairy. A bunch of dried flowers hanging from a beam in the roof. A sampler of Lloyd-George lying half-finished on a shelf by the doorway. Then there was a sudden rush of cold as the front door was opened and he was pushed outside into the snow. He stumbled a few feet, turned, fell flat on his back. Looking up, he saw Jamie standing full in the doorway, his arms stretched from doorpost to doorpost. Like a vision of Christ, Avram thought.

'Don't ye ever come here again,' Jamie screamed, his voice echoing across the yard. Avram heard the dog bark in response. 'Megan's no going to marry ye. She's getting engaged to Charlie Sinclair, ye wee Jew tinker. Charlie Sinclair it will be.'

Avram heard the swish of his scarf and jacket landing beside him, the door slamming shut, loosening some snow from the roof in a rush to the ground. Shouts from inside the cottage, Jamie's voice dominating the rest. Then everything quietened to a murmur. Charles Sinclair. Charlie fucking Sinclair. He should have known. Or maybe he had known all along. Seen it in the sly way she had taken the pilot's arm on the stile at their first meeting. Sensed it from her constant refusal to never let him inside her. Saving herself. For Charlie Sinclair. Of the Royal fucking Flying Corps. Two massive spasms in his stomach. He couldn't hold back and twisted to retch on the ground. His eyes teared, he threw up his food until the painful coughing ceased and he was left to observe the colourful, steaming mass splattered across the snow. The muscles in his abdomen ached from the effort. Slowly, he turned away from his vomit, laid his head back in the snow. He lay still for several minutes, the pain behind his eyes forming a skin over his deeper pain. Such a clear night. So many stars. Such a vast universe. He waited until the moon reappeared from behind some scudding clouds. Waited until the chill began to pierce him. Waited for Megan's call to return to the cottage. But none came.

With difficulty, he raised himself to his feet, fumbled to put on his jacket and gloves. He thought about raising a fist to the cottage door but instead brushed the snow off his bicycle, dragged it out on to the roadway. Several times he tried to mount and ride but his drunken state and the thickness of the snow prevented any success. He pushed it through the village but about a mile further up the road he decided to leave it hidden behind a tree. For a good while, he stood in front of the hiding place trying to make sure he would remember the spot when he returned.

The snow had stopped falling and the whole countryside was shrouded by an eerie light. It was as if all the cracks in the earth, all the divisions in humanity, all his feelings of loss, rejection and humiliation, were healed over by this unblemished sheet of whiteness. And then there was the deafening silence. He stopped and listened. Not an echo. Just pure, deadened, muffled landscape. Until a slurry of snow fell to the ground with a swoosh from an overladen branch. And then silence again. Despite all that had happened back at the cottage, he felt his soul light.

The cloudiness lifted from his brain and there was clarity of thought as he concentrated on surviving his situation. The alcohol in his bloodstream may have sustained him the first two miles, but now he felt the cold begin to claw its way into his bones, to chill the marrow, to clog the flow of blood. He had another six miles or so to trudge in the freezing cold, and he was not sure if he had the energy or will to sustain himself. He half-hoped, half-imagined he heard the whinnying of a horse behind him, and Megan would be there to rescue him. For she could not possibly leave him to walk home like this. Or maybe it was Jamie he heard, coming to beat him senseless. Or perhaps it was the chariot of the Lord, waiting like a divine vulture for his demise.

The snow came again, thicker this time, in a blinding swirl all around him. He found it difficult to keep to the road, wandering off from time to time on to the grass verges, once lurching into a ditch and through a coating of ice. His boots were soaked through, his feet and hands were numb, his finger ached, his cheeks and lips were chafed to a prickling iciness, the taste of stale sick coated his mouth. But he had no choice except to plough on. For there was not a household or a barn for shelter between where he stood and his uncle's cottage.

He plodded onwards, each step heavier than the next, his breath rasping cold in his chest. The snow came faster, heavier, blinding his eyes, tiring his feet. He tucked his hands into his jacket but there was no warmth to be found there. A total lack of heat anywhere. A cold world steeped in blue moonlight. He tried to keep standing but it was no use. There was no more strength in his limbs, no more desire to continue. Just an awful heaviness. He stopped trying any more. He let himself fall on to his knees, then tipped over on to the ground by the side of the road.

Again, silence. A thick muffled quiet. And such a pleasant stillness. There was no chill now. Just a sensation around his body that could be hot or cold. He touched his face with his frozen gloves. Nothing. No sensation. He laid his head back down, turned one cheek to his pillow of snow. This was where he would die. On the road between Lorn and Glenkura, in the shire of Argyll. Avram Escovitz, son of Rachel. Father unknown. Who fled Russia for Scotland and the Gorbals. Son in all but legal name to Herschel and Martha Kahn. Avram Escovitz. Who could have been as great a footballer as Patsy Gallacher. Who could have made his fortune from the manufacture and sale of waterproof clothing. Let down financially by Mendel Cohen. Forbidden to play the game he loved by Papa Kahn. Rejected as worthless by Celia Kahn. Deceived and humiliated by Megan Kennedy. Frozen to death as a credit draper in the Western Highlands. Avram Escovitz. This was he. Avram Escovitz. Who died a nothing.

CHAPTER FORTY

Avram opened his eyes. Heavy lids. Closed and opened again. Such an effort. Shadows danced across the hewn beams and thatch. He tried to move his arms but they were pinned to his side by the tight wind of the blankets. He remembered there had been a cold so terrible the blood had frozen in his veins, the air had iced up his lungs, the skin had rubbed raw on his cheeks and lips. But now he was warm again. Blood-warm. Bed-warm under these unfamiliar blankets. Bottle-warm from the earthenware container nestling cozy by his feet. But at his core there was still a slab of coldness. And in his head throbbed a dreadful ache.

He heard a breathing and a stirring beside him. With difficulty he turned his head. His cheek grazed sore against the pillow. No candles. No cruisie. Just the light of the fire. The deep earthy smell of the peat. The frost etched in a sworled glow on the window pane. Frost. Jack Frost. And a figure huddled on a stool by the hearth.

He tried to mouth the words of recognition. But his throat scratched dry. He tried again.

'Baird,' he managed in a rasp.

'Aye.' Baird moved in close, bringing with him the dry musty odour of horse hair.

'Here. Drink. It'll warm you.'

He smelt the whisky, shook his head. 'Water.'

Baird scratched his bald mound and disappeared from view.

Avram heard the sound of the pitcher pouring and soon there was a tin cup before his lips. Baird's rough hand was at the back of his neck as his head was lifted to the rim. The rawness of the metal edge grazed his cracked lips and the liquid washed against his tongue. The water was freezing cold. He tried not to swallow. Tried not to extinguish this savoured warmth in his belly. But Baird tipped the cup further, forcing more water into his mouth while drops dribbled down his chin and on to the coverlet. His parched throat ached to be soothed. He swallowed. Shivered and swallowed again. The cold pierced his stomach for an instant then there was warmth again. A small victory for the heat of his body. He relaxed, drank some more until his head was laid back on the pillow.

'Where am I?'

'My place. I'll make you some tea.'

He watched as Baird fixed up a brew from a kettle already boiling in the hearth. The man hummed as he worked.

'I thought ye were dead,' Baird said, looking up from his task. 'No, that's no true. First, I thought ye was just a sack of something. Then when I saw it was a body, I was sure it was a corpse. The corpse of a deer or some other stricken beast. Another while and I wouldnae have seen ye at all. Covered up with snow ye would have been. Just like a wee cairn. But I saw ye.' Baird raised a finger to his eyes. 'Nothing much gets passed these. I can spot a fox tail at twa hundred paces. Just ask the gamie.'

'When?'

'A good four or five hours ago. I managed to get a wee dram between yer lips. And lucky there were covers on the cart. Drove like the devil to get ye here. The road was almost snowed over. But Bessie's got me through worse.'

Baird approached the cot and loosened the blankets. Avram raised himself up, took the offered mug of tea. He was glad to hold the heat in his hands, press it against his chest. He closed his eyes. Such a weight of tiredness. He tried to think back those four or five hours. Baird was right. Another few minutes and he would have just been a snowy mound invisible to rescue. Baird from the Laird had saved his life.

'Warming up?'

Avram nodded.

'So what was ye doing out there in weather fit for no man or beast? My good self and Bessie excluded, who are used to such extreme conditions. Which is just as well, given yer predicament.'

'I was thrown out by the Kennedys.'

Baird stared at the glass in his hands, gently rolling it between his fingers.

'Can't imagine that. Good people, so they are. Hard to see them throw a soul to the mercy of weather such as this.'

'There was … a misunderstanding.'

'I see. A misunderstanding, is it? No more than that?'

'No more.'

Baird picked up the poker, fiddled with the peat on the fire. A burst of smoke billowed out into the room.

'Damp,' Baird observed, but continued poking.

Avram drank his tea. A strong brew. He felt his strength returning.

And a hunger too.

'Must have been some misunderstanding,' Baird said.

'It was.'

'It's no like Kenny Kennedy to shove a man out into such a cold.'

'It was Jamie that did it.'

'Aye, Jamie. Well, that's different then.'

'Why is that different?'

'Jamie Kennedy has a hardness in him.' Baird vigorously scratched the stubble on his cheek. 'If ye don't mind, I'll see to Bessie. Get some more peat.'

While Baird went out into the cold, Avram found the strength to get out of bed and sit by the fire. Baird came back with some apples that had run loose in the cart.

'It's beautiful out there,' Baird said. 'All of a whiteness. You wouldn't know where land ends and loch begins.'

Avram knew the beauty of that whiteness. He had been prepared to let it swallow him up in its silence.

'There's some bannocks there for toasting,' Baird said.

Avram was glad to oblige, prodding a fork into one of them and holding it to the flame.

'So what happened to Jamie Kennedy?' he asked Baird. 'You said there was a hardness.'

'That's a story for a long night.'

'A long night is what we have, Mr. Baird.'

'Ye could say that.'

'I do say that.'

'Ye've never heard it before? Jamie Kennedy and Jean McKenzie. Jean now married to Donald Munro. Jamie and Jean Munro?'

'No. I never knew there was a connection.' Although he did remember the laughter on Jean's face that day of the procession in Oban when Jamie lifted her up on his return from the war.

Baird poured a good few fingers of whisky into his mug, poked the fire, settled on his stool. 'It's a sad tale to tell,' he sighed. 'They were the best of friends. Jamie and Jean. Since they were bairns. Always together. Like they were joined together. Like these twins I read about in the papers. The ones that came from America to see the King. Did ye read about them? Siamese. Like the cats. Can ye imagine that? One of them even got married.' Baird slapped his thigh. 'Now that sets the mind thinking.'

'What were you saying about Jamie and Jean?'

'Like I says, Jamie and Jean were like brother and sister, never saw one without the other, that's the honest truth. Twa peas in a pod. Everyone says they'd get married. Even when they were little 'uns. Just as easy as putting one foot in front of the other.' Baird sipped at his whisky. Slowly. Savouring each mouthful. And then peering over the rim of his glass, he said: 'Until the fire, that is.'

Avram pulled the toasted bannock away from the flame, took a bite out of the warm oatcake. Baird watched him eat, anxious to continue the telling.

'And what fire was that?' Avram asked, after a couple of mouthfuls.

'The fire at McKenzie's farm. Must be over ten years ago now. No-one ever knew what really happened that night. Both Jean's parents burned to death in their croft. Jamie was there, too. He got out straight away. But Jean was trapped. They say beams fell all around her. Her screams could be heard for miles. Even Mad Aggie said she heard the shrieks. But there might be a doubt to that claim, given the distance. More like she heard the screaming in her own head. Anyway, that was the last time anyone heard any sound from Jean. Jamie went back in to get her. A brave wee lad so he was. There was not a scratch on her. But she never spoke again.'

'What happened after that?'

'The whole community was in shock, as you would expect from such an awful event. And what with Jean having no kin, being left an orphan like. Everyone thought the Kennedys would take her in. But they didn't. And no-one knows why. It's no as though they were unkind folk, being good people, like I said previous. But they kept the twa youngsters apart. It could be they just didnae have the resources to bring up another child. There were rumours, of course. Some say it was Jamie who started the fire, accidental like, that killed her parents. And that's what made her dumb, so she wouldna have to speak the unspeakable. Others say it was Jean herself that did it, and Jamie witnessed it. A turned-over cruisie perhaps. People here just wanted the story buried, anyway. I don't even think the constable was called from the town. Accidental death. A big shock to us all.'

'So who brought up Jean?'

'It was Helen Munro who fetched her. Donald's mother. She had just lost her husband, and what with Donald staying away at the pharmacy in Oban most of the time, the old woman was lonely out there on the point. Jean got a home and Helen Munro got company until she died. And then Donald got a young wife.'

'Not a very happy one, from the looks of it.'

'Aye,' Baird yawned. 'She's had a bit of a tragic life, that young Jean. Anyway, I'm going to turn in.'

Baird reclaimed his cot and soon the man was rattling away in a snore. Avram stayed up the night, wrapped up warm in the rocker, staring at the dancing, dying flames, imagining the tiny figure of Jean Munro trapped within. Screaming. Jean Munro. Who had locked away her voice the way he would try to lock away his pain.

CHAPTER FORTY-ONE

The small hut serving as the dressing room and kit store of the Argyll Thistle stank of its usual stale sweat and cheap hair oil. In the corner stood the hamper for the next day's match. Avram had already stolen a look under the lid at the new strips, specially purchased. Dark blue. All neatly pressed and folded in a tension for the important occasion. There was to be a full house, and the biggest gate receipts since the club was founded in 1900 by the team posing stiff and stern in the only photograph hanging on the wall. Argyll Thistle – as old as he was, as old as the century – had won nothing in all its history. Not even the Laird's Challenge Cup, which had gone to Glenkura Athletic every season but the war years. All the resources of the town's youth and patronage had been channelled into the shinty. But still the tight-lipped faces in the photograph stared down at him in defiance of their betrayal of the Highlands' traditional sport. And he thought that if they could smile, they would do so now. The team they had founded might be odds-on favourites to lose the morrow's game, but the club wouldn't lose money. The match was to be the club's biggest, a most prosperous moment for the town, and a chance to get one-over on the shinty lovers and the supporters of Glenkura Athletic.

He peeled off his boots, rubbed the soil and grass off his legs with a piece of damp rag he found among the studded cakes of mud littering the floor like dried-up wedges of cheese. He then eased himself back on the bench, head against the wall's loose planks, listening to his team-mates outside getting on with the practice session. A tap dripped cold water into a rusted sink. The Celtic players would be excused such primitive facilities. They were to change in their hotel in the town, then be ferried to and from the ground by charabanc.

The whole shire was thought to be turning out. Then there were the Celtic supporters coming up from Glasgow. Archie thought there might be more than five thousand in total. A makeshift stand had been built to seat a few of the local dignitaries. The nets had been patched up. Avram had even helped paint the white lines across the freshly-cut, rolled grass. Stewards had been hired to police the fenced-off areas around the perimeter allocated to Celtic supporters paying good money in advance for tickets to stand in a muddy field.

The local folk would be happy clambering up for a free view from the hill overlooking the pitch.

Avram stirred from his day-dreaming, glanced at the wall-clock. He was going to be late.

He managed to push his way through the mob to the little square outside the station entrance until the sheer mass of bodies stopped his progress. A large banner had been spread across the station wall: *ARGYLL THISTLE FOR THE CUP*. A couple of constables and a band of railway officials had linked arms in an attempt to form a clear passage for the visitors.

The Celtic players looked huge, like prize bulls in for market, luminous in their fame, but all slightly awkward in their shining white collars and tight-fitting suits. They moved slowly through the crowd, growing confident as a result of the adulation, shaking outstretched hands, signing autograph books or whatever was thrust in front of them, exchanging cheeky banter with the ladies. Only a few of the team stood off shyly, flinching from the camera-flash set off at the tripod of the local press, ignoring the shouts of recognition, waving at the crowd as if to wave them away.

Avram spotted Uncle Mendel standing out among them in his black garb and sidelocks, his arms grasped desperately around his brown-paper parcels, wandering around the station forecourt in bemusement at the groups of protesters berating the Celtic contingent.

'Go back to Ireland, Fenians! Hands off the shipyards, ye Papist shites! Go home, ye Fenian bastards, go home!

Uncle Mendel, taking up the socialist cause, shouted back at them. 'Workers unite! Workers unite!'

The jeerers answered him with a hurl of abuse.

'Catholics and Protestants unite,' he shouted again over his parcels. 'Workers unite. Unite against the enemy.'

'You're the enemy, ye daft German Jew.'

Avram tried to push through the bodies in front of him. But Uncle Mendel was not to be shouted down. 'The Catholics are not the enemy. The Jews are not the enemy. The landlords are the enemy. The employers are the enemy. The Laird is the enemy. Ah, *boychik*.' Uncle Mendel half-ran towards him, then tripped over the kerb sending his parcels scattering over the station forecourt, delighting the protesters. Someone from among the crowd assisted him to his feet.

'Thank you, sir, thank you,' Uncle Mendel said in a bluster to his helper as he brushed the dust off his jacket, hurriedly reassembled his parcels. 'The kerb I didn't see ... so many people. Thank you. I am Mendel Cohen. And this is my nephew Avram.'

There was a hand stretched out for Avram to take. He saw the fine fingers with the clusters of hair around the knuckles, the starch white of the escaped cuff with the Celtic insignia stamped on the links. He nervously put his hand forward, accepted the grip of the man who had won five league championships, two Scottish cups, three Glasgow cups, eight Glasgow Charity cups and two Irish international caps. The grip was as firm as it should be.

'Avram Escovitz, Mr.Gallacher. I play for the Thistle.'

Patsy was fuller than he remembered. Filled out from the skin and bones he used to be, his suit stretching in a shine over his stocky frame.

'What position?' The voice was warm. Broad. Irish.

'Inside forward. Like you.'

Patsy eyed him up and down, pausing at the mud-caked boots, smiling.

'Getting ready for us, then?'

'We need the practice.' He searched for something else to say. 'Where are you staying?'

The Celtic player cocked his head vaguely in the direction of the town.

'Caledonian.'

'Good hotel,' Avram said, although he had no idea if it was. 'Excellent view.'

'Pleased to hear it. I'm going to need a wee rest after this welcome. Well, look after your uncle, lad.'

'This man I should know?' Uncle Mendel asked as Avram led him away from the crowd.

'Only if you follow football,' he replied, still buoyed by the thrill of meeting his hero, actually shaking his hand, talking to him man-to-man about the accommodation in town. 'That was Patsy Gallacher. The greatest footballer to play for Celtic.'

'Ah yes,' Uncle Mendel sighed. 'The football. Avram the footballer.

In the Gorbals, all the Jews talk about this game.'

Avram hadn't thought of that. That word of his playing might be of interest to the Jewish community in Glasgow. Solly would know, of course. But he wondered if Papa Kahn stood among his admirers. Or even Celia. Or would she be too involved with her politics to know that the young boy she rejected was going to be stepping out on the same playing field as Glasgow Celtic?

'What do they say about me?'

'They say they are proud. Even if on a *Shabbos* you play.'

'I have my own life here now, uncle. And it's nothing to do with being a Jew playing on a Saturday.'

Uncle Mendel shrugged. 'What do I care?'

'What you need to care about is how you speak to these protesters. Feelings run high. Even up here, away from the shipyards. Away from Glasgow. It's the Church that binds here. You know that. Not your socialism.'

'Bah. They have to understand. The workers have to stand together. Not with this religion to divide themselves.'

'How can you say that? Look at you. Look at the way you are dressed. With your *yamulke*. And your *tsitsis* hanging out from under your waistcoat. Look how you divide yourself from the rest.'

'In my clothes, perhaps I am different. But in my heart, there is no hate for others not like me.'

CHAPTER FORTY-TWO

The Oban Arms was heaving with Celtic supporters. A jagged current of excitement ran through the place combining with the hum of the electric lamps recently installed. The regulars had surrendered to the invasion, closed up their domino-boxes, joined in the banter. Except Uncle Mendel. He sat twisted away in a corner, one hand clasping a parcel, the other clutched around his very own shot glass. He had knocked back two whiskies in ten minutes and was now on his third. Avram wondered why his uncle hadn't just bought a half-pint glass of the spirit. It would have saved him these trips to the bar through the crush.

'Are you all right, uncle?'

Uncle Mendel tapped his fingers on the knot of the parcel. His face was flushed but cheerless.

'What you were looking for I found.'

'You found the fabric?'

'Yes, yes, the airplane fabric. All as you said. From an airplane manufacturer in Carmunnock. Rolls of it, he had in stock. All his advance orders gone *kaput* now the war is over. So the fabric we can have. Cheap. And the lacquer too. Barrels of it.'

'Lacquer? You mean the fabric isn't already waterproofed?'

'Na, na, na. You have to paint it on yourself. It is not easy. But Sadie at the shop, she knows how to do this. Her sister was … how does Sadie tell it? … yes, a doper. She was a doper during the war. Painting the lacquer on the planes. A doper. Yes, that's it.'

'So what's difficult about it?'

'If you want to make clothing, not airplanes, it is difficult. But Sadie, she knows. The cloth shrinks with the painting, so you have to cut it a size bigger. Then you need to stretch it over the shape you want. Then you paint it. But not too much, or the fabric becomes too stiff. Just two coats. That's all. Sadie, she does this. Her sister was a doper.'

'And this is it?' Avram asked, pointing at the parcel.

'Smocks, leggings, hats. From the sketches you gave me. Sadie made them up. The cost is very cheap. Much cheaper than these coats from Macintosh. But one thing you must know.'

'What?'

'It is very easy to go on fire. Whoosh! Just like that. Because of this lacquer. Waterproof maybe. But not fireproof.'

'Let me see.' Avram quickly fished out his penknife but Uncle Mendel kept his hand on the knot.

'There is something else, Avram. Something else to tell you about this waterproof clothing. Herr Stein says he will help us. The idea he likes. The capital he will lend us in exchange for a share of the profits.'

'That depends. How much of a share?'

'This we need to work out. It will be reasonable. But there is a condition.' Uncle Mendel picked up his third whisky, drank back half. 'And you will not like it.'

Avram thought of the warehouse owner ensconced in his leather chair, cigar wedged between his fat fingers, staring at his portrait likeness as he tried to squeeze the best deal out of Uncle Mendel. 'I knew with Jacob Stein there would be something.'

'A good Jew I try to be, Avram. Others I try to help. But myself I cannot help. Please forgive me.'

'What are you talking about?'

Uncle Mendel turned in his chair, waved at two men sat in a huddle at a table behind. The older man Avram remembered. Hard to forget a face so red-ravaged from drink, the large tuberous nose. Avram guessed he was a local bookie from the surreptitious way he'd seen Uncle Mendel hand over money in the past in this very same pub. But the younger man also looked familiar. It was he who stood at the beckoning, walked over in a swagger, pushing carelessly between tables. A double-breasted suit hung too loose on his skinny frame.

'Remember me, Escovitz?' His thin lips parted into a sneer of broken teeth.

Avram scanned the long, sickly face. A face that looked as if it had never seen sunlight. The red-hair was swept back in a slick from a corrugated forehead, the cold, green eyes slit into a permanent squint. But it wasn't any physical feature that jogged Avram's memory. It was the sheer sense of tight, screwed-up menace in this young man's wiry frame that sent his mind back to a dreary winter's afternoon on a cinder football pitch.

'Dodds,' he said, recalling his vicious opponent from that day. 'Ginger Dodds.'

'Very good, Escovitz. But William Dodds, it is tae ye. Now that we're all grown up and doing business.' Dodds pulled out a chair in a scrape, twirled it round so the back faced the table, sat down in a straddle across the seat. He dug a hand into his pocket, scattered some coins at Uncle Mendel. 'Get us a drink, old man. And one for yerself.'

Dodds waited for Uncle Mendel to leave. 'We could've won a lot of money back then. If it wasnae for ye, Jew boy.'

'I don't know what you're talking about.'

'That schoolboys semi-final.' Dodds scratched vigorously at a cheek, scraping off white flecks of skin on to his suit lapel. 'It was Victoria and Cathcart supposed to go through tae the final. Not yer team of gobshites. Until ye scored that fucking goal frae the corner.'

'What do you mean Victoria and Cathcart was supposed to win?'

'Our money was on the V and C. I was tae put ye out the gemme. And yer goalie got two shillings for his trouble. Goal in the first minute. Remember?' Dodds laughed. 'Then that fucking gym teacher whacked me.' He opened his mouth wide, pointed to an ugly space where a tooth should have been.

'Begg,' Avram said. 'Didn't think you knew who or what hit you.'

'I knew it was Roy Begg, all right. The wan-eyed monster himself. Interfering fucker.'

'So if the game was supposed to be fixed, who fixed it?'

'Can ye no guess?'

'Haven't a clue.'

'Yer man Stein.'

'What?'

'Aye. The wan and only. Grand bailie of the City of fucking Glasgow.'

Avram sat back in his chair. Jacob Stein. Mr. front-seat-in-the-synagogue, closer-to-God, larger-than-life Jacob Stein. Jacob Stein betting on schoolboy football matches.

'I don't believe you.'

'Ask yer man here.'

Uncle Mendel, returned from the bar, searched to find a space on the table for the drinks. His hands shook as he placed the glasses on the table.

'What Mr. Dodds says is true, Avram.'

'What's Jacob Stein doing betting on football matches? Never mind fixing them?'

'There was no much horse racing then,' Dodds said. 'With the war and that. No trains to take the punters tae the track. So yer man Stein got intae betting on the football. Some bookies came up with the odds, took the bets. Like yer man back there.' Dodds jerked his head in the direction of his table. 'As for influencing the result? Well, the rich aye want tae get richer.'

'Is that why you're here now?'

'Clever boy.'

'So what's there to fix? Celtic will win. Only a few local romantics would bet on the Thistle. Don't tell me you've bribed the Celtic players to lose?'

Dodds wriggled his chair closer to the table. 'Of course, yer right. Celtic will thrash ye. They aye do against these wee teams. Eight-nil, nine-nil, ten-nil, twenty-nil. Disnae matter how many. Whit we need is a goal against them.'

'That's the bet?'

'Aye, that's the bet. A goal against Celtic.'

'And that's what you want me for? To score against Celtic? Just like that. You think I can just waltz around a bunch of internationals and bang the ball into the net whenever I want to?'

'Disnae have tae be ye personally.'

Avram laughed. 'I don't think a bunch of coopers and fishermen will score against Celtic, either. We just want to keep the hammering down to a decent level.'

'Yer no understanding me, Jew boy. There has to be a goal.'

'I understand you very well, Dodds. And what I'm saying is I don't know where that goal will come from.'

'And whit I'm saying is this. Yer a good player, Escovitz. I have tae admit that. And considering the Celtic know fuck all about ye, their marking will be slack. And that should give ye a chance to dribble yer way into their penalty area at least once in the ninety minutes. And if ye can get a shot in and score, well that would be very nice. I'm sure ye would be delighted with such a result yerself. But if yer finding there isnae a goal being scored, there are other things ye could do when yer visiting their penalty area.'

'You want me to take a dive?'

'Ye never heard me utter such a word. I'd just like ye to shift the odds a little in our favour, that's all.' Dodds stood up, placed a hand on Uncle Mendel's shoulder. 'And if there's a goal, well this man's debt's clear. And if there isnae, dinnae think the stakes aren't high. Just remember, Escovitz. A goal against the Celtic. And yer man here will be fancy free to make a business. Good idea. Waterproof clothing for the farmers. Shows yer smart. So think smart about whit I said.' Dodds rolled his shoulders, spun on his heels and moved off to his table.

'My God, uncle. How could you do this?'

'I am weak. So weak.'

'Forget about being weak. How much do you owe?'

'A lot. Too much for me to say. From the horses. A run of very bad *mazel*. From Herr Stein I borrowed to pay off my debts. And then I lose this money too. I'm sorry, *boychik*. But it is only a game of football. You can do it. This Celtic don't know how good you are. Do as he says and a clean start we have. A business we have. Clothes against the rain.' Uncle Mendel started tearing the paper off the parcel on the table. 'Look, a waterproof hat. And a smock. With pockets. Clothes against the rain, Avram. Just like you said. Your idea. Such a business we will make. You and me.'

Avram stared at the waterproof samples as they were held up before him. Like pathetic white flags of surrender.

CHAPTER FORTY-THREE

'It's just like going over the top,' Bobby Logan the goalkeeper said. 'Over the top of the trenches.' He stood in the centre of the tiny dressing room, gleaming like a bumble bee in his new yellow jersey. 'It's opening that door and going out there, not knowing what will happen.'

Avram sat with the rest of the team, squeezed tight in the row of benches round the hut, glad for the closeness of the bodies against the cold. Until Logan had got to his feet, the room had been silent but for the chants of the crowd filtering in from the outside. Some of the players smoked cigarettes, others swigged whisky from a flask passed around, but most just stared at their feet. Avram watched the minutes clunk by on the wall clock. The faded photograph of the founders looked down at him.

'Ye mean, not knowing if ye'll come back with all yer body parts, if ye come back at all,' said Sandy Balfour, the left full-back. 'That's a fine fucking comparison, Logan. Why don't ye sit doon and shut up.'

'Steady, Sandy,' said Archie Campbell, the cooper's son, captain for the day. 'Steady.'

Avram thought of Bobby Logan going over the top. What it must have been like for him, looking up to the rim of the trench wall at that horizontal line marking the difference between the earth and the sky, between waiting and weaving, between life and death. He remembered how he used to ponder over the lists of the numbers of British casualties in the newspapers:

Somme – 500,000;
Arras – 190,000;
Messines – 108,000;
Third Ypres – 400,000;
Amiens – 360,000.

But it was the Russians who had lost the most men. One million seven hundred thousand in total. And he could have been one of them. He and Bobby Logan could have been fighting together in the trenches of the Western Front instead of on a football pitch in the Western Highlands. He wanted to tell that to Bobby Logan now. To go over and say how a worrying mother had stopped him seeing what he must have seen. Yet how strange it was that Bobby

Logan should be a goalkeeper when what had kept him alive was his destiny to miss bullets rather than to catch them.

Logan sat down as a knock at the door split the tension.

'Come in,' Archie shouted.

The door creaked open. Avram saw it was Willie Maley himself standing at the entrance wrapped up in a large camel-coloured overcoat. The Argyll Thistle players hushed at the sight of the legendary Celtic manager.

'I'd come in,' the big man laughed. 'But there's no any room.'

It was Archie who stood up, went over to the doorway. 'Archie Campbell. Captain.'

Maley shook the proffered hand. 'Thought I'd pop in to wish you well.' He pulled out a notebook from his pocket, flicked through the pages. 'Is there an ... an Escovitz here?'

All attention in the room turned on Avram. Then a hard poke in the ribs from Sandy Balfour beside him. 'Go on.'

Avram stood up. 'That's me, sir.'

'Just wanted to see your face. And your number.'

He turned round to show him.

'Good,' Maley said. 'There's someone outside for you to meet.'

Roy Begg stood with arms in a relaxed fold across his chest, one shoulder hard up against a side wall, as if his muscular frame were stopping the hut from falling over. He was no longer the sad drunk Avram had last seen in Valentino's ice cream parlour. The war was over, the man's dignity had returned, his eye-patch now as much a testament to battles fought as to any real reason for its loss. Begg and his bravado were back. The man who had pulverised the stuffing out of a punch-bag every day at the rear of the school gym had re-emerged with all his former menace intact. Avram could see it in the tautness in the neck, the jut of the jaw, the stab of the good eye, as the man surveyed the ground like a proud hawk searching for sight of its prey. A scout hungry for talent.

'Escovitz.'

'Mr. Begg.'

'Playing on Saturdays now?'

He tried not to rise to the bait. Solly's ancient advice. Keep quiet. Minimum politeness. Don't give him a way in.

'Lightning isn't going to strike you down, or anything like that?

Or is the Angel of Death going to swoop over you?' Begg waved a hand at the sky as if to signal the direction from which such an avenger might come.

'It hasn't happened until now,' Avram couldn't resist saying. He bit his lower lip. Mistake.

'Oh, it hasn't has it?' Begg said, rising from his lean against the shed. 'God looking after you, is He? The little runt who wouldn't play in the final?'

'I didn't mean it like that. Anyway, I wasn't the one who didn't want to play on Saturdays. Mr. Kahn stopped me.'

'That self-righteous bastard with his Jew ways. Sunday is the day of rest in this country. Isn't that right, boy?' Begg poked a finger directly at him.

Avram shut up this time and to his surprise Begg relaxed, dug his hands into his pockets, hitched up his trousers. Pulled out a pack of cigarettes. Offered him one.

'No, thanks.'

'Heard you're still useful.'

'Maybe.'

'Told them all about you.'

'Told who?'

'The gaffer. Willie Maley. Could have another Patsy Gallacher on our books, I told him.' Begg sucked deeply on his cigarette, looked him up and down. 'You've put on a bit of weight. But Patsy started off light, too, then beefed up. A wee runt, he was. Five foot six. Eight and a half stone, if he was that. But he could still leave them standing. Hard to believe. What do you say, lad? You're not going to let me down again, are you?' Begg glanced at the referee, a wee stoat of a man who had trotted up to the hut. 'You'd better get back inside.'

'Ready, lads?' the referee asked.

'Ready,' Archie said, squeezing to the front.

As soon as Archie set foot out of the clubhouse, a tremendous roar soared through the valley. Avram felt the excitement too, felt it ripple through his stomach, tunnel down into his bowels. Bobby Logan, who was second in line, turned back to the rest of the players with a smile across his face as wide as the Connel Bridge.

'Come on, you miserable bastards,' he shouted. 'We're going

over the top.'

The afternoon sun stabbed straight into Avram's eyes as he stepped on to the playing field. The Celtic players, bussed in from the Caledonian Hotel, stood waiting, silhouetted in various positions across the field. The rest of the scene was just a haze of light. He wondered if Kenny Kennedy was out there among the spectators. And his son Jamie come to watch the wee tinker Jew not good enough to marry his sister. And Donald Munro with his pharmacy reluctantly closed for the day. And the Captain, hoping for a victory for the United Free over the Catholics. And wasn't that Tam MacIsaac who had trekked down to the town, abandoning his flock on the hillsides just to witness the 'big gemme'?

An army band accompanied their march on to the pitch. With each beat of the drum, Avram picked up his step while the pipes brought a stirring to his heart he could not readily explain. Was this his music now? Or was he stepping to a universal beat and drone that could not help but move even a poor Jewish boy from Russia? He strode on towards the half-way line.

He could feel Begg's one-eyed bigoted stare on his back, Ginger Dodd's spiteful glare. And the venom of Wallie MacPhee, the quarry guard, who knew not whether to cheer or curse the nephew of the German Jew. There was a warm shout of encouragement from Davey, the driver of the Rail-Motor Service, glad for the time off granted to members of the Caledonian Railway. Over in the make-shift stand, The Laird sat stiff and haughty with the rest of the dignitaries. He saw Willie Maley take his seat on a bench by the touchline. Thanks to Roy Begg, there was not much chance of being loosely marked now. But there could be a trial for Celtic at the end of it. If he managed to score. Just one goal. One goal to save his uncle, to start a business, to play for Celtic.

But even with all the cheers and pressures swirling around him, Avram's attention extended beyond the pitch, up over the hillsides of spectators, above the folly that was McCaig's Tower, across the rooftops of the Oban Distillery and the Oban Arms, past the station and the fishyards and out across the yellow of the stooping whin that spread across the moors to the swirling waters of the Firth of Lorn. From there, his mind's eye took him across the Connel Bridge to Benderloch and a few miles further to the church at Lorn and to the Kennedy's cottage where no doubt Mrs. Kennedy was frying up her rashers of succulent bacon, and perhaps where Megan had found in her traitorous heart a wish of success for him on this auspicious day. Further north, his spirit rose to the sight of Glenkura with wooded Glen Etive off to the east, while to the west he could hear the wind stroking the harp strings in the abandoned keep in accompaniment to Jean Munro's silent vigil out on the peninsula. At Glenkura, he followed the path that was nothing more than a sheep track to the small cottage by the loch. There he could see Uncle Mendel seated at the table by the window. The candles that had welcomed in the Sabbath dwindled to a hardened wax, and any warmth would have long disappeared from a fire that had burned out and was forbidden to be lit. And Uncle Mendel's mind would not be on any football match or any wagers or any fancy business project to make waterproof clothing out of airplane fabric. Instead, his lips would move silently as he pronounced the words of the sacred text in front of him; his heart would be fixed on the peace of the Sabbath and his soul would be uplifted by the wondrous God-given beauty of the Scottish countryside that stretched before him bathed in unseasonable winter sunshine.

Oban

1923

CHAPTER FORTY-FOUR

Depending on the direction of the wind, Avram could smell either the fishyards or the Oban Distillery. Herring or whisky. Mackerel or malt. In the broad east-to-west split of the town this polarisation of odours was the unique distinction of the High Street. As well as hosting the most established shops, of course. He had insisted on the High Street. If there was to be a shop, then it had to be there on the grandest street in town. Not North Street, South Street, George Street or Stafford Street. But Glenkura Waterproofs of the High Street, Oban. The name had been his idea as well. Glenkura. Uncle Mendel had wanted it to be Escovitz. After all, credit where credit due, the elder credit draper had laughingly suggested. But he had overruled his uncle. It was easy to do that then, in the beginning, when Uncle Mendel had been so contrite, so ready to please, so damn grateful. The name was too foreign-sounding anyway, too Jewish, too German. Glenkura. So much better. A sense of place. The setting for Uncle Mendel's cottage. As well as the name of one of the two distilleries in the region. Not the one at the far end of the High Street, but the Glenkura Distillery inland across the Connel Bridge. Yes, Glenkura Waterproofs. 'You cannae be surer – than when yer wearing Glenkura.' That was the slogan. His idea again. Printed on all posters, advertisements and business stationery.

On this unusually hot afternoon the breeze was coming from Avram's preferred direction. Off-shore. Bringing with it the distinctive fumes rising from the chimney of the distillery kiln. At some part of each day, the air revealed a certain stage of the mysterious process that turned the barley in the storage towers into the bottles of amber liquid lining up like proud soldiers along the shelves of the Oban Arms. Sometimes it was the clean dusty smell of the stored barley sweeping down the High Street, as if cartloads of newly-cut hay had just trundled past his shop. Or perhaps it was the mouldy aroma of the germinating seeds being turned on the stone floors by the maltmen with their wooden skips. At other times, it was the earthy reek of the peat drying the green malt. Or the thick yeasty odour of the ferment that clogged his nostrils and hovered in a cloud over the town until every particle of breath he inhaled was suffused with the sweet cloying taste of distilling alcohol. The angels' share.

That was what the townfolk called the spirit evaporating from the densely-packed casks in the warehouses. But it was not just the angels who shared in this tax-free blessing. For he could always detect a sudden cheer in the voice and a colour to the cheek of the shoppers as they entered the High Street. It was either the angel's share or the bottled lemonade Donald Munro sold as a successful sideline to his pharmacy business across the street. The secret ingredient to Munro's brew was just enough whisky to ensure his young customers always came back for more, although they were never quite sure why.

And here was the man responsible for leading these children to rack and ruin, pig-trotting his frame across the High Street with those small, hurried steps of his, a bottle of whisky in his hand.

'Is he back?' Munro asked, dressed down to his shirtsleeves but still perspiring in the heat. 'I've brought him an Islay to taste.'

'He got back about an hour ago. He's upstairs.'

'I'll join him, if ye don't mind.'

'I didn't think you'd be over so early in this thirsty weather.'

'Dinnae worry on my account. Jean's over there minding the counter.'

'You're the lucky one. I'll sell nothing in this weather. Look, I'll be up shortly. But don't you two go arguing again.'

'We'll be fine,' Munro said, disappearing into the shop.

He wasn't so sure if Munro and Uncle Mendel would be fine. It was the whisky that drew the two men together, but pushed them apart at the same time. Uncle Mendel drinking more of it than ever these days, until he got himself well wound up with his talk of politics and religion, Munro pushing and prodding him with his opposite views like a needle poking a scab. Still, he could hardly complain about Uncle Mendel and his drunken evenings. The man was hardly ever in Oban, splitting his sober time between his socialist work in Glasgow and selling waterproofs on credit to his rounds of customers in the Western Highlands.

Mail-order. That had been the way forward. Killed any instinct Avram had to continue with his uncle in the credit drapery business. His idea again. Advertising in the local papers and the national farming magazines. The orders coming in faster than expected, until the demand was too much for Kahn & Co in Glasgow. He had opened this shop here in the High Street, both as a retail showroom and a workshop, point-blank refused any investment from Jacob Stein, would have gladly spat on any bank-draft from the warehouseman had it been offered. He hadn't needed the money anyway. The Bank of Scotland had been happy to provide him with the capital, a million pounds interest-free if he had wanted, what with the manager being a big fan of the Argyll Thistle. With the new showroom on the High Street drawing in the tourists as well as the locals, business had trebled. Mrs. Wallace from Papa Kahn's shop in Glasgow sent up her daughter Jessie to be the chief seamstress. He'd taken on another three girls locally, what with all the doping of the fabric to be done. Four, sometimes, if there had been a lot of rain.

'Goodbye, Mr. Avram,' Jessie said, squeezing past him now. 'Nice to be off early on such a day.' Pleasant lass. Face plain and wholesome like an oatcake. Soft lips. Round hips. Wondered what she got up to at nights when she wasn't in her bed-sit across town. But he knew the score. 'Don't go fouling your own nest.' Good advice, those words of wisdom from the Glasgow steamie.

'Nice day for a picnic, Jessie,' he called after her. 'But not for Glenkura Waterproofs.'

He sniffed the air. As dry as unleavened bread. Downpours, deluges, cloudbursts, drizzles, mizzles and the famous Scotch mist. That was what he needed. It only took a few drops of rain these days to send farmers and shepherds scurrying for an order form in the latest issue of *Farming Monthly, Scottish Agricultural* or the *Oban Gazette*. But these last two weeks of incessant sunshine had not been good for business. Mail orders were down and passers-by did just that – passed by on their way for a cooling bottle of Munro's refreshing lemonade, hands swatting at the midgies, and never a thought to prepare for the inevitable rain with the purchase of a Glenkura waterproof jerkin.

It was the perfume he noticed first. That same smell of lavender Madame Kahn had so insisted upon, even when she was away in an internment camp. Then came the shadow cast by the parasol protecting her fair skin from the sun. Pretty, she still was, although the lines of fear and sorrow had etched deeper into her skin. No verbal greeting of course, just the flash of a smile that painted itself quickly on her lips then disappeared. She held out her small gloved hand for him to take and the grip was tight. After all, these were hands that lashed harshly at horses as they swept her carriage out to her lonely mansion on the peninsula. He felt the small wad of paper pressed into his palm. Her grip released and she touched a finger to her lips. Then Jean Munro turned and crossed back over the street to her husband's shop. He locked the door, switched the sign to 'Closed'.

The paper was packed hard and he had to pick it apart carefully with a fingernail until he had a full sheet spread across his desk. The page was blank but for two delicate lines of handwriting across the fold in the middle.

Megan Kennedy needs to see you. Urgent.
Come to my house tomorrow if you can. 3pm.

CHAPTER FORTY-FIVE

Upstairs in the small flat, the windows were propped open on the necks of beer bottles. Also open were three bottles of whisky set out on the table in an informal tasting – an *Oban*, a *Glenkura* and Munro's Islay. Avram grabbed the nearest one – the Islay – poured out a glass, swigged it down, nearly spat it right out again.

'Good God. It tastes like medicine.'

'An acquired taste that requires no blaspheming,' Munro said, pouring a shot for himself.

'A certain peatiness there is to the *Oban* malt,' Uncle Mendel observed in the swirl of a glass containing a darker liquid than the Islay. The man was stripped to his vest, yet his black hat still clung in a sweat to his head. 'Add the *geshmekt* of the sea air, a whiff of herring ... and that dry, rounded taste you get with just a hint of bitterness.'

'A whiff of herring?' Munro snorted. 'Is that what ye think, ye daft Jew? It's the brine that does it. That's what sets it apart from those land-locked upstarts.'

'Who are you calling a daft Jew?' Uncle Mendel protested. 'Let me tell you something, you Christian ... you Christian *schlemiel* ... yes, that's it. You *schlemiel*. The finest *schnapps* of Europe we Jews were drinking long before this Scotland was a nation. Tell him, *boychik*.'

Avram refused to be drawn into his uncle's arguments, re-filled his glass instead – this time with the *Oban* – sat down in an old armchair by the window, lit up a cigarette. Through the shop-glass across the street, he could see Jean Munro serving a group of schoolchildren, all lined up proper in a queue outside the door. No doubt glad to have Munro out from under her feet. Soon, she would lock up and head-off homewards alone. He wondered if Uncle Mendel did her a service, getting her husband so drunk he had to kip down for the night in the pharmacy. He thought of the note in his pocket. He sucked in the smoke, spat out strands of tobacco. Another gulp of the *Oban*.

'... Haud on, Moses,' Munro said. 'Ye Jews might have a taste for all these fruity liqueurs but there's no many of yer tribe who have known the magnificent combination of Highland spring water, peat and ripe barley. Especially at the hands of Alex Duthie, the master stillman himself. It is he who kens when the whisky runs true from the still. It is he who kens how not to pollute our grand *Oban* product with the foreshots and feints of the low wines. To Alex.' Munro raised his glass. 'But even the master stillman can't keep the salt out of the water. It's the brine, I tell ye. That's the distinctive taste.'

'Now, a truth there is in what you say,' Uncle Mendel reflected. 'But you can't tell me, Herr Munro, that a barrel you can stand for three years less than a quarter of a mile from the fishyards, without a whiff of the herring creeping in.'

'Och mon, leave the *Oban* alone then, and taste the Islay.'

'I will not. Avram's right. It tastes like iodine. Too much of the brine. Not enough of the herring, Herr Munro. Why not try the *Glenkura*? It is both salty and sweet, don't you think?'

Avram let them continue with their baiting and their bantering. Blew out a couple of smoke rings. Almost perfect circles. Solly had taught him that.

Megan Kennedy. Just the thought of her caused his stomach to clench over the stir of emotion. He hadn't seen her since her brother Jamie had turfed him out into the snow, must be almost four years past. He hadn't heard of any marriage to Charles Sinclair, either. He'd looked out for that. One eye on the banns, another on the local papers. But he'd lost an ear for the gossip of the shire now he was located in the town. She, in her turn, must have known about the clothing business, the Glenkura range, the shop in the High Street. After all, the Laird himself was a customer. There had to be a time when she was in town on a day off from the castle, visiting her best friend Jean. Yet not once had she appeared at his doorway. Even now, staring out across the street at the Munro's shop as he did on many a day, he felt he might catch sight of her hair reflecting golden in the sunlight.

It was her mother who had come. Just that one time. He had heard the tinkle of the shop-bell and gone out to serve. No-one there. He was just about to return to the workshop when he heard the bell again. Mrs. Kennedy stood unsure in the front entrance in her best coat, her fingers scraping at the clasp of her black leather handbag with its brown lines of wear cracked across the surface. He was too surprised to be angry, so his first words had come out with shopkeeper politeness.

'Is there something I can do to help you?'

'He won't come in,' she said, her mouth twisting somewhere between a grimace and a smile.'

'Who?'

'That big lump.'

He had glanced out of the window. Kenny Kennedy paced the street in gamekeeper tweeds, his hands clasped behind his bent back, bony fingers locked together in a tension. Despite what had happened, he couldn't help but feel a morsel of affection for the stooped figure.

'What are you after, Mrs. Kennedy? A jerkin for your husband? Shall I call him? Try one on him?'

'Naw, naw,' she said, a sudden panic her eyes. 'Dinnae do that. He won't come.' Again the fingers working at the clasp. 'He sent me instead.'

'Why would he do that?'

She ran her hand over the counter. 'Ye've done it nice. The glass displays. All these ... dummies ... is that whit ye call them? ... in the windae. It looks grand.'

'Why won't he come in, Mrs. Kennedy?'

'To tell the truth, we've been meaning to drop by for a while. Heard ye'd set up in the toon. Baird frae the Laird telt us whit happened that night.' And then her face collapsed into a sobbing. 'We shouldnae have stood by, Avram. It wasnae right. Ye could have died that night. We shouldnae have stood by and let it happen.'

Another swig of the *Oban* to shake off the memory. Uncle Mendel was right. There was a whiff of the herring to it.

'Hey *boychik*. From Glasgow you heard the good news?'

'What are you talking about? Family or politics?'

'Politics.'

'I don't want to know then.'

'Anyway, I'll tell you.'

'I don't want to hear it.'

'To these matters you shouldn't close your ears. Ten seats we won for the Labour party in the General Election. To Central Station we went with our new members of parliament. And to Westminster we sent them with the sound of the Red Flag ringing in their ears. Ringing in their ears.' Uncle Mendel hummed the first few bars, then raised his glass in a toast. 'To the Glasgow Ten.'

'What do ye mean? To the Glasgow Ten,' Munro said. The colour of the Red Flag itself could not have matched the choler boiled up in his cheeks. 'The Glasgow Ten. I spit on them.'

'Spit on them? Spit on them,' Uncle Mendel responded. 'Bah! You prefer a Government that failed on council housing and unemployment? And to Ireland sent troops? And on whisky tripled the tax?'

Munro jumped to his feet. 'Rather that than a government spending taxpayers' money on schools for the Papists.'

'Aha! Now I see. That's what this is all about. You and your Protestant hatred.'

'Rome on the rates, is what I call it.'

'I cannot sit with a man who by religion divides people,' Uncle Mendel said, sitting down again.

'And I cannot drink whisky with a Jewish Bolshevist,' Munro said, also sitting. 'And what is that infernal ringing?'

'Ah! The telephone,' Uncle Mendel said. 'Go get it, *boychik*.'

The telephone. Avram had arranged for its installation a few weeks ago, yet he still wasn't used to the urgent, beckoning sound of the contraption. He jumped up from the armchair and ran downstairs. With each jingling sound the shiny black device seemed to leap up and down on his desk, begging to be answered. He picked up the earpiece and mercifully the ringing stopped.

'Hello?' he shouted close into the mouthpiece. 'Hello. This is *Glenkura Waterproofs*.'

A crackle. 'Hello,' came the reply. 'Is that Avram? Avram Escovitz? Over.'

'Yes, it is. Avram Escovitz is speaking.'

'It is me, Avram.'

'Who is me?'

'Papa Kahn is speaking here. From Glasgow. Can you hear me? Over.'

Too much interference made the voice unrecognisable. Hollow. Distant. Carved out of the past. 'Oh,' was all he could manage. And then the worry of his worst fears. 'Something has happened?' he shouted down the line.

'Na, na, na. Don't worry. Nothing has happened. Nobody is ill. Nobody has died. We have just got a telephone. Mendel gave us your number when he was here. He showed me how to use it. To dial this number. It's a miracle, don't you think? Over.'

'You don't need to say "over" every time you're finished, Papa. And it's not a miracle. It's science.'

'Maybe, maybe. Can you still hear me?'

'I can still hear you.'

'Good. Avram. How are you? Uncle Mendel tells us you are a *ganze macher* up there in Oban.'

'I am fine, Papa. Business is good, too.'

'It has been too long. Too long away from us. We want you to come back. Come back to visit us, Avram. Come back for the High Holidays. Come back for *Yom Kippur*.'

'I can't, Papa. I have a business here.'

'Mendel says the sun is shining like the Sinai desert up there. And the midgies are like a plague of locusts. He says you could close down the shop. Take a week off. Even if you don't come for us, come back to be a Jew for the Holidays. Over. Sorry.'

'Tell me, how is Madame Kahn?'

'She is well.'

'And Celia? How is Celia?'

There was a long pause and he thought the line must have been disconnected.

'Celia? We hardly see her,' Papa Kahn said eventually.

He gazed at the black funnel of the mouthpiece waiting for the explanation that never came.

'Avram? Are you still there?'

'Yes. I am still here. And Nathan?'

'Nathan is a fine boy. You wouldn't recognise him. He asks for you all the time. *Komm*, Avram. You cannot stay away forever.'

'I will think about it.'

'Promise me you'll come. Promise me.'

Before he had time to answer, the line went dead, leaving him listening to the lonely buzz of disconnection. He fumbled with the earpiece, finally managing to replace it on its hook. His drenched shirt clung to him in this airless room. Difficult to breathe.

A clumping on the stairway.

'I cannae stay here one minute longer with that man,' Munro shouted, rattling the front door hard. 'Come on. Open up. Open up and let me out of this fucking place.'

'Calm yourself, Munro. You know what it's like with the two of you. Like red rags to a bull.' He went over and unlocked the door. 'Careful as you go. You've had too much to drink.'

'And yer no much fucking use either. Red flags to a bull, my arse!'

The door slammed shut, leaving the pane shaking in its casing.

CHAPTER FORTY-SIX

His brain told him that going to see Megan would only hurt him. His body, meanwhile, rose early and soaked in a hot bath. His brain told him not to bother with this woman who had deceived and humiliated him. His body, meanwhile, shaved, searched out fresh underwear, put on his laundered collar and cuffs. But not his best suit. He didn't want to appear too smart, too full of himself. Still, as his hands knotted the tie Jessie and the girls had given him for Christmas, it was quite the prosperous young businessman who looked back at him from the shop mirror. But there was something unsettling about his reflection. He peered closer, relaxed his shoulders, smiled at himself, crinkled up his cheeks. It was in the eyes. Perhaps only he could recognise it. He was sure he hadn't suffered any less in this world from his habit of sealing into little boxes those who had caused him pain. But somehow he grasped the notion that as these boxes piled up, they turned into the building bricks of the young man he had become. A man whose emotions were buried deep but flickered occasionally to the surface. As they did now.

He allowed himself plenty of time for his walk across the moors, strolling leisurely with his jacket overarm, careful not to work up a sweat in the steamy heat. At Connel, he was the only passenger for the Caledonian Railway Rail-Motor Service with little patience for driver Davey's teasings about where he might be going midday dressed up to the nines. Over on the other side of the Firth at Benderloch, he hired a horse and buggy for the ride out to the peninsula. It was a lonely drive without sight nor sound of a soul on the way until he reached Lorn. He lingered outside the Kennedy's cottage, the horse steaming breathless in a jangle of its reins, as he imagined Mrs. Kennedy heating up some lard on a skillet waiting for her husband to return from the shoot. For it was that time of year when Kenny Kennedy would be out on the moors as a ghillie with his beaters rousing up the grouse for the Laird and his party. As if to confirm his thoughts, somewhere off in the direction of Glen Etive a sequence of shots rifled across the sky in their search of a kill.

From Lorn, he turned west towards the sea, urging on his mare harder, keeping his thoughts for the drive rather than on any reason why Megan might want to see him after all this time. He sped through the forest close to the abandoned castle, the buggy lurching and swaying on the dried-up path until emerging from the tree-lined corridor, he could see the Munro mansion in the distance. Even in the sunlight, even with the cool blue waters stilled on the shore, the place looked gloomy and foreboding. A mounted figure swung out of the gates, galloped down the road towards him. At first, Avram thought it must be Jean Munro riding out to meet him. But as the horse approached, he realised it was a man's frame in the saddle. He slowed up his own approach to the horseman, holding up his hand against the glare of the sun, an arm ready against the churned up dirt and flailing stones from the galloping hooves. But the rider did not veer from his path, forcing Avram to steer his own horse and wagon off to the side of the road. Yet, still he had time to recognise the man as he passed. The man he had last seen as a vision of Christ standing arms outstretched in a lighted doorway on Christmas day. Jamie Kennedy.

Jean Munro did not return his greeting, but hastened him instead into the front room. The French windows were open and she left him to wander out on to the lawn as she went to fetch Megan. The grass had been trimmed fine and rolled where Donald Munro had cut out a few holes and pinned them with flags to make a small putting green. He located the first pin, wandered across the parched lawn following the numerical order of the flags, his attention focused on nothing more than the black tips of his shined-up brogues as they appeared, then disappeared from his line of vision. The afternoon hummed heavy and still. A few gulls cackled off the rocks. Gun shots popped in the distance.

'Avram.'

Flag number four. Grass patched yellow here and there, neatly trimmed cup, turn towards flag number five, her voice more persistent now.

'Avram.'

He hardly recognised her. Her long hair, that one memorable feature, cropped short into the kind of bob he knew was fashionable from sketches he'd seen alongside his advertisements in clothing catalogues. Her face, the full outline exposed now by the loss of its frame, was rounder, less defined. She trod barefoot to a halt beside him. Despite the heat, she had draped a tartan shawl over her shoulders. His body wanted to grab her and shake her. But he kept his distance.

'Thank ye for coming.'

'I wasn't sure if I would.'

'I'm glad ye did. Ye look grand. A proper gentleman.'

More gunshots. He looked away in their direction, imagined the feather burst, the stone-dead fall of the grouse, the retrievers in a lather bounding through the heather.

'Ye dinnae have to say anything. I ken I look like a midden.'

'You look different, that's all.' And then for the want of conversation: 'I passed your brother on the way here. Did he bring you over?'

'No. He was here to see Jean. He comes to visit sometimes.'

'When her husband's away in Oban?'

She pulled her shawl tighter. 'Come inside,' she said. 'I brought us some lemonade.'

Two wicker chairs had been drawn up close to the French windows, a tray with a pitcher and two glasses set down on a small table between them. He sat down, watched her pour. She struggled with the jug, spilling lemonade over the side of his glass and on to the table, dabbing up the liquid with a corner of her shawl. He glanced at her hand, skin tanned from the last fortnight's sun. No sign of a ring on her finger, not even the mark where one might have been. He picked up his glass. The drink washed cool and slightly bitter over his tongue. He wondered if she had made it herself or whether this was Munro's very own whisky-laced brew. She picked up her glass in the clasp of her two hands, all the time staring at him over the rim as she drank. He let the silence linger between them.

'I want tae apologise for what happened.'

'That would be a decent start. At least your mother came by to…'

'I ken ye must've felt hurt…'

'Of course, I felt bloody hurt. It wasn't enough you led me on without a word about Sinclair. You let that brother of yours throw me out into the snow like some useless rag. I nearly died that day. If it hadn't been for Baird…'

'Ye think I didnae care about ye? T'was Jamie stopped me from going after ye. He has such a hold. It's true I was seeing ye and Charlie at the same time. There's no excuse for that. But I didnae go out in search of his courting. Jamie kept pushing him at me. They'd become great pals at some ex-servicemen's club in the toon and Jamie had this fancy vision he'd make a grand brother-in-law. But at the time ye came for Christmas, I was no more promised tae him than I was tae ye, I swear it, Avram. Jamie made the decision there and then. Not me. He said Charlie had the better prospects over a Jew tinker. And he'd made faither think similar, with no mind for what was in my heart.'

He took another sip of lemonade, searching for the slightest taste of the whisky in it to sour away thoughts of Jamie and Charlie Sinclair. 'So is this why you brought me out here? To apologise?'

'Partly.' She drew her bare feet up on to the chair. Plucked off some stray blades of grass sticking to her soles and toes. It was an innocent act, but somehow it stirred a passion in him. He stood up, walked over to the sideboard, poured out a whisky from Munro's crystal decanter. A *Glenkura* malt. He helped himself as well to a cigarette from the man's engraved silver cigarette case. Silver lighter to match. Inhaled deeply. A couple of smoke rings on the exhale. He felt better now. More in control.

'So what else is there?'

'I'm pregnant.'

'I see,' he said, trying to hold his voice steady. He was surprised this piece of news could still affect him. 'Sinclair's the father, I assume?'

'Aye, Sinclair.'

'So what's the problem? There'll be a wedding.'

'A wedding?' she screamed. 'Aye. That would be a fine thing.'

'But you've been seeing him all these years?'

'Aye. Off and on. He wasnae a bad sort at first. Until he became wan of these big shots in the Royal Air Force, what with him flying in the war. A test pilot, he is now. Always off testing something or other. Never time for his wee sweetheart at the Laird's castle. Keeping me hanging like forgotten washing on the line. So I let him do what I said I'd never let anyone do until I was married. I thought it might make a difference.' She patted her belly. 'Aye, it's made a fine difference, all right.'

'So where is he now?'

'Once he had his way with me, he was off. Gone for good. I've no seen the bloody Sassenach since. And as for this baby – I cannae have it.' She was close to tears now. Chewing at her lip to hold them back, her fingers in a nervous pick at the hem of her shawl. Just like her mother's on the clasp of a handbag. 'Father would kill me if he found out. He'd kill Charlie too, if he could get his hands on him. So would Jamie. I'm going to ... to someone. One of the Laird's maids had it done. A woman in Glasgow. She says it's no so bad if it's caught early.'

The heat rose in his cheeks. He turned away from her in a walk to the window. He knew nothing of these matters. Women's talk.

'Avram. Listen to me. I know it's no right to ask ye after what I done. But I've no choice.'

'Ask me what?'

'I need some money.'

Outside, the pin flags struggled to life in a snatch of breeze then died again. He sucked slow on his cigarette, feeling the burn of the flake flood his lungs, then exhaled into a mist on the pane. 'What about Jean? She'd be your obvious choice.'

'Avram.' He sensed a harshness in her voice now. 'Does that mean ye won't help me?'

'I didn't say that. I was only wondering why bother with me when your best friend can help you.'

'That lass disnae have twa sticks of her ain to rub together. All this is Donald's. She came here with nothing after the fire. And every ha'penny and farthing she spends has to be accounted for. She cannae buy a needle or a grain of sugar without Donald wanting to see the receipt. How is she going to find me the money to pay for an abortion? And the fare to Glasgow? And a place to stay in the city till it's all over?'

'I'd still think she'd be smart enough to squirrel away a few bob from that drunk of a husband.'

'All right, then. If ye must know. She disnae approve. She says it's too dangerous.'

'And is it?'

'There's a chance of infection. Or I could bleed tae death.'

'These seem good reasons not to go ahead.'

She shook her head, bit down hard on her lip, pulling away the surface skin until just the hint of bleeding showed. 'I dinnae want any fatherless bairns running around the place. And anyway, what other choice have I got? It's either that … or I can throw myself down the stairs. I know I dinnae have the right to ask. But can ye please help me? I dinnae know where else to turn.'

He continued his stare out of the window. The sun made it so that partly he could see just his reflection, partly he could see beyond the glass. The sea was so calm, throwing out just the faintest shrug of a wave to the shore. Almost as if it was resting, waiting for something to happen, caught between tides perhaps. He turned back to Megan. 'I'll give you whatever you want. But on one small condition.' He paused, heard the crackle of Papa Kahn's voice among his thoughts. 'I'm coming with you.'

CHAPTER FORTY-SEVEN

The train was well past Stirling, and the urban blight of the Glasgow outskirts began to creep into view. Megan sat opposite, asleep, her face returned to the flush of a motherhood soon to be cut painfully short. Only one hour previously she had sat milk-white and drained after vomiting in the water-closet on Stirling station platform. She told him the sickness was normal. Avram reckoned it must have been the fear of what was to come, making her ill.

He thought about his return to Glasgow. Does everyone return? Returning was in his blood, for the Jews were in a constant state of returning. Returning from their exile. The children of Israel returning to the land of Canaan from Egypt. Only to be expelled again. And now, two thousand years later, Uncle Mendel telling him about Theodore Herzl and his Zionist descendants wanting to return to that very same land. Does everyone return to the source? Would he return, not only to Glasgow, but some time later retrace his steps back to Russia? Mother Russia. The Russia of his mother. The Russia of revolutions.

The Scots. They never seemed to return. They went to far-flung places like Canada and New Zealand and India and there they stayed. They colonized, they set down roots, they established their church, they taught people their proud ways, they sang their songs that seemed to long for the return they would never make. They lived life in straight lines, seeds in a furrow ready to seize the soil with a fervour and send up shoots from wherever they scattered. The Jews were different. They trod lightly on the land. Their suitcases were always packed. Their return tickets were forever hidden under the mattresses. They kept their songs to themselves. The Jews were forever moving in circles.

But there was a tangent yet, where linear Scot met circular Jew. He only had to look to Uncle Mendel as living proof. Not just with the common love for the herring, the betting, the fiddle and the *schnapps*. But a thirst for education and social justice. The Scots and the Jews. Karl Marx and John MacLean. A Scottish Jew. A Jewish Scot. With his *tallith* and his kilt. His *yarmulke* and his sporran. His *vursht* and black sausage.

He watched Megan sleep. Her mouth slightly open, a bubble of saliva escaping her lips to dampen the cushion she had put between her cheek and the glass. He thought of the baby inside her. The baby that would never return. He only prayed she would.

'If it was yours, I wouldnae do this,' she had told him at the start of the journey.

The words had moved him terribly.

'You don't think I'd have left you like Sinclair?'

'Yer here now,' she had said.

He flicked a loose thread off the sleeve of his new suit. A blue three-piece, with a fob watch to set it off nicely. His collar was freshly starched, his hair oiled and slicked back in the current style, his shoes polished to a shine. The credit draper was returning as a West Highland business man with his own store and his own product. *You cannae be surer – Than when yer wearing Glenkura.* He had brought gifts for the Kahns. Pebble jewellery, a bottle of malt, linen handkerchiefs. He looked forward to the look on their faces when he gave them.

The train drew close to Glasgow's Buchanan Street Station. He noticed the sky darken, the trees hanging weary, the birds flying sluggish. Warehouses and tenement buildings crowded closer to the track. Some of the passengers, restless now, stood up to unload their luggage from the overhead racks, only to sit back down with a load on their laps as the train wheezed to a halt in an approach tunnel. He could feel the excitement of the city waiting for him, this second city of a Great British Empire stretching pink on a school map of his memory from New Zealand to Canada. Here, there were tramcars and dance halls and picture houses and theatres. Here, there were broad avenues and bridges, foundries and shipyards, a university and an art gallery Here was the home of Rangers and Clyde and Third Lanark and Partick Thistle. And Celtic.

He gently shook Megan awake.

'We're almost there,' he said.

'I know.'

The man behind the reception desk of the Great Northern Hotel scratched his jaundiced cheek hard as he looked them up and down.

'You want a single room? Just for the lady?'

'That's what I said.'

'Well, no gentleman callers. It is a rule of the establishment.'

'I will have to visit Miss Kennedy during her stay.'

'I meant staying the night.'

Avram helped Megan to her room. It was on the third floor at the rear of the building. The view was not pleasant – a window onto a back court full of ash cans, empty bottles and the hotel's refuse. But at least they were high enough for the smell not to reach them. She checked the bed linen, fluffed up the pillows, adjusted the coverlet.

'It's clean enough,' she pronounced, sitting down on the bed.

'What will you do now?'

'I might have a nap. Then a wee walk around the shops. Just have to wait till the evening, that's all.'

He pulled out his wallet, picked out a note, crisp from the bank yesterday morning. 'Get yourself something nice.'

'Ye've done enough,' she said. But she took the money anyway.

'Do you want me to leave?' he asked.

'In a while.'

He sat down on the bed beside her. She gave him her hand, but continued to stare ahead. The wardrobe door was half-open and he could see their reflections in the mirror. He might as well have been a doctor taking her pulse. Her skin was rough and cold under the stroke of his fingertips. Behind the cupboard door, empty coat-hangers, shelves covered with newspapers, the smell of camphor.

'Come to bed with me,' she said. 'Will ye?'

The request took him off guard. He thought to refuse, just to spite her, just to show her where the power lay now. 'Yes,' he said, hearing the excitement in his voice.

She began to undress and he stood up to do the same. She didn't look at him as she folded her skirt and blouse in a professional neatness over the chair. He hung up his suit in the wardrobe, placed his shoes under the bed. She pulled back the bedclothes, lay down on the sheet in her shift and he moved in beside her. The linen felt slightly damp. He kept a distance, refraining from touching her, not knowing what she wanted.

'Ye can do it.'

'Are you sure?'

'Go inside me. It disnae matter any more.' She searched out his hand, clenched it. He suddenly realised he wanted her. He wanted her badly. She turned on her side towards him and stroked the hair off his forehead, running her fingers lightly across his cheek, her eyes full of questions. He put a hand on her hip, felt the cold beneath the coarse cloth, knew he wanted her hot before he would be ready. A hand on her buttock now, pressing her into his hardness, kissing her neck. She was grasping him tightly, her shift riding high on her thighs and his fingers pushing the cloth up further. He smelled the familiar odour of her sweat, the dampness underarm, but he missed entwining his fingers in the thick winding of her long hair. Her arms were around him now, nails digging deep into the back of him, legs kicking against his calves. Grasping and pushing away at the same time. He eased open her thighs. His own confidence surprised him. There was no nervousness, no fumbling, no hard push against her membrane of resistance. No blood. Instead, he slipped in warm and easy in a liquid flow, moving slowly and gently in a rhythm. She relaxed now, her hands caressing his, massaging desperate affection into skin. He felt himself tighten, ready to explode. She tensed underneath him in an arch of her body upwards, grinding herself closer to him. Her teeth bit into his shoulder. He heard a scream of release and realised it came from his own mouth. His body shuddered and he collapsed on top of her. He could hear her heartbeat against his chest. He looked at her, saw she was crying.

'What's wrong?'

She rubbed one eye, then the other with the back of her hand. 'It's nothing,' she said.

He eased himself off her. She turned away from him and he lay down beside her, drawing his arms around her belly, thinking for the first time about the child that had lain silently between their lovemaking.

CHAPTER FORTY-EIGHT

He had always cherished an image of how it would be. Drawing up front in a hansom, or even at the wheel of his own shiny motor car. He saw children in a scamper after his vehicle, rewarding their chase with scattered handfuls of sweets and farthings. Tenement windows thrown open for housewives to gape at the parked automobile outside the close at number 32. And wasn't that Rabbi Lieberman stepping out of the synagogue to admire the passing procession, and Mrs. Carnovsky gawking behind a tobacco cloud? Papa and Madame Kahn, Celia and Nathan, standing outside the close, lined-up spit and polished as if for a photograph.

But showing up and showing off like that was no longer in his mood. Shanks's pony was how he set himself across the city. It felt better to walk, even in the thick hot city air, his feet pounding out the memory of his journey from the docks so many years before. The banks, the hotels, the fancy stores and posh tea-rooms, all less intimidating to him now, but nevertheless still grand and imposing in their watch of his progress from the Saltmarket, along Argyll Street to the Adelphi Hotel, then south to the Gorbals. Half-way across Glasgow Bridge he stopped, set down his case, stood up on his toes and looked over the parapet at the sluggish swirl of the Clyde beneath. The water ran the colour of milky tea.

He thought of Megan curled up under the blankets in her dull hotel room, listening to the cats scrabbling for scraps down among the rubbish in the courtyard. The stain of their lovemaking remaining on the sheet as the birthmark of their consummation. He thought of the Kahn family waiting nervously for his return. He saw the table set with linen cloth in the front room, laid out for the early dinner before the Fast. A bottle of sweet red wine and glasses glistening ready for the blessings, the oily smell of the silver-polished candlesticks still lingering, Madame Kahn fussing with the table arrangements, Papa Kahn keeping to himself in his study, one eye on the Talmudic tract in front of him, the other on the clock. And Nathan? How had that sickly, bed-ridden child grown to be a young man ? And Celia? How would he feel when he saw her again?

A train pulled out in a slow steamy churn from Glasgow Central along the bridge opposite. He could feel the agitation in his limbs, his legs wanting to go this way and that, anywhere and everywhere but back to the Gorbals. He had a desire to pick up his case, return to the hotel, lie down by Megan's side, wrap his arms fiercely around the unborn child in her belly.

'Avram? Avram Escovitz? For God's sake, Patsy, is that you?'

He turned round. Solly standing there in front of him in a felt hat, filling out a fine double-breasted pinstripe, leather gloves despite the warm weather, a smile as broad as the Clyde splitting his fleshy jowls.

'It is you, isn't it, ye daft bampot? I hardly recognised you.'

Avram grabbed at Solly's outstretched hand, eagerly shook the leather-clad fingers. 'It's so good to see you, Solly.'

'It's grand to see you too. You're looking the right little business man.'

'You're looking prosperous yourself.'

'You mean I've got fat.'

'You never were a skinny one'

'The betting business has been good to me.' Solly adopted a boxer's crouch, sent a slow hooked delivery to pad at his shoulder. 'You've filled out a bit yourself.'

'No longer Begg's little runt.'

'That's for sure.' A tram swung on to the bridge in a clatter of metal, swinging pantograph, and a scatter of sparks. Like an elephant on the rampage.

'I heard you were coming to visit for Yom Kippur,' Solly shouted over the noise.

'Who told you?'

'Celia.'

'How is she?'

'Who knows, with Celia? She's one of these suffragettes. When she's not chaining herself to one thing or another, she's burning down the stands at the races. She is definitely not good for my business.'

'Do you have time for a drink?'

Solly laughed. 'Aye, a wee dram or two before the Fast would be a grand idea.' Then an arm round his shoulder. 'See how we've grown. It used to be a game of fitba' on the streets. Now, it's off to the pub.'

The *Rabbie Burns* was next to the railway bridge. Frosted windows to above eye-level, then topped with stained-glass panels boasting various coats of arms. *Rabbi Burns*, he and Solly used to call it, the joke doing nothing to diminish their fear of the place on their rush past after school. Frightened they were to bump into the occasional pallid customer emerging bleary-eyed, staggering and impatient from an establishment always reeking of beer, unemployment and serious drinking. Especially on schoolday afternoons when there was no darkness to disguise the air of sin about the place. Avram used to think a boy could get drunk just from the stench, waiting outside for a drinking father.

Yet, here he was entering the pub as a working adult with money in his pocket and Solly leading the way, of course. For that was Solly. Even today, when Megan had made him feel more of a man than any *barmitzvah* ceremony, Solly was in charge, ordering the drinks, half of heavy and a wee dram for them both, paying with a flourish, choosing a table. Solly holding court, full of the quick patter, offering him a cigarette from a case, silver-plated, nothing flash. Wouldn't want the punters to think he was doing too well. Still the same Solomon Green. Like father, like son. *Morris Green & Son, Bookmakers*. That would be the name above a permanent shop if his business were ever allowed to go legal. Although the betting shop did somehow exist inside Solly's head and in the heads of the punters slipping him a bet on the day's dogs and horses. Despite the work being 'not strictly *kosher*', Solly telling him how he had moved the business forward, setting up a network of agents in the shipyards, running a sideline in coupon betting.

'And do you know what?' Solly said, pinching his waistcoat pockets between thumb and forefinger, the first time his hands resting since he had sat down. Solly looking much older than his years, hair receding fast towards his father's bald dome. 'Dog racing is really taking off. They've just put in electronic traps at Glenburn. Next year, they're introducing electric hares at Carntyne. Should bring in the punters in droves.' He paused to gulp out two perfect smoke rings. 'And another thing you should know. I'm getting married.'

'*Mazeltov*. That Molly you used to winch?'

'Not Molly. Someone of the faith.'

'Anyone I know?'

'Aye.'

'So, you're not telling me then?'

'See if you can guess.'

'I'm not in the mood.'

'All right then. Judith Finkelstein.'

'Ah. Judith Finkelstein.' Avram remembered her from Hebrew classes. A short, timid creature with just a hint of a moustache over thick lips. Lips that seemed permanently curled up in a distaste for something. A distaste for what she was about to eat, for what she was about to hear, for what she was about to touch. But obviously not a distaste for Solly.

'She's blossomed,' Solly added.

'I'll look forward to seeing her, then.'

'I'll invite you to the wedding. It'll be a grand affair. At the Grand Hotel.'

'I'll drink to that.' Avram chased down the ale with a nip of the local blend that burned his throat with the coarseness. 'Old friends.'

'Lest they should be forgot.' Solly tossed back his whisky. 'And how is the clothing business?'

'Slack. With weather like this, waterproofs are not the first thing on people's minds. But I cannot complain. Things have moved fast the last few years. Faster than I dared expect when we started up.'

'You were always good with figures. I would have had you for my betting business if you'd stuck around. And what about the football?'

'I used to play for Argyll Thistle for a few years after the war. But I don't play any more.'

'I'm sorry to hear that. You always had a talent.'

'No time for it, really.'

'I see.' Solly scrunched out his cigarette in an ashtray the size of an automobile hubcap, immediately lit up another. No fancy rings this time. Just an ordinary cloud of smoke breathed out on a heavy sigh. 'I was there, you know.'

'Where?'

'In Oban. For the match against Celtic.'

'You were there? Why the hell didn't you tell me?'

Solly shrugged. 'You're not going to like this, Avram. But you see, the business with Stein was all my idea.'

'What? The betting?'

'Aye, the betting. I knew your Uncle Mendel was in trouble. He owed me a bundle and he was intae Jacob Stein and a few nasty types for a hell of a lot more. The Celtic match was a godsend. Punters are always looking for a bit of excitement away from the usual win, lose or draw bets on the football. So I thought, why not a punt on a goal against Celtic. No Highland league team had put one past them in the history of the Cup. I sold the idea to Stein. Told him you played for the Thistle and with Celtic not knowing a thing about you, I thought a goal against was a useful tip. I think Stein got three-to-one for it around the town. I knew he might get his wee hard man Dodds to lean on you a bit. Use your uncle as bait to secure his investment. But I thought you could handle it. Especially if it got your uncle off the hook.'

'You didn't count on Begg evening out the odds, did you?'

'I'm sorry about that. Best laid schemes, as Rabbie Burns would say.'

Begg blabbing his big mouth off to Willie Maley meant Avram was marked tight right from the off, tighter even than the time Ginger Dodds tailed him. Fergus Connelly was the Celtic right-back that day, Scottish international with around sixteen caps. A lumbering lump of a player with feet that looked as if they'd been launched down a Clydeside slipway but what Big Fergie lost on grace, he made up in knowing what to expect from his opponent. Whichever way Avram tried to twist and turn the Celtic defender, Big Fergie had him covered close with a leg outstretched as thick as a caber to take the ball away. The goals were going in fast the other end with Bobby Logan the goalie missing the ball like he used to miss German sniper bullets. It was eight-nil to the Celtic at half-time, Avram only seeing the ball a couple of times in the first forty-five minutes with Big Fergie taking care of him nice and easy on both occasions. Ginger Dodds was fuming at the break, his lips all wound up tight, mouthing obscenities. And Begg, poking his good eye at him as if he were wagging a finger. 'You're letting me down again, Jew boy. You're letting me down.'

The second half wasn't much better, except that the Celts eased off slightly, what with an Old Firm game the following week, so the score steadied at twelve-nil with about the same number of minutes to go. It was then that the ball finally came to Avram, landing snug on his instep like it deserved to be there, just as it had that very first time on a cobbled street right around the corner from where they sat now when Solly had called on him to play. This time he managed to drag the ball past Big Fergie's lunge and he was off on a run. It was a blessed few moments when all of his senses sharpened to a fineness, so that even now, sitting in this Glasgow pub, he could hear the noise from the crowd all swirled up in that valley, Fergie breathing heavy behind him. He jinked between another two Celtic players, dribbled into the penalty area. But the ball had skipped just that little bit too far ahead of him. Fergie was back on top of him and he knew the full-back's tackle would be good. That was when he made his decision. Not many could have seen it and no-one clearly if they had. He was surrounded by players when it happened. And even Fergie seemed unsure if he had taken him clean or not. But the referee blew his whistle. Penalty.

As Avram lay breathless on the turf, he thought he had got off easy, marking off his successes in his head – duty done for Uncle Mendel, money for a business, hopefully a trial for Celtic. After all, what was one goal against Celtic's twelve. Hardly a dent in their pride, never mind the scoreline. But he sensed a figure hovering, blotting out the winter sunlight in a stoop over him.

'That wasnae right, son,' was all Patsy said. 'That wasnae right.'

At the end of the game, a few of the Celtic players came over to shake his hand, even Fergus who had made the tackle, but Patsy Gallacher cut him off dead, turned his back, walked away from his approach. It was like a knife going into Avram's gut, twisted deep, almost doubling him over from the pain of it. He never heard from Begg or any other Celtic scout again, never told Uncle Mendel what had happened. That goal was the one glorious moment for the Argyll Thistle and he wouldn't have been able to tell anyone any different and no-one would have listened even if he did. Never once did he hear a suggestion he had taken a dive. *The Oban Gazette*, its motto of *Only the Truth and Nothing But* writ proud above its banner, recorded the moment:

Then with twelve minutes to go, Thistle inside-forward

Escovitz set off on a mazy run to match the best of anything produced by Celtic legend Patrick Gallacher. He dribbled past three players but was fouled in the area by Scottish international, Fergus Connelly. Thistle captain Archie Campbell scored with the resultant penalty kick. Twelve-one to Celtic.

He kept the clipping in his wallet. He had an inkling to show it to Solly now, but then thought better to keep it hidden away.

'I was right behind the Celtic goal,' Solly said. 'It was a brilliant run ye did.'

'What about the tackle?'

'Penalty was the shout. And penalty was what they got.'

'But what did you think?'

'I'm a practical man, Avram. I know you used to worry yourself sick with all that "God is watching me" stuff. But sometimes you just have to do what's best for everyone. Even if it's not always the right thing to do.'

'I never got my trial for Celtic. Patsy put the kibosh on that, I'm sure of it.'

'Aye, but you put your Uncle Mendel before yourself. That's got to count for something.'

CHAPTER FORTY-NINE

There had only been a couple of drinks, three at most, but Avram found it hard to focus properly on the stained-glass panel framed in the centre of the doorway. Strange, that in all his years of coming and going, he had never really paid the design much attention before. Perhaps it was because of the dull light in the close that the panel remained unappreciated. The image was of a bird in flight, its wings raised stiff to the vertical, set against a background of branches and berries. There was a border of slim rectangles in vague shades of pale yellows and greens. One of the rectangles had been broken and replaced by a segment of clear glass. He grasped the brass knocker, rapped hard, the sound of his arrival echoing up the stairwell. He waited. He was about to knock again when he heard movement and voices behind the door. A shadow behind the stained-glass panel. He wiped his feet on the mat. The door opened.

The young man before him stood tall. The dark circles of sorrow around the eyes had disappeared to reveal a shining brightness, the face was filled out and there was a stain of colour to the cheeks. But there remained one testament to the moroseness that had overwhelmed this boy Avram used to think of as a *lamed vav*, as one of the thirty-six righteous men placed on this earth to bear the overwhelming burden of suffering. Nathan's hair was completely white.

'You used to tell me you stole my words,' Nathan said. 'Now it seems I've stolen yours.'

'I just didn't…'

'It's all right, Avram. It's the hair, I know. Don't worry, I'm used to it. Come on in. We've been expecting you.'

He let Nathan take his case and lead him into the hallway as his eyes adjusted to the dimness. Madame Kahn was there – thinner, smaller, greyer. Shrinking as Nathan had grown. She wore a Paisley-patterned apron, her hands lightly dusted with flour.

'Avram.' She leaned forward, pecked each of his cheeks. Her lips felt cold and she smelled of lavender. But underneath her familiar scent, a powdered staleness lingered over her skin. 'You're late. And you've been drinking,' she said.

'I'm sorry. I met Solly. We had a couple of drinks.'

'Martha, Martha, Martha.' Papa Kahn emerged out of his study, hobbling on a cane. 'He hasn't even got both feet through the doorway and you're telling him off.'

Avram noticed the man's bloodshot eyes, the skin a yellowish vellum, the backs of the hands brown-spotted. No longer a man of contrasts, of blacks and whites, but of sickly pastels. 'Papa Kahn. Are you well?'

'As well as can be expected.'

'He should be in his bed,' Madame Kahn said. 'It is the time for his nap. He should be lying down. Not standing around in freezing hallways.'

Papa Kahn shook his head, pointed with his stick to the front room. 'Go. Go in there. So we can see you properly.'

The room was exactly the same as when Avram had left, each item of furniture remaining anchored to its chosen spot. He cleared his throat.

'Is Celia home?' he asked.

'How are we supposed to know?' Madame Kahn said. 'She comes and goes as she pleases. She treats this place like a bed and breakfast. Kahn's Bed and Breakfast. I should charge her. Bed and board.'

'Martha,' Papa Kahn said firmly.

'Celia has her work to do,' Nathan said. 'She will be here soon.'

'Bah. You call what she does work,' Madame Kahn snapped. 'Bed and board she should pay. And why not?'

Nathan turned away from his mother. 'Celia is very involved in politics. Not just with the suffragettes, but the socialists as well. There are meetings. Many meetings. They go on until very late. Usually on the other side of the city. It is safer for her to stay there than to try and come home in the dark. This is what mother means.'

'A father should stop a daughter doing such things,' Madame Kahn muttered.

Papa Kahn ignored her. 'Let me have a look at you,' he said. 'You have grown into a young man. Don't you think so, Martha? A young *mensch*.'

'A *mensch*? I don't think so. A young *mensch* doesn't drink in the afternoon. A *shiekerer,* maybe.'

'I only had a couple of drinks,' Avram protested.

'And you know from whom he gets such habits?' Papa Kahn said to his wife.

Madame Kahn folder her arms high on her chest. 'I have better things to do than listen to insults against my brother. There are cakes to bake.' And she left the room.

Papa Kahn shrugged. 'A *schnapps*. That's what I need. Not the naps but the *schnapps*, eh? Now where is that decanter?' He looked around the room on the swivel of his cane before settling himself down in a lean against the piano stool. 'I still see your mother in you, Avram. I can still see her. In the eyes and forehead. A beautiful woman she was. But there is no news of her. Nothing. After all these years. We would have told you, of course. Even though you stay away, we would communicate such things. And your teeth? How are your teeth?'

Avram smiled for the first time since his arrival. 'My teeth are fine.'

'See. What did I tell you? Bicarbonate of soda. It's good you listen to such an old man.'

'I listened to you about my teeth. But I'm not listening to you calling yourself an old man.' Yet he saw the frailty in Papa Kahn. Not just the physical weakness, but the loss of confidence in the dart of the eyes, their unwillingness to focus, their knowing that the body had let him down once already and would inevitably do so again.

'The body is weak, Avram. But the mind is still sharp, eh?' He tapped at his temple. 'Numbers. I'm still good with numbers. Go on. Test me. Fractions. Square roots. Go on. The mind is still sharp, I tell you. Sharp like a razor.'

Nathan came over, took his father by the arm. 'Come, Papa. It is time for you to rest. You are becoming over-agitated. A nap before *shul*, Papa. Time to lie down.'

'What I need is a *schnapps*. Where is that decanter?'

'Come, Papa,' Nathan quietly insisted. 'Come with me. Time for the naps. Not the *schnapps*.'

Avram pulled back the net curtains, hauled open a window, loosened his tie, brought a chair up close to the cool breeze. He sat down, only to stand up again, longing for another drink, a cigarette, anything to stop the fidget in his hands. He noticed the newly-installed telephone shiny-black on a table in the corner, thought to call Megan at the Great Northern. He had the number somewhere in one of his pockets. Instead, he lifted up the piano lid, randomly picked out two adjacent keys from the ivory mass. Back and forward with the same notes, trying to find a rhythm to calm himself. Nathan came back into the room.

'It certainly isn't Mozart.'

'Tell me what is going on here. Are they all right?'

'Not really. Mother has never got over the camps. And Papa has never really recovered from his illness. They both live in constant fear. Mother of recapture, Papa of death. Mother thinks she sees spies everywhere. For Papa, the slightest pain signifies a heart attack. They are going quite mad. And taking it out on each other, of course.'

'How can you stand it?'

Nathan shrugged. 'I just laugh.'

'You just laugh?'

'What else can I do? You saw what happened to me before. There is so much suffering in the world. Laughter is the only response, don't you think? Otherwise, we would die from the pain.'

Avram slowly brought down the piano lid. A cushioned thud where the baize kissed baize. He couldn't remember the last time he had laughed. Really laughed. Out of pure joy. 'You know, I used to think you were a *lamed vav*.'

Nathan chuckled. 'The legend of the thirty-six just men.'

'I envied you for that.'

'Why? Being chosen by God to carry the burden of the world's suffering is hardly something to envy.'

'I just thought it must be wonderful to be able to feel things so strongly. I used to think I stole your words. Sometimes I thought you stole my feelings.'

'Nobody could steal your feelings, Avram. You have them locked away too tight.'

* * *

Everyone was getting dressed for *shul*, Avram was sitting alone in the front room, half-dozing, when suddenly she was there. No time to button up his collar. No time to smooth down his hair. No time to guard against the sudden lurching sensation in his stomach. She was smiling. Breathless. No make-up. A beret perched on her dark curls. Belt twisted loosely and carelessly around a green woollen coat. Her arms stretched around a leather bag crammed full of notebooks and pamphlets. She quickly dumped the bag down on a chair.

'Do you not have a hug for me?' she asked.

He stood up, slipped his hands inside her coat, clasped her around her waist. She felt light. Skinny. Not like Megan. When did she become like this? So thin that he felt he could toss her high in the air. Like a bride. He imagined her sitting in bleak tenement rooms with fellow revolutionaries, debating issues, discussing tactics, printing off pamphlets. No time to eat. This Fast would be easy for her.

Her arms grabbed around his neck and she kissed him on the cheek. On both cheeks.

'Is that a kiss for a comrade?' he asked.

'That's a kiss for someone I've missed very much.'

She pushed away from him, looked him up and down. Confidently. He wondered if there had been lovers.

'You've grown up,' she said.

'So have you. You look beautiful.' He didn't mean to be so forthright, but he too felt confident. Revelling in the strength gained from sex with one woman as a defence against another.

'Thank you.' She danced around him as if he were a model on display. 'A brotherly compliment, I assume.'

'I'm not your brother.'

'Might as well be.' She dropped down into an armchair, took out a packet of cigarettes from one of her pockets. There was a slight tear in one of her stockings, just above the ankle. 'Smoke?'

'They let you?'

'They can't stop me.' She picked up a chunky solid-silver lighter usually reserved for guests. She flicked at the lever several times but the fuel had run dry. 'Damn,' she said, rummaging again in her coat pockets until she found a box of matches. 'Why are you staring?'

'You've changed.'

'You mean I smoke and swear.'

'Maybe.'

'Maybe you are wondering what happened to darling little Celia?'

She puffed several times on her cigarette. Some ash dropped on to her coat, which she quickly swept aside.

'Not really,' he said. 'You always were different.'

'Not "always", surely.'

'Yes, always. You wanted to be a clippie when the war started. You could only have been fifteen then. The last time I saw you, you were off to a demonstration in George Square.'

From between her lips she released little kisses of smoke to the air. 'I'm committed, Avram. That's the difference. Not like them.' She waved a hand behind her.

'They're committed to Judaism,' he offered.

'Hah,' she sniffed. 'They pay lip-service to Judaism. I don't think they really have a clue what's at the heart of their religion. Or what their prayers mean. Tell me, Avram. What are you committed to these days? What do you really care about? Is it still the football?'

That was Celia. No small talk. No 'Hello, how are you?' No 'What are the Highlands like?' With Celia, there was no beating around the bush. It was straight to the core. Like a Grand Inquisitor. And suddenly he found himself talking not about the football but about Megan. How they had met, the way her hair used to be, the songs she sang, the time spent out on the peninsula. Telling her everything. Sharing secrets like they used to do. All the words stored up for so long coming out in a rush, sometimes not knowing if it was Megan or Celia he was really talking about. He even told her what had happened with Sinclair. And the abortion.

'Megan said there was a good chance,' he said. 'If it was done early.'

'That's her just being brave. It's a bad business. You've got to be lucky to survive, early or not. If she doesn't bleed to death, the infection can kill her.'

'How do you know so much about it?'

'It's my business to know these things. Are you sure this child isn't yours?'

'I told you already.'

'Well, you're going to an awful lot of bother for someone not carrying your own.'

He shrugged. 'Like I said. It's not my child.'

'So why are you doing this?'

'I don't know.'

'Oh, Avram. What are you afraid of? Why don't you just admit that sometimes you have feelings for people?'

He was ready to hit back with some smart retort. But he felt an unfamiliar scratching in his throat, had to gulp it down, hold back the churn of emotion. For Celia's question had probed deep and all he could think of at that moment was a vision of his mother turning her back on him on a cold Riga pier. Celia appeared to guess the answer to her own question for she didn't wait for his response. But her tone had softened when she asked:

'When is the appointment?'

'I don't know ... about half-past seven, I think.'

'Right in the middle of the *Kol Nidre* service.'

'She didn't want me around anyway. But I'll try to get away when the service is finished. Just to check she is all right.'

'And I'll come with you. This is women's work, Avram. You wouldn't have a clue what to do.'

CHAPTER FIFTY

Avram's head ached, his dinner lay heavy in his stomach. All he wanted to do was close his eyes, wait for his food to lurch towards digestion, let what remained of this intense day flow past him. Yet here he was, stuck in full view of the congregation, with no place to hide. All the pew seats were reserved, but Papa Kahn had managed to book him a seat in the overflow – the several rows of folding chairs set out on the floor space between the Ark and the *bimah*. This was where he joined the other nomadic Jews. Those visiting their families in the city, those passing through from Edinburgh and onwards to America. Or those too poor to pay the synagogue's seat-rental charge.

Even in this painful exile, mercilessly exposed to the curious eyes sweeping over him, some sizing him up as future son-in-law material, he remembered how he used to enjoy being in the synagogue on *Yom Kippur* eve. Sitting in the twilight waiting for the *Kol Nidre* service to begin. Such an earnestness about the place as congregants assembled in a rush from their early suppers, souls primed for spiritual examination, hearts aching for forgiveness. Pew ledges clicking back, seat-lids opening and closing in the search for *tallithim* and prayer books, handshakes all round. Good *Yom Tov*, Good *Yom Tov*, Well over the Fast. The settling down into a time for contemplation. A time for repentance. A time to ask to be written into the Book of Life for yet another year. To discover who shall live and who shall die. Who by fire. Who by water. Who by the sword. Who by wild beasts. Who shall be at rest. And who shall wander.

This evening he wasn't the only curio on display. Up on the *bimah* stood Cantor Levy, dressed in white robes and a white silk Cossack-style hat. Much was expected of the new *chazan*, leased like some milk-cow from a synagogue in London, this squat, baby-faced man with a roly-poly figure perfectly proportioned to be a chamber for the voice.

'A great milestone in the history of our synagogue,' Papa Kahn had explained to Avram over dinner. Papa Kahn grabbing his arm, talking as if he were addressing the *shul* committee of which it seems he was still treasurer. 'Having our very own *chazan* represents the reaching of maturity for our Jewish community in the Gorbals.'

'But Uncle Mendel told me the Jews are moving out of the Gorbals. Further south. To Queens Park. To Langside.'

'What does Mendel know? He doesn't even return home for *Yom Kippur*. What kind of a Jew has he become? Listen, Avram. The Gorbals will always be the heart of the Jewish community in Glasgow. Garnethill may be the head. But the Gorbals is the heart. The rest of the body can go wherever it pleases.'

'I'm just glad we don't have to listen to Lieberman,' Celia said. 'I don't know what made me feel worse. His singing or the fasting.'

Avram scanned his fellow-congregants, exchanged silent greetings with Solly, seated beside his father, the recently-retired bookmaker Morris Green – Lucky Mo, with his bald head glistening under the newly-installed electric lights. Further along sat Old Man Arkush, the baker who used to store Madame Kahn's *cholent* pots in his ovens over the *Shabbos*, probably still did for all he knew. And there in the front row in his fine blue-mohair suit, fending off the outstretched hands of well-wishers, reigned Jacob Stein. Yes, of course, Jacob Stein – the *ganze macher*. The warehouse owner, his former employer, a city bailie, a founder of this very synagogue. And the organiser of betting syndicates. Shaking hands, bestowing his patronage, a firm grip here, a touch to the upper arm there, his shiny little moustache working overtime as it curved and straightened over the smile of his upper lip, the tobacco-stained teeth revealed. Avram realised he hadn't actually seen Jacob Stein in person since before the war had ended, since the day he'd been told he had to work with Uncle Mendel as a credit draper. Yet somehow the man had always been there in the background. Pulling strings.

Jacob Stein donned his *tallith*, lowered his bulky frame into his seat, an action that appeared to galvinize the other congregants into doing the same. Avram turned his attention to Rabbi Lieberman, his old *barmitzvah* teacher wedged into his single pew by the side of the Ark, hooded under his white garments, the weary eyes peering out from beneath his veil of silk, waiting patiently for his flock to settle. Then the rabbi's finger arched ever so slightly to signal commencement to his usurper on the *bimah* opposite. The *chazan* clasped his arms to his stomach, his flushed jowls trembled as he sang the first words of the *Yom Kippur* service.

Kol Nidre…

The notes were good, Avram thought. A mellifluous tenor voice as crisp and sweet as apple dipped in honey, soothing even to the pain inside his head, and he muttered his response along with the rest of the congregation. He tried to read on but the pounding behind his eyes made it difficult to focus on the text. Instead, his thoughts drifted back to the dinner table.

'… and not only a *chazan*,' Madame Kahn had continued. 'Soon we will have a *kosher* restaurant in the city.'

'And then you'll want your own *kosher* public house,' Celia said.

Papa Kahn turned to her. 'You might reject our ways, young woman. You might think all our customs mean nothing. That we ramble on with our prayers in a language most of us do not understand. But what is important is that we sit down in the synagogue as a community.'

'Papa,' Nathan said. 'You are becoming too excited.'

Papa Kahn brought his fist down on the table. His wife covered her face with her hands. 'Tell him to calm down,' she wailed. 'Tell him to stop.'

'No, I want Celia should understand this. It was the community that helped me when I arrived here. It was the community that helped your mother, the community that gave your uncle a job. Community, community, community. This Jewish community. It is not so different from this socialism.'

For once, Celia said nothing. But Madame Kahn rose from the table, strode over to the piano. She lifted the lid and began to play. A Scottish melody.

'Martha, please,' her husband called to her. 'Come and sit down.'

Madame Kahn continued, banging out the notes with an unnecessary harshness.

'Martha. We are in the middle of dinner.'

Madame Kahn stood up, walked calmly over to the open window.

'Only Scottish songs heard in this household,' she shouted out into the street until Nathan pulled her back. 'No German music. No Bach or Beethoven here. Only Scottish songs.'

Avram rose with the congregation for the *Amidah* prayer. A time to repent. A time to forgive and to ask for forgiveness. To rock back and forth in rhythm to his own silent mouthing of the words in front of him. To pound a fist into his chest above his heart as a symbol of atonement for his sins. So many sins.

Profanation of the Divine Name.
Wronging one's neighbour
Despising parents and teachers
Violence
Envy
Effrontery
Evil inclination
Unchastity
Denying and lying
Scoffing
Slander
The taking of bribes
Vain oaths
Breach of trust
Causeless hatred
Wanton looks
Haughty eyes
Turning aside
Being stiff-necked
Hardening of the heart

He stopped there, snapped his prayer book shut. If there was another sin to add to the list he had just read, he knew it would be the one he was about to commit now. Only sudden illness or death itself could excuse a person during the utterance of the *Amidah* prayer. And this was a matter of life. He squeezed himself to the end of the row. He saw the rabbi pushing aside the veil of his *tallith*, the look of shock on Cantor Levy's face. Suddenly, an arm shot out to block his path. Avram looked down at the blue-mohair sleeve then up to the face of the suit's owner.

'Where do you think you're going?' Jacob Stein hissed at him. 'It's the middle of the *Amidah*. Have some respect.'

Avram looked straight back at his obstructor, taking in the oiled-back hair, the fleshy lips, the lack of recognition in the man's stare.

'Let me be,' he said, angrily pushing away the hand.

Jacob Stein's hard little eyes lit up. 'Ah yes, now I see. Avram. Avram Escovitz. The footballer. Who never got to play for Celtic.' He leaned forward to whisper close to Avram's ear. 'Don't blame me. It was your decision in the end. Just remember that. Your decision.'

Jacob Stein pulled back, returned his attention to his prayer book, waved a hand of dismissal. But Avram didn't move. Instead, in the same way he'd earlier seen Stein bestow his little kindnesses on his fellow congregants, he took hold of the warehouse owner's upper arm. But firmly. Feeling the soft, fleshy muscle give way easily under his grasp. Like a woman's arm, Avram thought, as he saw Jacob Stein's face wince to his grip.

'And I forgive you, Herr Stein,' he said calmly. 'I forgive you.'

And with that remark he let go his hold, continued down the aisle beside the *bimah*, suddenly aware of the sound of his heartbeat and the certain lightness to his step. He glanced up at the gallery where Celia stood in a broad-rimmed hat, her head bowed over in prayer. He thought she might not have seen him, that he would have to aggravate his sin even further by calling out her name. But she lifted her face. Without hesitating, she closed her prayer book, and despite her mother's protests, she too made her way to the exit.

'Let me ask you again,' Celia said to him in the vestibule. 'This is definitely not your child?'

'Definitely not.'

'And now you want to stop this?'

'I'm sure. Will you come with me?'

'Of course.'

'Good. Let's find a hansom.'

'A hansom? On *Yom Kippur*?'

'We could be sent to hell for less.'

'To the *fabriken*.'

It had started to rain.

'A tram might be quicker,' Celia said, pulling her hat tight around her face.

'Whichever comes first.'

The cab came first.

'Trongate,' he told the driver, then sank back into the leather seat. Celia took his hand.

'You're shaking,' she said.

He held the small hand tighter. Somehow he had imagined this scene before. Hand in hand with Celia, seated in the back of a hansom. A slight drizzle outside. Both of them dressed in their best. A sense of common purpose to their journey. He thought it was to their wedding they were going.

'Do you love her?' Celia asked.

'I don't know. Maybe I just don't want to abandon her. Anyway, I always thought it was you I loved.'

He felt the pressure of her hand increase. 'I know you did. But now?'

'If the world were the walls of this carriage, and we could just sit here holding hands like this, then yes, I could say I love you.'

'And outside this carriage?'

'Too much has changed.' He felt her grip tighten again. Those tiny fingers. Leading him once to the top landing of the close. Childhood games. 'And you are so committed now, Celia. You have all these causes. You know what you want. I cannot compete with that. I feel like a nothing beside you. I only ever wanted to prove to you I could be a somebody.'

'But you are a somebody in my eyes. Look at what you are doing now.'

'I think it will be too late for that.' He pulled down the window, shouted to the driver. 'Hurry, please. This is urgent.'

CHAPTER FIFTY-ONE

The driver stopped at the end of a dim lane, lit at the entrance by a solitary gas lamp.

'Ye'll have tae walk frae here,' the cab driver said. 'But go careful.'

The whole length of one side of the lane seemed to consist solely of the back ends of pubs. The air reeked of alcohol from empty barrels piled high. Avram could hear the voices of male drinkers. Not cheery sounds. But harsh swearing. Shouting. A window slammed from somewhere above them. More shouting. A woman's voice this time. He stumbled on something underfoot. He heard a groan, stopped and peered into the shadows. He had tripped over someone's outstretched legs.

'What is it?' Celia asked.

'Somebody lying in the gutter.'

'Is he all right?'

A mumbling from the prostrate body. 'Drunk,' Avram said.

'Come on, then. Look for the numbers on the doors. There's another lamp further up.'

A figure emerged out of the greyness. 'Lookin' for something?' A woman's voice. Warm in the questioning, but cold underneath.

'Number sixteen,' Celia said.

The woman stepped back. 'Thought you was on yer own,' she said to Avram.

'Help us,' Celia said. She took the woman's arm, led her into the light. Avram could see her full now. Lank hair. Smudges of powder on a pasty face. Coat wrapped tight over her small body. She was probably eighteen, maybe less, looked a lot older. Lamb dressed as mutton.

'This is the address,' Celia said, showing her a piece of paper.

The woman laughed. 'I cannae read.'

'It says: Number sixteen. Saracen's Lane.'

'This is Saracen's Lane alright. I dinnae ken about no number sixteen.'

Celia leaned forward, whispered something into the woman's ear.

'I ken whit yer after' She pointed somewhere up to the left in the darkness. 'Three doors up. But I havenae seen her all day. I might have missed her but. I've had my busy times, ye ken.'

Celia reached into her coat pocket for her purse, pressed a few coins into the woman's hand.

Avram moved further up the lane, feeling his way along the dank, slimy walls. An invisible animal brushed by his ankle. He kicked out. Nothing.

He turned back to Celia. 'Give me your hand.'

'I can't see it.'

He poked his hand about in the darkness until he located her arm, moving down the sleeve of her coat to her fingers. They were cold and clammy. He stumbled on. No air came from above. The sweat was dripping off him.

'How can people live here?' he said but Celia didn't answer. He counted off three doorways and stopped.

'This must be it.'

'Let me see.'

She moved passed him, struck a match, held it up to the doorway. He saw the number sixteen chalked on the stone and knocked on the damp wooden door. Silence. He knocked again. There were no windows to the front, if there were any at all, but he thought he glimpsed a slither of light from under the door. He was sure he heard movement. He held his breath.

'Whit?' a voice said sharply from behind the door.

'Is Megan Kennedy there?'

No response. He could hear Celia's breathing behind him. Swollen drops of rain falling from a gutter into a puddle. He knocked again.

'I'm looking for Megan Kennedy.'

'Who?' came the voice.

'Megan Kennedy.'

'I dinnae ken names.'

'We're friends,' Celia said.

'How do I ken that?'

'You'll have to trust us.'

The clunking of a key in the lock. The door opened slightly, the light of a candle washed out into the lane. The woman came up no higher than Avram's chest. The candle glow showed a square face, the top of a head sparsely covered with clumps of reddish hair. He recognised the smell about her. Ether.

'Is that her?' she said tilting the candle towards Celia.

'Who?' Avram asked.

'The Oban lass.'

'That's who we're looking for.'

The woman peered up at them both. She had no eyebrows, her thin lips drooped at the corners in a terrible sadness.

'She's no been,' she sighed and quickly withdrew the candle. 'She should be here by now. But she's no been.' The door closed in their faces.

'Thank God,' he said. A feeling of nausea passed over him. He leaned forward until his brow touched the dampness of the stone wall. The slimy coolness slightly soothed his aching head.

'I'll let the lady up,' the man at the reception desk of the Great Northern Hotel said. 'But not you.'

'I'm the one paying the bill.'

'Changes nothing. Rules is rules.'

'It's probably better I go alone,' Celia said.

'I'll wait here.'

Avram settled down into an old leather sofa in the foyer. The concierge had stayed at his desk, flicking from page to page of his vast ledger, running a yellow-stained finger fast down the columns. Avram wanted to ask him for a cigarette but Celia was back at the top of the stairs.

'The door's locked,' she shouted. 'She's not answering.'

The concierge looked up from his books. 'I'll bring a key.'

'I'm coming with you,' Avram said.

The concierge looked at him, sniffed hard. 'Aye. All right then.'

Celia rattled the handle while Avram pounded the door.

'Let me,' the concierge said, catching up, breathless, finding the master key.

The door opened. The room was empty. Celia rushing to the open window.

'Nothing,' she said. 'Just the yard.'

'Must be out,' the concierge said. 'Although I didnae see her pass. And I've been sat there all day, what with my books to do and everything.'

'Bathroom,' Avram shouted. 'Where is it?'

'On yer left. Last door along the corridor.'

It was locked too. Avram knocked hard, grazing his knuckles but still no answer. 'Do you have a key for this one?'

'Aye. Just let me find it.'

The concierge opened up. Megan lay slumped in the bath. Still in her slip, skin bluish, wrinkled. A half-empty bottle of gin on the floor. Celia was there first. Head close in.

'She's still breathing. Help me get her out.'

The water was tepid. Avram took her under the shoulders, Celia took the feet. She lifted out nice and easy, laid on to a towel, cotton fabric clinging to her skin, cold nipples poking through.

'What's all this about?' The concierge pushed in, getting a good look. 'She's no dead, is she?'

'It's nothing to worry about,' Avram told him, fearing the lie in his words. 'She'll be fine.'

'She disnae look fine to me'

'She's drunk that's all. Fell asleep in the bath. Help me take her back.'

'I'm no touching her.'

Avram fished out his wallet, handed over a note. 'Take this.'

'I don't know. I might need to alert the polis.'

He pressed another ten shillings note into the concierge's hand. 'We can handle this ourselves. If there's a problem, I'll let you know.'

Celia, on the floor now, rubbing Megan hard with the towel. 'Old wives tales,' she said. 'Soak in a boiling hot tub. Flush it out with gin.'

'Will she be all right?'

'Let's carry her through. Get her warm first.'

'What about the baby?'

'We won't know for sure till the morning.'

Celia helped him carry her into the bedroom, bundled her up tight under the blankets. 'I'll see if I can fetch a hot bottle,' she said. 'You watch her.'

He watched her all night. Paid for another room on the same floor to keep the concierge off his back. Celia went home. When he wasn't in a guard by her bed, he was up by the window. It was a clear night and he could see the familiar glow from the foundry chimneys smeared against the starless sky. It was as if, many years ago, the City of Glasgow had lit a cigarette that had never gone out. A groan from Megan brought him back to her bedside. She had stopped shivering, there was even a smidgen of colour to her cheeks. Her breathing came easier and there was no fever. He took her hand, kneaded some warmth into her skin, watched the thick wrinkles disappear from her fingertips.

CHAPTER FIFTY-TWO

Avram helped Nathan bring out the card-table, folded out the legs until they locked, then placed it square in the centre of the room. Celia came in for the game. She strode around the room barefoot, her grey silk blouse hanging loose from the waistband of her skirt. Outside, a cut of lightning sliced through the hot heaviness of the evening. A thunder-boom and the rain streamed down. As if the confessions of the Jews had been too much for God to take, and now He was weeping at the failings of His people. Better God than Nathan, Avram thought as he prised open the window.

'Thank goodness,' Celia said, fanning her face with her free hand, flicking ash on to the carpet with the other. 'It's as hot as a bloody foundry in here.'

She took up her place at the table. Avram sat opposite, set an ashtray by her hand. A thin film of sweat had formed on her upper lip. Nathan dealt.

'I thought they accepted your situation quite calmly, don't you think?' she said, snatching up her cards from the baize. The green cloth was rubbed raw in places by impatient fingers, a couple of cigarette burns brown-spotted the surface close to where she sat. 'Considering your belle is not Jewish.'

'If almost complete silence means accepting the situation calmly,' Avram said, 'then they were very considerate.'

He had waited until the Fast was over before returning to the Kahn household. Apologised immediately for walking out of the *Kol Nidre* service, explained to Papa and Madame Kahn what had happened with Megan, what was going to happen with her. He wasn't sure why he had told them, letting them preside over his actions in their after-the-Fast bloatedness like some rabbinical court. But what could they do? Even in their disapproval, they had no power over him. He was not their son. He did not need their money. He wasn't even sure if he needed their blessing.

'At least she's British,' Madame Kahn had said before retiring to her bedroom. Papa Kahn had remained for a while, sitting silently in the tension, scraping patterns of loose sugar on the table-cloth with the edge of a butter knife. Avram thought perhaps he hadn't heard or fully understood what he had told him. Then the man had risen wearily from the table and disappeared into his study.

'It is all right for the both of you,' Nathan said. 'You go off and abandon them to me. I'm the one who gets all the complaints.'

'I can't help it if you never leave the house,' Celia snapped as she plucked and placed her cards within their fan. 'You see, Avram. That's why the poor boy's hair turned white.' She leaned over and ruffled Nathan's hair. 'They never saw the light of day, did they, these poor curls. They just drained of colour.'

Avram began to pick up his cards, one by one, sorting them into potential runs and trebles. 'Do you have any beau in your life?' he asked her. 'Or do you just sit in your own dark rooms plotting revolutions?'

'I will never marry,' she declared. 'I might love a man. But I will never be his property. Anyway, I'm thinking of emigrating to Palestine.'

'Palestine? Why would you do that?'

'Jews from Russia are building communities there,' she said. 'Socialist communes. *Kibbutzim*. There they have equality between men and women.'

'She wants to work on the land,' Nathan interjected, dealing out the last of the cards. 'This urbane miss intends to become a Zionist spinster.'

'I am going to build a Jewish state from the toil of these fair hands,' she said, scrubbing out her cigarette in the ashtray. Her nails were buffed and painted rosy red in the modern style.

Avram tried to imagine her milking cows or tying up the stooks or bent over stiff from the planting. He picked up the last of his cards. He couldn't believe what he had been dealt. No clubs or spades. Just hearts and diamonds. Love and money. A blood-red hand.

'And Avram is leaving us also,' Nathan said. 'The Jews of the Gorbals are not good enough for this young clothing tycoon.'

'I left the Gorbals a long time ago, my little *lamed vav*. And I left my Judaism behind too. The only difference now is I'm finally making a commitment to somewhere else. To someone else.'

'Well, you are always welcome here if you should choose to return. As Papa says, this is your community.'

Somewhere in the house a bell rang. Avram thought it must be the telephone but Celia looked up worried from her cards. 'I'll go and see what he wants.'

'It's Papa,' Nathan explained when she had left. 'It's Papa's bell.'

'He wants to see you,' Celia said to Avram on her return. 'Try not to keep him long.'

So many of the important events of Avram's life had taken place in this study. It had witnessed his arrival in this country, the night before his *barmitzvah*, the banning of the football. It was as if from their high position on the shelves all these Talmudic tracts inscribed with their laws and their ethics had stood forever in judgement of him. Papa Kahn now sat in the midst of all this inherited wisdom, his face glowing ghostly behind the solitary desk lamp, his fingers playing with the shiny ivory beads of the abacus. Click. Click. Click. It was a soothing sound. Regular. Predictable. Counting. Numbers.

'Lock the door.'

The request surprised Avram but he did what he was told. Then he moved some bolts of waterproof cloth off the only other seat in the room, sat down. He watched Papa Kahn follow the path of the beads, his yellowish eyes hypnotised by the movement. Click. Click. Click. Eventually the man spoke, talking as if he were continuing a conversation he had been having with himself for a very long time.

'...how they came for us these Cossacks. Like pigs sniffing out truffles. And each time, the Jewish elders had to hand over another few males to the army. Like a tithe. Or a sack of wheat. I escaped the first few visits but I knew it would soon be my turn. And it wasn't just the young men they were after. It was the young women, too. Not just like pigs now. But like hungry wolves. Do you remember your mother, Avram? How beautiful she was.'

Avram tried to remember, tried to form the features of her face from the haziness of his memory. The exact shape and colour of her eyes, the breadth of her forehead, the tone of her skin, the length of her hair. But there was no longer an image of Rachel Escovitz to be salvaged. All that remained was the smell of the skin on her neck.

The door handle shook. Madame Kahn's voice.

'Who locks a door in this house? What is going on in there? He is not to get excited? Do you hear, Avram? Herschel? Who locks a door in a house?'

'Everything is all right, Martha. Isn't it, Avram?'

'Everything is all right.'

'Now, leave us.'

The handle shook one last time.

Papa Kahn shifted in his chair and continued.

'You see, Avram, I loved your mother. I loved Rachel very much. But not enough.' Papa Kahn closed his eyes, hooded them from the desk-light with the cup of his hand. The fingers were almost without flesh. 'For they were coming after me too, these Cossacks. Closing in with their quotas. Quotas, quotas and more damned quotas. Quotas to stop me from studying. More quotas for the army. And what did I do? What did I do?'

Papa Kahn let the question hang, as if he was testing himself again, perhaps hoping this time for the answer to be different. Avram waited too, listening to the rain battering against the window, the click, click, click of the abacus beads marking out the passage of time. Papa Kahn cleared his throat.

'I ran away, Avram. Nothing more than a coward. I abandoned her, even though I loved her. The curse of a fearful man.' A long sigh. The tired escape of breath from withered lungs. 'I had heard the stories, of course. A man from a nearby village who had made his fortune in America. How that word sounded to me then. America. America. Like Paradise itself. Like a pot of gold. America.' He slumped back in his chair. 'I came here first, as you know. And while I was waiting for a ship to take me to this Paradise across the ocean, I started to like it here. This Glasgow with its little community of Jews. The *kosher* food. The *Yiddish*. The Scots with their tolerance for our ways. Our shared respect for education. For social justice. Of course, I wrote to your mother for a while. For a year perhaps we corresponded. And then nothing. Time passed, things changed. Until you and your letter.' Papa Kahn took off his glasses, rubbed his eyes with the back of his hand. 'And then we never hear from her again.'

'But what about the thimble?' Avram asked. 'The thimble. She sent you the thimble for my *barmitzvah*.'

'Forgive me, Avram. But I lied to you. Your mother gave the thimble to me when I left. A small token of her affection. Dmitry never came that time of your *barmitzvah*. He never came. I just wanted you to have something from your mother.'

Avram looked around him. The bolts of cloth, the abacus, the crumpled figure in the chair opposite. The rows upon rows of books, stacked high, pressing down him. The airlessness of the room making him feel nauseous. 'I must go,' he said.

'No, no, wait. I just want to say one more thing. One more thing. Please listen to a dying man.' With enormous effort, Papa Kahn raised himself from his slump. Avram noticed the loose fit of the suit, the wide gap between shirt collar and throat. A child in adult's clothing. 'About this matter at hand. About this girl.'

'Megan.'

'Yes, Megan. You are not running away like I did, Avram. Not running away. This is good. I want you to know this is what I think. It is something good that you do.'

Avram rose from his seat, backed slowly away from the desk, unlocked the door. Closed it softly behind him. Madame Kahn stood across the hallway in her dressing gown. Her hair was down in a ragged greasy mass of grey-white tresses. Her face ashen and greasy from the smear of some recently applied lotion. She held a hairbrush in her hand.

'Now you know,' she snarled, brandishing the brush at him as if to ward off a curse. 'Now you know all the trouble you brought. This memory of ... of her. Of that woman. It was better when you were away. Much better. So, go now. *Gie avek*. Get out of here. Go back to the Highlands with that *shiekse* of yours.'

He felt his legs heavy, powerless to move from the orbit of this woman's venom. He saw Celia and Nathan come out from the living room, the two of them together, almost a blur, Celia's dark hair merging with Nathan's whiteness.

'*Gie avek*,' Madame Kahn kept on saying. '*Gie avek*.'

He was gulping for breath now as his lungs tried to shift this incredible weight from somewhere deep in his stomach. Faster, harder, this struggle for air. He managed a step forward. And it was Nathan who took him. Nathan who had always been there to give sanctuary to his pain. Nathan who held him in his arms. As the tears started to come. His body shuddering, spasms coarsing through him, ripping him apart. This tremendous release. As the various compartments he had carefully constructed began to collapse in on themselves. Freeing their prisoners to run riot inside of him, to dance over that open sore of a moment when his mother let go of him and disappeared into the mist.

CHAPTER FIFTY-THREE

'They're introducing electric hares at Carntyne,' Solly tried to explain to Megan. 'That should bring back the punters. Then I'll have less to do with the horses and more to do with the dogs.' Solly sank back in the leather upholstery, flicked some cigar ash out of the cab's open window. 'I always liked dogs.'

'When have you ever liked dogs?' Avram remarked. 'I've never seen you with a dog in your life.'

'I have a dog,' Megan said.

'You see, Avram. A woman with my own pleasures at heart. Now are you still coming to my wedding?'

'Send me an invitation and I'll come.'

'You are first on my list. And bring this beautiful lassie with you.'

But both he and Solly knew the truth. There would be an invitation, of course. Followed by a polite refusal and an expensive gift. Better to refuse than try to explain to Megan the fuss he would cause bringing a pregnant Highland girl to a grand Jewish wedding at the Grand Hotel.

At Queen Street station, she complained of a slight nausea, some pain in her abdomen. Quite natural, she said. Just needed to sleep it off. He worried about any damage caused, but she reassured him enough time had passed for her to know the baby was fine. Celia had told him the same, although how women knew these things was a mystery.

He watched her as she slept, her head rolling this way and that with any strong movement of the train. This was his task now, to guard over her and this unborn child in her womb. Feeling all the better for making this commitment to her, crossing an invisible line to leave all that was unresolved, untidy and painful behind. A fresh start. With a wife and child and a good business to build on. But there would be no synagogue or kirk ceremony to mark this transition. Just a declaration before two witnesses. Jean Munro and Archie Campbell would do nicely.

Megan slept right past Stirling and Callander. It was only when the train was climbing its route towards Crianlarich that she awoke, as if roused by the sense of her return to the Highlands. He could smell the freshness himself. The pine. The heather.

'Are ye all right?' she asked him immediately.

'I'm fine. It's you I'm worried about.'

'I meant about the bairn. Saying it's yer ain.'

'If it makes things easier.'

'Stops a lot of wagging tongues is whit it does. It means I can tell Jamie. And mither and faither.'

'Jamie won't be happy we're to be married.'

'He'll be furious. Ye need to set yerself ready for that. But Jamie has his secrets too, there's no point in him trying to be all high and mighty. And in the end he has no choice. Yer making an honest woman of me after all. There will be no bastard child in this family.' She smiled to herself in the comfort of her thought. 'My folks will be happy. A chance for them to make it back to ye for whit happened. Only Jean knows different. I need to tell her what went on in Glesca. She'll be worried.'

'We can stop by to see her now. I'm going to check on the cottage for Uncle Mendel on my way back.'

Megan patted her belly, looked out of the window. 'There's the town,' she said. 'And those big merchant houses on the esplanade look just grand. A fine fit for a merchant family, don't you think?'

Jean was in a distressed state when they arrived. Avram left Megan to sit with her, tell her what had happened. He took a putter and golf ball out of Munro's bag of clubs by the French windows, went out into the garden. The grass was parched yellow in places. Red marker flags danced in the stiff breeze. The waves crashed up against the peninsula boulders not far off, so that he could taste the brine in the wind. He lined up a shot, felt the weight of the putter sit nicely in his hands. A gentle pull back of the club, the sweet sound and feel of a true shot. The white ball spun firmly towards the hole, hit the base of the flag pole, jumped to about three feet from its target. He strode across the turf in the track of the ball. He felt light, light enough for the words of a song to come to his lips. One of Megan's favourites.

I'm o'er young, I'm o'er young
I'm o'er young to marry yet!
I'm o'er young, 't wad be a sin

To tak me frae my mammie yet.

Still humming to himself, he pulled out the flag, lined up his second shot. The ball dropped straight into the hole. Not a roll and a spin around the rim like water down a drain. But a clean plop into the embrace of the cup. So satisfying, that sound. Perhaps this was the game for him now the football was gone. A pair of plus-fours and a tweed jacket, a daily stroll around the links, wife and child waiting at home. A merchant house on the esplanade.

Megan stood at the French windows, beckoning him over. Jean behind her, a worry in her eyes.

'She thinks Donald kens about Jamie coming to visit,' Megan told him.

'What makes her think that?'

'She thinks he's been waiting in the grounds around the house instead of going into Oban. She checked once with Davey the driver of the Cally Rail. Donald hadnae taken the train when he said. She thinks he's out there now. Spying on her.'

'Is Jamie coming over now?' he asked.

Jean shook her head.

'Then there's nothing to worry about. I'm taking a ride out to the cottage. I'll keep a look-out for Donald as I go. Megan can stay here with you.'

With the setting sun on his back, he set out for Lorn and Uncle Mendel's cottage beyond. He kept a watch out for Munro, but soon the road ploughed through the forest and any real chance of sighting the man was gone. At Lorn, he hastened past the Kennedy's cottage, then turned north to Glen Etive and the croft. The gloaming was approaching, bringing with it the mist over the mountains, the diffused light and the muted colours, the chill off the streams and the settling of the animals in the field. Off the main road and half-way down the rutted path to the cottage he pulled up the cart, stepped down to take in the silence. The surface of the loch shone flat, grey-pink clouds barely moved across the sky. He walked the rest of the way, happy to lead the horse by the reins in a loose pull. It was only when he was close to the cottage did he notice the door wide open.

'Is anyone there?' he called.

'Aye, there's someone.'

The squat figure of Donald Munro emerged from the cottage. Another man followed. The quarry guard, Wallie MacPhee. Avram recognised the ugly white scar that rose out of the man's beard and along the side of one eye. Uncle Mendel's angry work. Both men were carrying shotguns.

'Donald Munro. What are you doing here?'

'Waiting.'

'How did you know I'd be coming?'

'Spotted you riding out from my place.' Munro held his gun low to the ground. MacPhee carried his loose underarm but pointed in his direction. 'Saw the shop closed up in the town. Yer lass Jessie didnae seem to ken where you were.'

'I've been in Glasgow for a few days. Just got back.'

MacPhee tensed, tightening the grip on his gun. Munro stretched out a hand as he might to calm his horse or dog. 'Easy, Wallie.'

'What do you want, Donald? And what's he doing here?'

Munro ignored the questions. 'Been to see my wife, then?'

'I dropped Megan Kennedy off at your house, if that's what you're asking.'

'I'm no asking,' said Munro. 'I'm telling. Wallie here says he seen ye coming and going an awfy lot from my place the last couple of weeks.'

'Wallie should mind his own bloody business.'

The blast hit Avram full in his chest, sending him reeling backwards and stumbling towards the ground. He clutched his shattered rib cage where the bullet had pierced, feeling the warmth of his blood flood over his fingers, soaking into his shirt. He tried to raise his head off the ground but the pain held him back. The echo of the shot died away. A moorhen screeched somewhere out beyond the loch. Silence again.

'What the fuck did ye do that for?' he heard Munro scream.

'There's no use to talking. We know what the Jew was up to.'

'I wanted him to tell me himself. For fuck's sake. I didn't want ye to kill him. Go see if he's still alive.'

He could hear the crunch of MacPhee's footsteps approaching. Everything was so clear now. A symphony of sounds. The vibration of the earth. The smell of the rich loam, the wild grass. Why had he not paid attention before? Why did he have to wait until this moment to sense these things so vividly? This flow of breath, this vigorous pumping of his heart, this blood gurgling up in his chest, this moaning on his lips. A shadow. MacPhee stood over him. He winced to the kick in his side.

'Aye. The bastard's alive.'

'Christ, Wallie. What do we do now?'

'We? We do nothing. It's up to ye.'

Not a sound. Just the hard breathing of MacPhee above. Then the stench of the quarry guard as he knelt to place the gun by his body, to unfurl his fingers, tuck a cloth into his grip.

It hurt hard but he managed a breath. 'Help me.'

'Aye, sure.' And then the voice turned away towards Munro. 'It'll look like an accident if any soul should ever find him out here. Cleaning the gun, so he was. The crows should get him first, though.'

The shadow cleared.

'Finish him off.' Munro's words.

'Naw,' said MacPhee. 'Ye do it. I'm off.'

'Ye can't leave him,' Munro shouted after the retreating footsteps.

'I just did.' MacPhee laughed.

'Ye'd leave a man to bleed to death?'

'I'm leaving ye to let him bleed to death.'

'For Christ's sake, Wallie.'

'Oh, come on, Munro. Did ye think I'd let ye pin this all on me? Ye have to play yer part too.'

'I could shoot ye.'

'Ye don't have the guts to shoot a man cold. Ye're too much of a church-goer for that. Even with all yer blasphemin'.' MacPhee's voice died away.

Avram found that if he held still, somehow the agony stayed still too, and he could just observe it. Dispassionately. This gaping chasm of a wound in his chest. The blood clogging his lungs. The rasp in his breath. Another shadow. Munro. Gun barrel wafting above his head, blocking out the sun, then clearing again. A glinting light and then blackness. Horse snorting close by.

'We're in this together, Munro,' MacPhee shouted as he swept past on his mount. 'Ye, me and the devil. I might have shot him, but ye let him die.'

The clatter of hooves, kicking up the earth, Avram feeling the sprinkle of dirt on his face.

Donald Munro peered down at him. 'Say ye did it,' he said, then knelt down on his haunches, moved in close. 'Say ye lay with my wife. Say it.'

He tried to find the strength in his lungs to breathe out the one word that might save him. Jamie. This was what he wanted to say. He could picture the letters in his mind. JAMIE. Jamie. Jamie.

'Say ye did it. Go on, lad. Say ye lay with her.'

Avram began to shiver. Warm blood on his hands, the rest of him cold.

'Suit yourself, then.' Munro rose to his feet. Avram could hear him walk back to the cottage. The snort of horse breath. The jingle of a harness. Munro galloped off. He followed the sound until it faded away into nothing.

His hand put pressure on the wound and the bleeding seemed to ease. He flitted in and out of consciousness, not knowing whether he had passed out for seconds or minutes. Had the sky darkened, or was it his vision that had blurred? He thought he saw a thimble lost among a clog of reeds, he smelled a whiff of lavender from a bar of soap, he could hear a violinist playing on a Riga street and the clanging of a tramcar as it swept into the avenue below Jacob Stein's office. He tried to cling to memories of Megan, of his mother, of Nathan. Of Papa Kahn. Of Celia. Dear Celia. But it was the minute and the mundane that bubbled up in his consciousness. The taste of *cholent* fresh out of the oven, the aroma of herring baking on a fire, the yellow backs of the whin bent to the wind, a slice of sunlight on an aeroplane wing, a stick for a sword and a pole for a Cossack horse. He saw a young girl with fair hair clinging to her doll telling him she was on her way to America. America. America. Two men standing over the dead body of a stag, a biscuit tin with a picture of Queen Victoria on the lid, a football stretching a patched up net, a pink cigarette with a gold filter. These were the things that made up a life.

A cold fear began to seize him. Not a fear of death, but a fear of God. Was it too late to ask for forgiveness? To ask for a writing in the Book of Life. To start to pray. To pray to the One God that was the God of Moses and the God of David. Hear O Israel, the

Lord is One. Please do not abandon me now, O Lord. Please do not abandon me again, mother.

His mind clawed itself back to conscious thoughts of survival and he wondered if he had the strength to drag his body the short distance to the cottage, to staunch his wound with a strip of sheet, to cauterize it with boiling water. But as he eased himself over on to his side, he caught sight of the pool of dark red liquid escaped from the flesh-torn hole in his chest. The open door of the croft beckoned, yet he remained still, watching with fascination the stain of his blood as it seeped into the Highland earth.

Fiction from Two Ravens Press

Love Letters from my Death-bed: by Cynthia Rogerson
£8.99. ISBN 978-1-906120-00-9. Published April 2007

Nightingale: by Peter Dorward
£9.99. ISBN 978-1-906120-09-2. Published September 2007

Parties: by Tom Lappin
£9.99. ISBN 978-1-906120-11-5. Published October 2007

Prince Rupert's Teardrop: by Lisa Glass
£9.99. ISBN 978-1-906120-15-3. Published November 2007

The Most Glorified Strip of Bunting: by John McGill
£9.99. ISBN 978-1-906120-12-2. Published November 2007

One True Void: by Dexter Petley
£8.99. ISBN 978-1-906120-13-9. Published January 2008

The Long Delirious Burning Blue: by Sharon Blackie
£8.99. ISBN 978-1-906120-17-7. Published February 2008.

Auschwitz: by Angela Morgan Cutler
£9.99. ISBN 978-1-906120-18-4. Published February 2008

The Last Bear: by Mandy Haggith
£8.99. ISBN 978-1-906120-16-0. Published March 2008

Double or Nothing: by Raymond Federman
£9.99. ISBN 978-1-906120-20-7. Published March 2008

The Falconer: by Alice Thompson
£8.99. ISBN 978-1-906120-23-8. Published April 2008

Vanessa and Virginia: by Susan Sellers
£8.99. ISBN 978-1-906120-27-6. Published June 2008

Short Fiction & Anthologies

Highland Views: by David Ross
£7.99. ISBN 978-1-906120-05-4. Published April 2007

Riptide: New Writing from the Highlands & Islands: Sharon Blackie & David Knowles (eds)
£8.99. ISBN 978-1-906120-02-3. Published April 2007

Types of Everlasting Rest: by Clio Gray
£8.99. ISBN 978-1-906120-04-7. Published July 2007

The Perfect Loaf: by Angus Dunn
£8.99. ISBN 978-1-906120-10-8. Published February 2008

Cleave: New Writing by Women in Scotland: Sharon Blackie (ed)
£8.99. ISBN 978-1-906120-28-3. Published June 2008

Poetry

Castings: by Mandy Haggith
£8.99. ISBN 978-1-906120-01-6. Published February 2007

Leaving the Nest: by Dorothy Baird
£8.99. ISBN 978-1-906120-06-1. Published July 2007

The Zig Zag Woman: by Maggie Sawkins
£8.99. ISBN 978-1-906120-08-5. Published September 2007

In a Room Darkened: by Kevin Williamson
£8.99. ISBN 978-1-906120-07-8. Published October 2007

Running with a Snow Leopard: by Pamela Beasant
£8.99. ISBN 978-1-906120-14-6. Published January 2008

In the Hanging Valley: by Yvonne Gray
£8.99. ISBN 978-1-906120-19-1. Published March 2008

The Atlantic Forest: by George Gunn
£8.99. ISBN 978-1-906120-26-9. Published April 2008

Butterfly Bones: by Larry Butler
£8.99. ISBN 978-1-906120-24-5. Published May 2008
